Frederick

A Treatise on the Principles and Practice of Levelling

Showing the Application to Purposes of Railway Engineering and the Construction of Roads, etc

SALZWASSER
VERLAG

Frederick W. Simms

A Treatise on the Principles and Practice of Levelling

Showing the Application to Purposes of Railway Engineering and the Construction of Roads, etc

1st Edition | ISBN: 978-3-75257-720-4

Place of Publication: Frankfurt am Main, Germany

Year of Publication: 2022

Salzwasser Verlag GmbH, Germany.

Reprint of the original, first published in 1866.

A TREATISE

ON

THE PRINCIPLES AND PRACTICE

OF

LEVELLING.

SHOWING ITS APPLICATION TO PURPOSES OF

RAILWAY ENGINEERING AND THE CONSTRUCTION OF ROADS, &c.

BY

FREDERICK W. SIMMS, F.G.S., M.INST.C.E.

CIVIL ENGINEER.

FIFTH EDITION, REVISED AND CORRECTED.

WITH THE ADDITION OF

MR. LAW'S

PRACTICAL EXAMPLES FOR SETTING OUT RAILWAY CURVES

AND

MR. TRAUTWINE'S

FIELD PRACTICE OF LAYING OUT CIRCULAR CURVES.

With Plates and Woodcuts.

LONDON:

LOCKWOOD & CO., 7 STATIONERS'-HALL COURT.

1866.

ADVERTISEMENT.

THE FOLLOWING PAGES were written at the request of the Publisher,* in consequence of the very numerous applications he had received for a book upon this subject. In doing this, it was suggested that, in addition to explaining the method of taking levels in the field, and afterwards transferring them to paper in the form of a section, I should add an example of their application to practical purposes: I have accordingly inserted an example of road-work, wherein the necessary calculations of earth-work are shown, and worked out in full, both by the Prismoidal Formula, and the shorter process by the use of the Tables of Mr. Macneill †; and, as in a manner connected with the subject, it was also suggested that I should add some particulars upon the choice of a line of direction through a country for a road or railroad, preparatory to taking levels. In conclusion, I have given an abstract of the late Mr. Telford's rules for making and repairing roads, as contained in full in the valuable work of 'Sir Henry Parnell on Roads.'

F. W. S.

* The late Mr. Weale.

† Now Sir John Macneill.

ADVERTISEMENT TO THE FIFTH EDITION.

THIS WORK having been out of print for some time, and numerous enquiries having been made for it, the present Publishers have decided to reprint it in the same form. They have not done this, however, without submitting it to a searching revision, which has led to the detection and correction of several important errors. It is believed that this has added considerably to the value of the book.

March 1866.

CONTENTS.

PART I.

ON THE PRINCIPLES OF LEVELLING.

PART II.

THE PRACTICE OF LEVELLING.

PART III.

COMPUTATION OF EARTH-WORK, ROAD-MAKING, THE CLINOMETER, &c.

TABLES.

A TREATISE

ON

LEVELLING.

PART I.

ON THE PRINCIPLES OF LEVELLING.

LEVELLING is the art of tracing a line at the surface of the earth which shall cut the directions of gravity everywhere at right angles. If the earth were an extended plane, all lines representing the direction of gravity at every point on its surface would be parallel to each other; but, in consequence of its figure being that of a sphere or globe,* they everywhere converge to a point within the sphere which is equi-distant from all parts of its surface; or, in other words, the direction of gravity invariably tends towards the centre of the earth, and may be considered as represented by a plumb-line when hanging

* The figure of the earth is not exactly that of a sphere, but of an oblate spheroid flattened at the poles; the length of the equatorial diameter being 7924 miles, and that of the polar diameter 7898 miles. For our present purpose, it is sufficiently correct to consider it as a sphere.

freely, and suspended beyond the sphere of attraction of the surrounding objects.

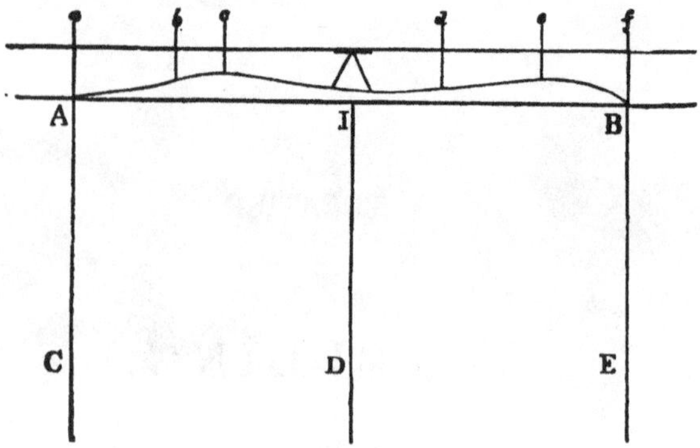

In the above diagram let the *straight* line A B represent the surface of the earth, upon the supposition of its being an extended plane, the direction of gravity at the points A, I, and B, would be represented by the lines A C, I D, and B E, all parallel to each other, and at right angles to the horizontal line A B. Now if the surface was undulatory, as shown by the curved line A B, and it was required to make a section representing it; an instrument capable of tracing out a line parallel to the horizontal line A B (as a spirit level), might be set up any where on the surface, as at I, and staves being placed or held along the line, as at *a*, *b*, *c*, *d*, &c., the different heights above the ground where such staves were intersected by the line so traced out, would at once show the relative level of all those points, with regard to the horizontal line, as a datum or standard of comparison.

But as the earth is a globe, its circumference must be

circular, as I K L in the annexed figure; the straight line A B will therefore not represent the surface of the

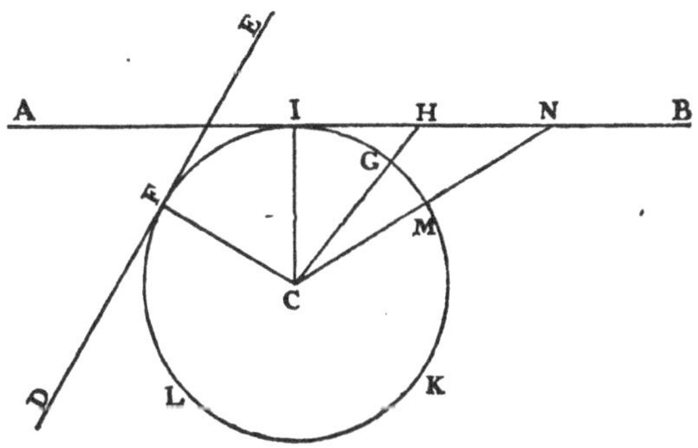

earth, but the sensible horizon of an observer stationed at the point I, to which point it is a tangent, being at right angles to the radius of the circle (or semi-diameter of the earth), I C. A line which is parallel to the sensible horizon of the observer, is the line traced out by our spirit-levels; it is parallel to a tangent to the earth's surface at that point only where the instrument is set up,—thus A B is a tangent at I, and D E a tangent at F; such being the fact, the difference of level between any two points cannot be determined by simple réference to a horizontal line, since every point on the surface of the globe (however near to each other) has a distinct horizon of its own.

If the earth were everywhere surrounded by a fluid at rest, or that its surface was smooth, regular, and uniform, every point thereon would be equally distant from the centre; but in consequence of the undulating form of the surface, places and objects are differently situated, some further from, and others nearer to, the centre of the earth, and consequently at different levels.

The operation of levelling may therefore be defined as the art of finding how much higher or lower any one point is than another, or, more properly, the difference of their distances from the centre of the earth.

Referring to our last figure, we have seen that the line A B is a true horizontal or level line at the point I, but being produced in the direction A or B, rises above the earth's surface; and although it may appear to be level as seen from I, yet it is above the true level (which is represented by the circumference of the circle) at every other point, and continues to diverge from it the further it is produced; at G, the apparent line of level, as the horizontal line A B is called, is above the true level, by the distance G H, and at M by the distance M N, *the difference being equal to the excess of the secant of the arc of distance above the radius of the earth.*

The difference, G H, or M N (see last figure), between the true and apparent level may be thus found: put t in the adjoining diagram for the tangent I H, r for

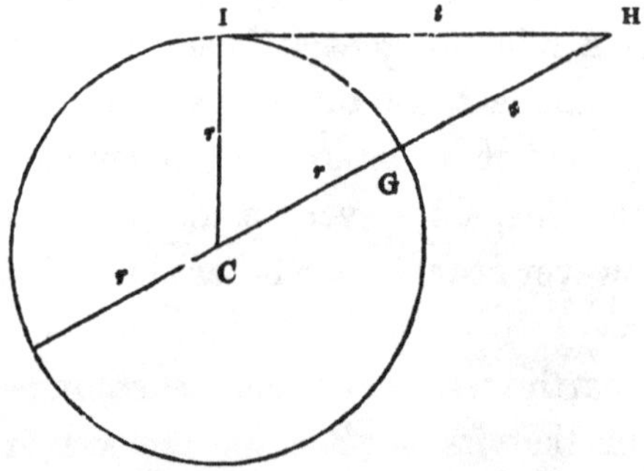

the radius C I of the earth, and x for G H, the excess of the secant of the arc of distance above the radius; I H being considered as equal to I G; then

$$(r+x)^2=r^2+t^2$$
$$\text{or } r^2+2\,r\,x+x^2=r+t^2$$
$$\text{and } 2\,r\,x+x^2=t^2$$
$$\text{or } (2\,r+x)x=t^2$$

But because the diameter of the earth $2\,r$ is so great with respect to the quantity (x) sought, at all distances to which a common levelling operation usually extends, that $2r+x$ without sensible error may be replaced by $2r$, we then have

$$2\,r\,x=t^2$$
$$\text{and } x=\frac{t^2}{2\,r}.$$

Or in words: *The difference* (x) *between the true and apparent level is equal to the square of the distance* (t^2) *divided by the diameter of the earth* ($2\,r$), *and consequently is always proportional to the square of the distance.*

The mean diameter of the earth is 7916 miles, and the excess of the apparent above the true level for one mile $\frac{t^2}{2r}=\frac{1}{7916}$ of a mile, or 8·004 inches. At two miles, it is four times that quantity, or 32·016 inches; at three miles, it is nine times that quantity, or 72·036 inches; and so on increasing in proportion to the square of the distance. If we reject the decimal ·004, and assume the difference between the true and apparent level for one mile to be exactly eight inches, or two-thirds of a foot, there arises the following convenient form for computing the correction of level due to the curvature of the earth, for distances given in miles, which may easily be remembered:

$$\text{correction} =\frac{2\text{ D}^2}{3},$$

D being the distance in miles. Or in words: *Two-thirds of the square of the distance in miles will be the amount of the correction in feet.*

Example.

From a point on the Folkstone road, the top of the keep of Dover Castle was observed to coincide with the horizontal wire of a levelling telescope when adjusted for observation, and therefore was apparently on the same level; the distance (D) from the instrument to the Castle was four miles and a half: consequently,

$$D^2 = 20{\cdot}25$$
$$2\,D^2 = 40{\cdot}50$$
$$\frac{2\,D^2}{3} = 13{\cdot}5 \text{ feet, the correction required.}$$

From this it appears, that the keep of Dover Castle was 13·5 feet higher than the centre of the telescope on the Folkstone road; but on account of the curvature of the earth, it was apparently depressed to the same level.

But the effect of the earth's curvature is modified by another cause, arising from optical deception; namely, Refraction. An object is never seen by us in its true position, but in the direction of the ray of light which conveys the impression or image of the object to our senses. Now the particles of light, in traversing the atmosphere, are, by the force of superior attraction, refracted or bent continually towards the perpendicular, as they penetrate the lower or denser strata; and consequently they describe a curved track, of which the last portion, or its tangent, indicates the apparent elevated situation of a remote point. This trajectory, suffering almost a regular inflexure, may be considered as very nearly an arc of a circle, which has for its radius seven times the radius of our globe; in consequence of which, the distance at which an object can be seen by the aid of refraction, is to the distance at which it could be seen without that aid, nearly as 14 to 13, the refraction augmenting the distance at which an object can be seen by about a thirteenth of itself. Hence, to correct the error occasioned by refraction, it will only be requisite to diminish the effects of the earth's curvature, or height of the apparent above the true level, by one-seventh of itself. Thus for our example of Dover Castle, $\frac{1}{7}$ of 13·5, or $\frac{13 \cdot 5}{7} = 1 \cdot 93$ feet nearly, to be substracted from 13·5, which leaves 11·57 feet for the height of Dover Castle above the level of a certain point on the Folkstone road.

The following Tables show the reduction of the apparent to the true level, both for the curvature of the earth only, and also for the combined effects of curvature and refraction. The first gives the corrections corresponding to distances expressed in miles, and the second for distances in chains.

Table of the Difference of the Apparent and True Level for Distances in Miles.

Distance in Miles.	CORRECTION.			
	Curvature.		Curvature and Refraction.	
	feet.	inches.	feet.	inches.
¼	0	0·5	0	0·4
½	0	2·0	0	1·7
¾	0	4·5	0	3·9
1	0	8·0	0	6·9
2	2	8·0	2	3·4
3	6	0·0	5	1·7
4	10	8·1	9	1·8
5	16	8·1	14	3·5
6	24	0·1	20	7·0
7	32	8·2	28	0·2
8	42	8·3	36	7·1
9	54	0·3	46	3·7
10	66	8·4	57	2·1
11	80	8·5	69	2·1
12	96	0·6	82	3·9
13	112	8·6	96	7·4
14	130	8·8	112	0·7
15	150	0·9	128	7·6
16	170	9·0	147	2·3
17	192	9·2	165	2·7
18	216	1·3	185	2·8
19	240	9·4	206	4·7
20	266	9·6	228	8·2

Table of the Difference of the Apparent and True Level for Distances in Chains.

Distance in Chains.	CORRECTION.	
	Curvature in decimals of feet.	Curvature and Refraction in decimals of feet.
1	·000104	·000089
2	·000417	·000358
3	·000938	·000804
4	·001668	·001430
5	·002605	·002233
6	·003752	·003216
7	·005107	·004378
8	·006670	·005717
9	·008442	·007236
10	·010422	·008933
11	·012610	·010809
12	·015007	·012863
13	·017613	·015097
14	·020427	·017509
15	·023450	·020100
16	·026680	·022869
17	·030120	·025817
18	·033767	·028943
19	·037623	·032248
20	·041687	·035732
21	·045960	·039394
22	·050442	·043236
23	·055132	·047259
24	·060031	·051455
25	·065137	·055832
26	·070452	·060388
27	·075975	·065121
28	·081708	·070036
29	·087648	·075127
30	·093798	·080399

The correction for distances greater than those given in the latter Table may be computed by the following rule, the same by which the Table itself was computed:

Rule.—*To the arithmetical complement of the logarithm of the diameter of the earth, or* 2·3788603, *add double the logarithm of the distance in feet, the sum will be the logarithm of the correction for curvature in feet and decimals; from which, if one-seventh of itself be subtracted, the result will be the combined correction for curvature and refraction.*

The practice of levelling is one of the most delicate operations that fall within the province of a surveyor, requiring the utmost possible circumspection to avoid the numerous sources of error to which he is liable. More especially, as it is seldom possible for him, after levelling over a long tract of country, to conjecture in what portion of the work his error lies, if he should then find that he had been so unfortunate as to commit any, and, not unfrequently in such cases, sufficient time cannot be spared to go over the ground again; as, for instance, when a section is required within a very limited time to produce before a parliamentary committee, either to support or oppose any measure submitted to their consideration. We have witnessed an instance where such a committee, during their inquiry into the merits of a certain proposed line of railroad, had brought before them a *rival contemplated line* with *pretensions* to *great superiority*; but it had been so hastily surveyed, that the learned counsel who had the supporting of the measure, acknowledged, in his opening address, that a trifling error at some unknown part of the line had been detected, which did not exceed fifty feet. We hardly need add, that the rival line was rejected.

The importance of extreme accuracy may also be felt, when it is known that from the section, the engineer has to make his calculations of the quantity of earthwork, in cuttings and embankments, necessary to carry into execution the intended measure, whether of a canal, a railway, or turnpike road, and of course the accuracy of the estimated expense is involved in it; and further, the fitness of the ground itself for such works is determined from the section; that is, whether the inclinations, which the undulations of the ground admit of being introduced, are suitable for the purpose either of a railway or turnpike road. And if the object be the formation of a canal, the section must show what extent of lockage will be required; not only affording a key to the expense, but also the possibility of its execution. We do not throw out these suggestions to alarm the mind of the young beginner, by bringing before him a fearful responsibility, but that he may understand the ultimate object of his labours, and to induce him, by carefulness and attention, to merit that confidence which is sure to be reposed in those who are known to possess such habits.

LEVELLING INSTRUMENTS.

It is essential to the good execution of work, that the surveyor should possess instruments most proper for the purpose, and of the best construction. Upon the subject of instruments, we shall generally refer the reader to a cheap work, entitled, "A Treatise on the principal Mathematical Instruments employed in Surveying, Levelling, and Astronomy, explaining their construction, adjustments, and use;" where the various kinds of spirit-levels, and levelling staves, together with the method of performing their several adjustments, &c., are minutely detailed, and represented by engravings; * and as the work alluded to contains also a similar account of the most important instruments used in surveying and astronomy, and has had an extensive sale, we presume it to be in the hands of most beginners in the profession; we shall, however, give some particulars in this place, and annex a description of the cause of, and a remedy for, the *parallax* between the wires of a levelling telescope, and the levelling staves, which is the cause of much annoyance to observers.

SPIRIT-LEVELS.

The Y *level*, so called from the supports in which the telescope rests, resembling in shape the letter Y, is the oldest construction of the spirit-level now in use: its adjustments are convenient to be performed, but, on the other hand, this kind of instrument seldom retains its adjustments perfect for any length of time; besides, there are conditions in its construction which are assumed to be perfect, but which practical men know to present difficulties in the manufacture. The use of this instrument is now very much superseded by those of modern construction.

Troughton's Improved Level.—This instrument has

* Also a Work published by Mr. Weale, on Drawing Instruments, with Instructions for Field Work, in 12mo., price 3*s.* 6*d.*

been a very general favourite among engineers for a length of time: its construction renders its adjustments much more permanent than those of the Y level, and it is altogether a more stable instrument. The telescope, which, in the former instrument, is capable of reversion on its supports, for the adjustment of the line of collimation, is, in Troughton's construction, firmly fixed in its place, as is also the glass tube of the spirit bubble. The verification and correction of the adjustments are performed very differently, and may at first appear more complex and difficult than those of the other; yet when a person has once mastered and become familiar with his instrument, these apparent difficulties vanish.

The Dumpy Level.—This modification of the spirit-level has but recently been introduced by William Gravatt, Esq., and bids fair to become the favourite instrument among civil engineers. In its general figure it does not differ very essentially from the level last spoken of, but it possesses many decided advantages. The aperture of the object glass is much larger for the same length of telescope; consequently more rays of light are admitted to the eye, producing the advantages of greater distinctness. We lately tried a *fourteen-inch* level, constructed upon Mr Gravatt's principle, and found that we could distinctly read the levelling-staff at twenty chains (a quarter of a mile) distant, which was the utmost we could do with a *twenty inch* level upon the old construction: we have, therefore, the advantage of a more portable instrument, fourteen inches in length, capable of performing the same work as a more cumbersome one of twenty inches. Besides this advantage, the instrument in question is more complete in its details.

It possesses a cross level, placed at right angles to the principal level, which affords very great facility in setting up the instrument, and adjusting for observation, as will be hereafter described: it likewise has a reflecting mirror, mounted with a hinge joint, and capable of being placed on the principal level tube, and adjusted, to show the observer if the instrument shifts from its horizontality whilst he is noting the observation: it also possesses other important though minor additions, all of which, in fact, could be applied by the maker to the other kind of instruments, if ordered, and for the particulars of which we refer to the work before alluded to.

From the large aperture and short focal length of the telescope, the instrument has altogether a dumpy appearance, and hence it is generally known by the cognomen of "Gravatt's Dumpy Level:" usually of nine or fourteen inches. We have seen some beautiful specimens of this kind of levelling instrument constructed for I. K. Brunel, Esq.

LEVELLING STAVES.

In the Treatise on Mathematical Instruments, will be found a description of the different kinds of levelling staves in use. The former construction, even as improved by Troughton, was decidedly defective in practice, inasmuch as the staff had to be read off by the assistant, who had then to communicate the result to the observer; or, if he was not sufficiently intelligent to be intrusted with so responsible a duty, he was obliged, after the observation was made, to carry the staff to the observer, or wait for him to come and read off the height of the vane, and register it in his field-book. This occasioned great loss of time and uncertainty in the results, for the vane on the staff might possibly be shifted in the mean time. We remember an instance of an ignorant attendant holding the staff upside down, which at once introduced an error of several feet in the result. To obviate this, a new staff has been contrived, originally, we believe, by Mr. Gravatt, and subsequently by Mr. Hennett, Mr. Bramah, Mr. Sopwith, &c., each varying the mechanical arrangements, but all agreeing in retaining the main advantage, viz. a sufficiently distinct graduated face for the observer to read off the quantities himself through the telescope of his instrument: the sliding vane is therefore dispensed with, and the only dependance to be placed on the staff-holder is, that he may hold it perpendicularly. To assist him in this, a small plummet is suspended in a groove cut out in the side of the staff, by which its verticality can be determined in one direction, and the observer himself can detect if it be held aslant in the other direction, as may be understood from the diagram at page 21, which represents the staff *e* as it appears in the field of the telescope, which shows objects inverted. If the staff be held perpendicularly, it will appear between and equally distant from each of the two vertical wires *c d* fixed in the telescope; consequently, if it be held aslant, it will cross the wires obliquely, and any want of verticality in the staff will be immediately detected, and the observer must signal to the staff-man accordingly. The advantages from the use of the modern staves, over those of the old construction, are so great, especially in saving of time, that we have no doubt of their general adoption.

THE IRON TRIPOD.

Another instrument of simple construction is represented in the above figure: its use is to rest the staff upon when held at any station. By this means the staff is sure to be kept on the same spot, and at the same height from the ground, while the observer is reading the staves both at the back and forward station on each side of the spirit-level: it is at present not generally used, but we consider it of more importance than is usually attached to it. It consists of a triangular piece of sheet iron, of about one-tenth of an inch in thickness, having the corners turned down to form the feet of the tripod, which are to be pressed into the ground by the foot of the staff-holder; a rounded piece of iron is riveted on the upper surface, to present a clean spot to rest the staff upon when held at the station; the chain with the attached ring is for the convenience of the staff-holder in lifting it from the ground, and carrying it from station to station.

THE MEASURING CHAIN.

In levelling operations it is in most cases necessary to note the relative distances of the staves from each other, from the spirit-level, or from some given point or place, otherwise no section of the ground levelled over can be made. For this purpose a measuring tape may be employed where the distances are short, but in most cases the means employed is a chain; the one commonly used is 4 poles in length, called Gunter's chain, which is divided into 100 links of 7·92 inches each. In many cases, however, this will not be found so convenient as the use of a chain with links of 1 foot in length; but there is a practical inconvenience attending these long links where the ground is rough and uneven, as the links are likely to get bent in being drawn through the hedges and rough places: whenever this occurs the chain is reduced in length, and, unless discovered and rectified, a considerable error in distance will very soon result. When we have had occasion to use such a chain over rough ground we have had the links made 6 inches long, and although it occasioned more trouble in noting and registering the distances, yet the liability of the links to become bent was greatly diminished. No measurements are required in taking what are called running or check levels, the object of which is merely to test the accuracy of a section previously made, by finding the difference of level between certain points on the section, to see if the results are identical with the former determination; which is the same thing as ascertaining the whole difference of level between distant places. Neither are any measurements required to produce a section if you possess a correct map or plan of the district or line, for if the level points are noted on the said plan, their relative distances can be taken therefrom by its scale; this, however, can only be considered as an approximate operation as far as the horizontal measures are concerned. In this way, however, many extensive trial sections for long lines of railway have been made by means of the Ordnance maps, and will, if properly done, determine the general features of the country sufficiently for the engineer to choose the best route for a minute and detailed survey, which would cost too much time and money to undertake in the first instance where there exists any doubt between two or more routes as to which it would be most judicious to adopt.

ON INSTRUMENTAL PARALLAX.

The foregoing is an account of the instruments necessary for the purposes of levelling ; but before closing this part of our subject, we think it may be useful to add some particulars respecting instrumental parallax, which we have occasionally found to be the source of much annoyance to the surveyor. This has invariably arisen from ignorance of the principles of the telescope, and hence, not knowing how the parallax arises, the means of removing it have not been understood ; we shall endeavour to explain, in a popular manner, both the cause and the remedy.

The rays of light which proceed from surrounding objects, and which, by entering our eyes, convey to us the sense of vision, move in perfectly straight lines, unless turned from their rectilineal course by the intervention of a refracting or reflecting medium, and whatever portion of such rays as can enter our eyes may (without sensible error) be considered as moving not only in *straight*, but *parallel* lines; the more remote the object is, the more nearly this will be the case. In the adjoining diagram, let A B represent the section of a

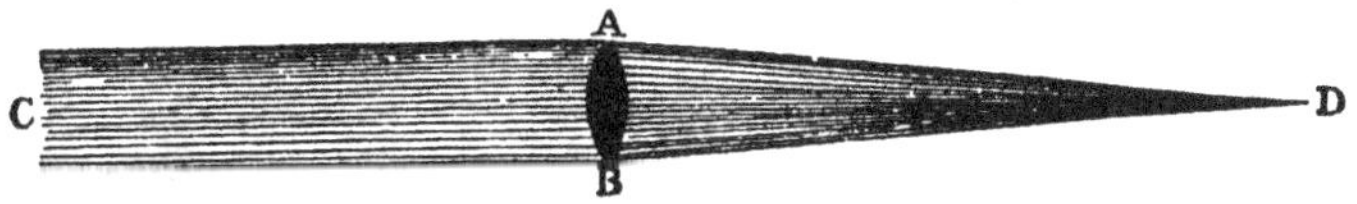

lens (or object glass of a telescope) ; let the parallel lines on the left represent the rays of light coming from some distant object in that direction ; the instant they impinge upon the glass, and in passing through it, they suffer refraction—that is, they are bent out of their former rectilineal path—and on leaving the lens at the opposite side, they converge to a certain point D, which is the focus of the object glass (in this point *all* the rays passing through a *perfectly formed* glass meet, and it is situated on the line C D, the direction of the ray which passes through the centre of the glass, the only one that continues its former course, and is called the axis of the lens) ; the concentration of the rays form an image of the distant object in the focal point D, "and if a piece of ground glass, transparent paper, or a plate of glass having one surface covered with a dried film of skimmed milk, be held up at D, a person looking at it from a few inches behind would see a perfect image of the distant object formed on the ground glass ; and by steadily keeping the eye in the same position, the ground glass may be removed, and the image will appear in the same spot suspended in the air."

Now let us imagine the lens applied to the construction of a telescope, and the adjoining diagram to represent a section of it ; the image of a levelling staff held at a distance, in the direction of C, would be formed at the point W, the focus of the object glass; let D F represent the eye-glass, which is fixed in a sliding tube, and together called the *eye-piece.* The eye-piece may be

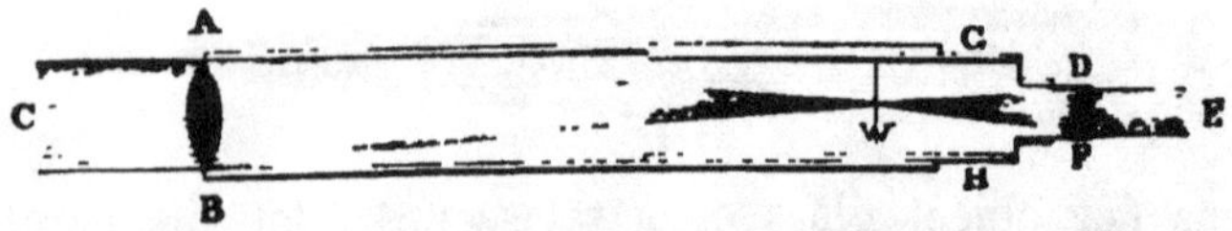

considered as a microscope, with which the observer magnifies the image of the object formed at W; to do this, it will readily appear to the reader that its distance from the image at W must be such as to cause its focal point to coincide therewith, making that point the common focus of the two glasses: for the purpose of effecting this, the eye-piece is made to slide either in or outwards, and the observer can tell when it is at the proper distance, for he will then obtain a perfectly distinct view of the object. The axis of the two glasses forms a continued straight line C E, which in a telescope is technically termed the optical axis of the instrument, or line of collimation; this imaginary line is, in levelling telescopes, the zero, from whence the readings on the staff are taken. It is therefore necessary to represent it by something tangible, that shall at the same time not interfere with the rays of light passing through the telescope to the eye; this is done by fixing across the interior of the telescope very fine wires, or threads from a spider's web, so that their intersection may not only coincide with the axis C E, but cross it precisely at W, the common focus of the two glasses, where the image of the staff (or distant object) is formed, and therefore the wires and the staff will appear to an observer as one object, or, at least, equally distant from him. The following diagram shows the appearance of the wires and the staff as seen through an inverting telescope; where *a b* represents the horizontal wire, *c* and *d* two

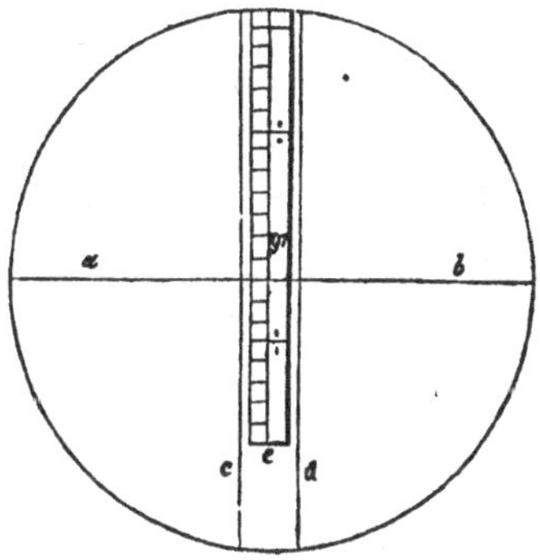

wires placed at right angles to it, and separated so as to admit, at usual distances, the staff *e* to appear between them, by which the observer can always tell if the staff-man holds it erect in a lateral direction, as before explained. The staff is represented as seen at the moment of completing an observation; the horizontal cross wire coinciding with the division ·20 above 16 feet, the staff being read downwards in consequence of its apparent inversion; the reading therefore, of such an observation, to be entered in the field-book, would be 16·20 feet.

The adjustment of the line of collimation consists in making the centre of the horizontal wire (or intersection of the wires in instruments intended for measuring angles) coincide with the optical axis of the telescope; this, when once accomplished, will, with care, keep correct for a long time, but the placing it in the common focus of the two glasses requires attention at every observation. For detailed instructions upon the former, we refer to the treatise on Mathematical Instruments, &c.; but as the latter forms part of every observation, and is the source of the perplexing parallax, we shall speak of it in this place.

The cross wires are fixed to a plate, called a diaphram, attached by screws to the slide G H, which also carries the slide D F of the eye-piece. The point W, or focus of the object glass, does not remain constant for terrestrial objects, but varies with every change in the distance of the staff; if it be brought closer to the instrument, the image, or focal point, will recede further from the glass, and *vice versâ*; therefore, the wires and the focus of the eye-piece must be brought to coincide with that of the object glass by their respective slides; and first, the eye-piece should be moved in its slide till its focus coincides with the wires in the tube G H; when this is accomplished, the observer will see the wires perfectly sharp and well-defined; next, motion must be given to the slide G H, by turning a milled head attached to the telescope, which gives motion to the slide by rack work; this will carry both the wires and the focus of the already adjusted eye-piece to coincide with the focus of the object glass, on whatever part of the optical axis of the instrument it may be situated. When this is done, the adjustment of the telescope for observation will be complete, and its proof consists in the observer having at the same time a clear and well-defined image both of the staff and the cross wires, which will be the case if they seem to be *attached* to each other,—or, in other words, appear equally distant from him; and the moving about of the observer's eye does not detect any apparent displacement of the staff, with respect to the wires. Such a displacement, or relative motion, is what is meant by *parallax*; and when it exists, it must be got rid of by a repetition of the adjustment of the glasses as above described, till the motion of the eye will no longer detect the least apparent movement, or passing and repassing of the wires and the staff: till this is done, no correct observation can be made.

From what has been advanced on the subject of the corrections for curvature and refraction, it may be necessary, before entering upon any practical examples, to remark, that such corrections are very seldom applied in practice, the observer, by the arrangements of his operations doing away in a great degree their injurious effects, which we will endeavour to explain.

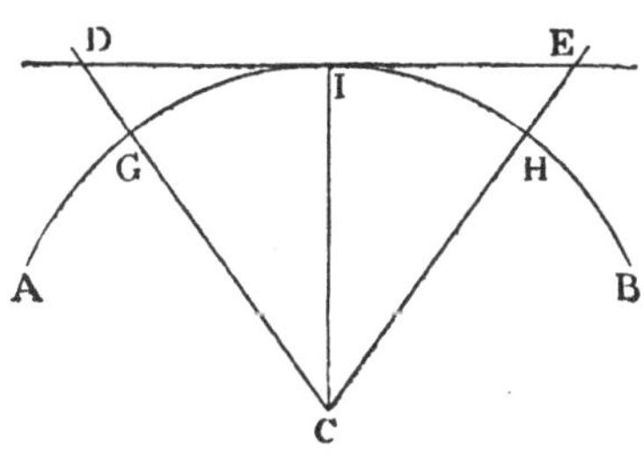

Suppose it were required to find the difference of level between any two points G and H in the preceding figure; let AB represent a portion of the earth's surface, let C represent the centre, and CG, CI, and CH the radii of the earth. Now a spirit-level being set up and adjusted at I, an observer looking through the telescope would see objects in the direction of the horizontal line DE only, and a staff held upright at H would be read off in the point E on the horizontal line; but this point is higher than the true level by the distance HE, which is the correction for curvature due to the distance IH (see page 5); and if that quantity be subtracted from the reading of the staff, the remainder will show the difference of level between the points I and H. If the same process be gone through by holding a staff at G, then the difference of level between G and I will also be ascertained, which being compared with the former difference, will show how much higher one of the points G or H is above the other; but it must be evident, that if G and H be equally distant from I, the horizontal line DE, being a tangent to the surface at the middle point I, must cut the staff at D on the same level with the point E;—that is, CD is equal to CE, therefore D and E are level points, being equi-distant from the centre of the earth; and if the reading of one staff above the ground is greater than the reading of the other, the difference will at once show the variation of level between the points where the staves were held, viz. G and H; the effect of curvature is thus removed by *simply placing the instrument midway between the station staves.* The effects of the atmospheric refraction will likewise be done away with in the same process, because it will affect both observations alike, unless under peculiar circumstances of the weather, &c., over which the observer has no control.

The above method of finding differences of level, by placing the instrument as near as possible midway between the two staves, and noting their readings, is the one adopted in practice; but as it can scarcely ever happen, on account of the extent of the work, that one placing of the instrument will complete it, a succession of similar operations must be performed, as shown in the annexed engraving.

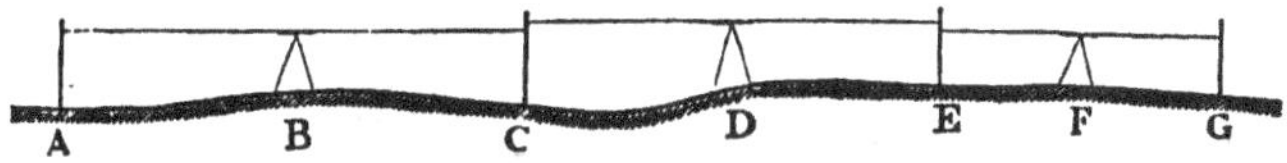

Suppose it were required to find the difference of level between the points A and G; a staff is erected at A, the instrument is set up at B, another staff at C, at the same distance from B that B is from A. The readings of the two staves are then noted; the horizontal lines connecting the staves with the instrument represent the visual ray or line of sight. The instrument is then conveyed to D, and the staff which stood at A is now removed to E, the staff C retaining its former position, and from being the forward staff at the last observation, it is now the back staff: the readings of the two staves are again noted, and the instrument removed to F, and the staff C to the point G; the staff at E retaining the same position, now becomes in its turn the back staff, and so on to the end of the work, which may thus be extended many miles: the difference of any two of the readings will show the difference of level between the places of the back and forward staff; and the difference between the sum of the back sights and the sum of the forward sights will give the difference of level between the extreme points: thus,

	Back sights. ft. dec.	Fore sights. ft. dec.
A and C	10·46	11·20
C „ E	11·33	8·00
E „ G	7·42	7·91
Sums	29·21	27·11
	27·11	
Difference of level	2·10	

showing that the point G is 2 feet and $\frac{1}{10}$ higher than the point A.

The foregoing process is called compound levelling. The following is an example of simple levelling, being performed at one operation, and therefore subject to the correction for curvature and refraction to obtain a correct result.

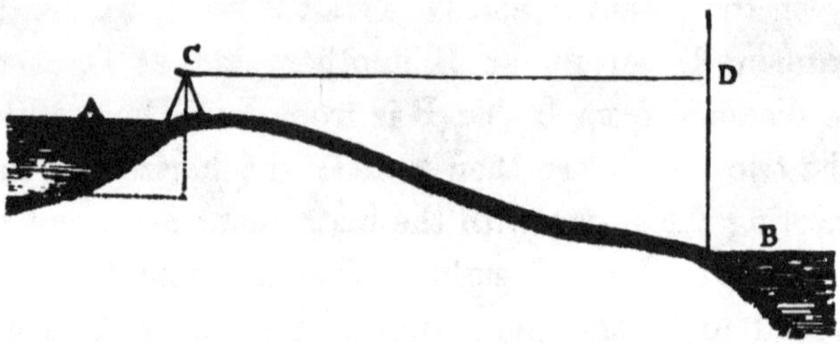

Suppose it were required to drain a pond and marsh A, by making a cut to a stream at B, a distance of thirty chains: let a level be set up at C, and directed to a staff held upright at the edge of the water at B. The horizontal line CD represents the line of sight which would cut the staff at D, the reading being 17·44 feet; the height of the instrument above the ground was 4 feet, and the depth of the pond 10 feet; therefore the difference of level between the bottom of the pond and the surface of the stream was as follows:

		ft. dec.
Reading of the staff		17·44
Height of instrument	4·00	
Depth of pond	10·00	
Curvature and refraction for 30 chains (see Tables, pages 8 and 9)	0·09	
		14·09
Difference of level		3·35

PART II.

THE PRACTICE OF LEVELLING.

ON RUNNING OR CHECK LEVELS.

To present, in the clearest possible manner, the practical application of the principles of levelling, we propose describing some operations in detail. We shall, therefore, commence with a case of a simple kind, which will prepare the way for more complicated examples. When a section of a line of country has been completed (for any purposes whatever), it is in most cases necessary to check its accuracy by repetition; but in doing this, it is seldom requisite to level over precisely the same line of ground, unless there is cause to suspect its general correctness, but to follow the most convenient and nearest route, and at intervals to level to some known points on the exact line of section, which will give *their* differences of level: the points thus selected are generally what are called bench marks, and are nothing more than marks or notches cut upon gate-posts, stumps of trees, mile or boundary stones, or any similarly immoveable objects, contiguous to the line of section, and at frequent intervals. These bench marks are made by the person who takes the section in the first instance, and are sometimes previously determined upon. When the section is complete, their relative heights with regard to the base line or datum of the section become known; consequently, they may be considered as so many zero or fixed points on the line, easily recognisable, from whence any portion of the work may be levelled over again; or branch lines of level may be conducted in any direction, and the levels of such branches be comparable with those of the main line.

When, in checking the principal levels, by proceeding in the most convenient direction from bench mark to bench mark, it is found that the differences of level prove identical with those on the section, or within the limits of probable error, it may be presumed that all the intermediate heights are likewise correct: it is, however, just possible that equal errors of an opposite kind may have been committed, when, the *sum* of each being of the same magnitude, a balance of errors would cause the extreme points to be right, whilst the intermediate levels would be incorrect; but the probability is so much against such an occurrence, that we believe, unless there be some particular reasons for so doing, the whole exact line of a section is seldom levelled a second time for the purpose of checking the former results only.

From what has been remarked, it will appear evident that in taking running or check levels, there is no necessity for the use of the chain, or the compass attached to the instrument, the distances and bearings having all been determined at the time the principal levels were taken.

The example we are about to give of this kind of operation is represented in the engraving, Plate I., which shows both the ground plan and the section. The strong black line on the plan is that of the section to be checked, and proceeds from a bridge in the town of A, in a circuitous direction along a valley, and nearly parallel to the course of a river, to a bench mark in the town of B: this originally formed a portion of a more extensive survey. We have selected this portion of the line as explanatory of our present subject; the route taken in proving the work is represented by the dotted line, and was confined to the public roads, that being considered the most convenient, because it would altogether exclude the necessity of passing through private property, as the surveyor would most likely have been ordered off, a great feeling of opposition existing among the owners and occupiers of the said lands; and further, the public road crossed the line several times, by which a number of intermediate points could be checked. Before giving the particulars of this example, we shall explain in detail the method of conducting the necessary observations.

In the first instance the staff-holder must place his staff on the bench mark from whence the levels are to commence. (In the case of our example the staff was first placed on a peculiarly shaped stone on the crown of the bridge at A, which could easily be recognised from description at any future time, if ever it should be necessary to refer to this spot again: it therefore answered as a bench mark.) The surveyor must next set up his spirit-level in the most suitable spot which presents itself, from whence he can have an uninterrupted view, not only of the staff at the back station, but also for a considerable distance in the direction he wishes to carry his levels. The station selected should not in any case exceed four or five chains, and if it be only half that quantity, there will be less likelihood of error; for when long sights (as they are usually termed) are taken, unless both the back and forward stations are equally distant from the instrument, errors will gradually creep in upon the results, which, in a long series of levels, are liable, by their accumulation, to become of serious consequence. The proper station being determined upon,* and the tripod legs of the instrument spread out and thrust into the ground sufficiently to ensure its stability, the observer must adjust his level for observation in the following order:—First, he must draw out the eye-piece of the telescope till he sees the cross wires perfectly well defined; then, directing it to the staff, he must turn the milled-headed screw, on the side of the telescope, till he can likewise distinguish with the utmost possible clearness the smallest graduations on the staff: that these two adjustments be very carefully and completely performed, is of more consequence than is generally supposed, for upon them depends the existence or non-existence of parallax. If any parallax is detected, it must be removed, or the observations will be incorrect: its existence may be detected by the observer moving his *eye* about at the same time that he is looking through the telescope at the staff; and if he sees that the cross wires do not appear to have the least motion with regard to the divisions with which they are coincident, then no parallax will exist; but if any motion appears to take place between the wires and the staff, it is a proof that

* It must be borne in mind, when we thus minutely detail what may appear to the practical man as naturally obvious, that we are writing for the information of those who have never had any practice whatever.

one or both of the foregoing adjustments have been imperfectly made.

To remedy this inconvenience the eye-piece should first be moved to try and improve the distinct appearance of the cross wires. The observer will be greatly assisted in this operation if he holds a sheet of white paper before the object glass, which, at the same time that it prevents other objects from attracting his attention, presents a clean white disk, or ground, for the wires to be seen upon; and when he is satisfied that they are as sharp and well defined as possible, he must repeat the movement of the milled head by the side of the telescope till he is equally satisfied of the distinct appearance of the graduations on the staff; then let him again move his eye about before the eye-glass to see if any parallax still exists, and if so, he ought to repeat the above simple operation until it is removed. We have known the parallax of a telescope to be a source of great annoyance to persons in the profession, which has led us to be thus minute upon what to some would appear very simple. We have for the like reason given an explanation of its nature, &c. at page 18.

The turning the milled head to obtain distinct vision of the staff, in the old construction of instruments, communicated motion to the object glass; but in those of recent contrivance, it moves the whole of the eye end of the telescope, and with it the cross wires. In either case, the distance between the object glass and the wires is increased to a proper extent; the modern contrivance appears to be the most approved. The adjustment of the eye-piece for distinct vision when once made, is not likely to require alteration the whole day, unless it be accidentally deranged; but that of obtaining distinct vision of the distant staff (together with the one we shall next describe) must be performed at every station, as it varies with the distance of the staff, as explained at page 22.

Having made the above adjustments perfect, bring the spirit-bubble into the centre of its glass tube, which position it must retain unmoved in every direction of the instrument; or in other words, the bubble must indicate a true level during the time the telescope is turned completely round horizontally on its staff head: this is accomplished by bringing the telescope successively over each pair of the parallel plate screws, and giving them motion, screwing up one while unscrewing the other to a corresponding extent; but if the telescope is supplied with a cross level, as in that contrived by Mr. Gravatt, the two bubbles, being at right angles to each other, will at once show which pair of screws require turning, in order to produce an indication of level in both bubbles. In the Treatise on Mathematical Instruments there is given an ample explanation of the adjustment of levels in all their details: upon such subjects we shall once for all refer to that work.

Having adjusted the level for observation, it must be directed to the back staff, of which a clear view must be had; then note with all possible exactness the foot, and decimal fraction of a foot, with which the central part of the horizontal wire appears to be coincident, which enter in the proper column of the field or observation book. This column should be headed "Back Sight," or "Back Station," as in the example given at page 38. As soon as it is registered, look to see that the spirit-bubble has not removed from its central position, and then repeat the observation, to ensure that no mistake had been made in noting it: this should be invariably done, to guard against errors.

The back observation being made, turn the telescope round in the forward direction, and obtain a distinct view of the staff, by turning the milled head at the side of the telescope; then look at the spirit-bubble, and if it has at all changed its position, by receding towards either end of its tube, bring it back to the centre by the parallel plate screws, as before described (this can be done so readily, and without moving the telescope, when a cross level is attached, and having likewise other advantages, that we recommend its universal application to spirit-levels); then, by looking through the telescope, observe what division on the staff is intersected by the cross wire, and enter the reading in the proper column of the field-book, which should be headed "Fore Sight," or "Fore Station." Having entered it, look to see that the bubble is still correct, and then verify the observation by noting it again, which will complete the first levels.*

It may be worth remarking that, in setting the level up, the pointed legs should be pushed into the ground sufficiently to ensure the stability of the instrument, and likewise that the observer should move himself about the instrument, whilst taking the levels, as little as possible, taking care not to strike the legs with his feet. Caution in these matters is required, for sometimes the least

* When taking levels for the formation of a section, it is sometimes necessary to note the bearing of the compass needle, and to measure distances, as will be explained hereafter.

movement of the person will derange the levels of the instrument, particularly on loose or elastic ground;—to do away the inconvenience arising from this source, a reflector has been contrived to fix on the top of the telescope tube, by which the observer can see both the staff and the reflected image of the spirit-bubble at the same time, and then he can make his observation at the instant he sees the bubble in its proper position. The foregoing description of the method of taking levels is general, and applies equally to every kind of levelling operation, with whatever additional matters may require attending to, when taking levels for the formation of a section, &c., which we shall hereafter describe.

The first levels being completed, the surveyor must take up his instrument, and, passing the man who holds the forward staff, proceed to some convenient spot to set up the instrument a second time, which, as before remarked, should not be more than four or five chains distant; the other man, also, who held the staff at the back station, must likewise take up a new station still further onwards in the required direction, and as nearly as possible at the same distance from the instrument as the instrument is from the staff, which has now become the back station; it being in every case necessary, to ensure correct work, that the instrument should occupy very nearly the middle point between the staves, for reasons which will be understood by those who have perused the former part of this book. Having set the instrument up, adjust it for observation as before—viz. see that the cross wires are distinct; turn the milled head by the side of the telescope till the graduation on the staff is quite distinct, and no parallax exists; and, lastly, set the spirit-bubble level in every direction of the telescope by the parallel plate screws; which done, note the reading on the back staff, and enter it in the book; then examine the bubble, and again read the staff to ensure accuracy; then turn the telescope about, and do the same for the forward station, which will complete the second level. As the third and fourth, and all the following levels, are conducted in precisely the same manner, it will be unnecessary to repeat the instructions again.

The man holding the back staff should be instructed never to move it in the least from its position till the forward observation is completed, which he can always tell by seeing the surveyor carry his level onwards. It is sometimes the practice to use one staff only, and after taking the back observation, to cause the assistant to go on and take up a position suitable for a forward station; but besides the loss of time attendant upon such a process, if the instrument should in the interval get moved by accident, those two observations will be incorrect, unless the back sight be taken again, and this cannot be done unless the precise spot before occupied by the staff can be identified, which is sometimes uncertain. When this is the case, no alternative is left but to go back and renew the work at the last bench mark, or known station; and if none such exist, the whole operation will probably have to be gone over again, where great accuracy is required.

The iron tripod, described at page 16, should in all cases be placed on the ground by the staff-holder, to rest the staff upon, as it ensures to the observer the certainty of the staff keeping exactly the same spot when the face of it is presented to him in the two directions, forward and backward. The staff-holder should likewise be instructed to hold the staff perfectly upright, which he can himself determine, in one direction, by a little plumb-weight suspended in a groove in the staff; and as the observer can tell if he holds it upright in a lateral direction (as explained at page 15), he should frequently look to see if he signals for him to move the upper end of the staff to the right or left, taking care not to disturb its position on the iron tripod,

We have been supposing the use of the newly introduced staves, as we do not expect that those of the former construction will hold their ground against them, they having the advantage of providing to the observer the means of noting the reading of the staff himself. If however, from habit or otherwise, the use of the staff with the sliding vane should be preferred, the foregoing instructions equally apply; the only difference in its use is, that the observer must signal to the staff-holder to move the vane up or down on the staff, till it appears bisected by the cross wires of his telescope; then the reading of the staff must be noted, and entered by the assistant in a temporary book carried by him for the purpose: or if he cannot be trusted to perform so important a part of the business, he must convey the staff to the observer, or wait for him to come and read it himself. It requires no comment to show the uncertainty, and loss of time, in this method of proceeding compared with the use of the newly-contrived staves.

Having explained the method of taking observations for checking levels, we must refer to our example. The levels, as before stated, were taken along the public road shown by the dotted line, that being the most convenient route from the town of A to the town of B, avoiding the necessity of passing through private property; the strong black line on the plan shows where the original section was taken; the section itself is represented above the plan, and is drawn to two scales; the one giving the horizontal measure, is the same as that of the plan, viz. one inch to one mile; and the vertical scale, $\frac{1}{4}$ inch to 100 feet: from this section it appears that the crown of the bridge at A is fourteen feet above the datum line D E of the section, and that the bench mark (a stone by the road side) at B is 111 feet above the same datum; therefore the difference of level between the two places is $111 - 14 = 97$ feet. Now, by referring to our observation book, of which we have subjoined a copy, we make the difference of level to be 96·8 feet, differing from the original section no more than two-tenths of a foot, or 2·4 inches, a quantity that may be disregarded; the inference, therefore, to be drawn from such a coincidence in the two results is, that the whole of the section between the points in question is sufficiently correct.

Copy of Field-Book, for running or check levels.

Back Sights.	Fore Sights.	Remarks.
0·34	3·16	Back Θ on B. M. on the bridge at A.
5·86	5·61	
4·19	4·24	Forward Θ at corner of road leading to B.
5·44	1·20	
4·96	3·20	
4·73	1·32	At crossing of line.
6·10	2·00	
5·33	3·96	
5·91	1·83	
5·70	0·90	
6·02	1·21	Staff placed on post notched for B. M.
1·21	4·00	At crossing of line.
3·53	6·07	
3·96	5·34	
3·94	4·81	
3·98	6·08	
4·08	4·94	Upon line.
3·90	3·96	
4·84	2·42	
1·54	5·12	
4·69	4·97	
5·04	1·60	
2·24	3·86	Upon line.
7·25	1·89	
4·03	1·30	
9·54	0·19	
6·70	1·70	
9·40	4·06	
6·44	0·38	
11·00	0·46	
5·98	1·30	
11·12	1·78	
9·84	2·20	
0·18	0·32	Upon line.
4·72	0·10	
8·89	0·77	
10·02	0·92	
10·00	1·03	
8·58	1·19	
9·53	1·18	
230·75 102·57	102·57	Sums.
128·18		Difference.

Copy of Field-Book—continued.

Back Sights.	Fore Sights.	Remarks.
128·18		Brought forward.
9·90	0·68	
9·04	0·35	
10·00	8·52	
3·00	11·55	
3·68	0·88	
7·21	8·75	
1·99	10·48	
0·65	10·00	
4·48	10·44	
1·47	10·30	
1·55	11·70	
2·45	9·88	
3·78	1·04	
6·64	2·65	Forward ϴ on B. M. called B.
194·02	97·22	Sums.
97·22		
96·80	. . . . .	Difference=diff. of level between A and B.

The back sights being greater in amount than the forward sights, it is evident that the bench mark at B was higher than the bench mark at A by the difference of the two sums.

LEVELS FOR THE FORMATION OF A SECTION.

Next to the running levels, the most simple case that can occur is, to take the levels of a line of country where the ground plan is already made, and the exact line of section determined upon, and in some instances picketed out. It is then only necessary, in addition to what is required for running levels, that the distance between the levelling staves, or the whole distance at every station from the starting point, be measured. The instrument should be placed, as usual, as near as can be at an equal distance from each staff; but it is not essential that it be placed in the exact line between them, unless it should happen to prove the most advantageous position. Plate II. represents an example of this kind of work, the survey of the land having been completed, and the plan of the fields, &c. drawn: the strong black line A B was the direction determined upon as the most suitable for a portion of an intended line of railroad, and the section was accordingly taken; a bench mark had been previously agreed upon at each extremity (A and B), from whence other surveyors could take up the levels, and carry them onwards in both directions.

First a staff was placed on the bench mark at A for a back station, and another staff was held up for a forward station, in the adjoining field, but exactly on the line as marked down on the plan, a copy of which the surveyor had in his possession; the instrument was then set up, as near as could be estimated, or the level of the ground would admit, at an equal distance from each staff, so as to be able to read them both; the adjustment of the instrument for observation, as described at page 30, was carefully attended to, and the reading of the staves noted. As soon as the observations were made, the distance from staff to staff was measured with a Gunter's chain, which completed the first level.

The measurement of the distances can be more conveniently performed, and with a great saving of time, by two additional assistants, who can be measuring, whilst the surveyor proceeds to direct the man who held the back staff in the last case, to take up a forward station precisely on the line as laid down on the plan. The staff which was the forward station in the last case now becomes the back station, and the instrument must be set up so as to read both stations as before, and as nearly equi-distant from them as can be: by the time the instrument is adjusted, and both the staves read off, the assistants would have completed the measurement from the bench mark A to the first forward staff, and be ready to continue on to the second one: whilst this is doing, the instrument and back staff can be carried forward and set up, &c. as before: by a continued repetition of a similar process, the whole line A B was levelled.

The measuring assistant should report to the surveyor the total distance of each forward staff from the bench mark at A as soon as it is determined, or, if thought more convenient, he may keep a book to enter the distances in, which should be ruled in two columns, one for his distances, and the other for references to them, as *a*, *b*, *c*, &c., or the numbers 1, 2, 3, &c., placed opposite; and if the observer makes similar notes in his book to each pair of sights, there can arise no mistake in placing the correct distances opposite the corresponding levels, when the measurer makes his return.

The following is a copy of the field-book of the example given in Plate II.; showing the manner of keeping it, and also the method adopted of reducing the levels to obtain the actual heights of each station, with regard to the starting point, for the purpose of drawing the section; which we shall then explain.

LEVELLING FIELD-BOOK.

Distances.	Rise.	Back Sight.	Fore Sight.	Fall.	Reduced Level.	Remarks.
519	5·83	13·71	7·88	—	+ 5·83	
1315	—	9·40	16·30	6·90	− 1·07	
1542	—	3·87	11·71	7·84	− 8·91	
1850	—	2·63	12·41	9·78	−18·69	
2358	13·67	14·62	0·95	—	− 5·02	
2698	15·55	17·00	1·45	—	+10·53	
3357	—	10·66	15·40	4·74	+ 5·79	
3758	—	2·87	17·00	14·13	− 8·34	
3976	—	3·40	10·32	6·92	−15·26	
5077	3·49	5·73	2·24	—	−11·77	
5904	15 69	16·54	0·85	—	+ 3·92	
6124	15·19	16·08	0·89	—	+19·11	
6437	13·83	14·56	0·73	—	+32·94	
7467	—	10·36	14·06	3·70	+29·24	
8369	8·48	9·84	1·36	—	+37·72	
9303	2·80	9·80	7·00	—	+40·52	
	—	2·30	10·96	8·66	+31·86	Centre of road at 215 links.
9679	—	10·96	14·46	3·50	+28·36	
9936	—	2·08	15·05	12·97	+15·39	
10164	—	1·75	16·58	14·83	+ 0·56	
10576	—	1·84	17·10	15·26	−14·70	
11423	—	0·00	7·43	7·43	−22·13	Forward Θ at corner of Wood
13066	1·88	5·38	3·50	—	−20·25	
14954	4·00	8·50	4·50	—	−16·25	
15650	3·94	5·30	1·36	—	−12·31	
17345	0·80	10·20	9·40	—	−11·51	
19135	6·46	6·86	0·40	—	− 5·05	
19359	7·04	11·00	3·96	—	+ 1·99	
19631	8·27	11·80	3·53	—	+10·26	
19841	7·85	10·53	2·68	—	+18·11	Forward Θ at edge of Wood.
20561	6·84	8·22	1·38	—	+24·95	
21671	6·56	8·76	2·20	—	+31·51	
	—	14·00	14·50	0·50	+31·01	Road at 450 links.
22710	10·18	14·50	4·32	—	+41·19	
23221	8·14	9·14	1·00	—	+49·33	B above A.
Sums.	166·49	304·19	254·86	117·16		
	117·16	254·86				
	49·33	49·33				

The first column contains the measured distances from the starting point to every forward station expressed in links of Gunter's chain. The two central columns, headed "Back Sight" and "Fore Sight," contain the readings of the two staves at the back and fore observations respectively. The *difference* of such readings is placed in one of the two side columns headed "Rise" or "Fall," according as the ground at the forward station is higher or lower than that at the back station. If it be highest (or the ground rises, as it is called), then the forward reading will be the smaller of the two: but if it be the lowest (or the ground falls), then the forward reading will be the greater of the two: thus, in our first reading, the back observation is 13·71, and the forward observation 7·88, their difference = 5·83 feet, which is the difference of level between the two points; and as the forward reading was the smaller of the two, it is clear that the ground was rising at that place, and, therefore, the difference of the readings, viz. 5·83, is placed in the column of rises. In the next three successive pair of sights, the forward readings are the greatest, indicating a continued descent of the surface line, and the differences of those readings are inserted in the column of falls, viz. 6·90, 7·84, and 9·78. At the next following sight, the forward reading is again the smallest, therefore the difference 13·67 is placed in the column headed "Rise," and so on of the rest. No mistake can arise by placing the subtraction in the wrong column, as in every instance it must be placed in the column adjoining the larger quantity; thus if the fore sight is greater than the back sight, the resulting quantity must be placed in the column of falls, which is adjoining to that containing the reading of the fore sight, and *vice versâ*.

The adjoining column, headed "Reduced Levels," contains the absolute heights of each forward station above the datum line of the section, or a horizontal line passing through the starting point or bench mark A: these quantities, which are technically called the reduced levels, are obtained by the constant addition and subtraction of the numbers contained in the columns of "Rise" and "Fall," the former being considered as positive, and the latter as negative quantities; thus, assuming the level of the starting point A as the datum, we have the first forward station 5·83 feet higher than the datum, therefore in the column of reduced levels it is marked + (plus): next we have a fall or negative quantity of 6·90 feet, which must be subtracted; but as it is greater than 5·83, it shows that this station is below the datum line, by the difference between 5·83 and 6·90=1·07 feet, which is the depth of the second forward station *below* the datum line, and therefore is marked – (minus): the next is likewise a fall of 7·84, and as our last result was below the datum line, this additional negative quantity will take us still lower by its whole amount; it must, therefore, be added to 1·07, giving 8·91 feet for the depth of our third forward station below our datum, and it is therefore entered in the column of reduced levels with a minus sign. The next is also a fall of 9 78, which, applied as the last, gives 18·69 for the depth of the fourth forward station below the datum. The ground then rises again, and we have an ascent of 13·67 feet, which will bring us nearer to our datum; and as it diminishes our depth below the datum line, it must be subtracted from the last result; thus, 18·69 − 13·67 = 5·02 feet for the depth of the fifth forward station below the datum; we have then a rise of 15·55, which will carry us above the datum by the amount of difference between it and 5·02, leaving 10·53 feet for the height of the sixth forward station above the datum line: the next is a fall of 4·74, which diminishes our height by that quantity, and therefore must be subtracted from 10·53, leaving 5·79 as the height of the seventh forward station above the datum.

In like manner every other pair of sights in our example was reduced, applying each difference of the back and forward readings with their proper signs, until, at the close of the work, the point B (the last forward station) was found to be 49·33 feet above the datum line, or level of the starting point A.

The reduction of levels becomes a simpler operation when the height of the bench mark (used as a starting point) above the intended datum line is known: thus (in our example), suppose the height of the bench mark A was 100 feet above the level of high-water Trinity mark at London Bridge, and that it was intended to assume the level of that mark as the datum line of our section; then 5·83 feet, the rise to the first forward station, must be added to 100, giving 105·83 for the height of the ground at the point *a* above datum; next, from 105·83 subtract the fall 6·90, which gives 98·93 for the height of the point *b* above datum; then from 98·93 subtract 7·84, which gives 91·09 for the height of *c* above datum; and in like manner, by adding the quantities of rise, and subtracting those of the falls, the whole line of levels may be reduced to the line assumed as the datum.

As a proof of the accuracy of the arithmetical operation, the columns of back and fore sights should be added up, and the lesser sum subtracted from the former; the result of the agreement with that by the reduced levels is a proof of accuracy. Likewise another proof may be obtained by adding up the contents of the column of rise and fall; and if upon taking the lesser sum from the greater, the remainder represents the same quantity as obtained by both the other operations, there can be no doubt of the correctness of the reductions of the levels, as in our example. By the reduced levels, the height of B above A is 49·33 feet. The sum of the back readings is 87·95, and that of the forward readings 38 62; their difference also gives 49·33 for the height of B above A; and, lastly, the sum of the rises is 54·88, and that of the falls is 5·55, the difference giving, as before, 49·33 feet.

It is, perhaps, to be recommended, that the observer should reduce his levels as he proceeds in the field, as it will occupy but very little time, and can be frequently done while the staff-man is taking a new position; besides, the observer will frequently be able to detect by the eye if he is committing any glaring error, as, for instance, inserting a number in the column of rises, when it ought to occupy a place in that of the falls, the surface of the ground at once reminding him that he is going down hill instead of ascending.

If the foregoing method of reducing levels be found difficult or troublesome, on account of the introduction of plus and minus signs, they can be dispensed with, as well as the columns of "Rise" and "Fall," by proceeding in the following manner. Assuming the starting point to be any even number of feet high; or, what is the same thing, assume a datum line any even number of feet below the starting point, as 100 or 1000, taking care that your choice falls upon a number greater than the number of the whole fall you are likely to experience in the operation; then from this assumed height *subtract* the reading of the forward staff, and to the remainder *add* the reading of the back staff; the result will be the height of the first forward station above the assumed datum line; then from this height subtract the next forward reading, and to the remainder add the reading of the back staff; the result will be the height of the second forward station above the assumed datum, and so on throughout the whole levelling operation. The difference between any two of the readings will be the difference of level between the corresponding points on the ground.

By way of illustration, we will reduce part of the foregoing example after this manner, and the student can adopt whichever method he may consider the best.

Back Sight.	Fore Sight.	Reduced Levels.	Remarks.
		100·00	Assumed datum.
13·71	7·88	7·88	
		92·12	
		13·71	
		105·83	Height of 1st forward station above assumed datum.
9·40	16·30	16·30	
		89·59	
		9·40	
		98·93	Height of 2nd do. above do.
3·87	11·71	11·71	
		87·22	
		3·87	
		91·09	„ 3rd do. „ do.
2·63	12·41	12·41	
		78·68	
		2·63	
		81·31	„ 4th do. „ do.
14·62	0·95	0·95	
		80·36	
		14·62	
		94·98	„ 5th do. „ do.
17·00	1·45	1·45	
		93·53	
		17·00	
		110·53	„ 6th do. „ do.
10·66	15·40	15·40	
		95·13	
		10·66	
		105·79	„ 7th do. „ do.
2·87	17·00	17·00	
		88·79	
		2·87	
		91·66	„ 8th do. „ do.

The above will, we trust, be found sufficient to make ourselves understood upon the subject of reducing levels. If, after adopting the latter mode, it should be required to reduce them to the level of the starting point as a datum, nothing more is required than to take the difference between the height thus found and that of the assumed datum; thus, in our example, subtracting 100 (the assumed datum) from the height of the first forward station, gives 5·83 for its height above the starting point: next, from 100 subtract 98·93=1·07, making the second forward station that quantity below the level of the starting point, and so of the rest. But it may be done much easier after the section is made to the assumed datum, by drawing a line parallel thereto through the point A, or any other that may be determined on; thus the section may be at once adapted to any required datum line.

TO DRAW THE SECTION.

The levels being reduced, the surface line may be represented in the form of a section, as shown above the plan in Plate II. The vertical and horizontal scales of a section are seldom the same, which produces a caricatured representation; the vertical scale being so much greater than the horizontal, shows the depths of cutting and embankment required in the execution of road, railway, or canal works, with greater clearness than if both scales were equal. The plans and sections of projected works deposited with the Clerks of the Peace of counties, and in the Private Bill office, to obtain the sanction of the legislature, are mostly drawn to scales of four inches to one mile horizontal, and one hundred feet to one inch vertical: we have adopted these scales in our example, Plate II.

To make the section of our present example, first draw the horizontal line C D as the datum to which our levels were reduced, assume any point A as the starting point, then set off the measured distance from A to the first forward station $a = 519$ links (see levelling field-book, page 42), at this point erect a perpendicular, and mark on it the height 5·83 of the first forward station, and connect the point A with this mark, and the result will show the surface line of the ground in that interval: next, from the same starting point A set off the point *b*, the second forward station, with the distance of 1315 links, as given in the levelling-book; but as this point is a minus quantity (see reduced level, page 42), that is, below the datum line, let fall a perpendicular, and set off on it 1·07 feet, which connect by a line with the former level, and the surface line from A to *b* will then be represented; then with the distance 1542 set off the point *c*, and on a perpendicular let fall therefrom, set off 8·91, which connect as before, and the section will be complete from A to *c*. In like manner, proceed with the rest of the reduced levels at the points *d*, *e*, *f*, &c., till the whole section is drawn.

Although, for the sake of clearness of description, we have desired the person plotting the section to draw the perpendicular, and thereon define the level point of the surface as he proceeds with setting off the horizontal distances step by step, yet in practice he will find it most expeditious in the first instance to place the chamfered edge of his ivory scale for the distances along the datum line, and at once to prick off the whole of the distances (or any convenient portion of them) successively as the numbers appear in the field-book; then draw all the perpendiculars by means of a parallel ruler, or by a T square if the paper is properly fixed on a drawing table; and, lastly, from the vertical scale prick off all the perpendiculars and connect those points, and the section will be made.

The distances given in the proper column of the field-book are supposed to be horizontal distances, and, in measuring them, care should be taken that they are as nearly such as possible (or they must afterwards be reduced thereto), otherwise the section will be longer than it ought to be. For the purpose of assisting the surveyor in making the necessary reduction from the hypothenusal to the horizontal measure, when laying down his section, we annex the following Table, showing the reduction to be made upon each chain's length, for the following quantities of rise, as shown by the reading of the staves:—

Rise in feet for one chain.	Reduction upon one chain in links and decimals.
1	0·01
2	0·04
3	0·11
4	0·19
5	0·29
6	0·44
7	0·56
8	0·74
9	0·94
10	1·16
11	1·40
12	1·76
13	2·01
14	2·24
15	2·61
16	2·99
17	3·39
18	3·76
19	4·23
20	4·64

The section can be referred to any other datum than the one by which it was produced; as, for instance, let it be required to refer the section, Plate II., to a datum line 100 feet below the point A; all that is required to be done is, to draw a line E F parallel to C D, at 100 feet below it; then, by drawing perpendiculars from the surface line to this new datum, as shown by the dotted lines, the transfer will be complete, as the height of any point can be measured by the scale of the section. We need not go through a further explanation of this subject, as an inspection of our engraved example will explain whatever further may be required.

WORKING SECTION.

For the purposes of carrying into execution any work, the section should be much more minute than is requisite for general purposes; it is then called a working section. The following are the field notes taken for such a section, the line having first been carefully set out and a stake driven into the ground at the extremity of each chain's length: these stakes were about 18 inches long and 2 inches square (and were furnished by a country wheelwright at the price of ten-pence per dozen); every tenth stake was circular, and somewhat larger, and had an iron ring round its top, and together with every fifth stake had their tops painted white, the more easily to identify them; they were all numbered (or considered to be numbered) from one end of the line to the other. Plate III. shows the section of the ground and railway at the extreme end of the line where the numbers terminate at 1103 chains or 13¾ miles and 3 chains: we would recommend the student to plot this section from the notes several times, and to various scales, that he may not only better understand the subject, but also for the sake of practice, it being an actual example from the working section of a line of railway now completed and opened to the public.

FIELD NOTES—WORKING SECTION.

Rise.	Back sight.	Fore sight.	Fall.	Distance.	Reduced Levels.	Remarks.
feet.	feet.	feet.	feet.	Links.	feet.	
					270·72	Brought forward (from last page of NOTES).
	4·47	4·53	0·06	103300	270·66	
	4·53	9·22	4·69	103400	265·97	
4·15	9·22	5·07		103500	270·12	
4·83	5·07	0·24		103600	274·95	
4·49	6·36	1·87		103700	279·44	
4·67	6·14	1·47		103800	284·11	
4·52	6·62	2·10		103900	288·63	Side of clapping post of field gate in occupation road.
	2·10	2·24	0·14	103916	288·49	
0·95	10·42	9·47			289·44	Lower hanging hook of gate.
	9·47	13·22	3·75	103944	285·69	Centre of occupation road.
0·07	13·22	13·15		103956	285·76	Edge of road.
4·40	13·15	8·75		103966	290·16	Top of bank.
4·27	8·75	4·48		103976	294·43	Do. do.
0·16	4·48	4·32		104000	294·59	
	2·44	8·84	6·40		288·19	B. M. south side of line.
6·01	8·84	2·83		104100	294·20	
	0·74	2·18	1·44	104200	292·76	
	2·18	5·35	3·17	104300	289·59	
	6·77	7·28	0·51	104400	289·08	
0·03	7·28	7·25		104490	289·11	Edge of ditch.
	7·25	8·36	1·11	104492	288·00	Bottom of ditch.
4·79	8·36	3·57		104500	292·79	Stump, top of bank.
0·62	3·37	2·75		104600	293·41	
1·32	2·75	1·43		104700	294·73	
	1·10	2·25	1·15	104800	293·58	
	2·25	8·88	6·63	104900	286·95	Enter alder plantation.
	5·65	9·53	3·88	104920	283·07	
	9·53	11·50	1·97	105000	281·10	
0·33	5·85	5·52		105021	281·43	
	5·52	12·01	6·49	105100	274·94	
	12·01	12·87	0·86	105148	274·08	
2·10	12·87	10·77		105190	276·18	
2·18	10·77	8·59		105200	278·36	Foot of bank, which rises perpendicularly 1 foot.
7·19	8·59	1·40		105300	285·55	

FIELD NOTES—Working Section.

Rise.	Back sight.	Fore sight.	Fall.	Distance.	Reduced Levels.	Remarks.
					285·55	Brought forward.
3·80	8·22	4·42		105400	289·35	
1·45	4·42	2·97		105500	290 80	
	2 97	3·39	0·42	105600	290·38	
	3·39	5·51	2·12	105700	288·26	
	5·51	7·67	2·16	105800	286·10	
	5·41	6·68	1·27	105827	284·83	Edge of ditch.
	6·68	8·56	1·88	105832	282·95	Bottom of ditch.
2·48	8·56	6·08	6·30	105837	285·43	Top of bank.
	6·08	12·38	4·34	105854	279·13	Foot of bank.
	12·38	16·72	0·62		274·79	
	2·04	2·66	3·82	105900	274·17	
	2·66	6·48	2·38	105940	270·35	Edge of ditch.
	6·48	8·86		105944	267·97	Bottom of ditch.
2·86	8·86	6·00	1·58	105952	270·83	Top of bank.
	6·00	7·58	3·16	105960	269·25	Foot of bank.
	7·58	10·74	4·91	106000	266·09	
	3·33	8·24	0·91	106095	261·18	Top of bank.
	8·24	9·15	4·19	106100	260·27	Stump side of bank.
	9·15	13·34		106105	256·08	Bottom of ditch.
1·69	13·34	11·65	1·15	106110	257·77	Edge of ditch.
	11·65	12·80	0·51	106200	256·62	
	3·62	4·13		106300	256·11	
0·75	4·13	3·38		106349	256·86	Foot of bank.
2·88	3·38	0·50	3·85	106359	259·74	Top of bank.
	0·50	4·35		106368	255·89	Bottom of side drain.
0·27	4·35	4·08	0·23	106386	256·16	Centre of parish road.
	4·08	4·31		106405	255 93	Foot of bank.
3·74	4·31	0·57	2·45	106415	259 67	Top of bank.
	0·57	3·02	0·41		257·22	
	0·99	1·40	1·43	106430	256·81	Foot of bank.
	1·40	2·83	1·58	106500	255·38	
	2·83	4·41	0·07	106600	253·80	
	4·41	4·48		106700	253·73	
0·46	7·80	7·34		106800	254·19	(Crosses foot-path at 106831).
2·93	7·34	4·41		106900	257·12	
3·67	4·41	0·74		107000	260·79	
4·20	10·63	6·43		107100	264·99	
5·06	6·43	1·37		107200	270·05	
5·79	10·76	4·97		107300	275·84	
3·85	4·97	1·12	0·05	107400	279·69	
	5·42	5·47		107500	279·64	
0·91	5·47	4·56	04 4	107600	280·55	
	4·56	5 00	0·56	107637	280·11	Edge of ditch.
	5·00	5·56		107640	279·55	Bottom of ditch.

FIELD NOTES—Working Section.

Rise.	Back sight.	Fore sight.	Fall.	Distance.	Reduced levels.	Remarks.
					279·55	Brought forward.
3·16	5·56	2·40	0·56	107647	282·71	Top of bank.
	2·40	2·96		107654	282·15	Foot of bank.
1·58	2·96	1·38		107700	283·73	
8·84	9·45	0·61		107800	292·57	
5·11	8·44	3·33		107853	297·68	Enter plantation.
2·91	3·33	0·42	1·50	107857	300·59	B. M. on timber stub.
	12·78	14·28		107882	299·09	
4·27	14·28	10·01		107900	303·36	
8·75	10·01	1·26		107947	312·11	
10·42	14·49	4·07		108000	322·53	
1·21	4·07	2·86	0·49	108008	323·74	
	2·86	3·35		108024	323·25	
2·98	3·35	0·37		108047	326·23	
15·33	16·35	1·02		108098	341·56	Top of bank, edge of plantation.
	1·02	1·32	0·30	108100	341·26	
2·74	8·66	5·92		108200	344·00	
0 78	5·92	5·14		108300	344·78	
	5·14	8·43	3·29	108400	341·49	
	1·05	4·50	3·45	108500	338·04	
	4·50	4·94	0·44	108520	337·60	
	4·94	6·83	1·89	108530	335·71	Edge of bank.
	6·83	12·54	5·71	108540	330·00	Foot of bank.
	12·54	16·82	4·28	108600	325·72	
	1·11	9·04	7·93	108700	317·79	
	1·18	9·09	7 91	108800	309·88	
	1·57	9·70	8·13	108900	301·75	
	1·28	9·58	8·30	109000	293·45	
	1·44	9·41	7·97	109100	285·48	
	1·34	9·14	7·80	109200	277·68	
	1·15	8·12	6·97	109300	270·71	
	3·04	4·43	1·39	109386	269·32	Edge of ditch.
	4·43	6·22	1·79	109390	267·53	Bottom of ditch.
1·06	6·22	5·16		109400	268·59	Stump, top of bank.
	5·16	11·10	5·94	109405	262 65	Foot of bank.
1 81	11·10	9·29		109500	264·46	
3·10	8·87	5·77		109600	267·56	At post and rail fence.
1·17	4·63	3·46		109700	268·73	Edge of slope.
	3·46	7·06	3·60	109800	265·13	
	1·96	4·60	2·64	109900	262·49	Foot of slope.
	4·60	4·60		110000	262·49	
0·93	4·60	3·67		110149	263·42	
	4·58	5·03	0 45	110377	262·97	Stump, end of curve.
0·63	5·03	4·40			263·60	On rails at end of curve.
	4·40	4·58	0·18		263·42	B. M. foot of post.
3·53	4·58	1·05			266·95	Top of said post.

In taking levels for a minute section where the observations must be very numerous, and consequently the back and fore sights not very far from each other, the observer will frequently be able to make a number of observations at each setting up of the level at one side of his line, so that his instrument may be about equally distant from his back and fore observations. Due attention to this will save much time and labour, and experience will enable the surveyor at a glance to see where he can set up his level at every remove forward with the greatest advantage. Upon looking down our field notes above, it will be seen it seldom occurred that only one back and one fore sight was obtained at a setting up of the level, and this only took place where the ground was very steep: by the first setting up of the instrument four forward sights were observed, and of course as many back ones; thus the first back sight was 4·47, the corresponding fore sight 4·53; this latter number was also placed as the back sight for the next observation, which was 9·22; this number was in like manner placed as the back sight for the next forward observation, 5·07, which also became the back sight for the last forward observation we could obtain at that setting up of the instrument, namely, 0·24: it should here be remarked that there was a necessity to place each forward reading as a back observation to the next forward reading, otherwise the difference of level between each point of observation would not have been obtained without more arithmetical work; the numbers otherwise only show the difference of level between each and the first point of observation; besides, by this arrangement, the whole section is continuous, however numerous the intermediate observations may be, and having the distances opposite, the whole can be plotted off with facility. The columns of Rise and Fall need no observation after what has already been said upon this subject. The column of distances denotes the continuous measurements from the commencement, Gunter's chain being the unit employed. Our notes commence at the 1033rd chain, and terminate with the end of the work, 1103 chains and 77 links, which we consider an ample extract for the purposes of the student. The column headed "Reduced Levels" contains the height of each point of observation above the datum line, which in this case was Trinity high-water mark, London Bridge: these numbers are obtained by adding the "rises" and subtracting the "falls" from the preceding reduced level, which in our notes commence with 270·72 feet.

THE SECTION.—SEE PLATE III.

The datum line must be drawn, every chain should then be pricked off and the perpendiculars erected; the chains or stakes should then be numbered beneath the datum line, to prevent mistakes, and just above the datum line the height of the surface at each stake should also be inserted; then the said heights can be pricked off upon the perpendiculars respectively, and the intermediate heights plotted from the field notes without fear of error, which otherwise, without great care, would be likely to occur in consequence of so many points falling near to each other, unless the scale be very large: the horizontal scale of the example is 1 inch to 5 chains, and the vertical scale 1 inch to 25 feet. Having drawn the undulating line of the surface through these points upon the perpendiculars, the gradients or intended line of railway may next be laid down; the extreme left-hand point was given, being the level of the rails at the point of junction with another line. The railway is represented by two parallel lines, the upper one being the upper surface of the rails, and the lower one the bottom of the ballasting or formation level, being 2·25 lower than the surface of the rails: for a short distance the line is level, then it rises at the rate of 20 feet per mile, for the two-fold object of diminishing the great cutting and of getting sufficiently high over the road at stake 1064, to allow (with the lowering the surface of the said road a small quantity) of sufficient headway for the public carriages to pass under the railway: from this point the line falls at the rate of 20 feet per mile for a considerable distance, the object being to get as low down as possible further to the eastward, where there was to be a considerable embankment, and by these means such embankment was reduced in dimensions; and furthermore, the earth from the cutting to the right of the road was to be taken eastward to form the said embankment, and therefore the down-hill gradient was favourable for carrying on the work as well as for the drainage of the cutting. Part of the earth from the large cutting was also to be taken to the eastward; the ascending gradient, up to the bridge, was unfavourable for this purpose, however, so far as the bringing out the bottom of the cutting, the upper part being brought down by means of inclined planes: the ascending gradient was unavoidable in this case, but by judiciously working the excavation, little inconvenience and extra expense attended it. Each change of gradients is denoted by a strong vertical line from the datum to the point of change, and the height marked thereon. The quantity of earth-work to form the cuttings and embankments with different slopes should be written upon them, as shown in our example; also over the line of figures denoting the height of the surface above the datum should be placed the depth of the cutting from the surface to formation level at the same point, or the height of the embankment, as the case may be: these heights and depths are those from which the calculations of the quantities are to be made, and therefore must be strictly correct; they should not be taken from the section by the scale, but should be obtained by calculation: the former method being liable to error. The calculation may be thus performed. Let it be required to find the depth of cutting at stake No. 1083, where the height of the surface above datum is 344·78 feet; at stake No. 1064, the height of formation level above datum is 269·20, from which point the gradient descends at the rate of 20 feet per mile, or 0·25 feet per chain, towards No. 1083; the distance from 1064 to 1083 is 19 chains, which multiplied by 0·25, gives 4·75 for the fall of the railway in the interval between the two points; consequently the height of the railway above datum at No. 10·83 is 269·20, minus $4·75 = 264·45$; this sum, subtracted from the whole height of the surface, gives $344·78 - 264·45 = 80·33$, for the depth of the cutting at that point, and so of all the remaining numbers. After giving the above particulars nothing need be added upon this subject. It may be worth observing, that in laying down the gradients care should be had so to dispose them as to produce the minimum quantity of work in the execution, and that the cuttings should equalize the embankments, or, if anything otherwise, they should be a little in excess, to allow for subsidence or slips in the embankments. The facilities for working the excavations and carrying the earth to bank should also be considered; a down-hill gradient in that direction is most suitable, provided it can be obtained without interfering with other and often more important considerations: the drainage of the works during the formation and after the line is completed should also be considered at the time of determining the gradients. We have inserted (Table I. at the end of the work) a very extensive and useful Table of Gradients, which is sufficiently self-explanatory as not to require further notice.

When a surveyor is required to level through a country in a perfectly straight line, and has not the advantage of its being picketed or poled out, his only means to keep a rectilineal course is by ascertaining, as accurately as possible, the magnetic bearing of one extremity from the other, and work in that direction by means of a compass. We once had business of this kind, and determined the bearing of our intended line from the map of the Ordnance survey (allowing for the variation of the needle), and after pursuing the route thus determined, we were surprised and delighted at finding how exactly we came to our required point, convincing us (if a proof had been required) how justly the public confidence has been placed in our national survey.

It is seldom the case in practice that the instrument can be placed precisely equi-distant from the back and forward staves, on account of the inequalities of the ground, &c. It would appear, therefore, to be necessary, to make our results perfectly correct, to apply to each observation the correction for curvature and refraction, as explained in the early pages of our book; this, however, we believe, is seldom done unless in particular cases, where the utmost possible accuracy is necessary, on account of the smallness of such correction, as may be seen by referring to our Table, page 9, where the correction for eleven chains is shown to amount to no more than $\frac{1}{100}$ of a foot; and as the difference in the distances of the instrument from the back and fore staves can in no case equal that sum, it is evident that such correction may be safely disregarded in practice.

Several machines have been constructed or designed for the purpose of describing a section of any ground passed over by the instrument, which at the same time would register the distance passed over, as well as the undulations: perhaps the best of this kind was the one designed and constructed by George Edwards, Esq., Civil Engineer, of Lowestoff, which is fully described and illustrated in the forty-fourth volume of the "Transactions of the Society of Arts," page 123, to which we refer. The use of such machines, however, must, from the nature of the work to be performed, be of a very limited character.

We have now described the leading principles and practice of levelling as employed in engineering operations; and although our observations may appear to be confined to its applicability to railroad purposes, yet the intelligent student will find no difficulty in applying to practice the same principles to every other branch of the profession where levelling operations may be required. We might indeed have multiplied instances and examples which would in reality have had no other effect than to swell our volume, as it must have been, to a great extent, but simply a repetition of the details already given.

Before closing this subject we cannot refrain from stating, that it has long been our opinion that if a register could be kept by some public body (as the Institution of Civil Engineers) of the height of particular spots throughout the kingdom, above some given datum, as Trinity high-water mark, London Bridge, or any other that might be agreed upon, such a record would be invaluable both in a particular and national point of view: to the engineer and geologist it would be most important, and the whole register could be prepared from time to time at a trifling cost, if each engineer and surveyor would but contribute to the common stock by sending to head-quarters the level of any particular spots as he, in the course of his professional engagements, may have opportunity of determining them. We consider that no time is likely to be so favourable for the purpose as the present, as nearly the whole country has been levelled over for railway purposes within the last few years; and no doubt the field notes of the greater part are still in existence, from which a great many such standard levels could be extracted by the parties who took the levels, and which in a few years it will be impossible to eliminate. By way of showing more fully our meaning, we have extracted from our own levelling books a few such standard levels, and arranged them after the manner we have above alluded to.

COUNTY OF KENT.

	Height in feet above Trinity high-water mark, London Bridge.
Upper edge of tablet over door of No. 1 Martello Tower, near Folkstone	256·4
Top of first milestone on the road from Folkstone turnpike to Dover	402·9
Top of second milestone, do.	510·7
Surface of ground at Folkstone turnpike gate	534·6
Dock wall at Dover, opposite Railway Office	7·4

COUNTY OF SURREY.

Surface of ground at New Chapel Turnpike gate . .	188·0
Waste board of Godstone Ponds, back of White Hart Inn .	319·2
Top of twentieth milestone (from Westminster Bridge) on the road from Godstone to East Grinstead	287·6
River Medway (tributary stream) meadows, west side of turnpike road, at Blundley Heath	151·2
Broadham Green, near Oxted, foot of pointing post . .	268·2

COUNTY OF SUSSEX.

Honey-pot Lane, South Chailley Common	122·5
Gullage Farm, source of the Medway, near the barn . .	324·6
Waste weir canal (east side of Lindfield)	82·1
Summit of South Downs at Plumpton Plains	682·5
,, ,, at Mount Harry	573·3
Turnpike road, Brighton to Lewes, near the barracks . .	85·1
Cross roads, at Turner's Hill turnpike gate	535·2

LEVELLING WITH THE THEODOLITE.

The application of the theodolite to the practice of levelling is an operation of great simplicity. We must suppose the reader to be already acquainted with the construction and method of measuring angles with that valuable instrument; and those who have no such knowledge, we refer to the Treatise on Mathematical Drawing Instruments spoken of, where every particular respecting it may be found. The ordinary 5-inch theodolite, of the best construction, is the one we recommend to the use of the surveyor, it being sufficiently accurate for most purposes that fall within his province, and is convenient to use on account of its portability. A larger theodolite is seldom employed, except on surveys of great extent upon trigonometrical principles, as those of the United Kingdom under the direction of the Board of Ordnance, where theodolites of 3 feet diameter have been employed to obtain the requisite degree of accuracy.

To use the theodolite in the common purposes of levelling, it is only necessary to set the instrument up at every spot on the line of country to be levelled, where the inclination changes, without regard to the minor inequalities of the surface, taking care that the adjustments have been carefully examined and rectified, as explained in the book above alluded to, especially those adjustments which set the line of collimation, and the spirit-level attached to the telescope, parallel to each other. Then set the instrument level by means of the parallel plate screws, and direct an assistant to go forward with a staff, having a vane, or cross piece, fixed to it exactly at the same height from the ground as the centre of the axis of the telescope. Having gone to the forward station, the assistant must hold the staff upright, whilst the observer measures the vertical angle, which an imaginary line connecting the instrument and staff makes with the horizon; the instrument and staff should then change places, or, to save time, another staff should take the place of the instrument, and the instrument be removed to the former staff, and from thence the same angle should be taken back again, and the *mean* taken as the correct result.

The distance must then be measured, which will furnish all the data required to find the difference of level between the places of the instrument and staff; this, it will appear evident, is a matter of trigonometrical calculation,* the measured distance being considered as the hypothenuse of a right-angled triangle, of which the perpendicular is the difference of level. It scarcely appears necessary to give the rule for the calculation, but for the sake of uniformity we shall do so.†

Add together the logarithm of the measured distance, and the log. sine of the observed angle; the sum, rejecting 10 *from the index, will be the log. of the difference of level, in feet or links, &c., the same as the distance was measured in.*

If the distance be measured with Gunter's chain, the result (in chains) can at once be obtained in feet, by simply adding to the above two logarithms the constant 1·8195439, which (10 being rejected from the index) will give the log. of the height in feet.

In this manner, by considering the surface of every principal undulation as the hypothenuse of a right-angled triangle, the operation of levelling may be carried on with great rapidity, but, it must be remarked, without pretensions to great accuracy; in fact, in that particular, the use of the spirit-level will never be superseded.

* Capt. Frome's Work, in 8vo., published 1840.

† See Appendix I.

Another method of applying a theodolite to the purposes of levelling was introduced by Sir John Macneill. He caused to be constructed, by Messrs. Troughton and Simms, a more powerful instrument for the purpose. It was a combination of the level and the theodolite. He set it up at the foot of an inclination, and sent a man on with a staff, as above described; and whilst the observer was looking through the telescope, another assistant walked along the line, holding up another staff at every rise and hollow of the intervening surface, and thereby the observer could note how much such rises and hollows were below the line of his vision. The distances from the instrument to the points where the staves were held up could then be measured, and the section drawn by simply ruling a line at the angle of elevation given by the instrument (or, more correctly, by computing the total elevation and setting that up as a perpendicular, and drawing the hypothenusal line thereto), and marking thereon the measured distances, and from such marks drawing perpendiculars of the various lengths indicated by the staff at its different positions: a line connecting the extremities of the perpendicular will represent the section of the surface line.

Instead of measuring the distances, Sir John Macneill had attached to the eye-end of the telescope a beautifully made wire micrometer, similar to those applied to astronomical telescopes, by which he could tell with sufficient accuracy the distances required. This method of levelling, like the former by the theodolite, will give but a general approximation to the truth, depending in a great degree upon the quality of the instruments, and the care bestowed upon the operation.

PART III.

COMPUTATION OF EARTH-WORK—ROAD-MAKING—THE CLINOMETER, ETC.

We have now to show the manner of applying a section to practical purposes. If the object to be attained is the making of a railroad, it is essential that it be formed as nearly level, and as perfectly straight, as the surface of the ground will admit of; for the nearer it approximates thereto, the more profitably will it be worked when completed, as locomotive steam-engines perform the most work with the least expense when the resistance they have to overcome is uniform and invariable. The same remarks hold with respect to a turnpike road; but the inclinations on the latter may be made greater and more variable, being worked by animal power, which is capable of putting forth, on a sudden emergency, a greater exertion for a short time, which is not the case with elemental or mechanical power beyond limits much short of what an animal is capable of.

Sir Henry Parnell, in his valuable Treatise on Roads, recommends that a road should not be made steeper than 1 in 35; that is, for every 35 feet in length of road surface, the difference of level will be 1 foot, that being an inclination which presents no difficulty to fast driving either in ascending or descending. But on a line of railroad to be traversed by locomotive engines, no rate of inclination, or gradient, as it is called,* should exceed 20 feet in a mile, or 1 in 264. To draw the lines of proposed surface (or gradients) upon a section, which shall be the most suitable for the purposes intended, and at the same time to be the most economical in the execution, that is to say, to have the least possible quantity of earthwork in cuttings and embankments, requires judgment and experience: no definite rules can be given for this purpose, as no two sections present the same undulating surface. There is one material point we would suggest, and which should be carefully attended to; viz., that for every piece of cutting, there should be an equal, or *rather less*, quantity of embankment. We say rather less because every newly formed embankment experiences a settlement to a greater or less degree, and therefore more earth will be required to raise it to a proper level. The excess of the cuttings above the embankments should never be great, otherwise the surplus would have to be disposed of in mounds, termed spoil-banks. In no case whatever should the required embankments exceed in cubical contents the quantity of cuttings; for then a serious difficulty occurs—land has to be purchased for the purpose of digging earth to supply the deficiency, which is usually called side cutting.

* Sir John Macneill, in his preface to his valuable translation of M. Navier's little work on the "Means of comparing the respective Advantages of different Lines of Railway," says, "I have rendered the word *peute* by *slope*, in preference to *inclination*, *inclined plane*, or *gradient*, considering the two former, though generally used, as improper expressions; and the latter, to say the least of it, as having so little to recommend it, that I hope it will have an extremely short existence in our nomenclature."

Suppose in the cut below the upper figure to represent the section of an old line of road, and that it were required, by cutting and embankment, to reduce it from its present hilly surface to one uniform rate of inclination from the point A to the point B. The lower

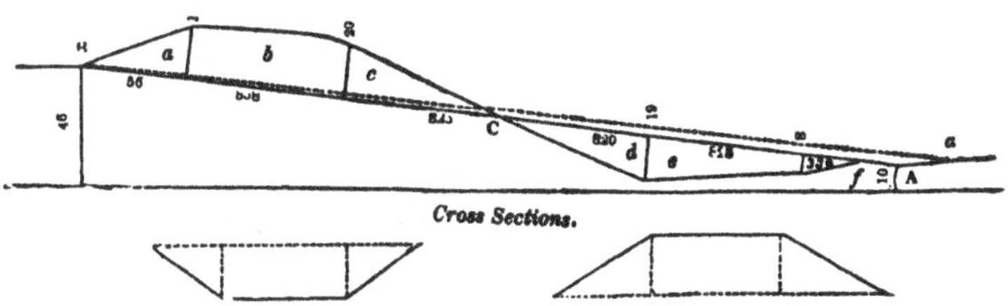

extremity A is 10 feet above the datum line of the section, and the higher point B 46 feet above the datum; consequently, 46 – 10 = 36 feet, the rise from A to B, and the distance 4356 feet, which, divided by the rise (36), will give 1 in 121 for the rate of inclination the road may be brought to.

Upon the section draw the straight line AB, which will show the extent of cutting and embanking to be made. The number of cubic yards of earth to be removed in the cutting between the points B and C, and the cubical contents, in yards, of embankment between C and A, may then be computed in the following manner:

Divide the quantities of cuttings and embankments, as shown upon the longitudinal section, into triangles and trapeziums, determined by the undulations of the surface lines, as shown in the above engraving, where, in the cuttings, *a* and *c* are triangles, *b* a trapezium; and in the embankments *d* and *f* are triangles, *e* a trapezium. The form of the excavation and embankment is shown by the transverse or cross sections. Let the width of the roadway (or base of the cutting, and top of the embankment) be 50 feet, including the foot-path, &c., on each side; the slope of the cutting to be 1½ to 1, that is, 1½ horizontal to 1 perpendicular: consequently, where the depth is 20 feet, the width of the slope at the surface will be 30 feet; the slope of the embankment to be 2 to 1, that is, for 19 feet perpendicular, the base is to be 38 feet. With these data, the cubical quantities, as computed by the valuable Tables of Sir John Macneill,* are as follows:

Excavation	. .	81517 yards.
Embankment	. .	57081 „
		24436 surplus cutting.

We have an excess of 24436 cubic yards of excavation, which is a quantity far too great. In order, therefore, to make the quantity of cutting and embankment more nearly balance each other, it would be necessary to continue the embankment beyond the point A, which would lengthen the inclination, as shown by the dotted line drawn from the point B to *a*; this dotted line would now represent the proposed surface of the road. By such means we diminish the quantity of cutting, and, at the same time, increase that of the embankments; and also by lengthening the inclination, we reduce its steepness. The alteration of the proposed surface line must be so made, that the cubical quantities of excavation and embankment are nearly equal;

* "Tables for calculating the cubic quantity of earthwork in the cuttings and embankments of canals, railways, and turnpike roads." By Sir John Macneill, Civil Engineer, F.R.A.S., &c.

leaving, however, a preponderance in favour of the latter of about 10 per cent. to supply the deficiency occasioned by the consolidation and shrinking of the earth; and if any portion of the excess be then remaining, it may be disposed of in flattening the slopes of the embankments, when no more convenient mode presents itself.

The quantities of earthwork on a given section depend upon the arrangement and disposition of the *gradients*, or proposed surface lines; and there is no practical consideration of more consequence to the engineer, in laying out a proposed line of surface upon a section, especially if it be of any great extent (as the present projected lines of railway), than the most judicious distribution of the cuttings and embankments, which should not only be nearly equal to each other in quantity, but the circumstances must be considered under which the various embankments have to be supplied, it not being alone sufficient that for every hollow on the section there should be a corresponding protuberance, but that such protuberances be advantageously situated for filling the hollows; for otherwise the work assumes a character of difficulty, in consequence of the great additional expense of removing the earth to a considerable distance; and if, in addition, the material has to be conveyed up an ascent, it will be more tedious in the execution.

Knowing the value of practical examples in elementary books, we shall here give the calculations of the above results in full, both by the common method; viz., *The Prismoidal Formula*, and Sir John Macneill's Tables, by which the saving of labour by the use of the Tables will be made apparent.

Prismoidal Formula.—The area of each end added to four times the middle area, and the sum multiplied by the length divided by 6, will give the solid content. If the measures used in the calculation are yards, the result will be the content in cubic yards; but if they are feet, the result must be divided by 27, to obtain the corresponding number of yards.

CALCULATION OF THE TRIANGULAR PORTION *a*.

		Height 0	
		2) 18	
Height . .	18	9	mean height.
Slope . . .	1·5	1·5	slope.
	9·0	4·5	
	18	9	
	27·0	13·5	
Base . . .	50	50·0	base (bottom of cutting, or top of embankment).
	77	63·5	
Height . .	18	9	mean height.
	616	571·5	middle area.
	77	4	
Area of greater end	1386	2286·0	4 times middle area.
		1386·0	area of greater end.
		3672	
		561	length.
		3672	
		22032	
		18360	
		6) 2059992	
		3) 343332	cub. content in feet.
		9) 114444	
		12716	cub. content in yards.

COMPUTATION OF *b*.

Height 18. Area, as before, 1386.

20 height.
1·5 slope.
———
10·0
20
———
30·0
50 base.
———
80
20 height.
———
1600 { area between *b* and *c*.
———

18 }
20 } heights.
—
2) 38
—
19 mean height.
1·5 slope.
———
9·5
19
———
28·5
50 base.
———
78·5
19 mean height.
———
7065
785
———
1491·5 middle area.
4
———
5966·0 4 times middle area.
1386 area of lesser end.
1600 area of greater end.
———
8952
858 length.
———
71616
44760
71616
———
6) 7680816
———
3) 1280136 cub. content in feet.
———
9) 426712
———
47412 cub. content in yards.

COMPUTATION OF *c*.

Area 1600, as before.

```
      20 }
       0 } heights.
      ---
   2) 20
      ---
      10   mean height.
       1·5 slope.
     ----
      50
     10
     ----
     15·0
     50    base.
     ----
     65
      10   mean height.
     ----
     650   middle area.
       4
    -----
    2600   4 times middle area.
    1600   area of greater end.
    -----
    4200
     825   length.
   ------
   21000
   8400
  33600
 --------
6) 3465000
 --------
3) 577500  cub. content in feet.
  -------
9) 192500
  -------
   21389   cub. content in yards.
  -------
```

a = cub. content	12716
b = cub. content	47412
c = cub. content	21389
Total cuttings	81517 cub. yards.

COMPUTATION OF EMBANKMENT *d*.

19	height.
2	slope.
38	
50	base.
88	
19	height.
792	
88	
1672	area.

0, 19	heights.
2) 19	
9·5	mean height.
2	slope.
19·0	
50	base.
69	
9·5	mean height.
34·5	
621	
655·5	middle area.
4	
2622·0	4 times middle area.
1672	area of greater end.
4294	
820	length.
85880	
34352	
6) 3521080	
3) 586847	cont. in cub. feet.
9) 195616	
21735	cont. in cub. yards.

COMPUTATION OF *e*.

Height 8. Area, as before, 1672.

8 height.
2 slope.
—
16
50 base.
—
66
8 height.
——
528 area.
——

19 } heights.
8 }
—
2) 27
——
13·5 mean height.
2 slope.
——
27·0
50 base.
——
77
13·5 mean height.
——
385
231
77
——
1039·5 middle arêa.
4
——
4158·0 4 times middle area.
1672 area of greater end.
528 area of lesser end.
——
6358
825 length.
——
31790
12716
50864
——
6) 5245350
——
3) 874225 cub. content in feet.
——
9) 291408
——
32379 cub. content in yards.
——

COMPUTATION OF f.

Area, as before, 528

8 } heights.
0

2) 8

4 mean height.
2 slope.

8
50 base.

58
4 mean height.

232 middle area.
4

928 4 times middle area.
528 area of greater end.

1456
330 length.

43680
4368

6) 480480

3) 80080 cub. content in feet.

9) 26693

2966 cub. content in yards.

d = cub. content 21735
e = cub. content 32379
f = cub. content 2966

Total embankment . . . . . . 57080 cubic yards.

The same quantities computed by Sir John Macneill's Tables.

THE CUTTINGS.

COMPUTATION OF *a*.

Tabular No.	= 22·67
Length	561
	2267
	13602
	11335
Cont. of *a* in cub. yards	= 12717·87

COMPUTATION OF *b*.

Tabular No.	= 55·26
Length	858
	44208
	27630
	44208
Cont. of *b* in cub. yards	= 47413·08

COMPUTATION OF *c*.

Tabular No.	= 25·92
Length	825
	12960
	5184
	20736
Cont. of *c* in cub. yards . .	= 21384·00

THE EMBANKMENTS.

COMPUTATION OF *d*.

Tabular No.	= ·3519
Base	50
	17·5950
Tabular No.	+ 8·914
	26·509
Length.	820
	530180
	212072
Cub. content .	= 21737·380

COMPUTATION OF *e*.

Tabular No.	= 5000
Base	50
	25·0000
Tabular No.	+ 14·247
	39·247
Length	825
	196235
	78494
	313976
Cub. content .	= 32378·775

COMPUTATION OF *f*.

Tabular No.	= ·1481
Base	50
	7·4050
Tabular No.	+ 1·580
	8·985
Length	330
	269550
	26955
Cub. content	2965·050

RESULTS BY THE TABLES.

CUTTINGS.	EMBANKMENTS.
a = 12717·9	d = 21737·4
b = 47413·1	e = 32378·8
c = 21384·0	f = 2965·0
81515·0	57081·2

By comparing these results with those obtained by the former process, it will be seen that the cubical quantity of cuttings differs but two yards, and that of the embankments but one yard. The computation by the Tables may be abbreviated by using but one place of decimals, which would be sufficiently accurate for practical purposes. Our object is to show the calculations, by the Tables, in their greatest extent, which even then produce a great saving of labour, and, of course, a much greater probability of accuracy, in consequence of the fewer figures employed than the former process.

It will be seen that the calculation of the embankments by the Tables is a longer process than that of the cuttings, the latter being done by simply multiplying a number taken from the Tables (answering to the height or depth at each end) by the length; whilst, for the embankments, the tabular number is first multiplied by the base (or width of roadway), and to the product is added a second tabular number taken out at the same time as the first. The first series of Sir John Macneill's Tables contain the numbers corresponding to a base of 50, and a slope of 1½ to 1 (which is the slope of the cuttings in our example). But for a slope of 2 to 1, reference must be had to the second series of the same Tables, which are applicable to every width of base, and from slopes varying from ½ to 1, to 3 to 1. We have adopted this example to show the calculations both by the *particular* and *general* Tables, as the first and second series of the valuable work referred to may be called.

The following is an extract from Sir John Macneill's preface to his Tables:—"All practical engineers are well aware, by experience, of the inconveniences which arise from the length of time necessary for calculating the cubic quantity of earthwork in the cuttings and embankments of canals, railways, and turnpike roads, especially when the section is of considerable extent, and the ground very uneven. As calculations of this kind are frequently, on a short notice, required to be completed within a limited period, the consequence is, that errors are almost sure to be made, as a multiplicity of figures is necessary, though the calculations in themselves are so very simple.

"To save time in making these calculations, and ensure accuracy in the results, were the principal objects I had in view in constructing the following Tables; how far I have succeeded, must be left to the decision of practical men, for whose use they were intended, and who are best able to judge of their utility.

"An advantage may arise from the use of these Tables, which I had not at first contemplated. By the common but erroneous method of calculation, the cuttings may appear to be equal to the embankments; yet when the work is carried into effect, a large quantity of earth may be required to make up the embankments, or there may be too much earth in the cuttings for the embankments, according to the shape or figure of the section, as will be shown hereafter. Such a circumstance as this cannot take place if the following Tables be used to ascertain the cubic quantities; for, as they are calculated from the prismoidal formula, they will give the true cubic quantity in any cutting or embankment; and consequently, if the cuttings be laid down on the section to balance the embankments, they will be found in practice to do so, when the work comes to be executed.

"Contractors very frequently find that they have more earth to move than they had previously calculated upon from the section, and are, therefore, often great losers. This, in most cases, arises from erroneous calculations; for the common practice is, either to add the two extreme heights together, and to take half the sum for a mean height; or to take half the sum of the areas at each end for a mean area. Both these methods are erroneous; one makes the quantity too much—the other too little."

SLOPES, ETC.

As connected with the subject of earth-work, we may insert in this place some particulars respecting the arrangement of slopes in cuttings and embankments. They are usually expressed in terms of the height or depth of cutting, as half to one, one to one, two to one, &c., signifying that for every foot perpendicular, the cutting shall batter half a foot, one foot, two feet, &c.

The slope adopted must depend upon the nature of the material worked upon. Solid rock may be left perpendicular, whilst loose friable material, or sand, will stand but at a very small angle with the horizon. The true criterion to judge of the proper slope to work to, is to observe, if convenient, what slope or angle the materials naturally assume when left to themselves. To determine this by measurement would be troublesome and tedious: but by the aid of a small instrument called a clinometer, the angle which any sloping surface makes with the horizon may be at once measured, and the ratio of the slope to the perpendicular, as one to one, &c., be readily deduced. As this very useful portable instrument is not generally known, we shall subjoin an engraving and description of it.

The following figure represents a clinometer, or, as it is called in some parts of the country, a *batter level.* It consists of a quadrant A B, of about two inches radius, attached to a flat bar C D, six inches long. The quadrant is graduated to degrees, from B towards A, and adjoining the divisions may be inserted, if required, the corresponding ratio of the slopes, one to one, &c.

An index bar, E, turns upon the centre of the quadrant, and carries a spirit-level by which the index may be set

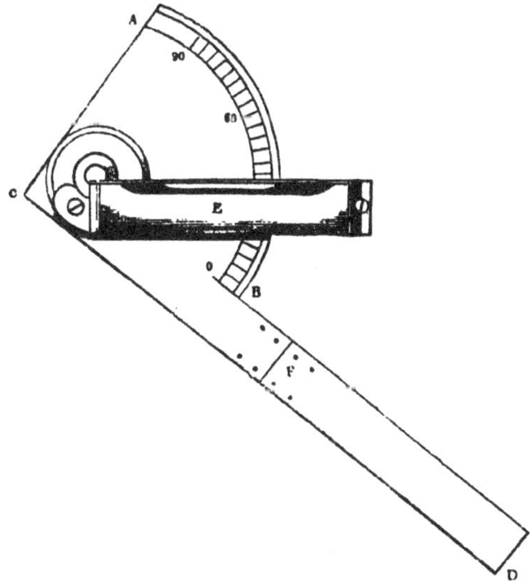

truly horizontal by the hand; and whatever angle is there denoted on the quadrant, will be that of the slope required. At F is a hinge-joint, by which the bar C D may be folded up, and the instrument can then be deposited in a box of very small dimensions, and carried in the pocket without inconvenience.

To use this instrument, open the hinge-joint, and rest the edge of the bar C D on the face of the slope to be measured; then gently move the index E round its centre until the attached spirit-bubble assumes a central position in its glass tube, and the angle, indicated by the index on the graduated arc, will at once measure the inclination. The ratio of the slope to the perpendicular is represented by the natural co-tangent of the angle thus measured; but as the observer may not have at hand a Table of natural co-tangents, &c., we have annexed a Table at once showing the slopes corresponding to the various angles of inclination likely to be required.

It will appear evident, that the longer the bar C D is, the more accurate will the measure of the slope be; but there is no necessity for the instrument to be encumbered with a long bar, which would destroy its portability, because it can easily be attached, by tying, to the end of a long straight rod, which can be furnished by any neighbouring carpenter, and the real slope of an undulating inclined surface can then be accurately measured.

Table of Slopes.

Slope or Batter to 1 foot perpendicular.	Ratio of Slope to perpendicular.	Angle of Slope.		Slope or Batter to 1 foot perpendicular.	Ratio of Slope to perpendicular.	Angle of Slope.	
		With vertical.	With horizon.			With vertical.	With horizon.
ft. in.		° ′	° ′	ft. in.		° ′	° ′
0 ¼	$\frac{1}{48}$ to 1	1 12	88 48	1 0	1 to 1	45 0	45 0
0 ½	$\frac{1}{24}$ „ 1	2 23	87 37	1 3	1¼ „ 1	51 20	38 40
0 ¾	$\frac{1}{16}$ „ 1	3 35	86 25	1 6	1½ „ 1	56 19	33 41
0 1	$\frac{1}{12}$ „ 1	4 46	85 14	1 9	1¾ „ 1	60 15	29 45
0 1¼	$\frac{1}{10}$ nearly 1	5 57	84 3	2 0	2 „ 1	63 26	26 34
0 1½	$\frac{1}{8}$ to 1	7 8	82 52	2 3	2¼ „ 1	66 2	23 58
0 1¾	$\frac{1}{7}$ nearly 1	8 18	81 42	2 6	2½ „ 1	68 12	21 48
0 2	$\frac{1}{6}$ to 1	9 28	80 32	2 9	2¾ „ 1	70 1	19 59
0 2½	$\frac{1}{5}$ nearly 1	11 46	78 14	3 0	3 „ 1	71 34	18 26
0 3	$\frac{1}{4}$ to 1	14 2	75 58	3 6	3½ „ 1	74 3	15 57
0 3½	$\frac{7}{24}$ „ 1	16 16	73 44	4 0	4 „ 1	75 58	14 2
0 4	$\frac{1}{3}$ „ 1	18 26	71 34	4 6	4½ „ 1	77 28	12 32
0 4½	$\frac{6}{16}$ „ 1	20 34	69 26	5 0	5 „ 1	78 41	11 19
0 5	$\frac{5}{12}$ „ 1	22 37	67 23	5 6	5½ „ 1	79 42	10 18
0 5½	$\frac{6}{13}$ „ 1	24 37	65 23	6 0	6 „ 1	80 32	9 28
0 6	$\frac{1}{2}$ „ 1	26 34	63 26	7 0	7 „ 1	81 52	8 8
0 7	$\frac{7}{12}$ „ 1	30 15	59 45	8 0	8 „ 1	82 53	7 7
0 8	$\frac{2}{3}$ „ 1	33 41	56 19	9 0	9 „ 1	83 39	6 21
0 9	$\frac{3}{4}$ „ 1	36 52	53 8	10 0	10 „ 1	84 17	5 43
0 10	$\frac{10}{12}$ „ 1	39 48	50 12	11 0	11 „ 1	84 48	5 12
0 11	$\frac{11}{12}$ „ 1	42 31	47 29	12 0	12 „ 1	85 14	4 46

It is very important, in fixing upon the slopes for the sides of an excavation or embankment, to approximate very nearly to the inclination at which the ground would naturally stand without slipping; for if they be made greater than necessary, a large quantity of labour, and of the surface of the ground, will be uselessly devoted. The proper slope for each particular soil can only be determined by observation and experience. "An embankment that would stand perfectly firm, and bear the action of the weather, when formed of sand, gravel, or the debris of rocks, and other materials that do not retain water in their fissures, would not last one winter, if it chiefly consisted of clay. The same remark applies with equal force to cutting, where it is made through a stratum of clay."* "A slope of 1 to 1, that is, a slope of 45°, is found sufficient for ordinary earth; for clay 1½ to 1, or a slope of 33° 41′ with the horizon, may often be required, unless it can be mixed with open materials to prevent water collecting in the fissures produced by its shrinkage in dry weather. In other cases, so steep a face may be left as ¾ to 1, or even ½ to 1; and the slope that will be likely to stand may easily be judged of, by knowing the nature of the strata which will be cut through, and examining its state when exposed in the surrounding district."

At Boughton Hill, near Canterbury, there is a large cutting through London clay, which, together with the embankment at the foot of the hill, formed of the same material, has been constantly giving way. The slopes of the embankment have been flattened from time to time, and now assume some appearance of consolidation; but the slopes of the cutting near the summit of the hill continue to slip down upon the roadway. From some cross-sections we were able to take a short time since, it

* Tredgold on Railroads, first edition, page 117.

appears that the original slope of the cuttings was about 2 to 1, forming an angle with the horizon of 26° 34′; but the natural slope assumed by the soft clay where it has slipped is about 9°, or a little more than 6¼ to 1.

ON SELECTING A LINE OF COUNTRY FOR A ROAD OR RAILWAY.

The choice of a suitable line of country for the formation of a turnpike-road, a railroad, or a canal, preparatory to the levels being taken, requires both judgment and care; otherwise a fruitless expenditure of time in taking a number of trial-sections may be the result, if attended with no more serious and permanent inconvenience. A person undertaking such a work should previously devote a little time to obtain a knowledge of the country, its localities, its structure, and geological character: such knowledge will lead to the choice of several lines of direction, which appear to the eye as equally favourable; it then becomes necessary to make such preliminary surveys as will enable the engineer to adopt the one which, under all circumstances, is likely to prove the most advantageous.

At p. 113 (1st edition) of the late Mr. Tredgold's work upon Railroads, we find the following observations upon this subject: "In order to facilitate the choice of a line as it regards the surface of the country, the engineer may be reminded, that even in the disposal which nature has made of hills and valleys there is much system. Those things which to the first glance of the better-informed, and at all times to the ignorant, appear to be without order or arrangement, are the result of the uniform action of natural causes, and are, in reality, capable of being traced and described with less difficulty than would be expected. Where a considerable tract of country is to be surveyed, the best index to its elevations and depressions is its streams and rivers; these indicate every change of inclination, and, to the experienced eye, with considerable precision. It will also be observed, that each river has its system of valleys; and except in a few instances, where the draining is effected by the outburst of an open stratum, a district, whose bounding ridge is easily traced, is drained by its river and system of valleys.

"Having formed a tolerable idea of the best direction for the road, the next step must be to make a more particular survey, with a view to fix nearly the precise line. We would recommend the principal engineer to have this done by rectangular lines, as infinitely superior to surveying by triangles, in giving him an exact knowledge of the surface of the country. Perhaps, with the assistance of a diagram, we shall be able to render the advantage of this method obvious.

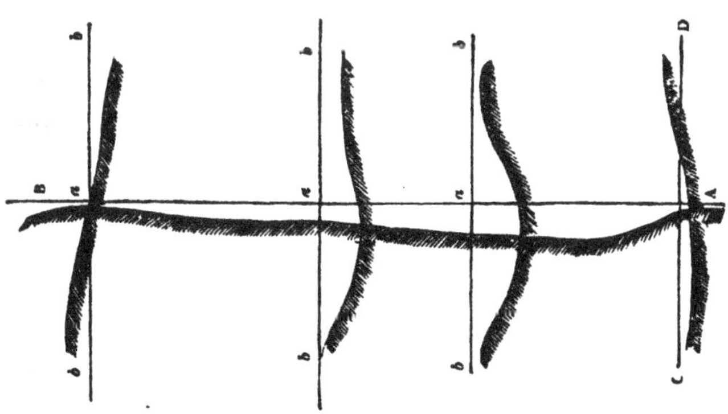

"Let A B be a portion of the intended line, and C D the breadth of the country to be included in the survey. At any suitable distances choose stations, *a*, *a*, *a*, their distances apart depending on the changes of level, and let the principal line A B, and also the cross lines *b b*, *b b*, &c., be accurately levelled, and then drawn, as shown in the figure, on the plan of the line of road. If the distance *b b* is required to be considerable, perhaps an additional line in the principal direction may be necessary. The etched lines show the form of the surface at the lines A B, *b b*, *b b*, &c., on the plan; and the latter being sections at right angles to A B, there is no difficulty in seeing the extent of cutting, or of embankment, that may be avoided by varying the position of the principal line. In fact, a plan of this kind, to a person familiar with sections, is better than a model of the country."

The most advantageous direction for a line, either of roadway or railroad, intended to connect two places, is evidently that of a right line, both horizontally and vertically: if one extremity of the line is more elevated than another, the straight line connecting them will be an inclined plane, having one uniform rate of inclination; but if a uniform slope cannot be obtained in the direct line, it is necessary to deviate therefrom to obtain, as nearly as the circumstances of the country will admit, such an inclined plane, or at least to obtain continued progressive rises, avoiding as much as possible the introduction of useless ascents, that is, ascending where we must descend again, and *vice versâ*. When a line of road is encumbered with numerous and extensive useless ascents, the wasteful expenditure of power in the conveyance of goods is very great, as the number of feet actually ascended is increased many times more than is necessary, if each height, when once gained, were not lost again.

Sir Henry Parnell, in his valuable treatise on Roads, gives the following instances of this kind of road-making:—"As one instance, amongst others, of the serious injury which the public sustain by this system of roadmaking, the road between London and Barnet may be mentioned, on which the total number of perpendicular feet that a horse must now ascend is upwards of 1300, although Barnet is only 500 feet higher than London; and in going from Barnet to London, a horse must ascend 800 feet, although London is 500 feet lower than Barnet."

Another instance of this defect in road-engineering is observable in the line of the old road across the island of Anglesea, on which a horse was obliged to ascend and descend 1283 perpendicular feet more than was found necessary by Mr. Telford, when he laid out the present new line, as shown by the annexed Table:

	Height of summit above high water.	Total rise and fall.	Length.	
			Miles.	Yards.
Old road .	339	3540	24	428
New road .	193	2257	21	1596
Difference	146	1283	2	592

In choosing the best direction for a line of roadway, the rate of inclination which can be obtained, with a moderate outlay in cuttings and embankments, is a consideration of greater importance than the mere maintaining of a direct line. For though the measured length of a circuitous route may be considerably greater than the length of a direct line, yet if the inclinations in the former case are much more favourable than those in the latter, it must be evident that more may be gained in speed, with the same expenditure of power, than is lost by the increase of distance. Thus, if two roads rise, one at the rate of 1 in 15, and the other at the rate of 1 in 35, the same expenditure of power will move a weight through 15 feet of the one and 35 feet of the other, at the same rate.

Upon the subject of the maintenance of turnpike roads, we shall annex an abstract of the General Rules for Constructing and Repairing Roads, laid down by the late Mr. Telford, and which is so fully treated upon in the important work of Sir H. Parnell on Roads.

SHAPE, OR TRANSVERSE SECTION.

The roadway should be 30 feet broad; the centre should be 6 inches higher than the level of the sides, where the junction of the surface, with the sloping edge of the footpaths, or other defining bounds of the road-way, form the side channels; at 4 feet from the centre (on each side) the surface should be half an inch lower; at 9 feet, it should be 2 inches lower; and at 15 feet, its extreme edge, it should be 6 inches lower: this will give the form of a flat ellipse, which is well adapted for carrying off the water to the side channels, without making the cross section of the road too round, and allow the sun and wind to have a greater effect in evaporation, and keeping the road dry. In giving the surface one uniform curvature from side to side, the surveyor should use such a level as is described at page 96.

The footpaths should be 6 feet broad, and have an inclined surface of 1 inch in a yard towards the road; its surface should not be lower than the level of the centre of the road, and the edge should be sloped down (and covered with green sod) to meet the roadway, and form the side channel to carry off the water from the surface.

DRAINAGE.

All open main drains should be cut on the field side of the road fences, and should lead to the natural water-courses of the country; in general, they should be 3 feet deep below the bed of the road, 1 foot wide at bottom, and from 3 to 4 feet wide at top. Stone drains and culverts should also be made under the road, and continued to the open side drains, or ditches; side channels (before named) must be made on the road side, with openings of masonry into the cross drains, to prevent any water lying on the road, it being necessary, in order to preserve the surface of a road perfect, that it be kept completely dry. All land springs ought to be carried from the site of the road by under-draining.

FENCES.

"All road fences should be kept as low as possible, never being allowed to exceed 5 feet in height, in order that they may not intercept the sun and wind, and diminish their effects in producing evaporation;" and for the same reason no trees should be allowed to grow by the side of a road; for by keeping the roads wet, they occasion the rapid wear of the materials of which they are formed.

ROAD MATERIALS.

The hardest description of stone should always be preferred, such as basalt, granite, quartz, &c. "The whinstones found in different parts of the United Kingdom, Guernsey granite, Mountsorrel and Hartshill stone of Leicestershire, and the pebbles of Shropshire, Staffordshire, and Warwickshire, are among the best of the stones now commonly in use. The schistus rocks, being of a slaty and argillaceous structure, will make smooth roads, but they are rapidly destroyed when wet by the pressure of the wheels, and occasion great expense in scraping, and the constantly laying on of new coatings. Limestone is defective in the same respect. Sandstone is generally much too weak for the surface of a road; it will never make a hard one. The hardest flints are nearly as good as the best limestone; but the softer kinds are quickly crushed by the wheels of carriages, and make heavy and dirty roads. Gravel, when it consists of pebbles of the harder sorts of stones, will make a good road; but when it consists of limestone, sandstone, flint, and other weak stones, it will not; for it wears so rapidly, that the crust of a road made with it always consists of a large portion of the earthy matter to which it is reduced, and prevents the gravel from becoming consolidated, and the road from attaining that perfect hardness it ought to possess."* When the materials are stone, they should be broken to a size of a cubical form not exceeding 2½ inches in their largest dimensions,

* Abridged from Sir H. Parnell on Roads, page 271.

and should be capable of passing through a ring of that diameter. When it consists of gravel, the pebbles which are from 1 to 1½ inch in size only should be used for the middle part of the road; all larger pebbles should be broken; the smaller stones may be used for the sides of the roads and the footpaths.

THE FOUNDATION AND DISPOSITION OF MATERIALS.

Before the foundation is laid, the surface on which it is to rest must be prepared, by making it level from side to side, and, if necessary, raising it so that the finished surface of the road may not be below the level of the adjoining fields. If the subsoil be wet and elastic, it must be rendered non-elastic by whatever means is best adapted to overcome the cause, as drainage, &c. The foundation should consist of a rough close-set pavement, of any kind of stones that can be most readily procured; those set in the middle of the road should be 7 inches in depth; at 9 feet from the centre, 5 inches; at 12 feet from the centre, 4 inches; and at 15 feet, 3 inches. They should be set with their broadest faces downwards, and lengthwise across the road; and no stone should be more than 5 inches broad on its face. "The irregularities of the upper part of the pavement should be broken off with the hammer, and all the interstices should be filled with stone chips, firmly wedged, or packed by hand with a light hammer; so that, when the pavement is finished, there may be a convexity of 4 inches in the breadth of 15 feet from the centre.

"The middle 18 feet of pavement should be coated

with hard broken stones, of the form and size described under the head 'Road Materials,' to the depth of 6 inches. Four of these 6 inches to be first put on, and worked in by carriages and horses; care being taken to rake in the ruts until the surface becomes firm and consolidated, after which the remaining 2 inches are to be put on.

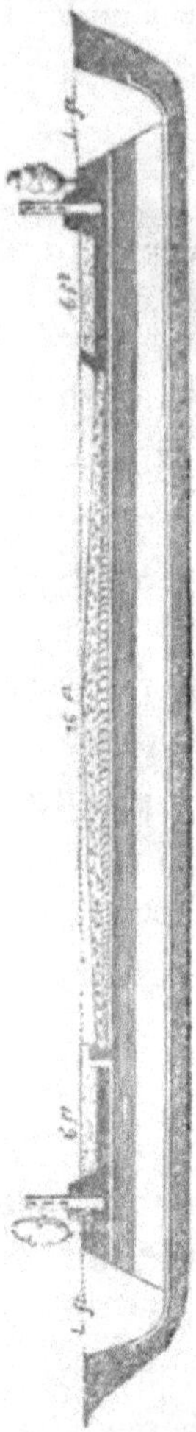

"The paved spaces on each side of the 18 middle feet should be coated with broken stones, or well-cleansed strong gravel, up to the footpath, or other boundary of the road, so as to make the whole convexity of the road 6 inches from the centre to the sides of it; and the whole of the materials should be covered with a binding of an inch and a half in depth of good gravel, free from clay or earth."

The footpaths should be made with a coating of strong gravel, or small broken stones, at least 6 inches deep. The annexed engraving exhibits a section of a road constructed according to the above rules.

REPAIRING ROADS.

Towards the latter end of the autumn of each year, a road should be put into a complete state of repair, to preserve it from being broken up during the following winter, between which time and the preceding spring, all repairs, by laying on of new materials, should be done. If thin coatings be laid on at a time, and when the ground is wet, they will soon be worked into the surface without being crushed into powder.

All ruts and hollows should be filled up as soon as they appear. The side channels and drains should be continually kept clean, and free from obstruction; and all damage they may have sustained be made good as soon as discovered.

"A road should be scraped from time to time, so as never to have half an inch of mud upon it; the mud should not be scraped into, or allowed to remain in, the side channels, so as to stop the running of water in them.

"The hedges should be kept constantly clipped and cut as low as possible, without rendering them unfit for confining cattle; and all projecting branches of the trees in the fences should be lopped."

In the minutes of evidence given before a Select Committee of the House of Commons on the subject of Steam Carriages, we find the following paragraph as part of the evidence given by Sir John Macneill:

"Well-made roads, formed of clean, hard, broken stone, placed on a solid foundation, are very little affected by changes of atmosphere; weak roads, or those that are imperfectly formed of gravel, flint, or round pebbles, without a bottoming or foundation of stone pavement or concrete, are, on the contrary, much affected by changes of the weather. In the formation of such roads, and before they become bound or firm, a considerable portion of the subsoil mixes with the stone or gravel, in consequence of the necessity of putting the gravel on in thin layers: this mixture of earth or clay, in dry warm seasons, expands by the heat, and makes the road loose and open; the consequence is, that the stones are thrown out, and many of them are crushed and ground into dust, producing considerable wear and diminution of the materials: in wet weather, also, the clay or earth, mixed with the stones, absorbs moisture, becomes soft, and allows the stones to move and rub against each other when acted upon by the feet of horses or wheels of carriages. This attrition of the stones against each other wears them out surprisingly fast, and produces large quantities of mud, which tend to keep the road damp, and by that means increase the injury."

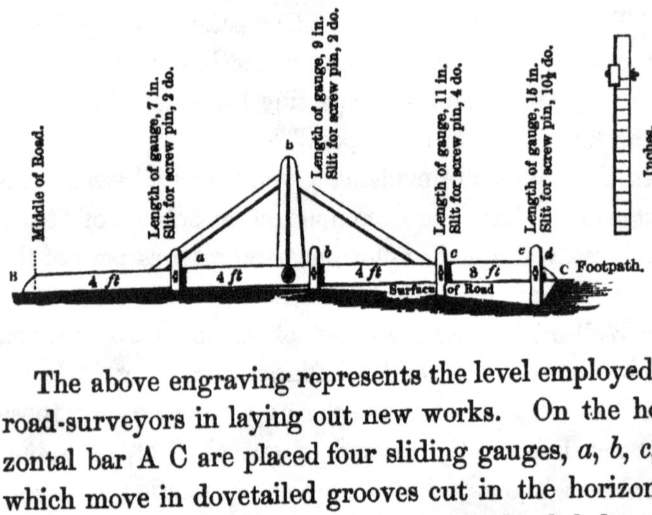

The above engraving represents the level employed by road-surveyors in laying out new works. On the horizontal bar A C are placed four sliding gauges, *a*, *b*, *c*, *d*, which move in dovetailed grooves cut in the horizontal bar, and when adjusted to their proper depth below the bottom edge of the level, can be firmly fixed in their position by a thumb-screw. A section of this portion of the instrument, taken through the line at *e*, is given on the right, drawn to a larger scale; the remaining parts of the instrument require no explanation.

For laying out slopes, the clinometer, described at page 82, is the best instrument that can be used.

TABLE I.—*Showing the reduction upon each chain necessary to reduce hypothenusal to horizontal measure.*

Angle of ascent or descent.	Reduction in links.	Angle of ascent or descent.	Reduction in links.	Angle of ascent or descent.	Reduction in links.
° ′		° ′		° ′	
4 0	¼	23 48	8½	33 55	17
5 44	½	24 30	9	34 25	17½
7 2	¾	25 11	9½	34 55	18
8 7	1	25 51	10	35 25	18½
11 28	2	26 30	10½	35 54	19
12 50	2½	27 8	11	36 24	19½
14 5	3	27 45	11½	36 53	20
15 13	3½	28 22	12	37 21	20½
16 15	4	28 58	12½	37 49	21
17 15	4½	29 33	13	38 17	21½
18 12	5	30 8	13½	38 45	22
19 6	5½	30 41	14	39 12	22½
19 57	6	31 15	14½	39 39	23
20 47	6½	31 48	15	40 6	23½
21 34	7	32 20	15½	40 33	24
22 20	7½	32 52	16	40 58	24½
23 5	8	33 24	16½	41 25	25

Table II.—*Gradients or Inclined Planes.*

Ascent or Descent.		Rate of inclination.	Angle of inclination.	Ascent or Descent.		Rate of inclination.	Angle of inclination.
In 1 mile.	In 1 chain.			In 1 mile.	In 1 chain.		
feet.	ft. dec.		° ′ ″	feet.	ft. dec.		° ′ ″
1	0·013	1 in 5280·0	0 0 39	51	0·638	1 in 103·5	0 33 12
2	0·025	... 2640·0	0 1 18	52	0·650	... 101·5	0 33 51
3	0·038	... 1760·0	0 1 57	53	0·663	... 99·6	0 34 30
4	0·050	... 1320·0	0 2 36	54	0·675	... 97·8	0 35 10
5	0·063	... 1056·0	0 3 16	55	0·688	... 96·0	0 35 49
6	0·075	... 880·0	0 3 55	56	0·700	... 94·3	0 36 28
7	0·088	... 754·3	0 4 34	57	0·713	... 92·6	0 37 7
8	0·100	... 660·0	0 5 13	58	0·725	... 91·0	0 37 46
9	0·113	... 586·7	0 5 52	59	0·738	... 89·5	0 38 25
10	0·125	... 528·0	0 6 31	60	0·750	... 88·0	0 39 4
11	0·138	... 480·0	0 7 10	61	0·763	... 86·6	0 39 43
12	0·150	... 440·0	0 7 49	62	0·775	... 85·2	0 40 22
13	0·163	... 406·1	0 8 28	63	0·788	... 83·8	0 41 1
14	0·175	... 377·1	0 9 7	64	0·800	... 82·5	0 41 40
15	0·188	... 352·0	0 9 46	65	0·813	... 81·2	0 42 19
16	0·200	... 330·0	0 10 25	66	0·825	... 80·0	0 42 58
17	0·213	... 310·6	0 11 4	67	0·838	... 78·8	0 43 37
18	0·225	... 293·3	0 11 43	68	0·850	... 77·6	0 44 16
19	0·238	... 277·9	0 12 22	69	0·863	... 76·5	0 44 55
20	0·250	... 264·0	0 13 1	70	0·875	... 75·4	0 45 34
21	0·263	... 251·4	0 13 40	75	0·938	... 70·4	0 48 50
22	0·275	... 240·0	0 14 20	80	1·000	... 66 0	0 52 5
23	0·288	... 229·6	0 14 59	85	1·063	... 62·1	0 55 20
24	0·300	... 220·0	0 15 38	90	1·126	... 58·7	0 58 36
25	0·313	... 211·2	0 16 17	95	1·188	... 55·6	1 1 51
26	0·325	... 203·1	0 16 56	100	1·250	... 52·8	1 5 6
27	0·338	... 195·6	0 17 35	110	1·375	... 48·0	1 11 37
28	0·350	... 188·6	0 18 14	120	1·500	... 44·0	1 18 7
29	0·363	... 182·1	0 18 53	130	1·625	... 40·6	1 24 38
30	0·375	... 176·0	0 19 32	140	1·750	... 37·7	1 31 8
31	0·388	... 170·3	0 20 11	150	1·875	... 35·2	1 37 38
32	0·400	... 165·0	0 20 50	160	2·000	... 33·0	1 44 8
33	0·413	... 160·0	0 21 29	170	2·125	... 31·1	1 50 39
34	0·425	... 155·3	0 22 8	180	2·250	... 29·3	1 57 9
35	0·438	... 150·9	0 22 47	190	2·375	... 27·8	2 3 39
36	0·450	... 146·7	0 23 26	200	2·500	... 26·4	2 10 9
37	0·463	... 142·7	0 24 5	220	2·750	... 24·0	2 23 9
38	0·475	... 138·9	0 24 44	240	3·000	... 22·0	2 36 9
39	0·488	... 135·4	0 25 23	260	3·250	... 20·3	2 49 9
40	0·500	... 132·0	0 26 3	280	3·500	... 18·9	3 2 8
41	0·513	... 128·8	0 26 42	300	3·750	... 17·6	3 15 7
42	0·525	... 125·7	0 27 21	320	4·000	... 16·5	3 28 6
43	0·538	... 122·8	0 28 0	340	4·250	... 15·3	3 41 4
44	0·550	... 120·0	0 28 39	360	4·500	... 14·7	3 54 2
45	0·563	... 117·3	0 29 18	380	4·750	... 13·9	4 6 59
46	0·575	... 114·8	0 29 57	400	5·000	... 13·2	4 19 56
47	0·588	... 112·3	0 30 36	425	5·313	... 12·4	4 36 7
48	0·600	... 110·0	0 31 15	450	5·625	... 11·7	4 52 17
49	0·613	... 107·8	0 31 54	475	5·938	... 11·1	5 8 26
50	0·625	... 105·6	0 32 33	500	6·250	... 10·6	5 24 35

TABLE III.—*To convert Links into Feet.*

Links	CHAINS.									
	0	1	2	3	4	5	6	7	8	9
	feet.	feet.	feet.	feet.	feet.	feet.	feet.	feet.	feet.	feet.
0	0·0	66·0	132·0	198·0	264·0	330·0	396·0	462·0	528·0	594·0
1	0·7	66·7	132·7	198·7	264·7	330·7	396·7	462·7	528·7	594·7
2	1·3	67·3	133·3	199·3	265·3	331·3	397·3	463·3	529·3	595·3
3	2·0	68·0	134·0	200·0	266·0	332·0	398·0	464·0	530·0	596·0
4	2·6	68·6	134·6	200·6	266·6	332·6	398·6	464·6	530·6	596·6
5	3·3	69·3	135·3	201·3	267·3	333·3	399·3	465·3	531·3	597·3
6	4·0	70·0	136·0	202·0	268·0	334·0	400·0	466·0	532·0	598·0
7	4·6	70·6	136·6	202·6	268·6	334·6	400·6	466·6	532·6	598·6
8	5·3	71·3	137·3	203·3	269·3	335·3	401·3	467·3	533·3	599·3
9	5·9	71·9	137·9	203·9	269·9	335·9	401·9	467·9	533·9	599·9
10	6·6	72·6	138·6	204·6	270·6	336·6	402·6	468·6	534·6	600·6
11	7·3	73·3	139·3	205·3	271·3	337·3	403·3	469·3	535·3	601·3
12	7·9	73·0	130·0	205·9	271·9	337·9	403·9	409·9	535·9	601·9
13	8·6	74·6	140·6	206·6	272·6	338·6	404·6	470·6	536·6	602·6
14	9·2	75·2	141·2	207·2	273·2	339·2	405·2	471·2	537·2	603·2
15	9·9	75·9	141·9	207·9	273·9	339·9	405·9	471·9	537·9	603·9
16	10·6	76·6	142·6	208·6	274·6	340·6	406·6	472·6	538·6	604·6
17	11·2	77·2	143·2	209·2	275·2	341·2	407·2	473·2	539·2	605·2
18	11·9	77·9	143·9	209·9	275·9	341·9	407·9	473·9	539·9	605·9
19	12·5	78·5	144·5	210·5	276·5	342·5	408·5	474·5	540·5	606·5
20	13·2	79·2	145·2	211·2	277·2	343·2	409·2	475·2	541·2	607·2
21	13·9	79·9	145·9	211·9	277·9	343·9	409·9	475·9	541·9	607·9
22	14·5	80·5	146·5	212·5	278·5	344·5	410·5	476·5	542·5	608·5
23	15·2	81·2	147·2	213·2	279·2	345·2	411·2	477·2	543·2	609·2
24	15·8	81·8	147·8	213·8	279·8	345·8	411·8	477·8	543·8	609·8
25	16·5	82·5	148·5	214·5	280·5	346·5	412·5	478·5	544·5	610·5
26	17·2	83·2	149·2	215·2	281·2	347·2	413·2	479·2	545·2	611·2
27	17·8	83·8	149·8	215·8	281·8	347·8	413·8	479·8	545·8	611·8
28	18·5	84·5	150·5	216·5	282·5	348·5	414·5	480·5	546·5	612·5
29	19·1	85·1	151·1	217·1	283·1	349·1	415·1	481·1	547·1	613·1
30	19·8	85·8	151·8	217·8	283·8	349·8	415·8	481·8	547·8	613·8
31	20·5	86·5	152·5	218·5	284·5	350·5	416·5	482·5	548·5	614·5
32	21·1	87·1	153·1	219·1	285·1	351·1	417·1	483·1	549·1	615·1
33	21·8	87·8	153·8	219·8	285·8	351·8	417·8	483·8	549·8	615·8
34	22·4	88·4	154·4	220·4	286·4	352·4	418·4	484·4	550·4	616·4
35	23·1	89·1	155·1	221·1	287·1	353·1	419·1	485·1	551·1	617·1
36	23·8	89·8	155·8	221·8	287·8	353·8	419·8	485·8	551·8	617·8
37	24·4	90·4	156·4	222·4	288·4	354·4	420·4	486·4	552·4	618·4
38	25·1	91·1	157·1	223·1	289·1	355·1	421·1	487·1	553·1	619·1
39	25·7	91·7	157·7	223·7	289·7	355·7	421·7	487·7	553·7	619·7
40	26·4	92·4	158·4	224·4	290·4	356·4	422·4	488·4	554·4	620·4
41	27·1	93·1	159·1	225·1	291·1	357·1	423·1	489·1	555·1	621·1
42	27·7	93·7	159·7	225·7	291·7	357·7	423·7	489·7	555·7	621·7
43	28·4	94·4	160·4	226·4	292·4	358·4	424·4	490·4	556·4	622·4
44	29·0	95·0	161·0	227·0	293·0	359·0	425·0	491·0	557·0	623·0
45	29·7	95·7	161·7	227·7	293·7	359·7	425·7	491·7	557·7	623·7
46	30·4	96·4	162·4	228·4	294·4	360·4	426·4	492·4	558·4	624·4
47	31·0	97·0	163·0	229·0	295·0	361·0	427·0	493·0	559·0	625·0
48	31·7	97·7	163·7	229·7	295·7	361·7	427·7	493·7	559·7	625·7
49	32·3	98·3	164·3	230·3	296·3	362·3	428·3	494·3	560·3	626·3

TABLE III.—*To convert Links into Feet* (continued).

Links	CHAINS.									
	0	1	2	3	4	5	6	7	8	9
	feet.	feet.	feet.	feet.	feet.	feet.	feet.	feet.	feet.	feet.
50	33·0	99·0	165·0	231·0	297·0	363·0	429·0	495·0	561·0	627·0
51	33·7	99·7	165·7	231·7	297·7	363·7	429·7	495·7	561·7	627·7
52	34·3	100·3	166·3	232·3	298·3	364·3	430·3	496·3	562·3	628·3
53	35·0	101·0	167·0	233·0	299·0	365·0	431·0	497·0	563·0	629·0
54	35·6	101·6	167·6	233·6	299·6	365·6	431·6	497·6	563·6	629·6
55	36·3	102·3	168·3	234·3	300·3	366·3	432·3	498 3	564·3	630·3
56	37·0	103·0	169·0	235·0	301·0	367·0	433·0	499·0	565·0	631·0
57	37·6	103·6	169·6	235·6	301·6	367·6	433·6	499·6	565·6	631·6
58	38·3	104·3	170 3	236·3	302·3	368·3	434·3	500·3	566·3	632·3
59	38·9	104·9	170·9	236·9	302·9	368·9	434·9	500·9	566·9	632·9
60	39·6	105·6	171·6	237·6	303·6	369·6	435·6	501·6	567·6	633·6
61	40·3	106·3	172·3	238·3	304·3	370·3	436·3	502·3	568·3	634·3
62	40·9	106·9	172·9	238·9	304·9	370·9	436·9	502·9	568·9	634·9
63	41·6	107·6	173·6	239·6	305·6	371·6	437·6	503·6	569·6	635·6
64	42·2	108·2	174·2	240·2	306·2	372·2	438·2	504·2	570·2	636·2
65	42·9	108·9	174·9	240·9	306·9	372·9	438·9	504·9	570·9	636·9
66	43·6	109·6	175·6	241·6	307·6	373·6	439·6	505·6	571·6	637·6
67	44·2	110·2	176·2	242·2	308·2	374·2	440·2	506·2	572·2	638·2
68	44·9	110·9	176·9	242·9	308·9	374·9	440·9	506·9	572·9	638·9
69	45·5	111·5	177·5	243·5	309·5	375·5	441·5	507·5	573·5	639·5
70	46·2	112·2	178·2	244·2	310·2	376·2	442·2	508·2	574·2	640·2
71	46·9	112·9	178·9	244·9	310·9	376·9	442·9	508·9	574·9	640·9
72	47·5	113·5	179·5	245·5	311·5	377·5	443·5	509·5	575·5	641·5
73	48·2	114·2	180·2	246·2	312·2	378·2	444·2	510·2	576·2	642·2
74	48·8	114·8	180·8	246·8	312·8	378·8	444·8	510·8	576·8	642·8
75	49·5	115·5	181·5	247·5	313·5	379·5	445·5	511·5	577·5	643·5
76	50·2	116·2	182·2	248·2	314·2	380·2	446·2	512·2	578·2	644·2
77	50·8	116·8	182·8	248·8	314·8	380·8	446·8	512·8	578 8	644·8
78	51·5	117·5	183·5	249·5	315·5	381·5	447·5	513·5	579·5	645·5
79	52·1	118·1	184·1	250·1	316·1	382·1	448·1	514·1	580·1	646·1
80	52·8	118·8	184·8	250·8	316·8	382·8	448·8	514·8	580·8	646·8
81	53·5	119·5	185·5	251·5	317·5	383·5	449·5	515·5	581·5	647·5
82	54·1	120·1	186·1	252·1	318·1	384·1	450·1	516·1	582·1	648·1
83	54·8	120·8	186·8	252·8	318 8	384·8	450·8	516·8	582·8	648·8
84	55·4	121·4	187·4	253·4	319·4	385·4	451·4	517·4	583·4	649·4
85	56·1	122·1	188·1	254·1	320·1	386·1	452·1	518·1	584·1	650 1
86	56·8	122·8	188·8	254·8	320·8	386·8	452·8	518·8	584·8	650·8
87	57·4	123·4	189·4	255·4	321·4	387·4	453·4	519·4	585·4	651·4
88	58·1	124·1	190·1	256·1	322·1	388·1	454·1	520·1	586·1	652·1
89	58·7	124·7	190·7	256·7	322·7	388·7	454·7	520·7	586·7	652·7
90	59·4	125·4	191·4	257·4	323·4	389·4	455·4	521·4	587·4	653·4
91	60·1	126·1	192·1	258·1	324·1	390·1	456·1	522·1	588·1	654·1
92	60·7	126·7	192·7	258·7	324·7	390·7	456·7	522·7	588·7	654·7
93	61·4	127·4	193·4	259·4	325·4	391·4	457·4	523·4	589·4	655·4
94	62·0	128·0	194·0	260·0	326·0	392·0	458·0	524·0	590·0	656·0
95	62·7	128·7	194·7	260·7	326·7	392·7	458·7	524·7	590·7	656·7
96	63·4	129·4	195·4	261·4	327·4	393·4	459·4	525·4	591·4	657·4
97	64·0	130·0	196·0	262·0	328·0	394·0	460·0	526·0	592·0	658·0
98	64·7	130·7	196·7	262·7	328 7	394·7	460·7	526·7	592·7	658·7
99	65·3	131·3	197·3	263·3	329·3	395·3	461·3	527·3	593·3	659 3

TABLE IV.—*To convert Feet into Links.*

Feet.	FEET.									
	0	100	200	300	400	500	600	700	800	900
	links.	links.	links.	links.	links.	links.	links.	links.	links.	links.
0	0·0	151·5	303·0	454·5	606·1	757·6	000·1	1060·6	1212·1	1363·6
1	1·5	153·0	304·5	456·1	607·6	759·1	910·6	1062·1	1213·6	1365·2
2	3·0	154·5	306·1	457·6	609·1	760·6	912·1	1063·6	1215·2	1366·7
3	4·5	156·1	307·6	459·1	610·6	762·1	913·6	1065·2	1216·7	1368·2
4	6·1	157·6	309·1	460·6	612·1	763·6	915·2	1066·7	1218·2	1369·7
5	7·6	159·1	310·6	462·1	613·6	765·2	916·7	1068·2	1219·7	1371·2
6	9·1	160·6	312·1	463·6	615·2	766·7	918·2	1069·7	1221·2	1372·7
7	10·6	162·1	313·6	465·2	616·7	768·2	919·7	1071·2	1222·7	1374·2
8	12·1	163·6	315·2	466·7	618·2	769·7	921·2	1072·7	1224·2	1375·8
9	13·6	165·2	316·7	468·2	619·7	771·2	922·7	1074·2	1225·8	1377·3
10	15·2	166·7	318·2	469·7	621·2	772·7	924·2	1075·8	1227·3	1378·8
11	16·7	168·2	319·7	471·2	622·7	774·2	925·8	1077·3	1228·8	1380·3
12	18·2	169·7	321·2	472·7	624·2	775·8	927·3	1078·8	1230·3	1381·8
13	19·7	171·2	322·7	474·2	625·8	777·3	928·8	1080·3	1231·8	1383·3
14	21·2	172·7	324·2	475·8	627·3	778·8	930·3	1081·8	1233·3	1384·8
15	22·7	174·2	325·8	477·3	628·8	780·3	931·8	1083·3	1234·8	1386·4
16	24·2	175·8	327·3	478·8	630·3	781·8	933·3	1084·8	1236·4	1387·9
17	25·8	177·3	328·8	480·3	631·8	783·3	934·8	1086·4	1237·9	1389·4
18	27·3	178·8	330·3	481·8	633·3	784·8	936·4	1087·9	1239·4	1390·9
19	28·8	180·3	331·8	483·3	634·8	786·4	937·9	1089·4	1240·9	1392·4
20	30·3	181·8	333·3	484·8	636·4	787·9	939·4	1090·9	1242·4	1393·9
21	31·8	183·3	334·8	486·4	637·9	789·4	940·9	1092·4	1243·9	1395·5
22	33·3	184·8	336·4	487·8	639·4	790·9	942·4	1093·9	1245·5	1397·0
23	34·8	186·4	337·9	489·4	640·9	792·4	943·9	1095·5	1247·0	1398·5
24	36·4	187·9	339·4	490·9	642·4	793·9	945·5	1079·0	1248·5	1400·0
25	37·9	189·4	340·9	492·4	643·9	795·5	947·0	1098·5	1250·0	1401·5
26	39·4	191·0	342·4	493·9	645·5	797·0	948·5	1100·0	1251·5	1403·0
27	40·9	192·4	343·9	495·5	647·0	798·5	950·0	1101·5	1253·0	1404·5
28	42·4	193·9	345·5	497·0	648·5	800·0	951·5	1103·0	1254·5	1406·1
29	43·9	195·5	347·0	498·5	650·0	801·5	953·0	1104·5	1256·1	1407·6
30	45·5	197·0	348·5	500·0	651·5	803·0	954·5	1106·1	1257·6	1409·1
31	47·0	198·5	350·0	501·5	653·0	804·5	956·1	1107·6	1259·1	1410·6
32	48·5	200·0	351·5	503·0	654·5	806·1	957·6	1109·1	1260·6	1412·1
33	50·0	201·5	353·0	504·5	656·1	807·6	959·1	1110·6	1262·1	1413·6
34	51·5	203·0	354·5	506·1	657·6	809·1	960·6	1112·1	1263·6	1415·2
35	53·0	204·5	356·1	507·6	659·1	810·6	962·1	1113·6	1265·2	1416·7
36	54·5	206·1	357·6	509·1	660·6	812·1	963·6	1115·2	1266·7	1418·2
37	56·1	207·6	359·1	510·6	662·1	813·6	965·2	1116·7	1268·2	1419·7
38	57·6	209·1	360·6	512·1	663·6	815·2	966·7	1118·2	1269·7	1421·2
39	59·1	210·6	362·1	513·6	665·2	816·7	968·2	1119·7	1271·2	1422·7
40	60·6	212·1	363·6	515·2	666·7	818·2	969·7	1121·2	1272·7	1424·2
41	62·1	213·6	365·2	516·7	668·2	819·7	971·2	1122·7	1274·2	1425·8
42	63·6	215·2	366·7	518·2	669·7	821·2	972·7	1124·2	1275·8	1427·3
43	65·2	216·7	368·2	519·7	671·2	822·7	974·2	1125·8	1277·3	1428·8
44	66·7	218·2	369·7	521·2	672·7	824·2	975·8	1127·3	1278·8	1430·3
45	68·2	219·7	371·2	522·7	674·2	825·8	977·3	1128·8	1280·3	1431·8
46	69·7	221·2	372·7	524·2	675·8	827·3	978·8	1130·3	1281·8	1433·3
47	71·2	222·7	374·2	525·8	677·3	828·8	980·3	1131·8	1283·3	1434·8
48	72·7	224·2	375·8	527·3	678·8	830·3	981·8	1133·3	1284·8	1436·4
49	74·2	225·8	377·3	528·8	680·3	831·8	983·3	1134·8	1286·4	1437·9

Table IV.—*To convert Feet into Links* (continued).

Feet.	FEET.									
	0	100	200	300	400	500	600	700	800	900
	links.	links.	links.	links.	links.	links.	links.	links.	links.	links.
50	75·8	227·3	378·8	530·3	681·8	833·3	984·8	1136·4	1287·9	1439·4
51	77·3	228·8	380·3	531·8	683·3	834·8	986·4	1137·9	1289·4	1440·9
52	78·8	230·3	381·8	533·3	684·8	836·4	987·9	1139·4	1290·9	1442·4
53	80·3	231·8	383·3	534·8	686·4	837·9	989·4	1140·9	1292·4	1443·9
54	81·8	233·3	384·8	536·4	687·9	839·4	990·9	1142·4	1293·9	1445·5
55	83·3	234·8	386·4	537·9	689·4	840·9	992·4	1143·9	1295·5	1447·0
56	84·8	236·4	387·9	539·4	690·9	842·4	993·9	1145·5	1297·0	1448·5
57	86·4	237·9	389·4	540·9	692·4	843·9	995·5	1147·0	1298·5	1450·0
58	87·9	239·4	390·9	542·4	693·9	845·5	997·0	1148·5	1300·0	1451·5
59	89·4	240·9	392·4	543·9	695·5	847·0	998·5	1150·0	1301·5	1453·0
60	90·9	242·4	393·9	545·5	697·0	848·5	1000·0	1151·5	1303·0	1454·5
61	92·4	243·9	395·5	547·0	698·5	850·0	1001·5	1153·0	1304·5	1456·1
62	93·9	245·5	397·0	548·5	700·0	851·5	1003·0	1154·5	1306·1	1457·6
63	95·5	247·0	398·5	550·0	701·5	853·0	1004·5	1156·1	1307·6	1459·1
64	97·0	248·5	400·0	551·5	703·0	854·5	1006·1	1157·6	1309·1	1460·6
65	98·5	250·0	401·5	553·0	704·5	856·1	1007·6	1159·1	1310·6	1462·1
66	100·0	251·5	403·0	554·5	706·1	857·6	1009·1	1160·6	1312·1	1463·6
67	101·5	253·0	404·5	556·1	707·6	859·1	1010·6	1162·1	1313·6	1465·2
68	103·0	255·5	406·1	557·6	709·1	860·6	1012·1	1163·6	1315·2	1466·7
69	104·5	256·1	407·6	559·1	710·6	862·1	1013·6	1165·2	1316·7	1468·2
70	106·1	257·6	409·1	560·6	712·1	863·6	1015·2	1166·7	1318·2	1469·7
71	107·6	259·1	410·6	562·1	713·6	865·2	1016·7	1168·2	1319·7	1471·2
72	109·1	260·6	412·1	563·6	715·2	866·7	1018·2	1169·7	1321·2	1472·7
73	110·6	262·1	413·6	565·2	716·7	868·2	1019·7	1171·2	1322·7	1474·2
74	112·1	263·6	415·2	566·7	718·2	869·7	1021·2	1172·7	1324·2	1475·8
75	113·6	265·2	416·7	568·2	719·7	871·2	1022·7	1174·2	1325·8	1477·3
76	115·2	266·7	418·2	569·7	721·2	872·7	1024·2	1175·8	1327·3	1478·8
77	116·7	268·2	419·7	571·2	722·7	874·2	1025·8	1177·3	1328·8	1480·3
78	118·2	269·7	421·2	572·7	724·2	875·8	1027·3	1178·8	1330·3	1481·8
79	119·7	271·2	422·7	574·2	725·8	877·3	1028·8	1180·3	1331·8	1483·3
80	121·2	272·7	424·2	575·8	727·3	878·8	1030·3	1181·8	1333·3	1484·8
81	122·7	274·2	425·8	577·3	728·8	880·3	1031·8	1183·3	1334·8	1486·4
82	124·2	275·8	427·3	578·8	730·3	881·8	1033·3	1184·8	1336·4	1487·9
83	125·8	277·3	428·8	580·3	731·8	883·3	1034·8	1186·4	1337·9	1489·4
84	127·3	278·8	430·3	581·8	733·4	884·8	1036·4	1187·9	1339·4	1490·9
85	128·8	280·3	431·8	583·3	734·8	886·4	1037·9	1189·4	1340·9	1492·4
86	130·3	281·8	433·3	584·8	736·4	887·9	1039·4	1190·9	1342·4	1493·9
87	131·8	283·3	434·8	586·4	737·9	889·4	1040·9	1192·4	1343·9	1495·4
88	133·3	284·8	436·4	587·9	739·4	890·9	1042·4	1193·9	1345·5	1497·0
89	134·8	286·4	437·9	589·4	740·9	892·4	1043·9	1195·5	1347·0	1498·5
90	136·4	287·9	439·4	590·9	742·4	893·9	1045·5	1197·0	1348·5	1500·0
91	137·9	289·4	440·9	592·4	743·9	895·5	1047·0	1198·5	1350·0	1501·5
92	139·4	290·9	442·4	593·9	745·5	897·0	1048·5	1200·0	1351·5	1503·0
93	140·9	292·4	443·9	595·5	747·0	898·5	1050·0	1201·5	1353·0	1504·5
94	142·4	293·9	445·5	597·0	748·5	900·0	1051·5	1203·0	1354·5	1506·1
95	143·9	295·5	447·0	598·5	750·0	901·5	1053·0	1204·5	1356·1	1507·6
96	145·5	297·0	448·5	600·0	751·5	903·0	1054·5	1206·1	1357·6	1509·1
97	147·0	298·5	450·0	601·5	753·0	904·5	1056·1	1207·6	1359·1	1510·6
98	148·5	300·0	451·5	603·0	754·5	906·1	1057·6	1209·1	1360·6	1512·1
99	150·0	301·5	453·0	604·5	756·1	907·6	1059·1	1210·6	1362·1	1513·6

APPENDIX.

IN the former edition of this work there was an error in the Rule which appears, in the present edition, at page 65, the word "tangent" having been written for "sine." A scientific friend, in noticing this mistake, has suggested a convenient method of arranging the figures of the calculation when the perpendicular and base of a right-angled triangle are *both* to be computed from the base-angle and hypothenuse. The directions are as follows:—

"1st. Write down the log. of the measured hypothenuse taken from the table of numbers.

"2nd. Over it place the log. sine of the measured angle from table of log. sines, &c., and draw a line *above*.

"3rd. Under the log. of the hypothenuse write down the cosine of the angle, and then draw a line *under* it. Add the hypothenuse to the sine *upwards*, and it will give the length of the perpendicular sought in the table of numbers. Add the hypothenuse and cosine together *downwards*, and it will give the length of the base in the table of numbers.

"NOTE.—I reject 10 from the log. index in both sums, because radius 10 stood in the first term, as a divisor, in both proportions.

" EXAMPLE.

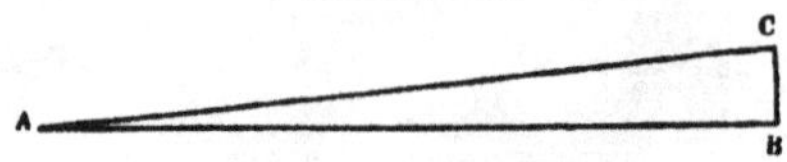

" From A to C, I found the angle to be 6° rising—and the length of the hypothenuse A C measured 1240 links.

" I state the calculation thus :

		2·112657 = log $129\frac{6}{10}$ the perp^{r}.
2nd, Sine of 6°	**=**	**9·019235**
1st, Hypothenuse 1240	**=**	**3·093422**
3rd, Cosine of 6°	**=**	**9 997614**
		3·091036 = log $1233\frac{2}{10}$ the base.

Answer :

Perpendicular . .	**$129\frac{6}{10}$**	**links.**
Base	**$1233\frac{2}{10}$**	**do.**
Hypothenuse . .	**1240**	**do."**

We may add here, in reference to the precept in italics, at page 65, that the constant number 1·8195439 is the logarithm of 66, the number of feet in a chain.

)N SETTING OUT THE WIDTHS OF GROUND REQUIRED

FOR THE WORKS OF A

RAILWAY OR CANAL,

ETC., ETC.

DEPENDING UPON THE DEPTH OF CUTTING OR HEIGHT OF EMBANKMENT, AND THE TRANSVERSE SLOPE OF THE NATURAL SURFACE.

BY

FREDERICK WALTER SIMMS, F.G.S., M.I.C.E.

ON SETTING OUT THE WIDTHS OF GROUND REQUIRED

FOR THE WORKS OF A

RAILWAY OR CANAL,

&c., &c.

WHEN the natural surface of the ground, both longitudinally and transversely, is upon the same level as that of the intended works, the process of setting and staking out the widths is very simple. Let us take, for example, the case of a railway, the base or bottom width of which, when prepared for the reception of the ballasting and permanent way, is to be 36 feet; the ratio of the inclination, or batter, of the slopes to the heights, both in the cuttings and the embankments, to be 2 to 1; beyond which, or at the outward edge, a slip of land 12 feet wide is to be taken on each side of the railway for the fences, &c. First, the centre line must be staked out and carefully levelled: it is customary to drive a stake, about 2 feet long and about 1½ inch square, into the ground at each chain's length, their tops to be upon the fair level of the natural surface, thus affording good stations for the levelling staves to be held upon; the relative level of each stake being then very accurately determined with respect to some given datum, they become so many zero points for reference in the subsequent operations. From each of the centre stakes a line must be set out on both sides, and at right angles to the centre line, or at right angles to a tangent to the centre line at that point, if the centre line be curved: upon these transverse lines the required widths of land must be set out. Now, if the ground at any of the centre stakes is upon the same level as the intended base of the railway, nothing more will be required than to measure on each transverse line, and in both directions from the centre stake, one half the required width, which, in our supposed case, is 18 feet for the half width of the railway, and 12 feet for the fences; in all 30 feet on each side of the centre. But when, as it mostly happens, the ground is not on the proposed level of the railway, the operation is not quite so simple; and if in addition thereto the ground slopes sidewise or at right angles to the general direction of the line, the business is still more complicated, and requires some skill and care to do the work correctly. The method of doing this it is now our business to explain.

The next most simple case to the above is when the cross section of the ground is horizontal, be the depth of cutting or height of embankment what it may.

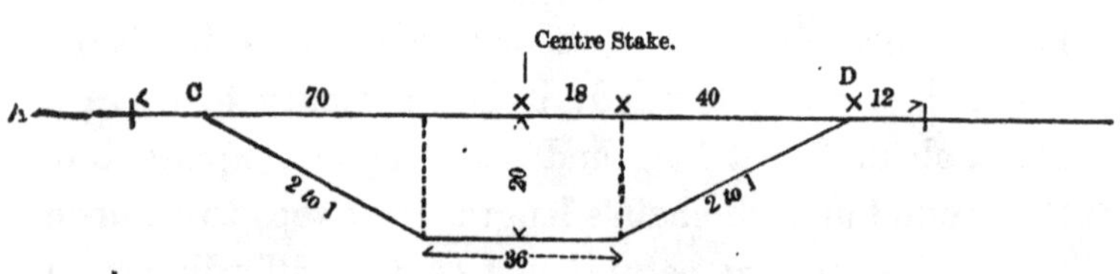

This is shown in the above diagram, which represents a cross section of a 20 feet cutting, with slopes of two horizontal to one perpendicular. The horizontal line A B at right angles to the centre line represents the natural surface of the ground. Under these circumstances it will readily be seen that the half width of the cutting, or the distance from the centre to the edge of the slopes C and D, equals the half width of the base (18) added to the batter of the sloping sides (40), and including the 12 feet for the fences, the total half width of land required for the purposes of such railway would be 18 + 40 + 12 = 70 feet, and consequently the whole required width to be appropriated and fenced in for a 20 feet cutting or embankment, when the ground does not slope sidewise, would be 140 feet.

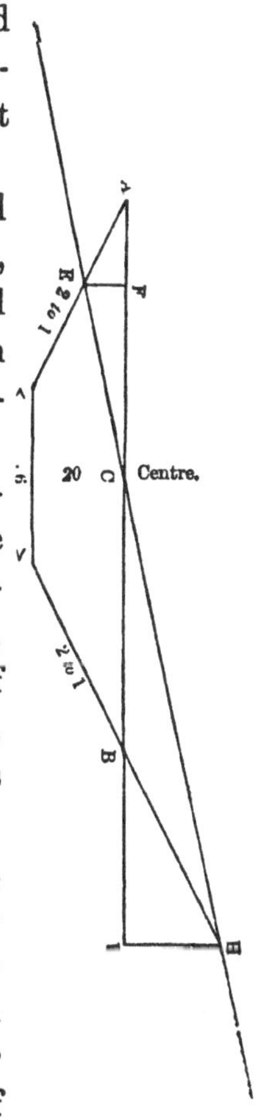

The next and more complicated, and also the most frequently occurring case, is, when the cross section of the natural surface is not horizontal, as shown in the annexed diagram, which also represents a cutting of 20 feet.

Let the line A B represent a horizontal line passing through the centre line C of the railway, which, if it coincided with the surface of the ground, would give A C and C B (each half width) 70 feet, as in the former example, the depth of cutting and the slopes being assumed the same.

Let the line E H represent the natural surface of the ground upon this transverse section; it will readily be perceived that the real half width C E (on the left of the diagram) is much shorter than the horizontal or computed half width A C, because the ground-line is depressed on that side of the centre; likewise the half width C H on the other side of the centre is greater than the said horizontal or computed half width, because the ground is there elevated above the horizontal line A B passing through the centre. To determine *exactly* the distances C E and C H in actual operations in the field, would be attended with some difficulty, and consume much time; but the following method, at the same time that it gives a sufficiently correct approximation in practice, is also a very expeditious one:

Let us suppose that the point E or distance C E be known, and that with a spirit-level we determine the difference of level between the points C and E, this difference is represented by the line E F, which suppose to be one foot; now we have a small right-angled triangle A E F, of which E F is determined, being the difference of level (one foot), and the slope or ratio of A F to E F also given (2 to 1), therefore the side A F is known (2 feet), which, subtracted from the computed half width A C, leaves F C approximately equal to E C, the required half width, sufficiently exact for all practical purposes, where the cross section of the ground does not differ materially from a horizontal line.

We have been supposing that the point E is known, whereas that point is the object of our search; in practice, therefore, we proceed thus:—Take the computed half width, and if the ground is *depressed*, let a levelling staff be held somewhat *nearer* the point C than the said computed half width, for a first approximation to the point E; then determine the *difference of level* between this assumed point and the centre point C, *multiply this difference of level by the ratio of the slopes* (which doubles it when the slope is 2 to 1), and *subtract* the result from the computed half width, which gives a more correct approximation to the point E; now hold the staff at this *new point* and find the difference of level as before, again multiply by the ratio of the slopes, and deduct the result from the computed half width, which second result will in most cases be sufficiently near the real half width for a *depressed* line for all practical purposes.

EXAMPLE.—Central height (or depth of cutting), 20 feet, slopes 2 to 1, base 36 feet; the computed half width was therefore 58 feet; the ground being depressed, we estimated that the point E might fall short of the computed half width 2 feet: we therefore directed a levelling staff to be held at 56 feet from the centre line (or stake) C, at which point another staff was held, and, by means of a spirit-level set up at a convenient distance, we found the difference of level between these points to be 0·87 foot, which, multiplied by the ratio of the slopes (2 to 1), gave 1·74 foot to be subtracted from the computed half width 58 feet, leaving 56·26 feet for a first approximation to the half width C E (see last diagram). Now, upon removing the staff to this new point, the difference of level was again taken (or rather we should say that the staff was again read off, as the level had not been disturbed), and found to be 0·91 foot, which, also multiplied by the ratio of the slopes (2 to 1), gave 1·82 foot to be subtracted from 58 feet, leaving 56·18 for the second approximation, and which was adopted as the correct half width for the depressed side of the centre; indeed, in such a case as is above given, where the ground is so nearly horizontal, the first approximation (taken by a person after a little practice) may be assumed as the correct result, for in the above example it differed but ·08 from the second determination, and if it had been taken a third time it could not have been more accurate as far as practice is concerned; this, however, is not the case where the inclination or slope of the ground is considerable, for then (if this method be followed) several approximations will be necessary to bring the result within admissible limits.

When the ground is *elevated* above the horizontal line, as shown on the right hand of the diagram, the mode of procedure will somewhat differ: thus, instead of holding the staff and finding the difference of level at a *less distance* than the computed half width, it must be held at a *greater distance* to obtain the point H by approximation; the difference of level between that point and the centre point C being equal to H I, which multiplied by the ratio of the slopes, will give the distance B I to be added to the computed half width C B, to obtain the half width C H; this may likewise be repeated to obtain a more correct result, as described for the other or depressed side of the centre C. It will also here be obvious to a person possessing but the smallest share of mathematical knowledge, that this result is not strictly correct, inasmuch as the line C H can never be equal to C I, but for practical purposes it is, as before observed, sufficiently correct. It may not be altogether unnecessary to observe, in this place, that the corrections B I, &c., as shown in the foregoing diagrams, are much exaggerated, being far greater in proportion to the computed half width C B, than ever occurs in ordinary practice, but this has been done to make our explanations more distinct than they otherwise would be.

The above particulars have been confined to the case of excavations; we must now show in what the process differs when the ground is to be covered with an embankment.

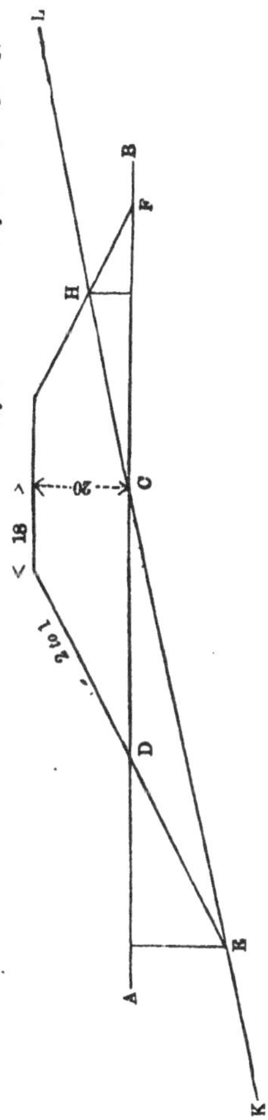

By reversing page 108 we invert the diagram, which then represents an embankment. The rule for finding the half width for an embankment where the transverse section of the ground is horizontal, remains the same as for the cuttings under like circumstances, as may be seen by an inspection of the inverted figure of the first diagram; but upon inverting the second diagram, it will at once be seen that some variation in the process is required. Thus:

The horizontal line is represented by that marked A B; C D and C F are the computed half widths; C E the required half width on the depressed side, and C H the required half width on the elevated side, the line K L representing the natural surface of the ground. In the case of an excavation, we have shown that the *real* half width is greater on the *elevated* side than the computed half width, and less on the *depressed* side; but it will be seen by the above diagram that for an embankment the *real* half width is *less* on the *elevated* side, and *greater* on the *depressed* side, than the computed half width; therefore, in determining the approximate place of the point E on the depressed side for an embankment, the staff must be held *further* from the centre than the computed half width; and for the point H, or the elevated side, it must be held *nearer* to the centre than the computed half width; and finally, for computing the real half widths from the differences of level between the points E and the centre, and H and the centre; on the *depressed* side the difference of level multiplied by the ratio of the slopes is to be *added* to the computed half widths to obtain the point E, and to be *subtracted* from the computed half widths to obtain the point H.

The process above described may appear to the reader a very tedious one; it perhaps is so to read; but a little practice will convince him that it is a very expeditious method, for in most cases one setting up of the level will answer for several stations, and the multiplication by the ratio of the slopes upon such small numbers as mostly occur is easily performed, especially if it be an even number, as 2 to 1. The columns of the field-book may be arranged as in the following example for making the calculations in the field, or may be abridged to suit a more convenient-sized book for the pocket, at the pleasure of the surveyor; indeed, all that can be accomplished now of this kind is to give general rules, which can be altered and arranged to suit the convenience of the surveyor, as experience may point out a more suitable mode of proceeding. The example is taken from an extensive field operation by the writer, and shows the work both for a cutting and an embankment; the change from one to the other, or the tailing out of the cutting, as it is called, being included therein. The slope of the cutting is calculated at $1\frac{1}{2}$ to 1, and that of the embankment at 2 to 1. The width of the railway was 36 feet, consequently half the said width was 18 feet.

EXAMPLE.

No. of Stake.	Depth of Cutting or Embankment.	Computed half width.	Section or Level Readings at right angles to Line.			Difference of Level. + −		Difference of Level, × ratio of Slope. + −		Required half width for edge of Cutting or foot of Embankment.	
			South.	Centre.	North.	South.	North.	South.	North.	South.	North.
EMBANKMENT.											
	Feet.	Feet.	Feet.	Feet.	Feet.	Feet.	Feet.	Feet.	Feet.	Feet.	Feet.
285	16·97	51·94	10·90	7·50	3·96	+ 3·40	− 3·54	+ 6·80	− 7·08	58·74	44·86
286	1·43	0·86	7·06	4·74	3·24	+ 2·32	{ + 0·07 − 1·50 }	+ 4·64	+ 0·11	25·50	20·97
287	2·77	23·54	8·00	5·80	4·26	+ 2·20	− 1·54	+ 4·40	− 3·08	27·94	20·46
288	3·06	24·12	8·82	6·42	5·12	+ 2·40	− 1·30	+ 4·80	− 2·60	28·92	21·52
289	2·01	22·02	7·02	5·13	3·74	+ 1·89	− 1·39	+ 3·78	− 2 78	25·80	19·24
290	1·22	20·44	6·00	4·10	2·76	+ 1·90	{ + 0·12 − 1·34 }	+ 3·80	+ 0·18	24·24	20·62
291	1·91	21·82	7·52	6·95	5·20	+ 0·57	− 1·75	+ 1·14	− 3·50	22·96	18·32
CUTTING.											
292	1·39	20·78	12·20	11·35	10·52	− 0·85	+ 0·83	− 1·27	+ 1·24	19·51	22·02
293	4·51	27·02	9·56	7·98	6·22	− 1·58	+ 1·76	− 2·37	+ 2·64	24·65	29·66
294	5·72	29·44	8·40	6·52	4·27	− 1·88	+ 2·25	− 2·82	+ 3·37	26·62	32·81
295	6·85	31·70	7·06	5·10	3·02	− 1·96	+ 2·08	− 2·94	+ 3·12	28·76	34·82
296	8·61	35·22	7·53	5·28	2·76	− 2·25	+ 2·52	− 3·37	+ 3·78	31·85	39·00

The first column contains the number of the central stakes, reckoned from the commencement of the work, which are convenient for reference.

The second column contains the depth of cutting or the height of embankment, as the case may be, at that point on the centre line.

The third column, the computed half width from the centre line to the edge of the cutting, or foot of embankment, upon the supposition that the ground is horizontal at right angles to the centre line; this half width, as before explained (p. 109), is found by multiplying the central height by the ratio of the slopes, and adding to the product half the width at the base of the railway.

The fourth, fifth, and sixth columns contain the readings from the levelling staves at the centre stake, and at the approximate points E and H (see last diagram).

The seventh and eighth columns contain the differences of level between the centre stake and the above approximate points. These numbers are simply the differences of the quantities in the three preceding columns (except at stakes 286 and 290, which we will presently explain), and the signs + and − denote whether they are positive or negative quantities, as respects the centre and the approximate points E and H.

The ninth and tenth columns contain the differences of level (contained in columns 7 and 8) multiplied by the ratio of the slopes, and must have the same signs + or − as the corresponding numbers in the preceding columns.

The last two columns contain the final half widths obtained by adding or subtracting, according to the prefixed signs + or −, the numbers in the two preceding columns to the computed half width contained in column 3.

After the explanations already given, the reader can find no difficulty in tracing the steps of the example, except perhaps with the stakes 286 and 290, where the difference of level on the north side is represented by two numbers bracketed together, one having the sign +, and the other −: for the stake 286 the real difference of level on the north side the centre is a rise of 1·50, that is, the approximate point H is 1·50 foot above the centre stake: but it happens that the height of the embankment itself at that point is to be but 1·43 foot (column 2); therefore the approximate point H is above the intended top of the embankment, and consequently will not represent the foot of an embankment, but the edge of a cutting, and therefore the calculation for the half width on the north side must be treated as for a cutting whose depth is equal to the *height of the approximate point* H *above the intended top of the embankment*; or, in other words, the *excess* of the difference of level between the centre stake and the approximate point H, above the intended height of the embankment, is the quantity to be entered in the column (7 or 8) "Difference of Level," and to be computed as for a cutting instead of embankment. In the case of stake 286 this excess is 0·07, to which is prefixed the sign plus; this sum multiplied by the ratio of the slope being additive (for a cutting) on the elevated side of the centre, as before explained.

For the stake 290, the north side of the line (column 6) is 1·34 higher than the centre stake, and it, being embankment, would have the sign − prefixed (as shown by the lower number, column 8): but the central height of the embankment at that point is but 1·22 (column 2); therefore, 1·34 − 1·22 = 0·12, which is the depth of cutting on the elevated side, and when multiplied by the ratio of the slopes is to be added to the computed half width to obtain the correct result. When the surface of the ground is much inclined at right angles to the centre line, the numbers to be operated upon become proportionally large.

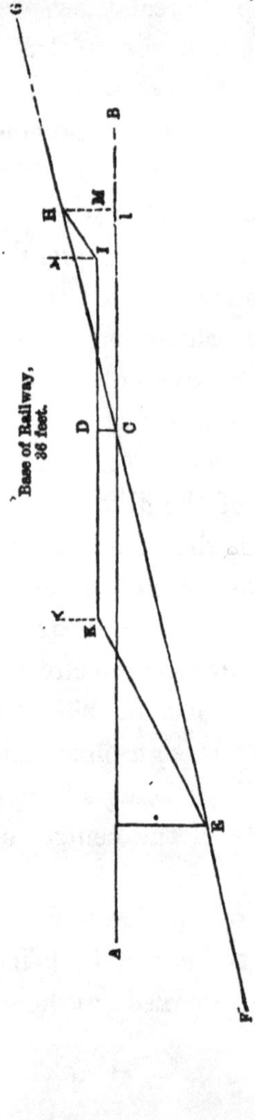

As it is a case of frequent occurrence that one side will be a cutting when the other is an embankment, we wish it to be well understood, and therefore annex the accompanying diagram to illustrate it.

The line F G represents the natural surface of the ground, A B the horizontal line at the centre stake, C D the intended height of the embankment, K L the width or base of the railway, 36 feet, part of which is an embankment and part a cutting; the point E, or foot of the embankment, will be determined in the usual way, as explained at page 113; but the point H, which is to be the edge of the cutting, must be found by subtracting D C (the height of embankment) from H I (the difference of level); the remainder, H M (which is *the excess of the difference of level between the centre stake and the approximate point* H *above the intended height of embankment*), multiplied into the ratio of the slope, must be added to the computed half width, or, in other words, treated as for a cutting, to obtain the said point H, as before stated. By reversing the diagram the corresponding case will become evident; namely, when the centre line is in cutting, and one side on embankment, while the other is in excavation; and the mode of proceeding will at once strike the reader after perusing what we have above written.

EXAMPLES OF THE MODES

OF SETTING OUT

RAILWAY CURVES.

By HENRY LAW.

EXAMPLES OF THE MODES OF SETTING OUT

RAILWAY CURVES.

THERE are very few lines of railway so favourably situated as to be free from curves of greater or less extent, and occurring more or less frequently in their course; and consequently a knowledge of the method of correctly and readily laying down these curves upon the ground becomes a very necessary and important qualification in those engaged in setting out lines of railway. It has not therefore been considered out of place to append to a work treating on one of the most important branches of railway surveying, a description of the various methods which may be employed for this purpose.

Previously, however, to proceeding to the more practical part of the subject, it may be desirable to make a few observations upon railway curves in general. The curve which has been almost universally employed in laying down lines of railway, is the arc of a circle, although it may be shown, that under certain circumstances this curve is not *theoretically* that which should be employed, as affording the least danger from the centrifugal tendency of the carriages. It has been generally considered, that the *true curve* was one which commenced with an infinite radius, decreasing in a regular manner in advancing on the curve, until the minimum radius of curvature required had been attained. This form of curve has, however, been deduced upon the assumption, that the *whole* of the centrifugal tendency of the carriages is balanced by the superelevation of the outer rail, an assumption which is only correct on the supposition of the wheels of the carriages being cylindrical, or no play being allowed between the flanges and the rails —conditions which are never fulfilled in practice. For it may be shown, that with conical wheels, and a certain amount of play, a portion of the centrifugal tendency will always be counteracted by the self-acting adjustment produced by the lateral deviation of the carriage on the rails, however small the radius of curvature may be; and that when the radius exceeds a certain limit, this adjustment is perfect, no superelevation of the outer rail being then required.

It is obvious, therefore, that in curves whose radii are *within* this limit, the true form for the curve is one whose radius of curvature at its commencement should equal this limit, and should decrease in advancing upon the curve, according to such a law, that (assuming the rise in the outer rail to form a regular inclined plane) the unbalanced centrifugal tendency should at every part of the curve be exactly counteracted by the amount of the superelevation of the rail at that part; until the top of the incline being reached, the radius of curvature should then remain constant, being such that the centrifugal tendency of the train should be exactly balanced by the combined effect of the lateral deviation of the carriages on the rails, and the superelevation of the outer rail. When, however, the radius of curvature exceeds this limit, it may be shown that the arc of a circle is preferable to any other form of curve.

Now, if we put d for the diameter of the wheels of the carriages, w for the width of the gauge of the line, and p for the lateral play allowed *on each side*, between the flanges of the wheels and the rails (all the dimensions being expressed in feet), and $\frac{1}{n}$ being the ratio of inclination of the tire of the wheel; then

$$\frac{n\,d\,w}{4\,p} = R \quad . \quad . \quad . \quad . \quad . \quad . \quad \text{I.}$$

will be the limit above referred to; that is, R will be the least radius of curvature which may be used without the necessity of raising the outer rail. And for any other smaller radius, putting v for the velocity of the train in miles per hour, and r for the radius of the curve in feet; then

$$\frac{\cdot 782\, v^2\,(n\,d\,w - 4\,p\,r)}{n\,d\,r} = \epsilon \quad . \quad . \quad \text{II.}$$

will be the superelevation of the outer rail in inches, which will be required for that radius, in order that the whole of the centrifugal tendency of the train may be destroyed.

Although we have thus shown, that for all curves having a smaller radius than R, it would not be correct, *theoretically*, to employ the arc of a circle, it is nevertheless very questionable whether it would be advisable, *in practice* (except under peculiar circumstances), to substitute the theoretical curve in its stead, inasmuch as the circular arc possesses the practical advantage of being laid down upon the ground with far greater facility; and the only real objection which can be made to its use—namely, that of requiring a sudden and instantaneous superelevation of the outer rail at the point where the curve commences—may in a great measure be removed by commencing to raise the rail before arriving at this point, and making the rise form a gradual inclined plane, whose summit shall be attained at the commencement of the curve. By the adoption of this plan, although the centrifugal tendency (as without it) commences suddenly, the counteracting force, produced by the superelevation of the outer rail, at the same instant attains its maximum, and the two forces therefore balance each other. Whereas, without it, the sudden commencement of the centrifugal force, being entirely unopposed, would at first tend to throw the carriages off the line, until, by the gradual elevation of the outer rail, it had been entirely destroyed.

Having thus far pursued the inquiry as to which form of curve it is most expedient to employ in practice in laying down a line of railway, and having shown that with hardly an exception the arc of a circle is practically the best, we shall confine ourselves to describing a few of the most generally applicable methods by which the circular arc may be traced on the ground.

The first method which we shall describe is that which has in practice been perhaps the most extensively used, although it possesses some objections, which we shall point out in the sequel. Let A B and C D (fig. 1, plate 6) be the two straight portions of the line which it is desired to connect by a curve, B and C being the two points at which the curve falls into the straight lines; and let B b_1, b_1 b_2, b_2 b_3, &c., be the distance which it is desired that the points to be found in the curve shall be apart: then measure upon the straight line A B produced, the distance B a_1, equal δ_1 in formula IV. below, and from the point a_1 set off, perpendicular to the same line, the distance a_1 b_1, equal to o_1 in formula III., which will give the first point required in the curve; then range a straight line through the points B, b_1, and upon this line lay off the distance b_1, a_2, equal to δ_2 in formula VI., and from the point a_2 set off, perpendicular to the line B a_2, the distance a_2 b_2, equal to o_2, in formula V., and the point b_2 will be the second point in the curve; then in a similar manner range another line through the points b_1 b_2, upon which measure the distance b_2 a_3, equal to the distance δ_2 or b_1 a_2, and from a_3 set off as before, perpendicular to the line b_1 a_3, the distance a_3 b_3, equal to o_2, which will determine the third point in the curve; and thus proceed until the whole extent of the curve has been set out.

In order to obtain the values of δ_1, δ_2, o_1, and o_2, let r equal the radius and d equal the distance B b_1, or b_1 b_2, &c., which it is desired that the points found in the curve shall be apart (both expressed in feet); then

$$\frac{d^2}{2\,r} = o_1 \quad . \quad . \quad . \quad . \quad . \quad . \quad . \quad . \quad \text{III.}$$

$$\sqrt{d^2 - o_1{}^2} = \delta_1 \quad . \quad . \quad . \quad . \quad . \quad . \quad . \quad \text{IV.}$$

$$\frac{d\,\delta_1}{r} = o_2 \quad . \quad . \quad . \quad . \quad . \quad . \quad . \quad \text{V.}$$

$$\frac{d\,(r - o_1)}{r} = \delta_2 \quad . \quad . \quad . \quad . \quad . \quad . \quad \text{VI.}$$

As an example of the application of this method, let the radius of the curve (r) be 15 chains or 990 feet, and the distance B b_1 (d) one chain or 66 feet; then from formula III.

$$\frac{66^2}{2 \times 990} = 2{\cdot}2 \text{ feet} = o_1$$

will be the first offset at a_1; and

$$\sqrt{66^2 - 2{\cdot}2^2} = 65{\cdot}963 \text{ feet} = \delta_1$$

will be the distance B a_1, to be laid off upon the line A B produced to give the place for this offset. Again,

$$\frac{66 \times 65{\cdot}963}{990} = 4{\cdot}397 \text{ feet} = o_2$$

will be the offset at a_2, a_3, a_4, &c.; and

$$\frac{66 \times (990 - 2{\cdot}2)}{990} = 65{\cdot}85 \text{ feet} = \delta_2$$

will be the distance $b_1\,a_2$, $b_2\,a_3$, &c., to be measured from the points b_1, b_2, &c., in order to give the points a_2, a_3, a_4, &c., from which the offsets o_2 are to be taken.

To this method there are, as has been already stated, some practical objections, inasmuch as any error which may be committed, in setting out only one of the points in the curve, will occasion a corresponding error in every succeeding one; and a very trifling inaccuracy in calculating either the distance δ_2, or the length of the offset o_2, from its being frequently repeated, may ultimately cause a very considerable deviation from the true curve. Both these objections, however, may be in a great measure removed by the adoption of the following method of checking the position of about every fifth point; or, which would be better, first determining the position of these points, and then filling in the intermediate ones; and as we consider this modification does away almost entirely with the above-mentioned sources of error, we shall give an example of its application.

Let us suppose r and d, or the radius, and the distance the points B, b_1, b_2, &c., are apart (see figure 2, plate 6), to be the same as in the last example—viz., 990 feet and 66 feet respectively, and let it be determined to check the position of every *fourth* point: then the values of δ_1, δ_2, o_1, and o_2, will be the same as before; but previous to setting out the points b_1, b_2, b_3, &c., we must calculate the distance B B_1 to be measured along the line A B produced, and the distance B_1 b_4 to be set off from the point B_1 to give the position of the fourth point (b_4) in the curve, which may be done as follows: Let the distance B B_1 equal Δ_1, and B_1 b_4 equal O_1; and let D_1 be the length of the chord line connecting the two points B and b_4, and β be the angle a_1 B b_1; then

$$\frac{o_1 \text{ rad}}{d} = \sin \beta,$$

and

$$\frac{2\, r \sin 4\, \beta}{\text{rad}} = D_1.$$

Then, by substituting D_1, O_1, and Δ_1, for d, o_1, and δ_1, in the formulæ III., IV., V., and VI., we shall obtain the values of O_1, Δ_1, O_2, and Δ_2, where Δ_2 is the distance b_4 B_2 to be measured upon the chord line B_1 b_4 produced, and O_2 is the distance B_2 b_8 to be set off from B_2 in order to give the eighth point (b_8) in the curve; for the values of r and d given above we shall obtain

Log o_1	=	0·342423 = log 2·2
Log rad	=	10·000000
		10·342423
Log d	=	1·819544 = log 66
Log sin β	=	8·522879

and $\beta = 1° \; 54' \; 37''$ ∴ $4\,\beta = 7° \; 38' \; 28''$; then

Log 2 r	=	3·296665 = log 1980
Log sin 4 β	=	9·123745
		12·420410
Log rad	=	10·000000
Log D_1	=	2·420410 = log 263·27.

Then from formula III.

$$\frac{263{\cdot}27^2}{2 \times 990} = 35 \text{ feet} = O_1;$$

from formula IV.

$$\sqrt{263{\cdot}27^2 - 35^2} = 260{\cdot}92 \text{ feet} = \Delta_1;$$

from formula V.

$$\frac{263{\cdot}27 \times 260\,92}{990} = 69{\cdot}4 = O_2;$$

and from formula VI.

$$\frac{263{\cdot}27 \times (990 - 35)}{990} = 253{\cdot}96 = \Delta_2.$$

These being obtained, the position of every fourth point, b_4, b_8, b_{12}, &c., should be first determined by the dimensions Δ_1, O_1, Δ_2, and O_2; and then the intermediate points b_1, b_2, b_3, b_5, b_6, &c., by δ_1, o_1, δ_2, and o_2, as first described.

The second method which we shall describe may be advantageously employed when the radius of curvature is large and the centre can be seen from every part of the curve.

Let the lines (figure 3, plate 6) A B and C D as before represent the two straight portions of the line required to be connected by a curve having a radius of 80 chains or 1 mile. First set up a theodolite at B and another at C (the two terminations of the straight portions of the line) and from each point range a line at right angles to the lines A B and C D respectively, and at the intersection of these lines (E), which will be the centre of the curve, put up a signal sufficiently conspicuous to be seen from any point between B and C. Then produce the straight lines A B and C D until they intersect in the point F, and on these lines drive in stakes at equal distances, a_1, a_2, a_3, &c., commencing from the points

B and C. If r equal the radius, and δ equal the distance between the points a_1, a_2, a_3, &c., both in feet, then

$$\sqrt{r^2+\delta^2} - r = o_1$$

will be the distance which must be set off from the first point a_1, not perpendicular to the line B F, but in the direction a_1 E; in like manner

$$\sqrt{r^2+\overline{2\,\delta}|^2} - r = o_2$$

will be the distance to be set off from the point a_2 in the direction a_2 E ; and generally

$$\sqrt{r^2+\overline{n\,\delta}|^2} - r = o_n$$

will be the distance to be set off at the nth points from B and C.

For example, let r be 5280 feet and δ equal 100 feet: then

$$\sqrt{5280^2+100^2}-5280 = \cdot 94 \text{ feet} = o_1$$

will be the distance a_1 b_1, which must be set off from a_1 in the direction a_1 E to obtain the first point b_1 in the curve; and proceeding in a similar manner with the others, the following Table will exhibit the distances to be set off at the respective points a_1, a_2, a_3, &c.:

At a_1 or	100 feet from B,	the offset will be		·94 feet
a_2	200	,,	,,	3·79
a_3	300	,,	,,	8·52
a_4	400	,,	,,	15·13
a_5	500	,,	,,	23·62
a_6	600	,,	,,	33·98
a_7	700	,,	,,	46·19
a_8	800	,,	,,	60·26
a_9	900	,,	,,	76·16
a_{10}	1000	,,	,,	93·86
a_{11}	1100	,,	,,	113·36
a_{12}	1200	,,	,,	134·65
a_{13}	1300	,,	,,	157·68
a_{14}	1400	,,	,,	182·45
a_{15}	1500	,,	,,	208·93

If the extent of the curve is such that the length of the offsets before reaching the point F, where the two tangent lines intersect, become inconveniently long, so as to occasion a loss of time in setting them off, it will be advisable to make use of another tangent line as shown at G I, fig. 4, plate 7; for determining the position of which line the following method may be made use of. Let r, as before, be the radius, ε the number of degrees contained by the angle B E C, and n the number of tangent lines (as B G, G H, H I, I C) intended to be employed; then

$$\frac{r \sin \frac{\varepsilon}{n}}{\cos \frac{\varepsilon}{n}} = r \tan \frac{\varepsilon}{n}$$

will be equal to the length of any one of these tangent lines. As an example, let r be equal to 5280 feet, ε equal to 60°, and n equal to 4, so that the quotient of ε divided by n will be 15°: then the calculation for the length of each of the lines B G, G H, &c., will be as follows :—

$$\begin{aligned} \text{Log } r &= 3{\cdot}722634 \\ \text{Log } \tan \frac{\varepsilon}{n} &= 9{\cdot}428052 \\ \hline & \quad 3{\cdot}150686 = \log 1414{\cdot}8 \end{aligned}$$

Hence the length of each of the lines B G, G H, &c. will be 1414·8 feet.

Now, having ascertained this length, nothing more remains than to set it off from B and C towards F, and then to range a line G I from the two points thus obtained, which will be the required tangent line : this line must then be bisected in the point H, which may readily be done by ranging a line from F to E, which having been done, proceed as already described to set off the equal distances a_1, a_2, a_3, &c., from B and H towards G, and from H and C towards I; and then by setting off the distances a_1, b_1, a_2, b_2, &c., contained in the Table already given, from the several points a_1, a_2, &c., in directions radiating to the centre E, the course of the curve will be marked by the points b_1, b_2, b_3, &c., thus obtained.

One advantage possessed by the above method is, that, knowing exactly the direction in which to lay off the offsets (and that by the range of a comparatively distant object), the errors which have frequently arisen from their not having been set off perpendicularly, where the eye has been the only criterion, are entirely obviated; and this method is also entirely free from the objections made to the former method.

When the centre point E cannot be seen from every part of the curve, so as to allow the offsets being laid off radially, the more usual method may be adopted of laying off the offsets perpendicularly to the tangent B F, but in this case a cross staff should always be employed to insure accuracy, and the distances to be set off from the points a_1, a_2, a_3, &c., will be greater than those employed in the previous method, and must be calculated from the formula

$$r - \sqrt{r^2 - \delta^2} = o_1$$

instead of that given at page 131.

The third method is most applicable where the radius of the curve is small as compared with its extent, and is deduced from the well-known theorem, that all angles contained in the same segment of a circle are equal to one another.* The method is as follows:—Place a theodolite at B and another at C (figure 5, plate 7), the two terminations of the straight portions of the line, setting the telescope of the instrument at B on C, and that at C on F, the point of intersection of the lines A B and C D produced; then if the former be moved through an arc of any number of degrees, towards F, and the latter the same number of degrees towards B, the point a_1, where the lines of collimation of the two telescopes intersect, will be a point in the curve; now let both theodolites be again moved the same number of degrees and in the same directions as before, and their axes produced, or lines of collimation, will again intersect at a_2, another point in the curve; and in fact, to whatever extent the theodolites are moved, so long as the arc described is equal in both, the point of their intersection will always be in the required curve. Or more generally, suppose the two theodolites to be placed as first described, and then simultaneously to commence to revolve with the same uniform angular velocity, the point of intersection of their lines of collimation will describe the circular arc C, a_1, a_2, a_3, ... B; and in equal intervals of time, equal portions of the arc will be described, which will be half as great as the arc, which would have been described in the same time, by the same angular velocity, at the centre of the circle (E); from which last-mentioned circumstance, we may readily calculate the magnitude of the angle through which the theodolites at B and C must be successively moved, in order that the

* Euclid, Book III., prop. 21.

points a_1, a_2, a_3, &c., at which their axes intersect, may be at the distance apart which it is desired that they should be. If r equal the radius of the curve, d the required distance, and β the angle a_1 B C; then

$$\frac{d \text{ rad}}{2 r} = \sin \beta \quad . \quad . \quad . \quad . \quad . \quad . \quad . \quad \text{VII.}$$

As an example of the application of this method, let r equal 20 chains, or 1320 feet, and let it be required to determine points in the curve at distances of about 100 feet; now, from the above formula we shall obtain

$$\begin{aligned}
\text{Log } d &= 2{\cdot}000000 = \log 100 \\
\text{Log rad} &= 10{\cdot}000000 \\
\hline
& \quad 12{\cdot}000000 \\
\text{Log } 2r &= 3{\cdot}421604 = \log 2640 \\
\hline
\text{Log sin } \beta &= 8{\cdot}578396 \therefore \beta = 2^\circ\ 10'\ 15''.
\end{aligned}$$

As it would be inconvenient, however, in practice, to lay off so frequently as would be required, an angle with odd minutes and seconds, we may instead of the above take an angle of 2 degrees, which will make the distance d equal 92·13 feet. Having thus determined the angle, and placed the theodolites as previously described—viz., that at B in the direction B C, and that at C in the direction C F—the former must be moved 2° towards F, and the latter 2° towards B, and a stake driven down at their point of intersection a_1; the former must then be moved 2° more towards F, and the latter 2° more towards B, and another stake put down at their point of intersection a_2, and so on until the theodolite at B is brought to the direction B F, and that at C to the direction C B, when the whole of the curve will have been staked out as required, the stakes being 92·13 feet apart. This method, the same as the last, is not liable to the objections that the first method was, and in addition possesses the very important practical advantage, that its accuracy is entirely independent of any undulation or change of level in the surface of the ground, an advantage which is not possessed by any of the other methods which we have described, the whole of which would require to have the distances and offsets corrected in proportion to the slope of the surface of the ground. In a hilly country—and it is in such districts that curves most frequently occur—this circumstance will render the last-described method far superior to either of those which precede it.

The next method which we shall give, is that described by Mr. Rankine, in a communication to the Institution of Civil Engineers, and depends on the theorem * that the angle subtended by any arc of a circle at the centre of a circle, is double the angle subtended by the same arc at any point in the circumference of the circle. The method of proceeding is as follows: first place a theodolite at B (figure 6, plate 7.), the point where the curve commences; and then lay off from the line B F the angle B, calculated from formula VII. (supposing as before r to represent the radius of the curve and d the distance required between the points in the curve), and in the direction of the axis of the instrument set off the distance d, which will give the first point a_1 in the curve; in the same manner lay off from B F the angle 2 β, and from a_1 set off the same distance d, and the point where it cuts the axis of the instrument

* Euclid, Book III., prop. 20.

produced will be the second point a_2; and generally by laying off the angle $n\beta$, and setting off from the preceding point a_m the distance d, the point a_n will be given.

As an example of the application of this method, let r equal 19 chains, or 1254 feet, and d equal 100 feet; then from formula VII. we obtain

$$\begin{aligned} \text{Log } d &= 2{\cdot}000000 = \log 100 \\ \text{Log rad} &= 10{\cdot}000000 \\ \hline &\ 12{\cdot}000000 \\ \text{Log } 2\,r &= 3{\cdot}399328 = \log 2508 \\ \hline \text{Log sin } \beta &= 8{\cdot}600672 \therefore \beta = 2^\circ\, 17'\, 6''; \end{aligned}$$

then having placed the theodolite at the point B, lay off this angle 2° 17′ 6″ from the line B F, and upon the line B a_1 thus obtained set off 100 feet, which will give the first point in the curve a_1; then with an angle of 4° 34′ 12″ or 2β set off another 100 feet from a_1, which will give the second point a_2, and thus proceed until the whole extent of the curve has been set out.

Having now pointed out several methods of procedure, in setting out the curved portions of a line of Railway, and having stated generally their relative advantages and disadvantages, we must leave it to the person using them to determine, from the circumstances attending any particular instance, which of these methods it would be preferable to employ. It may perhaps be necessary to add, that in passing from a curve of greater to one of less radius, and *vice versâ*, or in passing at once from a line curving in one direction to a line curving in the contrary direction, or a curve of contrary flexure, nothing more is requisite than to set off the tangent line to the curve at the point where the alteration occurs, and then to work from that line as from the line A B in any of the methods given above.

In conclusion, we would urge that too much care cannot be employed in the operations described above, much of the durability of the permanent way, freedom from jerks and uneasy motion, and also safety in travelling upon lines of Railway, depending upon the accuracy with which the rails are laid, the more especially on the curved portions of the line.

THE FIELD PRACTICE

OF

LAYING OUT CIRCULAR CURVES

FOR

RAILROADS.

By JOHN C. TRAUTWINE,

CIVIL ENGINEER.

PREFACE.

This little volume has been prepared almost entirely with reference to the wants of young men who desire to qualify themselves for field service in an Engineer Corps. On that account the plainest language has been used to render the subject intelligible,—dispensing with mathematical brevity.

The Table of Natural Sines and Tangents to single minutes, in a form sufficiently portable for field use, will supply a want which is frequently experienced, not only in the operation of laying out curves, but on many other occasions.

One object in preparing it, was to furnish the profession with a Table that should be not only portable, but *absolutely reliable.* Those whose occupations compel them to resort to the Tables in common use, must have frequently experienced the embarrassment which attends the inaccuracies to which they are all subject. So long as a Table is known to contain a single error, the position of which is not ascertained, its employment is attended with doubt in every instance in which we are obliged to refer to it.

As Hutton's Tables of Natural Sines and Tangents are those most in use among the profession, it will be desirable to those persons who possess them, to be able to correct the following errors, which I detected in comparing them.

In Hutton's Tables, Fifth Edition, 1811.

Sine of 6° 8′, for ·1063425, read ·1068425.
Page 328, at top, for 25 Deg., read 40 Deg.
Tangent of 44° 60′, for ·1000000, read 1·000000.
Tangent of 41° 60′, for ·8994040, read ·9004040.

In Dr. Gregory's corrected Edition (the 8th) of Hutton's Tables, 1838.

Sine of 49° 14′, for ·7576751, read ·7573751.

In Hassler's Tables, 1830.

Sine of 78° 24′, read ·9795752.
Sine of 20° 60′, „ ·3583679.
Sine of 66° 19′, „ ·9157795.
Sine of 56° 39′, „ ·8353279.
Sine of 55° 20′, „ ·8224751.
Sine of 53° 4′, „ ·7993352.
Sine of 48° 12′, „ ·7454760.
Sine of 45° 3′, „ ·7077236.

The discrepancies of 1 in the 7th decimal, are not considered as errors, as they are occasioned by a neglect of the value of the 8th decimal. For calculating curves, it is not necessary to use more than 4 decimals.

It is scarcely necessary to remark that, beyond 44°, the Sines, Tangents, &c. are read *upwards,* from the bottom of the page, using the corresponding column of minutes. To find the sine of an angle exceeding 90°, subtract the angle from 180°, and take out the sine of the remainder—because the sine of an angle, and that of what it wants of 180°, are the same.

J. C. T.

THE FIELD PRACTICE

OF

LAYING OUT CIRCULAR CURVES

FOR

RAILROADS.

ARTICLE I.

PRINCIPLES OF LAYING OUT CURVES.

METHOD 1.

To lay out a Curve by means of Tangential Angles.

IF from any point B, fig. 1, in a straight line A D, we lay off number of equal angles, as D B *s*, *s* B *t*, *t* B *u*, *u* B *v*, &c., and at the same time make the chords B *s*, *s t*, *t u*, *u v*, &c., equal to each other, then the points B, *s*, *t*, *u*, *v*, &c., will be situated in the circumference of a circle, which is tangential to the line A D at the point B.

Fig. 1.

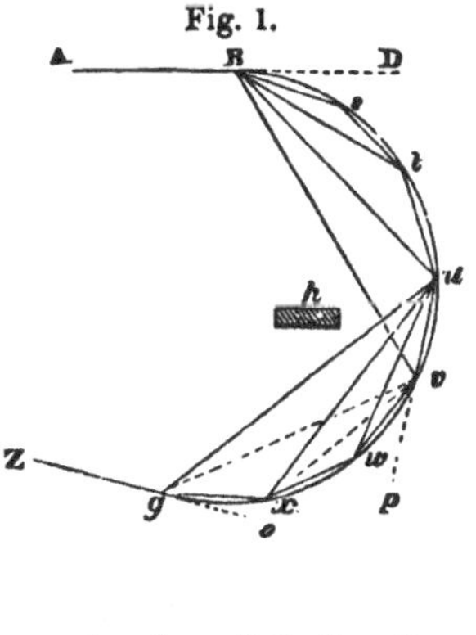

The first of these angles, D B *s*, is called the *tangential angle*, as being that by which the curve is connected with the tangent A D; but inasmuch as the others are all equal to it, they also are called tangential angles.

If any obstacle, as *h*, should prevent our seeing from B farther than to *v*, the curve may be continued by removing the instrument to *u*, the point preceding *v*: thence sighting first on *v*, continue to lay off additional tangential angles *v u w*, *w u x*, &c., as before. Or else, moving the instrument to *v* itself instead of to *u*, sight back to *u*, and lay off first the exterior angle *p v w*, equal to *double* the tangential angle, and afterwards continue the tangential angles *w v x*, *x v g*, &c., as before, to the end of the curve.

Finally, in order to pass from the end of the curve at *g*, on to a tangent *g z*, place the instrument at *g*, and sighting back to *x*, lay off the tangential angle *x g o*; then *o g* continued towards *Z* will be the required tangent. (See Art. IV.)

For the tangential angles corresponding to different radii, and chords of 100 feet, see page 160.

ARTICLE II.

METHOD 2.

To lay out a Curve by means of Deflection Angles.

Fig. 2. First, having, as in method 1, laid off a tangential angle D B *s*, and measured the chord B *s*, remove the instrument to the end *s* of the chord, and make the exterior angle *m s t* equal to *twice* the tangential angle, and measure the chord *s t*; and so on at the other points *t*, *u*, *v*, &c., making each of the exterior angles *n t u*, *o u v*, equal to twice the tangential angle, and all the chords equal; then will the points B, *s*, *t*, *u*, *v*, &c., be in the circumference of a circle which is tangential to the line A D at the point B, as by the first method.

Fig. 2.

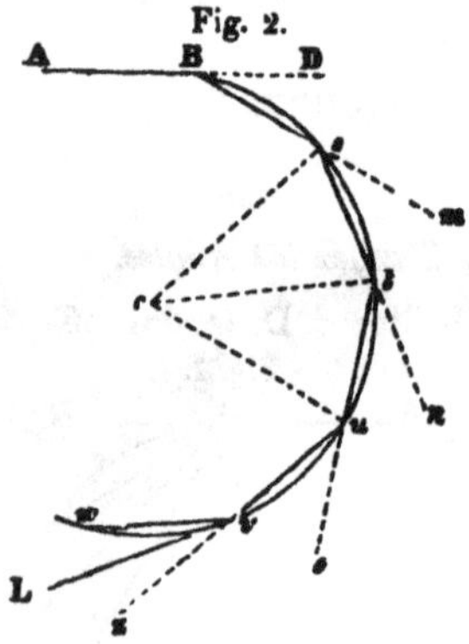

But if, at any of these points, as *v*, we wish to pass off to a tangent *v* L, employ at that point the *tangential* angle *z v* L, equal to half the deflection angle *z v w*. (See Art. IV.)

These exterior angles, included between any *chord* and the extension of the preceding *chord*, are called *deflection angles*, or *angles of deflection*, or *angles of curvature*. In any given circle, the angle of deflection is always precisely double the tangential angle, supposing the chords to be equal. At page 160, we give tables of the angles corresponding to circles of different radii, embracing the limits of railroad practice; and calculated for chords 100 feet in length, that being the usual length for a measuring chain on public works.

N.B. The deflection angle of any curve is equal to the angle *t c u*, or *t c s*, &c., at the centre of the circle, subtended by one of the equal chords *t u* or *t s*. This angle at the centre, so subtended, is called the *central* angle. The tangential angle, being always half the deflection angle, is, of course, always half the central angle.

ARTICLE III.

METHOD 3.

To lay out a Curve by Eye.

The *deflection* angles, fig. 3, *e s t*, *f t u*, *g u v*, *h v w*, &c., being double the *tangential* angle D B *s*, the *arcs* *e d t*, *f i u*, *g m v*, *h n w*, &c., are double the *arc* D *c s*, since the arcs of circles are proportionate to the angles which they subtend; but the *chords* *e t*, *f u*, *g v*, *h w*, &c., are *not* double the *chord* D *s*, since the chords of arcs are not proportionate to the arcs or to the angles which they subtend.

Fig. 3.

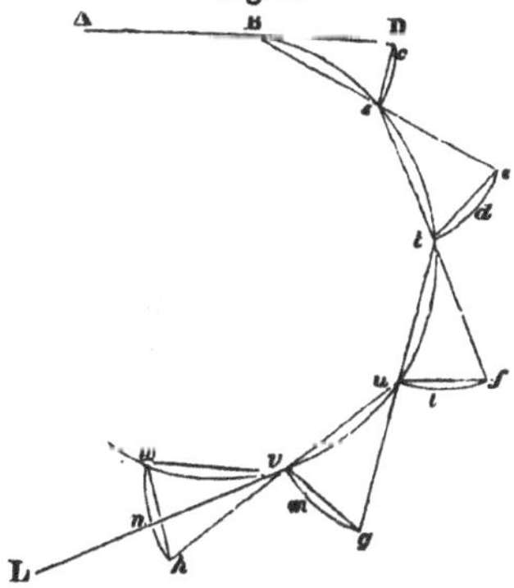

The chords *e t*, *f u*, *g v*, *h w*, &c., which subtend the deflection angles, are called *deflection distances*; and the chord D *s*, which subtends the tangential angle, is called the *tangential distance.*

But although, in any given circle, the deflection distance is not *truly* twice the tangential distance, yet the difference is so trifling in large railroad curves, with chords of but 100 feet, that it may generally be neglected in curves of more than 300 feet radius.

In our tables the *precise* length of both will be found for different radii, and for chords of 100 feet.

Having these respective distances, we may frequently trace a curve on the ground by the eye only, with very tolerable accuracy, sufficient for guiding the excavations and embankments, especially on nearly level ground. Suppose, for instance, it be required to lay out in this manner a curve of 5730 feet radius.

First, find by the table, page 160, or by Art. XVI., the deflection distance *e t* or *f u*, &c., corresponding to a radius of 5730 feet for a chord of 100 feet—viz., 1·745 foot; and also the tangential distance *D s*, ·873 of a foot.

Then from the starting-point B, and in line with A B, measure B D, equal 100 feet, and put a pin at D. Also from B, measure the chord B *s*, equal 100 feet; at the same time measuring with a graduated rod, from the pin D, the *tangential* distance D *s*, equal to ·873 of a foot; and place a stake at *s*. The pin at D may then be removed.

Next, make *s e* equal to 100 feet, placing a pin at *e*, precisely in line with *s* B; also from *s* measure *s t*, equal 100 feet; at the same time measuring with the rod, from the pin *e*, the *deflection* distance *e t*, equal to 1·745 foot. Place a stake at *t*, and remove the pin at *e*. In this manner proceed to find other points as far as the end of the curve at *v*.

In order to pass the curve, as at *v*, to a tangent *v* L, proceed as before, only using the tangential distance *h n*, instead of the deflection distance *h w*. (See Art. IV.)

This method is abundantly accurate for laying out curves on a canal or common road; and will occasionally answer very well, when carefully performed, for railroad curves, in the absence of an instrument. Thin straight rods, iron-pointed, and a plumb-line should be used for ranging the points in the latter case.

The transit instrument is the best for tracing curves, and running lines generally. I prefer the graduations to run from the same zero, right and left, to 180° each way. There should be two verniers, graduated to minutes; by their means half or even quarter minutes may generally be estimated with considerable certainty. The telescope, revolving in a vertical plane, greatly expedites the laying off of exterior angles, after having first sighted backward to the point behind.

The verniers are sometimes graduated to hundredths of a degree; and this division is, in certain cases, the best; but for *general* purposes, the division into minutes is to be preferred, as all the printed tables of sines, tangents, &c., are calculated for that division.

ARTICLE IV.

On Sub-Chords.

We have hitherto spoken of curves as if they were composed of equal chords, each of 100 feet in length. It frequently happens, however, that at the end of a curve, as at *e*, fig. 4, we are obliged to use a shorter or sub-chord, *d e*, in order to unite properly with the tangent *e f*.

Fig. 4.

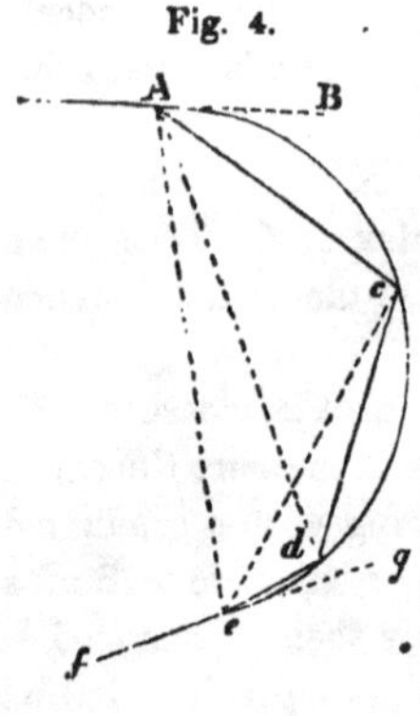

In that case, and *when using Method* 1, *Art.* I., *of laying out curves by means of tangential angles*, we must in order to fix the point *e*, lay off a *sub-tangential* angle, *d* A *e*, as much smaller than the entire tangential angle B A *c*, or *c* A *d*, &c., as the sub-chord *d e* is smaller than an entire 100 feet chord, *A c*, *c d*, &c. Thus, if the sub-chord be one-half, or one-fourth, &c., of the entire chord, the sub-tangential angle must be one-half, or one-fourth, &c., of the entire tangential angle.

This method is not mathematically exact, for the reason stated in Art. III. (viz., that the *chords* subtending different angles are not proportional to those angles); yet, for curves of 300 or more feet radius, and with chords not exceeding 100 feet in length, the error is not observable in practice.

In like manner, when we pass off from a sub-chord, as at *e*, to a second tangent, *e f*, we must place the instrument at *e*, and lay off the same sub-tangential angle *d e g*; or, which is better, take sight from *e* to *c*, and lay off the angle *c e g*, equal to the *sum* of a tangential and the sub-tangential angle.

But *when using Method* 2, *Art.* II., *of deflection angles, or Method* 3, *Art.* III., *of deflection distances, we may calculate the sub-deflection angle* a s e, *fig.* 5, *and sub-deflection distance* a e, *formed between a sub-chord* s e, *and the extension* s a, *of an entire chord* g s, *with sufficient accuracy for curves of* 300 *or more feet radius, and chords of not more than* 100 *feet, thus*:

Rule.—Say, As an entire chord of 100 feet is to the sub-chord *s e*, so is the *deflection* angle of the curve to a certain angle. Add these two angles together and divide their sum by 2, for the sub-deflection angle *a s e* of the sub-chord.

Fig. 5.

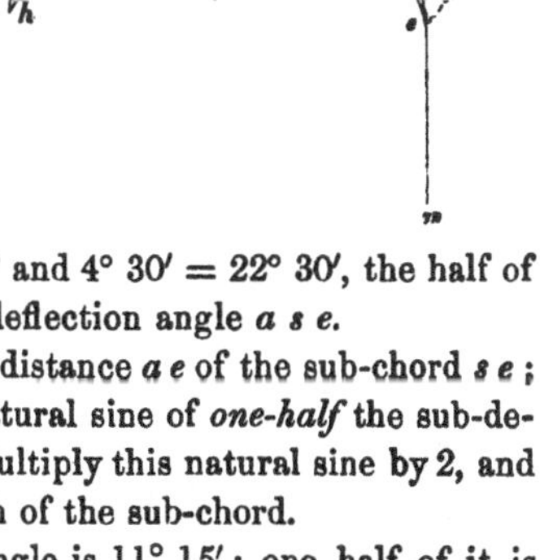

Example.—The curve, fig. 5, has a radius of 319·6 feet, and an angle of deflection, *f g s*, of 18° for chords of 100 feet. The sub-chord *s e* is 25 feet in length: what is the sub-deflection *angle a s e*; and also the sub-deflection *distance a e*, for the sub-chord *s e*?

	Chord.		Sub-Chord.
Here, as	100	is to	25;
	Def. An. of 100 feet chord.		Certain Angle.
So is	18°	to	4° 30′.

The sum of these two angles, 18° and 4° 30′ = 22° 30′, the half of which is 11° 15′, the required sub-deflection angle *a s e*.

Again, to find the sub-deflection distance *a e* of the sub-chord *s e*; take from the table of sines the natural sine of *one-half* the sub-deflection angle *a s e*, just found. Multiply this natural sine by 2, and multiply that product by the length of the sub-chord.

Example.—The sub-deflection angle is 11° 15′; one half of it is 5° 37½′, the tabular natural sine of which is ·0979, which, multiplied by 2, gives ·1958; this, multiplied by the sub-chord, 25 feet, gives 4·895 feet, the required sub-deflection distance *a e*.

Finally, to find the sub-tangential distance *s n*, by means of which to pass from *e* to the tangent *e m*, say, As 10000 is to the square of the sub-chord in feet, so is the *tangential* distance for 100 feet chord to *s n*. In this instance, we have, As 10000 is to 625, so is 15·69 feet to ·980 foot, or *s n*.

ARTICLE V.

Ordinates for Entire Chords.

It would be both tedious, and liable to inaccuracy, to attempt to fix all the necessary points in railroad curves by the foregoing means, which are employed only for entire chords, or for such sub-chords as may be required at the ends of curves.

The best method is to stretch a piece of twine, *a b*, fig. 6, 100 feet long, between two adjacent chord-stakes, and measure off as nearly as may be at right angles to it, with a graduated rod, the previously calculated ordinates *c d*, *e f*, *g h*, &c., placing pegs at *d*, *f*, *h*, &c.* Our table of ordinates, page 162, is calculated for distances apart, *b c*, *c e*, *e g*, &c., of 5 feet; and for all curves likely to occur in practice. The 5 feet distances on the twine should be marked by knots or otherwise; and those at the centre, and half way between it and the ends, be further distinguished by tying on pieces of tape.

Fig. 6.

The 5 feet distances are only used (after the excavations and embankments are finished) for placing pegs to guide the laying of the rails, and then only for very sudden curves; for those of large radii, distances of 10 feet are sufficiently near, or even 25 feet for very easy curves. For guiding the curves of the cuttings and fillings, it is not necessary to place the stakes nearer than 50 feet apart; unless for those of less than about 1000 feet radius, when they may be placed 25 feet apart. Ordinates for radii intermediate to those in the table, may either be calculated by the rules given further on, or they may be taken proportionally intermediate of the tabular ones, with sufficient accuracy for practice.

Ordinates for Sub-Chords.

These may readily be calculated *approximately enough for railroad practice*, for curves of over 300 feet radius, and for chords not exceeding 100 feet, thus: In a circle of given radius, not less than about 300 feet, the ordinates of an entire 100 feet chord may be as-

* On the tops of these stakes small tacks are driven, to define the precise point in the curve.

sumed to be to those of a sub-chord as the square of the chord is to the square of the sub-chord.

In all our tables the chord is supposed to be 100 feet, the square of which is 10000; the rule therefore becomes, As 10000 feet : square of sub-chord in feet : : Ord. of Chord : Ord. of Sub-Chord *approximately.*

Example.—In a curve of 5730 feet radius, the middle ordinate of a 100 feet chord is ·218 of a foot; what will be the length of the middle ordinate of a sub-chord of 50 feet? Here,

Sq. of 100 ft. :	Sq. of 50 ft. : :	Mid. Ord. of Chord.	:	Mid. Ord. Sub-Chord *approximately.*
10000 :	2500 : :	·218 ft.	:	·0545 ft.

And so of any other ordinate, always supposing the chord and sub-chord to be divided into the *same number of parts.*

ARTICLE VI.

Having given the angle a b d, *fig.* 7, *it is required to find the point* a *or* d, *at which to commence a curve of given radius.*

Rule.—Subtract half the angle *a b d* from 90°; the remainder will be the angle *b c a* or *b c d.* From the table of tangents take the natural tangent of *b c a*, and multiply it by the given radius; the product will be *b a* or *b d.*

Fig. 7.

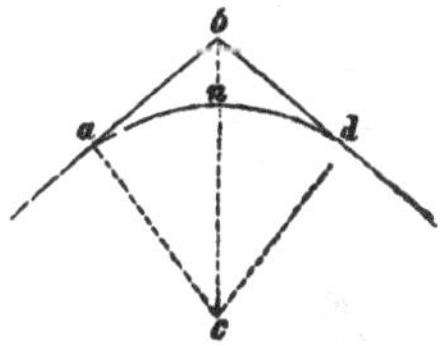

Example.—Let the angle *a b d* be 120°, how far from *b* must we begin, at *a* or *d*, to lay out a curve, *a n d*, of 2865 feet radius?

Here, half of the angle $a\ b\ d = 60°$, which taken from 90° leaves the angle $b\ c\ a = 30°$. The natural tangent of $30° = {\cdot}5773$, which, multiplied by the radius of 2865 feet, gives 1653·96 feet for *b a* or *b d.* (See Art. XII.)

ARTICLE VII.

Having given the angle a b d, *fig.* 7, *and the distance from* b *to* a *or* d, *at one of which we wish to commence a curve, it is required to find what radius,* c a *or* c d, *the curve must have, in order to unite with* b a *and* b d *tangentially at* a *and* d.

Rule.—Subtract the angle *a b c*, which is half the angle *a b d*, from 90°; the remainder will be the angle *b c a* or *b c d.* Then as natural sine of *b c a** is to natural sine of *a b c*,† so is *a b* to *a c*, the radius required.

* The angle opposite the given side, *a b.*

† The angle opposite the required side, *a c.*

Example.—Let the angle *a b d* be 120°, and the distance *b a* or *b d* 1654 feet; what will be the radius *a c* or *c d* of a circle that shall touch *a* and *d* tangentially?

Here, the angle *a b c* = half the angle *a b d*, is 60°, which, taken from 90°, leaves the angle *b c a* or *b c d* = 30°. Then, as the natural sine of *b c a* (30°) = ·5000 is to natural sine of *a b c* (60°) = ·8660, so is *b a* (1654 feet) to *a c* (2865 feet), the radius required.

ARTICLE VIII.

Having given the radius* a c, *fig.* 7, *of a curve, and the angle* a b d, *it is required to find the number of chords of* 100 *feet that will constitute the curve.

Rule.—Subtract the angle *a b d* from 180°, and divide the remainder by the angle of curvature, or deflection of the curve. The quotient will be the required number of chords.

Example.—Let the angle *a b d* be 120°, and the radius *a c* 2865 feet.

Here, the angle *a b d*, 120°, subtracted from 180°, leaves a remainder of 60°; which, divided by 2°, the angle of deflection for a curve of 2865 feet, gives a quotient of 30; which is the required number of chords of 100 feet.

N.B.—Had the quotient contained a *fraction* of a chord, it would have indicated that we should have had to employ a sub-chord at the end of the curve; for instance, had the number of chords been 30½, a sub-chord of 50 feet (very approximately) would have been necessary.

ARTICLE IX.

How to proceed when the end of a curve does not correctly join the tangent.

We sometimes find, in running out a curve for the number of chords determined by the Rule in the preceding Article, that, instead of uniting as it should with the previously determined tan-

Fig. 8.

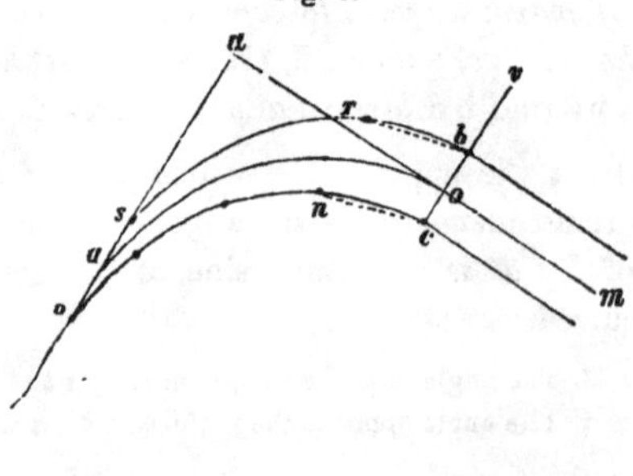

gent *d m*, fig. 8, at *o*, it ends tangentially to a line *parallel* to said tangent, either *within* it, as at *c*; or beyond it, as at *b*. Being first certain that no error has occurred in tracing out the curve, ascertain with the compass the bearing of the tangent *a d*, and, removing the compass to the end of the curve at *c* or *b* (as the case may be), run the line *b o* or *c o*, in the same course as *a d*, until it strikes the tangent *d o m*; which may be ascertained by ranging two stakes placed on the tangent.

Then measure *b o* or *c o* (as the case may be), and if the curve fall *within* the tangent *o m*, as at *c*, measure *forwards* from *t* towards *d* the distance *t a*, equal to *c o*; or if the curve fall *beyond* the tangent, as at *b*, measure *backwards* from *s* the distance *s a*, equal to *b o*. Then the curve retraced from *a* will terminate tangentially in *d m* at *o*.

N.B.—The direction of *c o* or *b o* may be ascertained without a compass, and better, thus: Multiply the *tangential* angle of the curve by *twice* the number of chords run, *less one*; subtract the product from 180°, and sighting back one chord to *n* or *r*, lay off the angle *n c b* or *r b v*, equal to the remainder. For example, if the tangential angle be 10°, and from *t* to *c* be 4 chords, then 7 times 10° taken from 180° leaves the angle *n c b* or *r b v* = 110°. When the product exceeds 180°, it must be subtracted from 360° for the angle *n c b* or *r b v*.*

This case occurs whenever an error has been made in measuring the distance from *d* to *a*. If *d a* be made too short, the curve *s b* is the result; and if too long, the curve *t c*.

If the error is small, it may be divided equally among the chords by measure without retracing the curve with an instrument. This method may be employed with perfect security so long as the error does not exceed 1 foot to every chord of 100 feet; and it will never be so great if moderate care be taken.

Thus, if the curve be 20 chords long, and the error 20 feet, the last stake may be moved 20 feet, the next 19, the next 18, &c., as nearly at right angles to the curve as can be judged by the eye.

The same ordinates that would have been used had the curve been correct will answer for the one so adjusted, without perceptible difference. For other cases, see Art. X.

ARTICLE X.

Again, it may happen that the error is not caused by a mismeasurement of the distance *a e*, figs. 9 and 10, as in the last case; but by mistake in obtaining the angle *a e f*.

* In both cases the angle is measured *outwardly* from the curve; but when the curve falls beyond the tangent, as at *b*, then *b v* must be continued inwardly, as *b o*.

If *a e f*, fig. 9, be measured in excess, as *a e g*, then the curve *a b c*,

Fig. 9.

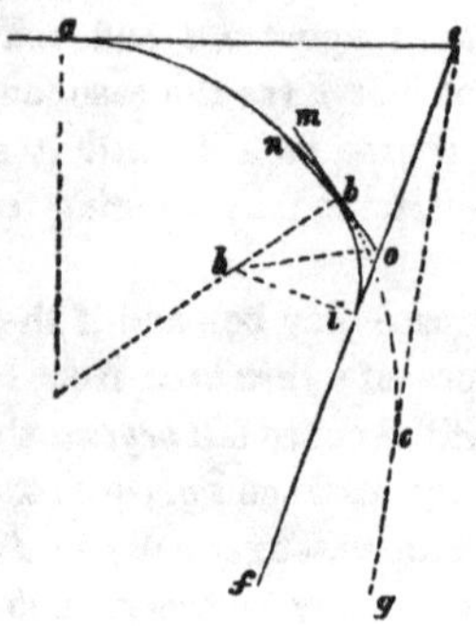

Fig. 10.

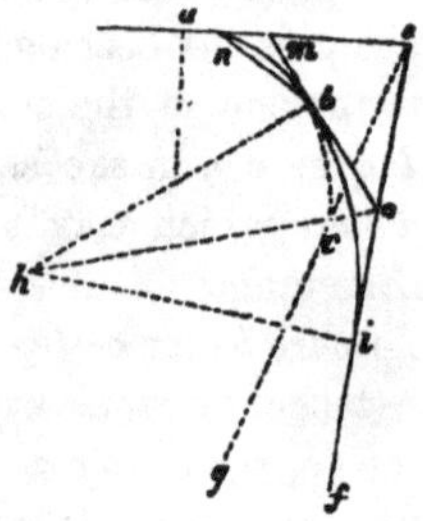

calculated for the incorrect angle *a e g*, will be found to fall *beyond* the true tangent *e f*, as at *c*; and the tangents *e g* and *e f* not being parallel, the curve cannot be adjusted by either of the methods given in the preceding Article, unless the error be within about 1 foot to each 100 feet length of curve; in which case (supposing no other error to exist), either of those methods may be employed with sufficient accuracy for practice.

Also, if *a e f*, fig. 10, be measured too small, as *a e g*, then the curve *a b c*, calculated for the incorrect angle *a e g*, will be found to fall *within* the true tangent *e f*, as at *c*; when so, the remarks contained in the preceding sentence are equally applicable here. If the error be within 1 foot to 100 feet length of curve, it may be equally divided among the chords. But if greater, we must either remeasure the angle *a e f* correctly, and go over the whole work again, or resort to some other mode of obviating the difficulty. The angle *a e f* may be difficult of access; or the curve may be so long that to retrace it would be a work of much labour. We may then adopt the method of *compound curves* (see Art. XIII.), by which much trouble will be avoided, and a considerable portion of the first part of the curve be allowed to remain as it is.

Thus, whether the curve *a b c* fall beyond the true tangent *e f*, as in fig. 9, or inside of it, as in fig. 10, place the instrument at *b*, figs. 9 and 10 (the point at which the change of radius is to take place), and sighting back one chord to *n*, lay off the tangential angle *n b m* of the curve *a b c*, and observe where the tangent *m b* continued strikes *e f*, as at *o*. Measure both *b o*, and the angle *b o f*. Half the angle *b o f* taken from 90° gives the angle *b h o*; then say,

As the $\left\{\begin{array}{l}\text{Nat. Sine of angle } b\ h\ o \text{ op-}\\ \text{posite the given side } b\ o\end{array}\right\}$ is to $\left\{\begin{array}{c}\text{Nat. Sine of angle } b\ o\ h\\ \text{opposite the required}\\ \text{side } b\ h,\end{array}\right.$

So is The given side *b o*, to The required side or new radius *b h*.

Ascertain from the table, or by calculation, the angle of deflection and the tangential angle corresponding to this new radius *b h*; and the new curve commencing at *b* will terminate tangentially to *e f* at *i*, as far from *o* as *o* is from *b*.

For the mode of uniting two curves of different radii, so as to form a *compound* curve, see Art. XIII.

It will be observed, that when the first curve *a b c*, fig. 10, falls *inside* the tangent *e f*, the new curve must be of *greater* radius; and when *beyond*, fig. 9, of a *less* one.

ARTICLE XI.

Having given the angles a b c *and* b c d, *fig.* 11, *and the distance* b c, *it is required to find the greatest radius*, g i *or* h i, *that can be employed in a* REVERSE *curve* (*see Art.* XIV.), f o i n m, *for uniting* a b *to* c d.

Rule.—Half the angle *a b c* taken from 90° leaves the angle *b g i*; and half the angle *b c d* taken from 90° leaves the angle *i h c*.

Fig. 11.

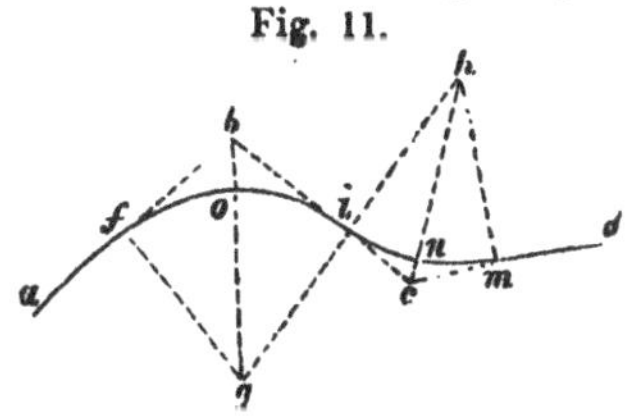

From the table of tangents take the natural tangent (*b i*) of the angle *b g i*; and that (*i c*) of the angle *i h c*; and add them together.

Then as the sum of these two natural tangents is to the natural tangent of *b g i*, so is *b c* to *b i*: and *b i* taken from *b c* gives *i c*.

Again, in the triangle *b g i*, as the natural sine of the angle *b g i*, opposite the given side *b i*, just found, is to the natural sine of the angle *g b i*, opposite the required side *g i*, so is *b i*, the given side, to *g i*, the required side or radius.

Example.—Let the angle *a b c* be 71° 40′, the angle *b c d* 129° 15′, and the distance *b c* 950 feet. What is the length of radius *h i* or *g i*, of the easiest reverse curve that can be traced for uniting *a b* to *c d*?

Here, half the angle *a b c* (35° 50′) taken from 90° leaves the angle *b g i* 54° 10′; and half the angle *b c d* (64° 37½′) taken from 90° leaves the angle *i h c* = 25° 22½′.

From the table of tangents, we have natural tangent of *b g i* (54° 10′) = 1·3848; and natural tangent of *i h c* (25° 22½′) = ·4743; their sum being 1·8591.

Then as

Sum of Tangts. 1·8591 } is to { Tang. of 54° 10′ 1·3848, } so is { *b c* 950 feet } to { *b i* 707·63 feet,

and *b i* 707·63 feet, taken from *b c* 950 feet, leaves *i c* 242·37 feet.

Again, as the

Nat. Sine of angle *b g i* ·8107 } is to { Nat. Sine of angle *g b i* ·5854, } so is { *b i* 707·63 feet } to { *g* or *h i*, the required radius, 510·97 feet.

ARTICLE XII.

***To obtain the angle* d b e, *formed by two tangents,* d b *and* b c, *when the point* b *is inaccessible.* Figs. 12, 13, 14, and 15.**

This is of frequent occurrence.

CASE 1. When the included figure, fig. 12, has but *three* sides.

Rule.—Subtract the angle *a d e* from 180° for the angle *b d e*; and subtract the angle *d e c* from 180° for the angle *d e b*. Add together *b d e* and *d e b*, and subtract their sum from 180° for the angle *d b e*. Or, more briefly, subtract 180° from the sum of *a d e* and *d e c*.

Fig. 12.

Fig. 13.

Fig. 14.

Fig. 15.

CASE 2. When the included figure *d b e f* (13, 14) has *four* sides.

Rule.—Subtract the sum of the three *internal* angles of the figure marked by dotted segments of circle, from 360° for the angle *d b e*.

CASE 3. When the included figure, fig. 15, has *more than four sides.*

Rule.—Add together all the *internal* angles, marked by dotted segments of circles ; and subtract their sum from twice as many right angles as the figure has sides, less four, for the angle *d b e*.

Example.—Let the angles denoted by the dotted segments at the different letters be as follows: That at *d*, 70°; at *o*, 220°; at *i*, 150°; at *s*, 110° ; at *c*, 160° ; at *e*, 100°. The sum of these is 810°. The figure has 7 sides ; and twice 7 less 4 = 10; and 10 right angles = 900°; from which the sum of the designated internal angles (810°) being subtracted, leaves 90° for the angle *d b e*.

N.B.—When the angle *d b e* has to be deduced from a figure of many sides, as fig. 15, the errors spoken of in Articles IX. and X. are apt to occur, unless the several sides and the angles *o i s*, &c., be measured with much care. For tracing curves with any accuracy and satisfaction, the instrument should be divided at least into minutes ;

as before remarked, the transit instrument is the best for the purpose. With moderate care in the preparatory measurement of the sides and angles, errors will seldom occur that may not be adjusted with all the accuracy required in practice, by the very simple method of dividing them equally among the chords, as explained in Articles IX. and X.

ARTICLE XIII.

To pass from one curve, a m b, *fig.* 16, *to another,* b n c, *of different radius, but running in the same direction, constituting a* COMPOUND *curve.*

Rule.—Placing the instrument at *b*, sight back to the other end of the 100 feet chord at *a*; and lay off the *tangential* angle *a b d* of the curve *a m b*; then from the common tangent *d b e* lay off the *tangential* angle *e b c* of the curve *b n c*, making at the same time the chord *b c*, equal to 100 feet.

Fig. 16.

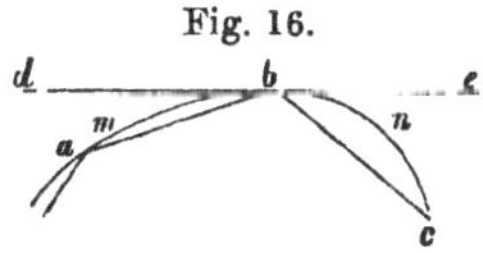

N.B.—If running the curve by eye, use the tangential *distances* instead of the angles.

ARTICLE XIV.

To pass from one curve, m n t, *fig.* 17, *to another,* t i o, *of either the same or of a different radius, but running in an opposite direction, constituting a* REVERSE *curve.*

Rule.—Placing the instrument at *t*, sight back to the other end of the 100 feet chord at *m*, and lay off the tangential angle *m t r* of the curve *m n t*; then from the common tangent *r t s* lay off the tangential angle *s t o* of the curve *t i o*, making at the same time the chord *t o*, equal to 100 feet.

Fig. 17.

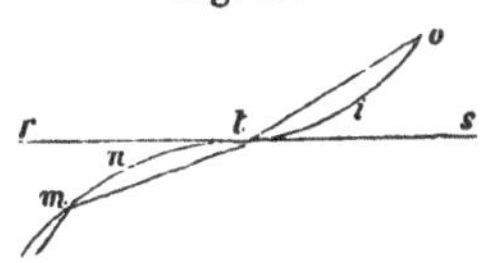

N.B.—If running the curve by eye, use the tangential *distances* instead of the angles.

ARTICLE XV.

RADII.

To find the radius corresponding to any given angle of deflection, and to equal chords of any given length.

Rule 1.—Subtract the angle of deflection from 180°, then say, As natural sine of angle of deflection is to natural sine of *half* the remainder, so is the given chord to the radius required.

Example.—Let the angle of deflection be 2°, and the chord 100 feet; required the radius.

Here, 2° subtracted from 180° leaves 178°, the half of which is 89°; and as

Nat. Sine of 2°	:	Nat. Sine of 89°	::	Chord	:	Radius
·034899		·999848		100 feet		2865 feet.

Rule 2.—The radius for 100 feet chords may be found *approximately*, by dividing 5730 by the deflection angle. This rule is very close for radii of not less than 500 feet. For 500 feet it gives eight-tenths of a foot too little, but is more approximate for larger radii.

Example.—What is the radius to a deflection angle of 2°, the chords being 100 feet long?

Here, 5730 divided by 2 gives 2865 feet, the radius required.

ARTICLE XVI.

TANGENTIAL AND DEFLECTION ANGLES.

To find either the Tangential or Deflection Angle corresponding to any given radius, and to equal chords of any given length.

Rule 1.—Divide *half* the chord by the radius; the quotient will be the natural sine of the *tangential* angle. Therefore the angle corresponding to this sine, in the Table of Natural Sines, will be the tangential angle required; and the tangential angle multiplied by 2 will give the deflection angle.

Example—Let the radius be 2865 feet, and the chord 100 feet; what will be the tangential and deflection angles?

Here, half the chord (50 feet), divided by the radius (2865 feet), gives ·01745; and the tangential angle in the Table corresponding to the natural sine ·01745 is 1°, twice which is 2°, the deflection angle required.

Rule 2.—The deflection angle for 100 feet chords may be found approximately by dividing 5730 by the radius. This is very close for curves of over 500 feet radius. For 500 feet it gives about one minute too little.

Example.—What is the deflection angle for a radius of 2865 feet, the chords being 100 each?

Here, 5730 divided by the radius 2865 gives 2°, the deflection angle required.

ARTICLE XVII.

DEFLECTION DISTANCES.

To find the Deflection Distance (exactly) for any given radius, when the chords are 100 feet long.

Rule.—Divide the constant number 10000 by the radius in feet; the quotient will be the deflection angle required.*

Example.—What is the deflection distance to a radius of 5730 feet, the chords being 100 feet long?

Here, 10000 divided by 5730 radius gives 1·745 foot, the deflection distance required.

To find the Deflection Distance for any given radius, and for equal chords of any given length.

Rule.—Divide half the given chord by radius, the quotient will be the natural sine of one-*half* the deflection angle; and *double* this natural sine, multiplied by the chord, will give the deflection distance required. By this rule our Table was prepared.

Example.—As before, what is the deflection distance to a radius of 5730 feet, the chords being 100 feet long?

Here, half the chord (50 feet), divided by radius (5730 feet), gives ·008727, which is the natural sine of half the deflection angle. Now ·008727, multiplied by 2, gives ·017454, which, multiplied by the chord (100 feet), gives 1·745 foot, the required deflection distance, the same as in the preceding example.

ARTICLE XVIII.

TANGENTIAL DISTANCES.

To find the Tangential Distance corresponding to any given radius, and to equal chords of any given length.

Rule.—First find the tangential angle by Art. XVI., and take from the Table of Natural Sines that corresponding to one-*half* of the *tangential* angle. Then multiply *double* this sine by the given chord for the tangential distance. By this rule our Table was prepared.

* Because the deflection distance to a radius of 10000 feet, with chords of 100 feet, is 1 foot; and the deflection distances for other radii increase *inversely* as the radii.

Example.—Let the radius be 2865 feet, and the chords 100 feet each; what will be the tangential distance?

Here we find, by Art. XVI., the tangential angle 1° for a radius of 2865 feet.

The natural sine corresponding to 30 minutes, or one-half of this tangential angle, is, by the Table of Sines, ·008727; the double of which is ·017454, which, multiplied by the chord, or 100 feet, gives 1·745 foot for the tangential distance required.

ARTICLE XIX.

ORDINATES.

To find the Middle Ordinate to any given radius, and to any given chord.

Rule 1.—From the square of the radius subtract the square of *half* the chord; and take the square root of the remainder from the radius, for the middle ordinate.

Fig. 18.

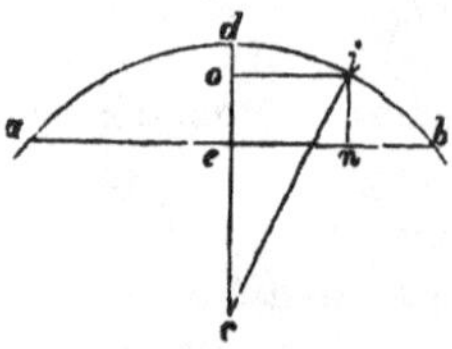

Example.—What is the length of the middle ordinate *d e*, fig 18, the radius *c a* being 819 feet, and the chord *a b* 100 feet?

Here, the square of *c a* (819) is 670761, and the square of *a e* (50) is 2500; which, being subtracted from the former, leaves 668261; the square root of which is *e c*, 817·472; which, taken from the radius 819, leaves 1·528 foot, the required middle ordinate, *d e*.

Rule 2.—Subtract the tabular cosine of the *tangential* angle from 1, and multiply the remainder by the radius.

Example.—Same as foregoing; namely, radius 819 feet, angle of deflection 7°, to chords of 100 feet. What will be the length of the middle ordinate?

Here, tabular cosine of $3\frac{1}{2}$° (the tangential angle) is ·998135; which, subtracted from 1, leaves ·001865; which, multiplied by 819, the radius, gives 1·527, the middle ordinate required.

ARTICLE XX.

Having given the Middle Ordinate d e, *fig.* 18, *it is required to find any other one, as* i n.

Rule 1.—Subtract the middle ordinate *d e* from the radius *d c*, the remainder will be *e c*: then from the square of the radius *c i* subtract the square of the distance *o i*, which the required ordinate *i n* is from the middle ordinate *d e*, and extract the square root of the remainder. This square root will be *o c*. From this square root *o c* subtract *e c*; the remainder will be *o e*, which is equal to *i n*, the required ordinate.

Example.—The middle ordinate *d e*, of a 100 feet chord *b a*, to a radius of 819, being 1·528 foot, it is required to find the length of the ordinate *i n*, 20 feet from the middle one.

Here, the middle ordinate *d e*, 1·528, subtracted from the radius 819, leaves *e c*, 817·472. The square of the radius is 670761; and the square of 20 (the distance of the required ordinate from the middle one) is 400; which, taken from 670761, leaves 670361; the square root of which is 818·756, or *o c*; from which take *e c*, or 817·472, and the remainder, 1·284, will be *o e*, which is equal to *i n*, the required ordinate.

Rule 2.—Multiply the ordinates of a 1° curve by the deflection angle of the curve whose ordinates are required (chords being 100 feet). This is a sufficiently close approximation for curves of not less than 500 feet radius; and for placing ordinates *for guiding the excavations and embankments*, it is close enough for the smallest curves in our Table.

I.—Table of Radii, &c.—*Chord* 100 *feet.*

The Tangential Angle is always one-half of the Angle of Deflection.

Angle of Deflection.	Radius in feet.	Deflection distance in feet.	Tangential distance in feet.	Angle of Deflection.	Radius in feet.	Deflection distance in feet.	Tangential distance in feet.
° ′				° ′			
1	343800	·029	·014	51	6741	1·482	·741
2	171900	·058	·029	52	6611	1·511	·755
3	114600	·087	·043	53	6487	1·540	·770
4	85950	·116	·058	54	6367	1·569	·784
5	68760	·145	·072	55	6251	1·598	·799
6	57300	·174	·087	56	6139	1·627	·813
7	49116	·203	·101	57	6032	1·656	·828
8	42975	·232	·116	58	5928	1·685	·842
9	38200	·262	·131	59	5827	1·715	·857
10	34380	·291	·145	1 0	5730	1·745	·872
11	31256	·320	·160	2	5545	1·802	·901
12	28650	·349	·174	4	5372	1·860	·930
13	26446	·378	·189	6	5209	1·918	·959
14	24558	·407	·203	8	5056	1·976	·988
15	22920	·436	·218	10	4912	2·036	1·018
16	21487	·465	·232	12	4775	2·094	1·047
17	20224	·494	·247	14	4646	2·152	1·076
18	19100	·523	·261	16	4524	2·210	1·105
19	18094	·552	·276	18	4408	2·268	1·134
20	17190	·581	·290	20	4298	2·326	1·163
21	16372	·610	·305	22	4193	2·384	1·192
22	15628	·639	·319	24	4093	2·443	1·221
23	14948	·668	·334	26	3998	2·501	1·250
24	14325	·697	·348	28	3907	2·559	1·279
25	13752	·727	·363	30	3820	2·617	1·308
26	13223	·756	·378	32	3737	2·676	1·338
27	12733	·785	·392	34	3657	2·734	1·367
28	12279	·814	·407	36	3581	2·793	1·396
29	11856	·843	·421	38	3508	2·851	1·425
30	11460	·872	·436	40	3438	2·908	1·454
31	11090	·900	·450	42	3370	2·967	1·483
32	10744	·930	·465	44	3306	3·025	1·512
33	10419	·959	·479	46	3243	3·083	1·541
34	10112	·988	·494	48	3183	3·141	1·570
35	9823	1·017	·508	50	3126	3·199	1·599
36	9550	1·046	·523	52	3069	3·258	1·629
37	9292	1·075	·537	54	3016	3·316	1·658
38	9047	1·104	·552	56	2964	3·374	1·687
39	8815	1·133	·566	58	2914	3·432	1·716
40	8595	1·162	·581	2 0	2865	3·490	1·745
41	8385	1·191	·595	2	2818	3·548	1·774
42	8186	1·221	·610	4	2772	3·606	1·803
43	7995	1·250	·625	6	2729	3·665	1·832
44	7814	1·279	·639	8	2686	3·723	1·861
45	7640	1·308	·654	10	2644	3·781	1·890
46	7474	1·337	·668	12	2604	3·839	1·919
47	7315	1·366	·683	14	2566	3·897	1·948
48	7162	1·395	·697	16	2528	3·956	1·978
49	7016	1·424	·712	18	2491	4·014	2·007
50	6876	1·453	·726	20	2456	4·072	2·036

I.—Table of Radii, &c.—*continued.*

Angle of Deflection.	Radius in feet.	Deflection distance in feet.	Tangential distance in feet.	Angle of Deflection.	Radius in feet.	Deflection distance in feet.	Tangential distance in feet.
2° 22′	2421	4·130	2·065	4° 15′	1348	7·410	3·708
24	2387	4·188	2·094	20	1322	7·563	3·781
26	2355	4·246	2·123	25	1298	7·708	3·854
28	2323	4·305	2·152	30	1274	7·853	3·927
30	2292	4·363	2·182	35	1251	7·998	3·999
32	2262	4·421	2·210	40	1228	8·143	4·071
34	2232	4·479	2·239	45	1207	8·289	4·145
36	2204	4·538	2·269	50	1185	8·432	4·216
38	2176	4·596	2·298	55	1166	8·577	4·288
40	2149	4·653	2·326	5 0	1146	8·722	4·361
42	2122	4·712	2·356	5	1127	8·869	4·434
44	2096	4·770	2·385	10	1109	9·014	4·507
46	2071	4·828	2·414	15	1092	9·159	4·579
48	2046	4·886	2·443	20	1074	9·304	4·652
50	2023	4·944	2·472	25	1058	9·449	4·724
52	1999	5·002	2·501	30	1042	9·595	4·798
54	1976	5·060	2·530	35	1026	9·740	4·870
56	1953	5·118	2·559	40	1011	9·885	4·942
58	1932	5·176	2·588	45	996·8	10·03	5·015
3 0	1910	5·235	2·618	50	982·7	10·18	5·090
2	1889	5·293	2·646	55	969·0	10·32	5·160
4	1868	5·351	2·675	6 0	955·4	10·47	5·235
6	1848	5·409	2·704	5	947·5	10·62	5·310
8	1828	5·468	2·734	10	939·7	10·76	5·380
10	1810	5·526	2·763	15	917·0	10·90	5·450
12	1790	5·584	2·792	20	905·0	11·04	5·520
14	1772	5·642	2·821	25	893·5	11·20	5·600
16	1754	5·700	2·850	30	882·0	11·34	5·670
18	1736	5·758	2·879	35	870·7	11·48	5·740
20	1719	5·817	2·908	40	859·5	11·63	5·815
22	1702	5·875	2·937	45	849·3	11·78	5·890
24	1685	5·933	2·966	50	838·9	11·92	5·960
26	1669	5·992	2·996	55	828·9	12·06	6·030
28	1653	6·050	3·025	7 0	819·0	12·21	6·105
30	1637	6·108	3·054	5	813·3	12·36	6·180
32	1621	6·166	3·083	10	807·4	12·50	6·250
34	1606	6·224	3·112	15	790·8	12·64	6·320
36	1591	6·282	3·141	20	781·9	12·79	6·395
38	1577	6·340	3·170	25	773·2	12·94	6·470
40	1563	6·398	3·199	30	764·5	13·08	6·540
42	1549	6·456	3·228	35	756·1	13·22	6·610
44	1534	6·515	3·257	40	748·0	13·37	6·685
46	1521	6·574	3·287	45	739·9	13·51	6·755
48	1508	6·632	3·316	50	732·0	13·66	6·830
50	1495	6·690	3·345	55	724·3	13·80	6·900
52	1482	6·748	3·374	8 0	716·8	13·95	6·975
54	1469	6·806	3·403	15	695·1	14·38	7·190
56	1457	6·864	3·432	30	674·6	14·81	7·405
58	1445	6·922	3·461	45	655·5	15·25	7·625
4 0	1433	6·980	3·490	9 0	637·3	15·68	7·840
5	1403	7·125	3·562	15	620·2	16·12	8·060
10	1375	7·270	3·635	30	603·8	16·55	8·275

I.—Table of Radii, &c.—*continued.*

Angle of Deflection.	Radius in feet.	Deflection distance in feet.	Tangential distance in feet.	Angle of Deflection.	Radius in feet.	Deflection distance in feet.	Tangential distance in feet.
° ′				° ′			
9 45	588·4	16·99	8·495	17 0	338·3	29·56	14·82
10 0	573·7	17·43	8·715	30	328·7	30·43	15·25
15	559·7	17·87	8·935	18 0	319·6	21·29	15·69
30	546·4	18·30	9·150	30	311·0	32·15	16·12
45	533·8	18·73	9·365	19 0	302·9	33·01	16·56
11 0	521·7	19·17	9·585	30	295·3	33·87	16·99
15	510·1	19·61	9·805	20 0	287·9	34·73	17·43
30	499·1	20·05	10·03	21 0	274·4	36·44	18·30
45	488·5	20·50	10·25	22 0	262·0	38·15	19·17
12 0	478·3	20·94	10·47	23 0	250·8	39·87	20·02
15	468·7	21·36	10·69	24 0	240·5	41·58	20·91
30	459·3	21·79	10·90	25 0	231·0	43·28	21·77
45	450·3	22·21	11·12	26 0	222·3	44·98	22·64
13 0	441·7	22·64	11·34	27 0	214·2	46·68	23·51
15	433·4	23·07	11·56	28 0	206·7	48·38	24·37
30	425·5	23·51	11·77	29 0	199·7	50·07	25·24
45	417·7	23·94	11·99	30 0	193·2	51·76	26·11
14 0	410·3	24·37	12·21	31 0	187·1	53·45	26·97
15	403·1	24·81	12·43	32 0	181·4	55·13	27·83
30	396·2	25·24	12·65	33 0	176·0	56·80	28·70
45	389·6	25·67	12·86	34 0	171·0	58·47	29·56
15 0	383·1	26·11	13·08	35 0	166·3	60·14	30·42
15	376·9	26·52	13·30	36 0	161·8	61·80	31·29
30	370·8	26·94	13·52	37 0	157·6	63·46	32·15
45	365·0	27·37	13·73	38 0	153·6	65·11	33·01
16 0	359·3	27·83	13·95	39 0	149·8	66·76	33·87
30	348·4	28·70	14·38	40 0	146·2	68·40	34·73

II.—Table of Ordinates.

Ordinates five feet apart.—Chord 100 *feet.*

	Distances of the Ordinates from the end of the 100 feet Chord.								
Angle of Deflection.	Middle, 50 feet.	45 feet.	40 feet.	35 feet.	30 feet.	25 feet.	20 feet.	15 feet.	10 feet.	5 feet.
° ′										
2	·007	·007	·007	·006	·006	·005	·003	·003	·002	·001
4	·014	·014	·014	·013	·012	·010	·008	·008	·005	·003
6	·021	·021	·021	·020	·019	·016	·013	·011	·008	·004
8	·029	·029	·028	·026	·024	·022	·018	·015	·010	·005
10	·036	·036	·035	·033	·031	·027	·023	·019	·013	·007
12	·043	·043	·041	·038	·037	·033	·028	·022	·015	·008
14	·050	·050	·048	·044	·043	·038	·032	·026	·017	·010
16	·058	·058	·056	·052	·049	·044	·037	·030	·020	·011
18	·065	·065	·063	·059	·055	·050	·042	·033	·023	·013
20	·073	·072	·070	·066	·061	·055	·047	·037	·026	·014
22	·080	·079	·076	·071	·067	·060	·051	·041	·029	·015

II.—Table of Ordinates—*continued.*

Angle of Deflection.	Middle, 50 feet.	45 feet.	40 feet.	35 feet.	30 feet.	25 feet.	20 feet.	15 feet.	10 feet.	5 feet.
	Distances of the Ordinates from the end of the 100 feet Chord.									
° ′										
24	·087	·086	·083	·077	·074	·066	·056	·045	·031	·017
26	·094	·093	·090	·084	·080	·071	·060	·048	·034	·018
28	·102	·101	·098	·092	·086	·077	·065	·052	·036	·019
30	·109	·108	·105	·099	·092	·082	·070	·055	·039	·020
32	·116	·115	·112	·106	·098	·088	·075	·058	·042	·022
34	·123	·122	·118	·111	·104	·094	·079	·062	·044	·023
36	·131	·130	·126	·119	·110	·099	·084	·066	·047	·024
38	·138	·137	·133	·126	·116	·105	·089	·070	·049	·025
40	·145	·144	·140	·133	·123	·110	·093	·074	·052	·027
42	·152	·150	·146	·138	·128	·115	·098	·077	·055	·028
44	·160	·158	·153	·145	·135	·121	·103	·081	·057	·030
46	·167	·165	·160	·152	·141	·126	·107	·085	·060	·032
48	·174	·172	·167	·158	·147	·132	·112	·088	·062	·033
50	·182	·180	·175	·166	·153	·138	·117	·092	·065	·034
52	·189	·187	·181	·171	·159	·143	·122	·095	·068	·035
54	·196	·194	·188	·178	·165	·148	·126	·099	·070	·036
56	·204	·202	·195	·185	·171	·154	·131	·103	·073	·038
58	·211	·209	·202	·192	·177	·159	·136	·107	·075	·039
1 0	·218	·216	·209	·198	·183	·164	·140	·111	·078	·041
2	·225	·223	·215	·204	·189	·169	·145	·114	·081	·042
4	·233	·231	·223	·211	·196	·175	·150	·118	·083	·043
6	·240	·238	·230	·217	·202	·180	·155	·121	·086	·045
8	·247	·245	·237	·224	·208	·186	·159	·125	·088	·046
10	·254	·252	·244	·231	·214	·191	·163	·130	·091	·048
12	·262	·260	·252	·237	·220	·196	·168	·133	·094	·049
14	·269	·267	·258	·244	·226	·202	·173	·136	·096	·050
16	·276	·274	·265	·251	·232	·207	·177	·140	·099	·052
18	·284	·282	·273	·257	·238	·213	·182	·144	·101	·053
20	·291	·288	·279	·264	·244	·218	·187	·148	·104	·055
22	·298	·295	·285	·270	·250	·224	·192	·151	·107	·056
24	·306	·303	·293	·277	·256	·229	·197	·155	·109	·057
26	·313	·310	·300	·284	·263	·235	·201	·159	·112	·059
28	·320	·317	·307	·291	·269	·240	·206	·163	·114	·060
30	·327	·324	·314	·297	·275	·246	·210	·167	·117	·062
32	·334	·331	·321	·304	·281	·251	·215	·171	·120	·063
34	·341	·338	·328	·310	·287	·257	·219	·174	·122	·065
36	·349	·345	·335	·317	·293	·262	·224	·178	·125	·066
38	·356	·353	·342	·323	·299	·268	·228	·182	·127	·068
40	·364	·360	·349	·330	·305	·273	·233	·185	·130	·069
42	·371	·367	·356	·337	·312	·278	·238	·189	·133	·070
44	·378	·374	·363	·343	·318	·284	·242	·192	·135	·072
46	·385	·382	·370	·350	·324	·289	·247	·196	·138	·073
48	·393	·389	·377	·356	·330	·295	·251	·200	·141	·075
50	·400	·396	·384	·364	·336	·300	·256	·204	·144	·076
52	·407	·403	·391	·370	·342	·305	·261	·208	·147	·077
54	·414	·410	·398	·376	·348	·311	·265	·211	·149	·079
56	·422	·418	·405	·383	·354	·316	·270	·215	·152	·080
58	·429	·425	·412	·389	·360	·322	·275	·219	·154	·082
2 0	·436	·432	·419	·397	·366	·327	·280	·222	·157	·083
2	·443	·439	·426	·402	·373	·332	·284	·226	·160	·084
4	·451	·446	·433	·409	·379	·338	·289	·230	·162	·086

II.—Table of Ordinates—*continued.*

Angle of Deflection.	Distances of the Ordinates from the end of the 100 feet Chord.									
	Middle, 50 feet.	45 feet.	40 feet.	35 feet.	30 feet.	25 feet.	20 feet.	15 feet.	10 feet.	5 feet.
2° 6′	·458	·454	·440	·416	·385	·343	·293	·234	·165	·087
8	·465	·461	·447	·425	·391	·349	·298	237	·167	·088
10	·473	·468	·454	·430	·397	·355	·303	·241	·170	·089
12	·480	·475	·461	·437	·403	·360	·308	·245	·173	·090
14	·487	·482	·468	·443	·409	·366	·312	·248	·175	·092
16	·495	·490	·475	·450	·415	·371	·317	·252	·178	·093
18	·502	·497	·482	·456	·421	·377	·321	·256	·180	·095
20	·509	·504	·489	·463	·428	·382	·326	·260	·183	·096
22	·516	·511	·496	·470	·434	·387	·330	·264	·186	·097
24	·523	·518	·503	·476	·440	·393	·334	·267	·188	·099
26	·531	·526	·510	·483	·446	·398	·338	·271	·191	·100
28	·538	·533	·517	·489	·452	·404	·346	·275	·194	·102
30	·545	·540	·524	·496	·458	·409	·350	·278	·196	·103
32	·552	·547	·531	·503	·465	·415	·355	·282	·199	·104
34	·560	·554	·538	·509	·471	·420	·359	·285	·201	·106
36	·567	·562	·545	·516	·477	·425	·364	·289	·204	·107
38	·574	·569	·552	·522	·483	·431	·368	·293	·206	·109
40	·582	·576	·559	·529	·489	·436	·373	·297	·209	·110
42	·589	·583	·566	·536	·495	·441	·378	·301	·212	·111
44	·596	·590	·573	·542	·501	·447	·382	·304	·214	·113
46	·603	·598	·580	·549	·507	·452	·387	·308	·217	·114
48	·611	·605	·587	·555	·513	·458	·391	·312	·219	·116
50	·618	·612	·594	·562	·519	·464	·396	·315	·222	·117
52	·625	·619	·601	·569	·526	·469	·401	·319	·225	·118
54	·632	·626	·608	·575	·532	·474	·405	·322	·227	·119
56	·640	·634	·615	·582	·538	·480	·410	·326	·230	·121
58	·647	·641	·622	·588	·544	·485	·414	·330	·232	·123
3 0	·654	·648	·629	·595	·550	·491	·419	·334	·235	·124
2	·661	·655	·636	·602	·556	·497	·424	·338	·238	·125
4	·669	·662	·643	·608	·562	·502	·428	·341	·240	·127
6	·676	·670	·650	·615	·568	·507	·433	·345	·243	·128
8	·683	·677	·657	·621	·574	·512	·438	·349	·246	·130
10	·691	·684	·664	·629	·581	·518	·443	·353	·249	·131
12	·698	·691	·671	·635	·587	·523	·448	·357	·251	·132
14	·706	·698	·678	·642	·593	·529	·452	·360	·254	·134
16	·713	·705	·685	·649	·599	·534	·457	·364	·257	·135
18	·720	·713	·692	·655	·605	·540	·462	·368	·259	·137
20	·727	·720	·699	·662	·611	·545	·466	·371	·262	·138
22	·734	·727	·706	·668	·617	·550	·471	·375	·264	·139
24	·742	·734	·713	·675	·623	·556	·475	·378	·267	·141
26	·749	·742	·720	·682	·629	·561	·480	·382	·270	·142
28	·756	·749	·727	·688	·635	·567	·485	·386	·272	·144
30	·764	·756	·734	·695	·642	·573	·489	·390	·275	·145
32	·771	·763	·741	·702	·648	·578	·494	·394	·278	·146
34	·779	·770	·748	·708	·654	·584	·498	·397	·280	·148
36	·786	·777	·755	·715	·660	·589	·503	·401	·283	·149
38	·793	·785	·762	·721	·666	·594	·508	·405	·285	·151
40	·800	·792	·769	·728	·673	·600	·512	·408	·288	·152
42	·807	·799	·776	·734	·679	·605	·517	·412	·291	·153
44	·814	·806	·783	·741	·685	·611	·521	·415	·293	·155
46	·822	·814	·790	·748	·691	·616	·526	·419	·296	·156

II.—Table of Ordinates—*continued.*

Distances of the Ordinates from the end of the 100 feet Chord.

Angle of Deflection.	Middle, 50 feet.	45 feet.	40 feet.	35 feet.	30 feet.	25 feet.	20 feet.	15 feet.	10 feet.	5 feet.
° ′										
3 48	·829	·821	·797	·754	·697	.621	·531	·423	·298	·158
50	·836	·828	·804	·761	·703	·627	·536	·427	·301	·159
52	·843	·835	·811	·768	·709	·632	·541	·431	·304	·160
54	·850	·842	·818	·774	·715	·638	·545	·434	·306	·162
56	·858	·850	·825	·781	·721	·643	·550	·438	·309	·163
58	·865	·857	·832	·787	·728	·648	·555	·442	·311	·165
4 0	·873	·864	·839	·794	·734	·655	·559	·445	·314	·166
5	·891	·882	·856	·810	·749	·668	·571	·454	·320	·169
10	·909	·900	·874	·827	·764	·682	·582	·464	·327	·173
15	·927	·918	·891	·844	·780	·695	·594	·473	·334	·176
20	·945	·936	·909	·860	·795	·709	·606	·482	·340	·179
25	·963	·954	·926	·877	·810	·723	·617	·491	·347	·183
30	·981	·972	·944	·893	·825	·736	·629	·501	·354	·186
35	·999	·990	·961	·909	·840	·750	·640	·510	·360	·189
40	1·017	1·008	·979	·926	·855	·764	·652	·519	·367	·193
45	1·036	1·026	·996	·943	·871	·777	·664	·529	·373	·196
50	1·054	1·044	1·014	·959	·886	·791	·676	·538	·380	·199
55	1·072	1·062	1·031	·976	·901	·804	·687	·547	·386	·203
5 0	1·091	1·080	1·048	·993	·917	·818	·699	·557	·393	·207
5	1·109	1·098	1·065	1·009	·932	·831	·711	·566	·400	·210
10	1·127	1·116	1·083	1·026	·947	·845	·722	·576	·406	·214
15	1·146	1·134	1·000	1·042	·963	·859	·734	·585	·413	·217
20	1·164	1·152	1·118	1·058	·978	·872	·746	·594	·419	·220
25	1·182	1·170	1·135	1·075	·993	·886	·757	·603	·426	·224
30	1·200	1·188	1·153	1·092	1·009	·900	·769	·613	·432	·228
35	1·218	1·206	1·170	1·108	1·024	·913	·781	·622	·438	·231
40	1·236	1·224	1·188	1·124	1·039	·927	·792	·631	·445	·235
45	1·255	1·242	1·205	1·141	1·055	·941	·804	·640	·452	·238
50	1·273	1·260	1·223	1·157	1·070	·954	·816	·649	·458	·241
55	1·291	1·278	1·240	1·174	1·085	·967	·827	·658	·465	·245
6 0	1·300	1·296	1·258	1·191	1·100	·982	·839	·668	·472	·248
5	1·327	1·314	1·275	1·207	1·115	·995	·851	·677	·478	·251
10	1·345	1·332	1·293	1·224	1·130	1·009	·862	·686	·485	·255
15	1·364	1·350	1·310	1·240	1·146	1·023	·874	·696	·492	·259
20	1·382	1·368	1·328	1·256	1·161	1·036	·886	·705	·498	·262
25	1·400	1·386	1·345	1·273	1·176	1·050	·897	·714	·505	·266
30	1·419	1·404	1·362	1·290	1·192	1·064	·909	·724	·511	·269
35	1·437	1·422	1·379	1·306	1·207	1·077	·921	·733	·517	·272
40	1·455	1·440	1·397	1·323	1·222	1·091	·932	·742	·524	·276
45	1·473	1·458	1·415	1·339	1·238	1·105	·944	·752	·531	·280
50	1·491	1·476	1·432	1·355	1·253	1·118	·956	·761	·537	·283
55	1·509	1·494	1·450	1·372	1·268	1·132	·967	·770	·544	·387
7 0	1·528	1·512	1·467	1·389	1·284	1·146	·979	·779	·551	·290
5	1·546	1·530	1·484	1·405	1·299	1·159	·991	·788	·557	·293
10	1·564	1·548	1·502	1·422	1·314	1·173	1·002	·798	·564	·297
15	1·582	1·566	1·520	1·438	1·330	1·187	1·014	·807	·570	·301
20	1·600	1·584	1·537	1·454	1·345	1·200	1·026	·816	·576	·304
25	1·618	1·602	1·555	1·471	1·360	1·214	1·037	·825	·583	·308
30	1·637	1·620	1·572	1·488	1·375	1·228	1·048	·835	·590	·311
35	1·655	1·638	1·589	1·504	1·390	1·241	1·060	·844	·596	·314
40	1·673	1·656	1·607	1·521	1·405	1·255	1·071	·854	·603	·318

II.—Table of Ordinates—*continued.*

Angle of Deflection.	Middle, 50 feet.	45 feet.	40 feet.	35 feet.	30 feet.	25 feet.	20 feet.	15 feet.	10 feet.	5 feet.
	Distances of the Ordinates from the end of the 100 feet Chord.									
° ′										
7 45	1·692	1·674	1·624	1·537	1·421	1·269	1·083	·863	·610	·321
50	1·710	1·692	1·641	1·553	1·436	1·282	1·095	·872	·616	·324
55	1·728	1·710	1·659	1·570	1·451	1·296	1·106	·881	·623	·328
8 0	1·746	1·728	1·677	1·587	1·467	1·310	1·118	·891	·629	·332
15	1·801	1·782	1·729	1·637	1·513	1·351	1·153	·918	·649	·342
30	1·855	1·836	1·782	1·687	1·559	1·392	1·188	·946	·669	·353
45	1·910	1·890	1·834	1·737	1·605	1·433	1·223	·974	·689	·363
9 0	1·965	1·944	1·886	1·787	1·651	1·474	1·258	1·002	·708	·373
15	2·019	1·998	1·939	1·837	1·696	1·515	1·293	1·030	·728	·384
30	2·074	2·052	1·991	1·887	1·742	1·556	1·328	1·057	·748	·394
45	2·128	2·106	2·044	1·937	1·788	1·597	1·363	1·085	·767	·405
10 0	2·183	2·161	2·096	1·987	1·834	1·637	1·398	1·114	·787	·415
15	2·238	2·215	2·148	2·037	1·880	1·678	1·433	1·142	·807	·425
30	2·292	2·269	2·201	2·087	1·926	1·719	1·468	1·170	·827	·436
45	2·347	2·323	2·254	2·136	1·972	1·761	1·503	1·198	·846	·446
11 0	2·401	2·377	2·306	2·186	2·018	1·802	1·538	1·226	·866	·457
15	2·456	2·432	2·359	2·236	2·064	1·843	1·574	1·254	·886	·467
30	2·511	2·486	2·411	2·286	2·110	1·884	1·609	1·282	·906	·478
45	2·566	2·540	2·464	2·336	2·156	1·926	1·644	1·310	·926	·488
12 0	2·620	2·594	2·516	2·386	2·203	1·967	1·680	1·339	·946	·499
15	2·675	2·649	2·569	2·436	2·249	2·008	1·715	1·367	·966	·509
30	2·730	2·703	2·621	2·485	2·295	2·049	1·750	1·395	·985	·520
45	2·785	2·757	2·674	2·535	2·341	2·091	1·785	1·423	1·005	·530
13 0	2·839	2·811	2·726	2·585	2·387	2·132	1·820	1·451	1·025	·541
15	2·894	2·865	2·779	2·635	2·433	2·173	1·855	1·479	1·045	·551
30	2·949	2·920	2·832	2·685	2·479	2·214	1·891	1·507	1·065	·562
45	3·000	2·974	2·884	2·735	2·525	2·256	1·926	1·535	1·085	·572
14 0	3·058	3·028	2·937	2·785	2·571	2·297	1·961	1·564	1·105	·583
15	3·113	3·082	2·989	2·834	2·618	2·338	1·996	1·592	1·124	·593
30	3·168	3·136	3·042	2·884	2·664	2·379	2·031	1·620	1·144	·604
45	3·222	3·191	3·094	2·934	2·710	2·421	2·067	1·648	1·164	·614
15 0	3·277	3·245	3·147	2·984	2·756	2·462	2·102	1·676	1·184	·625
15	3·332	3·299	3·200	3·034	2·802	2·503	2·137	1·704	1·204	·635
30	3·387	3·354	3·252	3·084	2·848	2·544	2·172	1·732	1·224	·646
45	3·442	3·408	3·305	3·134	2·895	2·586	2·208	1·760	1·244	·656
16 0	3·496	3·462	3·358	3·184	2·941	2·627	2·243	1·789	1·264	·667
30	3·606	3·571	3·463	3·284	3·033	2·710	2·314	1·845	1·304	·688
17 0	3·716	3·680	3·569	3·384	3·125	2·792	2·384	1·902	1·344	·709
30	3·826	3·788	3·674	3·484	3·218	2·875	2·455	1·958	1·384	·730
18 0	3·935	3·897	3·779	3·584	3·310	2·958	2·525	2·014	1·424	·751
30	4·045	4·006	3·885	3·684	3·403	3·040	2·596	2·071	1·464	·772
19 0	4·155	4·115	3·990	3·784	3·495	3·123	2·666	2·127	1·504	·793
30	4·265	4·223	4·096	3·884	3·588	3·205	2·737	2·184	1·544	·814
20 0	4·375	4·332	4·201	3·984	3·680	3·288	2·808	2·240	1·583	·836
21 0	4·595	4·549	4·412	4·184	3·864	3·454	2·950	2·353	1·663	·879
22 0	4·815	4·768	4·624	4·386	4·050	3·620	3·093	2·467	1·744	·922
23 0	5·035	4·986	4·836	4·587	4·237	3·786	3·236	2·581	1·824	·965
24 0	5·255	5·204	5·048	4·789	4·423	3·952	3·379	2·695	1·905	1·008
25 0	5·476	5·422	5·260	4·989	4·609	4·119	3·522	2·809	1·986	1·051
26 0	5·697	5·642	5·473	5·192	4·798	4·286	3·665	2·924	2·068	1·094
27 0	5·918	5·860	5·685	5·393	4·984	4·454	3·808	3·039	2·150	1·137

II.—TABLE OF ORDINATES—*continued.*

Angle of Deflection.	Distances of the Ordinates from the end of the 100 feet Chord.									
	Middle, 50 feet.	45 feet.	40 feet.	35 feet.	30 feet.	25 feet.	20 feet.	15 feet.	10 feet.	5 feet.
°										
28	6·139	0 079	5·898	5·596	5·171	4·622	3·952	3·154	2·232	1·181
29	6·361	6·298	6·110	5·796	5·357	4·790	4·095	3·269	2·314	1·224
30	6·582	6·517	6·323	5·999	5·544	4·958	4·239	3·385	2·396	1·268
31	6·804	6·737	6·537	6·202	5·733	5·127	4·384	3·502	2·481	1·312
32	7·027	6·957	6·751	6·406	5·922	5·297	4·530	3·619	2·565	1·356
33	7·249	7·178	6·965	6·609	6·111	5·467	4·676	3·737	2·649	1·401
34	7·472	7·398	7·179	6·813	6·300	5·637	4·822	3·854	2·733	1·445
35	7·694	7·619	7·393	7·017	6·489	5·807	4·968	3·972	2·817	1·490
36	7·918	7·841	7·609	7·222	6·679	5·978	5·115	4·090	2·901	1·535
37	8·143	8·063	7·825	7·427	6·870	6·149	5·262	4·209	2·985	1·581
38	8·367	8·286	8·041	7·633	7·060	6·320	5·410	4·327	3·069	1·626
39	8·592	8·508	8·257	7·838	7·251	6·491	5·557	4·446	3·153	1·672
40	8·816	8·731	8·474	8·044	7·442	6·663	5·705	4·565	3·238	1·718

ARTICLE XXI.

ON LONG CHORDS.

It is sometimes convenient, in preliminary locations, to lay off curves by chords longer than 100 feet. For instance, in fig. 19, instead of running from *a* by chords *a b, b c, c d,* &c., of but 100 feet, points *d, f, g,* &c., may be obtained with less trouble by using three times the tangential or deflection angles of the table (as the case may be), and employing chords *a d, d f, f g,* &c., *nearly* three times as long as the chords *a b, b c,* &c.; or if *a d, d f, f g* be either 2 or 4 stations apart, then 2 or 4 times the tangential and deflection angles would be used; and chords nearly 2 or 4 times 100 feet in length.

Fig. 19.

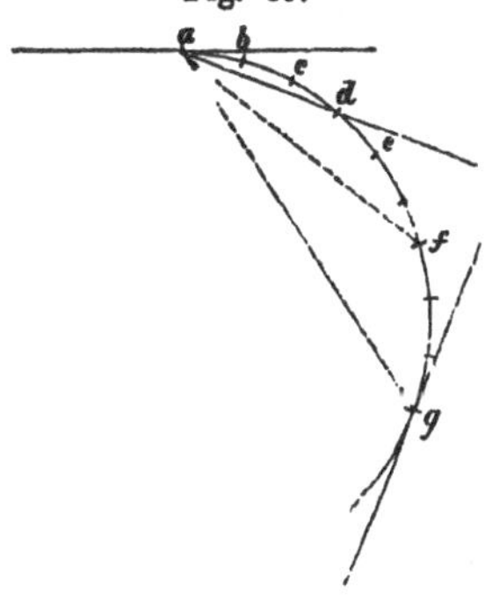

The following table contains the precise length of chord required to subtend respectively 1, 2, 3, or 4 stations. It is seldom desirable to exceed the latter limit.

III.—Table of Long Chords.

Radius in feet.	Angle of Deflection.	Length of Chord in feet required to subtend. 1 Station.	2 Stations.	3 Stations.	4 Stations.
5730·0	1°	100	200·0	300·0	400·0
4584·0	¼	100	200·0	300·0	399·9
3820·0	½	100	200·0	300·0	399·9
3274·0	¾	100	200·0	300·0	399·8
2865·0	2°	100	200·0	299·9	399·7
2547·0	¼	100	200·0	299·9	399·6
2292·0	½	100	200·0	299·8	399·5
2084·0	¾	100	200·0	299·8	399·4
1910·0	3°	100	200·0	299·7	399·3
1763·0	¼	100	200·0	299·7	399·2
1637·0	½	100	200·0	299·6	399·1
1528 0	¾	100	200·0	299·6	399·0
1433·0	4°	100	199·9	299·6	398·9
1348·0	¼	100	199·9	299·5	398·7
1274·0	½	100	199·9	299·4	398·5
1207·0	¾	100	199·9	299·3	398·3
1146·0	5°	100	199·9	299·2	398·0
1092·0	¼	100	199·8	299·1	397·8
1042·0	½	100	199·8	299·0	397·6
996·8	¾	100	199·7	298·9	397·5
955 4	6°	100	199·7	298·8	397·3
917·0	¼	100	199·7	298·7	397·0
882·0	½	100	199·7	298·6	396·7
849·3	¾	100	199·6	298·5	396·5
819·0	7°	100	199·6	298·4	396·2
790·8	¼	100	199·6	298·3	396·0
764·5	½	100	199·6	298·2	395·7
739·9	¾	100	199·6	298·1	395·4
716·8	8°	100	199·6	298·0	395·1
695·1	¼	100	199·5	297·9	394·8
674·6	½	100	199·5	297·8	394·5
655 5	¾	100	199·4	297·7	394·3
637·3	9°	100	199·4	297·5	394·1
620·2	¼	100	199·4	297·4	393·7
603·8	½	100	199·3	297·3	393·2
588·4	¾	100	199·2	297·2	392·8
573·7	10°	100	199·2	297·0	392·4
For radii less than 573·7 feet, it is never required to use longer chords than 100 feet.					

When this method of laying out curves by long chords is used, the instrument should be moved to each successive point after it is determined, in order to fix the next one, instead of attempting to obtain more than one point from one position of the instrument: because when the chords are longer than one chain, they cannot be measured in the right direction by eye, but must be guided by the instrument.

It must be especially borne in mind that, in any given curve, only the tangential and deflection *angles* increase in the same proportion as the number of 100 feet stations subtended by the long chord. Therefore, *these* long chords cannot be used for laying out curves *by eye*, as their tangential and deflection *distances* are not known.

When it is required to use long chords for turning a curve *by eye*, they must be composed of a number of *whole chains*, being made say 200, 300, or 400, &c., feet in length. The tangential and deflection *distances* of curves of more than 500 feet radius may then be assumed, in practice, to increase as the *squares* of the number of chains in the length of the long chord. For instance, to lay off a 5° curve by chords of 200, 300, or 400 feet in length, the tangential and deflection distances of the table must be multiplied by 4, 9, or 16, as the case may be. In this case the tangential and deflection *angles* are unknown.

This is not mathematically correct, but will answer in practice for the curves of a canal or common road, where great nicety is not needed.

The only proper instrument for running lines of survey is the *transit*, furnished with a compass and with a revolving telescope. The deflections, being measured in *angles*, serve as a check to the numerous sources of error to which the compass is liable, arising from local attraction, electrical action in the glass cover, diurnal variation, &c. Besides, when the compass alone is used, it is necessary to test every course or bearing from each end of each station; and this involves loss of time.

The following is a good form of field-book for the transit and compass combined:

Station.	Distance.	Total Distance.	Course.	Deflection in Degrees.		The right-hand page is left blank for Remarks, and Sketches of Topography.
				Left.	Right.	

In every locating party there should be one person whose duty is to obtain and record the transverse slopes of the ground at each station. His observations will usually extend to from fifty feet to one hundred yards on each side of the centre stakes, depending on a variety of circumstances of locality which cannot be alluded to here. In preliminary locations these slopes need not be taken with very great nicety, as they will be used chiefly for ascertaining, approximately, the amount of excavation and embankment.

After the final location is made, the slopes should be taken again, with great care, to the nearest quarter of a degree; but need not extend beyond the width actually occupied by the road. Their use in this second operation will be for determining the cubic contents with more precision than before, for final estimates; and also for obtaining the positions of the *side-stakes*.

Should the duty of *recording* these slopes devolve upon the compassman (which it should not), it will be necessary to add another column to his field-book after that containing the deflections. In this column he will insert the slopes thus (fig. 20), the dot representing the centre stake. The degrees of slope are written above the lines, and the distance in feet to which they extend below.

Fig. 20.

The slopes are taken by laying a long rod on the ground, at *right angles to the line of survey*, as nearly as may be judged by eye, and measuring the angles by means of a small *slope instrument* placed upon the rod. These are made by most of our instrument-makers.

ARTICLE XXII.

TO ADJUST A TRANSIT INSTRUMENT.

Having placed the transit firmly at *a*, fig. 21, and levelled it, clamp all fast, and direct the cross-hairs, by means of the tangent screw, to some convenient object, *b*. Then, revolving the telescope *vertically*, but without moving it in the least *horizontally*, let the cross-hairs fix upon a second object in the opposite direction, as *c*; or, if there be no such object, place one, as for instance a chain-pin, at any convenient distance. Then unclamp the *lower* clamp, and revolve *horizontally* the entire upper part of the instrument above the parallel plates. Clamp it again, and fix the cross-hairs upon *b*; then again revolve the *telescope* vertically. If the sight now strikes *c*, as before, it is in adjustment; but if not, place another object, *d*, where it does strike; and with the adjusting pin alter the vertical cross-hair so as to strike half-way between *d* and *c*. The instrument will then be in adjustment. Two or more trials will generally be needed before the adjustment is perfect.

Fig. 21.

With care, and on a firm floor, the operation may be performed in a long room, or by placing the instrument in a doorway communicating with two rooms of moderate size. Fine pins, or needles, should then be used as the objects to be sighted at. It is better, however, to adjust out of doors, with more distant objects. It is also a good precaution to hang up a long plumb-line, or select some vertical object, and see whether the vertical hair coincides with it, as the telescope is raised or lowered. If from any accident, or carelessness in its construction, it does not, the defect must be remedied by an instrument-maker.

IV.—Natural Sines and Tangents to a Radius 1.

0 Deg. 0 Deg. 0 Deg.

′	Sine.	Tang.	Cotang.	Cosine.	′	′	Sine.	Tang.	Cotang.	Cosine.	′	′	Sine.	Tang.	Cotang.	Cosine.	′
0	·0000000	·000000	Infinite.	1·000000	60	21	·0061086	·006108	163·70010	·9999813	39	41	·0119261	·011927	83·84350	·9999289	19
1	·0002909	·000291	3437·7460	1·000000	59	22	·0063995	·006399	156·25900	·9999795	38	42	·0122170	·012217	81·84704	·9999254	18
2	·0005818	·000582	1718·8730	·9999998	58	23	·0066904	·006690	149·46500	·9999776	37	43	·0125079	·012508	79·94343	·9999218	17
3	·0008727	·000872	1145·9150	·9999996	57	24	·0069813	·006981	143·23710	·9999756	36	44	·0127987	·012799	78·12634	·9999181	16
4	·0011636	·001163	859·4363	·9999993	56	25	·0072721	·007272	137·50750	·9999736	35	45	·0130896	·013090	76·39000	·9999143	15
5	·0014544	·001454	687·4588	·9999989	55	26	·0075630	·007563	132·21850	·9999714	34	46	·0133805	·013381	74·72916	·9999105	14
6	·0017453	·001745	572·9572	·9999985	54	27	·0078539	·007854	127·32130	·9999692	33	47	·0136713	·013672	73·13899	·9999065	13
7	·0020362	·002036	491·1060	·9999979	53	28	·0081448	·008145	122·77390	·9999668	32	48	·0139622	·013963	71·61507	·9999025	12
8	·0023271	·002327	429·7175	·9999973	52	29	·0084357	·008436	118·54010	·9999644	31	49	·0142530	·014254	70·15334	·9998984	11
9	·0026180	·002618	381·9709	·9999966	51	30	·0087265	·008726	114·58860	·9999619	30	50	·0145439	·014545	68·75008	·9998942	10
10	·0029089	·002908	343·7737	·9999958	50	31	·0090174	·009017	110·89200	·9999593	29	51	·0148348	·014836	67·40185	·9998900	9
11	·0031998	·003199	312·5213	·9999949	49	32	·0093083	·009308	107·42640	·9999567	28	52	·0151256	·015127	66·10547	·9998856	8
12	·0034907	·003490	286·4777	·9999939	48	33	·0095992	·009599	104·17090	·9999539	27	53	·0154165	·015418	64·85800	·9998812	7
13	·0037815	·003781	264·4408	·9999928	47	34	·0098900	·009890	101·10690	·9999511	26	54	·0157073	·015709	63·65674	·9998766	6
14	·0040724	·004072	245·5519	·9999917	46	35	·0101809	·010181	98·21794	·9999482	25	55	·0159982	·016000	62·49915	·9998720	5
15	·0043633	·004363	229·1816	·9999905	45	36	·0104718	·010472	95·48947	·9999452	24	56	·0162890	·016291	61·38290	·9998673	4
16	·0046542	·004654	214·8576	·9999892	44	37	·0107627	·010763	92·90848	·9999421	23	57	·0165799	·016582	60·30582	·9998625	3
17	·0049451	·004945	202·2187	·9999878	43	38	·0110535	·011054	90·46333	·9999389	22	58	·0168707	·016873	59·26587	·9998577	2
18	·0052360	·005236	190·9841	·9999863	42	39	·0113444	·011345	88·14357	·9999357	21	59	·0171616	·017164	58·26117	·9998527	1
19	·0055268	·005526	180·9322	·9999847	41	40	·0116353	·011636	85·83979	·9999323	20	60	·0174524	·017455	57·28996	·9998477	0
20	·0058177	·005817	171·8854	·9999831	40												
′	Cosine.	Cotan.	Tang.	Sine.	′	′	Cosine.	Cotan.	Tang.	Sine.	′	′	Cosine.	Cotan.	Tang.	Sine.	′

Deg. 89. Deg. 89. Deg. 89.

IV.—Natural Sines and Tangents to a Radius 1—*continued.*

1 Deg. | 1 Deg. | 1 Deg.

′	Sine.	Tang.	Cotang.	Cosine.	′	′	Sine.	Tang.	Cotang.	Cosine.	′	′	Sine.	Tang.	Cotang.	Cosine.	′
0	·0174524	·017455	57·28996	·9998477	60	21	·0235598	·023566	42·43346	·9997224	39	41	·0293755	·029388	34·02730	·9995684	19
1	·0177432	·017746	56·35059	·9998426	59	12	·0238506	·023857	41·91579	·9997156	38	42	·0296662	·029679	33·69350	·9995599	18
2	·0180341	·018037	55·44151	·9998374	58	23	·0241414	·024148	41·41058	·9997086	37	43	·0299570	·029970	33·36619	·9995512	17
3	·0183249	·018328	54·56130	·9998321	57	24	·0244322	·024439	40·91741	·9997015	36	44	·0302478	·030261	33·04517	·9995424	16
4	·0186158	·018619	53·70858	·9998267	56	25	·0247230	·024730	40·43583	·9996493	35	45	·0305385	·030552	32·73026	·9995336	15
5	·0189066	·018910	52·88211	·9998213	55	26	·0250138	·025021	39·96546	·9996871	34	46	·0308293	·030843	32·42129	·9995247	14
6	·0191974	·019201	52·08067	·9998157	54	27	·0253046	·025312	39·50589	·9996798	33	47	·0311200	·031135	32·11809	·9995157	13
7	·0194883	·019492	51·30315	·9998101	53	28	·0255954	·025603	39·05677	·9996724	32	48	·0314108	·031426	31·82051	·9995066	12
8	·0197791	·019783	50·54850	·9998044	52	29	·0258862	·025894	38·61773	·9996649	31	49	·0317015	·031717	31·52839	·9994974	11
9	·0200699	·020074	49·81572	·9997986	51	30	·0261769	·026185	38·18845	·9996573	30	50	·0319922	·032008	31·24157	·9994881	10
10	·0203608	·020365	49·10388	·9997927	50	31	·0264677	·026477	37·76861	·9996497	29	51	·0322830	·032299	30·95992	·9994788	9
11	·0206516	·020556	48·41208	·9997867	49	32	·0267585	·026768	37·35789	·9996419	28	52	·0325737	·032591	30·68330	·9994693	8
12	·0209424	·020947	47·73950	·9997807	48	33	·0270493	·027059	36·95600	·9996341	27	53	·0328644	·032882	30·41158	·9994598	7
13	·0212332	·021238	47·08534	·9997745	47	34	·0273401	·027350	36·56265	·9996262	26	54	·0331552	·033173	30·14461	·9994502	6
14	·0215241	·021529	46·44886	·9997683	46	35	·0276309	·027641	36·17759	·9996182	25	55	·0334459	·033464	29·88229	·9994405	5
15	·0218149	·021820	45·82935	·9997620	45	36	·0279216	·027932	35·80055	·9996101	24	56	·0337366	·033755	29·62449	·9994308	4
16	·0221057	·022111	45·22614	·9997556	44	37	·0282124	·028223	35·43128	·9996020	23	57	·0340274	·034047	29·37110	·9994209	3
17	·0223965	·022402	44·63859	·9997492	43	38	·0285032	·028514	35·06954	·9995937	22	58	·0343181	·034338	29·12200	·9994110	2
18	·0226873	·022693	44·06611	·9997426	42	39	·0287940	·028805	34·71511	·9995854	21	59	·0346088	·034629	28·87708	·9994009	1
19	·0229781	·022984	43·50812	·9997360	41	40	·0290847	·029097	34·36777	·9995770	20	60	·0348995	·034920	28·63625	·9993908	0
20	·0232690	·023275	42·96407	·9997292	40												
′	Cosine.	Cotan.	Tang.	Sine.	′	′	Cosine.	Cotan.	Tang.	Sine.	′	′	Cosine.	Cotan.	Tang.	Sine.	′

Deg. 88. | Deg. 88. | Deg. 88.

IV.—Natural Sines and Tangents to a Radius 1—*continued*.

2 Deg.

′	Sine.	Tang.	Cotang.	Cosine.	′
0	·0348995	·034920	28·63625	·9993908	60
1	·0351902	·035212	28·39939	·9993806	59
2	·0354809	·035503	28·16642	·9993704	58
3	·0357716	·035794	27·93723	·9993600	57
4	·0360623	·036085	27·71174	·9993495	56
5	·0363530	·036377	27·48985	·9993390	55
6	·0366437	·036668	27·27148	·9993284	54
7	·0369344	·036959	27·05655	·9993177	53
8	·0372251	·037250	26·84498	·9993069	52
9	·0375158	·037542	26·63669	·9992960	51
10	·0378065	·037833	26·43160	·9992851	50
11	·0380971	·038124	26·22963	·9992740	49
12	·0383878	·038416	26·03073	·9992629	48
13	·0386785	·038707	25·83482	·9992517	47
14	·0389692	·038998	25·64183	·9992404	46
15	·0392598	·039290	25·45170	·9992290	55
16	·0395505	·039581	25·26436	·9992176	44
17	·0398411	·039872	25·07975	·9992060	43
18	·0401318	·040164	24·89782	·9991944	42
19	·0404224	·040455	24·71851	·9991827	41
20	·0407131	·040746	24·54175	·9991709	40
′	Cosine.	Cotan.	Tang.	Sine.	′

Deg. 87.

2 Deg.

′	Sine.	Tang.	Cotang.	Cosine.	′
21	·0410037	·041038	24·36750	·9991590	39
22	·0412944	·041329	24·19571	·9991470	38
23	·0415850	·041621	24·02632	·9991350	37
24	·0418757	·041912	23·85927	·9991228	36
25	·0421663	·042203	23·69453	·9991106	35
26	·0424569	·042495	23·53205	·9990983	34
27	·0427475	·042786	23·37177	·9990859	33
28	·0430382	·043078	23·21366	·9990734	32
29	·0433288	·043369	23·05767	·9990609	31
30	·0436194	·043660	22·90376	·9990482	30
31	·0439100	·043952	22·75189	·9990355	29
32	·0442006	·044243	22·60201	·9990227	28
33	·0444912	·044535	22·45409	·9990098	27
34	·0447818	·044826	22·30809	·9989968	26
35	·0450724	·045118	22·16398	·9989837	25
36	·0453630	·045409	22·02171	·9989706	24
37	·0456536	·045701	21·88125	·9989573	23
38	·0459442	·045992	21·74256	·9989440	22
39	·0462347	·046284	21·60563	·9989306	21
40	·0465253	·046575	21·47040	·9989171	20
′	Cosine.	Cotan.	Tang.	Sine.	′

Deg. 87.

2 Deg.

′	Sine.	Tang.	Cotang.	Cosine.	′
41	·0468159	·046867	21·33685	·9989035	19
42	·0471065	·047158	21·20494	·9988899	18
43	·0473970	·047450	21·07466	·9988761	17
44	·0476876	·047741	20·94596	·9988623	16
45	·0479781	·048033	20·81182	·9988484	15
46	·0482687	·048325	20·69322	·9988344	14
47	·0485592	·048616	20·56911	·9988203	13
48	·0488498	·048908	20·44648	·9988061	12
49	·0491403	·049199	20·32530	·9987919	11
50	·0494308	·049491	20·20555	·9987775	10
51	·0497214	·049782	20·08719	·9987631	9
52	·0500119	·050074	19·97021	·9987486	8
53	·0503024	·050366	19·85459	·9987340	7
54	·0505929	·050657	19·74029	·9987194	6
55	·0508835	·050949	19·62729	·9987046	5
56	·0511740	·051241	19·51558	·9986898	4
57	·0514645	·051532	19·40513	·9986748	3
58	·0517550	·051824	19·29592	·9986598	2
59	·0520455	·052116	19·18793	·9986447	1
60	·0523360	·052407	19·08113	·9986295	0
′	Cosine.	Cotan.	Tang.	Sine.	′

Deg. 87.

IV.—Natural Sines and Tangents to a Radius 1—*continued.*

3 Deg. | 3 Deg. | 3 Deg.

′	Sine.	Tang.	Cotang.	Cosine.	′	′	Sine.	Tang.	Cotang.	Cosine.	′	′	Sine.	Tang.	Cotang.	Cosine.	′
0	·0523360	·052407	19·08113	·9986295	60	21	·0584352	·058535	17·08372	·9982912	39	41	·0642420	·064375	15·53398	·9979343	19
1	·0526264	·052699	18·97552	·9986143	59	22	·0587256	·058827	16·99895	·9982742	38	42	·0645323	·064667	15·46381	·9979156	18
2	·0529169	·052991	18·87106	·9985989	58	23	·0590160	·059119	16·91502	·9982570	37	43	·0648226	·064959	15·39427	·9978968	17
3	·0532074	·053282	18·76775	·9985835	57	24	·0593064	·059410	16·83191	·9982398	36	44	·0651129	·065251	15·32535	·9978779	16
4	·0534979	·053574	18·66556	·9985680	56	25	·0595967	·059702	16·74961	·9982225	35	45	·0654031	·065543	15·25705	·9978589	15
5	·0537883	·053866	18·56447	·9985524	55	26	·0598871	·059994	16·66811	·9982052	34	46	·0656934	·065835	15·18934	·9978399	14
6	·0540788	·054158	18·46447	·9985367	54	27	·0601775	·060286	16·58739	·9981877	33	47	·0659836	·066127	15·12224	·9978207	13
7	·0543693	·054449	18·36553	·9985209	53	28	·0604678	·060578	16·50745	·9981701	32	48	·0662739	·066419	15·05572	·9978015	12
8	·0546597	·054741	18·26765	·9985050	52	29	·0607582	·060870	16·42827	·9981525	31	49	·0665641	·666712	14·98978	·9977821	11
9	·0549502	·055033	18·17080	·9984891	51	30	·0610485	·061162	16·34985	·9981348	30	50	·0668544	·067004	14·92441	·9977627	10
10	·0552406	·055325	18·07497	·9984731	50	31	·0613389	·061454	16·27217	·9981170	29	51	·0671446	·067296	14·85961	·9977433	9
11	·0555311	·055616	17·98015	·9984570	49	32	·0616292	·061746	16·19522	·9980991	28	52	·0674349	·067588	14·79537	·9977237	8
12	·0558215	·055908	17·88631	·9984408	48	33	·0619196	·062038	16·11899	·9980811	27	53	·0677251	·067880	14·73167	·9977040	7
13	·0561119	·056200	17·79344	·9984245	47	34	·0622099	·062330	16·04348	·9980631	26	54	·0680153	·068173	14·66852	·9976843	6
14	·0564024	·056492	17·70152	·9984081	46	35	·0625002	·062622	15·96866	·9980450	25	55	·0683055	·068465	14·60591	·9976645	5
15	·0566928	·056784	17·61055	·9983917	45	36	·0627905	·062914	15·89454	·9980267	24	56	·0685957	·068757	14·54383	·9976445	4
16	·0569832	·057075	17·52051	·9983751	44	37	·0630808	·063206	15·82110	·9980084	23	57	·0688859	·069049	14·48227	·9976245	3
17	·0572736	·057367	17·43138	·9983585	43	38	·0633711	·063498	15·74833	·9979900	22	58	·0691761	·069342	14·42123	·9976045	2
18	·0575640	·057659	17·34315	·9983418	42	39	·0636614	·063790	15·67623	·9979716	21	59	·0694663	·069634	14·36069	·9975843	1
19	·0578544	·057951	17·25580	·9983250	41	40	·0639517	·064082	15·60478	·9979530	20	60	·0697565	·069926	14·30066	·9975641	0
20	·0581448	·058243	17·16933	·9983082	40												
′	Cosine.	Cotan.	Tang.	Sine.	′	′	Cosine.	Cotan.	Tang.	Sine.	′	′	Cosine.	Cotan.	Tang.	Sine.	′

Deg. 86. | Deg. 86. | Deg. 86

IV.—Natural Sines and Tangents to a Radius 1—*continued.*

4 Deg.

′	Sine.	Tang.	Cotang.	Cosine.	′
0	·0697565	·069926	14·30066	·9975641	60
1	·0700467	·070219	14·24113	·9975437	59
2	·0703368	·070511	14·18209	·9975233	58
3	·0706270	·070803	14·12353	·9975028	57
4	·0709171	·071096	14·06545	·9974822	56
5	·0712073	·071388	14·00785	·9974615	55
6	·0714974	·071680	13·95071	·9974408	54
7	·0717876	·071973	13·89404	·9974199	53
8	·0720777	·072265	13·83782	·9973990	52
9	·0723678	·072558	13·78206	·9973780	51
10	·0726580	·072850	13·72673	·9973569	50
11	·0729481	·073143	13·67185	·9973357	49
12	·0732382	·073435	13·61740	·9973145	48
13	·0735283	·073727	13·56339	·9972931	47
14	·0738184	·074020	13·50979	·9972717	46
15	·0741085	·074312	13·45662	·9972502	45
16	·0743986	·074605	13·40386	·9972286	44
17	0746887	·074897	13·35151	·9972069	43
18	·0749787	·075190	13·29957	·9971851	42
19	·0752688	·075482	13·24803	·9971633	41
20	·0755589	·075775	13·19688	·9971413	40
′	Cosine.	Cotan.	Tang.	Sine.	′

Deg. 85.

4 Deg.

′	Sine.	Tang.	Cotang.	Cosine.	′
21	·0758489	·076068	13·14612	·9971193	39
22	·0761390	·076360	13·09575	·9970972	38
23	·0764290	·076653	13·04576	·9970750	37
24	·0767190	·076945	12·99616	·9970528	36
25	·0770091	·077238	12·94692	·9970304	35
26	·0772991	·077531	12·89805	·9970080	34
27	·0775891	·077823	12·84955	·9969854	33
28	·0778791	·078116	12·80141	·9969628	32
29	·0781691	·078409	12·75363	·9969401	31
30	·0784591	·078701	12·70620	·9969173	30
31	·0787491	·078994	12·65912	·9968945	29
32	·0790391	·079287	12·61239	·9968715	28
33	·0793290	·079579	12·56599	·9968485	27
34	·0796190	·079872	12·51994	·9968254	26
35	·0799090	·080165	12·47422	·9968022	25
36	·0801989	·080458	12·42883	·9967789	24
37	·0804889	·080750	12·38376	·9967555	23
38	·0807788	·081043	12·33902	·9967321	22
39	·0810687	·081336	12·29460	·9967085	21
40	·0813587	·081629	12·25050	·9966849	20
′	Cosine.	Cotan.	Tang.	Sine.	′

Deg. 85.

4 Deg.

′	Sine.	Tang.	Cotang.	Cosine.	′
41	·0816486	·081922	12·20671	·9966612	19
42	·0819385	·082215	12·16323	·9966374	18
43	·0822284	·082507	12·12006	·9966135	17
44	·0825183	·082800	12·07719	·9965895	16
45	·0828082	·083093	12·03462	·9965655	15
46	·0830981	·083386	11·99234	·9965414	14
47	·0833880	·083679	11·95037	·9965172	13
48	·0836778	·083972	11·90868	·9964929	12
49	·0839677	·084265	11·86728	·9964685	11
50	·0842576	·084558	11·82616	·9964440	10
51	·0845474	·084851	11·78533	·9964195	9
52	·0848373	·085144	11·74477	·9963948	8
53	·0851271	·085437	11·70450	·9963701	7
54	·0854169	·085730	11·66449	·9963453	6
55	·0857067	·086023	11·62476	·9963204	5
56	·0859966	·086316	11·58529	·9962954	4
57	·0862864	·086609	11·54609	·9962704	3
58	·0865762	·086902	11·50715	·9962452	2
59	·0868660	·087195	11·46847	·9962200	1
60	·0871557	·087488	11·43005	·9961947	0
′	Cosine.	Cotan.	Tang.	Sine.	′

Deg. 85.

IV.—NATURAL SINES AND TANGENTS TO A RADIUS 1—*continued.*

5 Deg.						5 Deg.						5 Deg.					
′	Sine.	Tang.	Cotang.	Cosine.	′	′	Sine.	Tang.	Cotang.	Cosine.	′	′	Sine.	Tang.	Cotang.	Cosine.	′
0	·0871557	·087488	11·43005	·9961947	60	21	·0932395	·093647	10·67834	·9956437	39	41	·0990303	·099519	10·048280	·9950844	19
1	·0874455	·087781	11·39188	·9961693	59	22	·0935291	·093940	10·64499	·9956165	38	42	·0993197	·099813	10·018710	·9950556	18
2	·0877353	·088074	11·35397	·9961438	58	23	·0938187	·094234	10·61184	·9955892	37	43	·0996092	·100107	9·989305	·9950266	17
3	·0880251	·088368	11·31630	·9961183	57	24	·0941083	·094527	10·57889	·9955620	36	44	·0998986	·100400	9·960072	·9949976	16
4	·0883148	·088661	11·27888	·9960926	56	25	·0943979	·094821	10·54615	·9955345	35	45	·1001881	·100694	9·931008	·9949685	15
5	·0886046	·088954	11·24171	·9960669	55	26	·0946875	·095114	10·51360	·9955070	34	46	·1004775	·100988	9·902112	·9949393	14
6	·0888943	·089247	11·20478	·9960411	54	27	·0949771	·095408	10·48126	·9954794	33	47	·1007669	101282	9·873382	·9949101	13
7	·0891840	·089540	11·16808	·9960152	53	28	·0952666	·095701	10·44911	·9954517	32	48	·1010563	·101576	9·844816	·9948807	12
8	·0894738	·089834	11·13163	·9959892	52	29	·0955562	·095995	10·41715	·9954240	31	49	·1013457	·101870	9·816414	·9948513	11
9	·0897635	090127	11·09541	·9959631	51	30	·0958458	·096289	10·38539	·9953962	30	50	·1016351	·102164	9·788173	·9948217	10
10	·0900532	·090420	11·05943	·9959370	50	31	·0961353	·096582	10·35382	·9953683	29	51	·1019245	·102458	9·760092	·9947921	9
11	·0903429	·090713	11·02367	·9959107	49	32	·0964248	·096876	10·32244	·9953403	28	52	·1022138	·102752	9·732171	·9947625	8
12	·0906326	·091007	10·98815	·9958844	48	33	·0967144	·097169	10·29125	·9953122	27	53	·1025032	·103046	9·704407	·9947327	7
13	·0909223	·091300	10·95285	·9958580	47	34	·0970039	·097463	10·26024	·9952840	26	54	·1027925	·103339	9·676800	·9947028	6
14	·0912119	·091593	10·91777	9958315	46	35	·0972934	·097757	10·22942	·9952557	25	55	·1030819	·103634	9·649347	·9946729	5
15	·0915016	·091887	10·88292	·9958049	45	36	·0975829	·098050	10·19878	·9952274	24	56	·1033712	·103928	9·622048	·9946428	4
16	·0917913	·092180	10·84828	·9957783	44	37	·0978724	·098344	10·16833	·9951990	23	57	·1036605	·104222	9·594902	·9946127	3
17	·0920809	·092473	10·81387	·9957515	43	38	·0981619	·098638	10·13805	·9951705	22	58	·1039499	·104516	9·567906	·9945825	2
18	·0923706	·092767	10·77967	·9957247	42	39	·0984514	·098932	10·10795	·9951419	21	59	·1042392	·104810	9·541061	·9945523	1
19	·0926602	·093060	10·74568	·9956978	41	40	·0987408	·099225	10·07803	·9951132	20	60	·1045285	·105104	9·514364	·9945219	0
20	·0929499	·093354	10·71191	·9956708	40												
′	Cosine.	Cotan.	Tang.	Sine.	′	′	Cosine.	Cotan.	Tang.	Sine.	′	′	Cosine.	Cotan.	Tang.	Sine.	′
				Deg. 84.						Deg. 84.						Deg. 84.	

IV.—Natural Sines and Tangents to a Radius 1—*continued.*

6 Deg.

′	Sine.	Tang.	Cotang.	Cosine.	′
0	·1045285	·105104	9·514364	·9945219	60
1	·1048178	·105398	9·487814	·9944914	59
2	·1051070	·105692	9·461411	·9944609	58
3	·1053963	·105986	9·435153	·9944303	57
4	·1056856	·106280	9·409038	·9943996	56
5	·1059748	·106575	9·383066	·9943688	55
6	·1062641	·106869	9·357235	·9943379	54
7	·1065533	·107163	9·331545	·9943070	53
8	·1068425	·107457	9·305993	·9942760	52
9	·1071318	·107751	9·280580	·9942448	51
10	·1074210	·108046	9·255303	·9942136	50
11	·1077102	·108340	9·230162	·9941823	49
12	·1079994	·108634	9·205156	·9941510	48
13	·1082885	·108929	9·180283	·9941195	47
14	·1085777	·109223	9·155543	·9940880	46
15	·1088669	·109517	9·130934	·9940563	45
16	·1091560	·109812	9·106456	·9940246	44
17	·1094452	·110106	9·082107	·9939928	43
18	·1097343	·110401	9·057886	·9939610	42
19	·1100234	·110695	9·033793	·9939290	41
20	·1103126	·110989	9·009826	·9938969	40
′	Cosine.	Cotan.	Tang.	Sine.	′

Deg. 83.

6 Deg.

′	Sine.	Tang.	Cotang.	Cosine.	′
21	·1106017	·111284	8·985984	·9938648	39
22	·1108908	·111578	8·962266	·9938326	38
23	·1111799	·111873	8·938672	·9938003	37
24	·1114689	·112168	8·915200	·9937679	36
25	·1117580	·112462	8·891850	·9937355	35
26	·1120471	·112757	8·868620	·9937029	34
27	·1123361	·113051	8·845510	·9936703	33
28	·1126252	·113346	8·822518	·9936375	32
29	·1129142	·113641	8·799644	·9936047	31
30	·1132032	·113935	8·776887	·9935719	30
31	·1134922	·114230	8·754246	·9935389	29
32	·1137812	·114525	8·731719	·9935058	28
33	·1140702	·114819	8·709307	·9934727	27
34	·1143592	·115114	8·687008	·9934395	26
35	·1146482	·115409	8·664822	·9934062	25
36	·1149372	·115703	8·642747	·9933728	24
37	·1152261	·115998	8·620783	·9933393	23
38	·1155151	·116293	8·598929	·9933057	22
39	·1158040	·116588	8·577183	·9932721	21
40	·1160929	·116883	8·555546	·9932384	20
′	Cosine.	Cotan.	Tang.	Sine.	′

Deg. 83.

6 Deg.

′	Sine.	Tang.	Cotang.	Cosine.	′
41	·1163818	·117178	8·534017	·9932045	19
42	·1166707	·117473	8·512594	·9931706	18
43	·1169596	·117767	8·491277	·9931367	17
44	·1172485	·118062	8·470065	·9931026	16
45	·1175374	·118357	8·448957	·9930685	15
46	·1178263	·118652	8·427953	·9930342	14
47	·1181151	·118947	8·407051	·9929999	13
48	·1184040	·119242	8·386251	·9929655	12
49	·1186928	·119537	8·365553	·9929310	11
50	·1189816	·119832	8·344955	·9928965	10
51	·1192704	·120127	8·324457	·9928618	9
52	·1195593	·120423	8·304058	·9928271	8
53	·1198481	·120718	8·283757	·9927922	7
54	·1201368	·121013	8·263554	·9927573	6
55	·1204256	·121308	8·243448	·9927224	5
56	·1207144	·121603	8·223438	·9926873	4
57	·1210031	·121898	8·203523	·9926521	3
58	·1212919	·122194	8·183704	·9926169	2
59	·1215806	·122489	8·163978	·9925816	1
60	·1218693	·122784	8·144346	·9925462	0
′	Cosine.	Cotan.	Tang.	Sine.	′

Deg. 83.

IV.—Natural Sines and Tangents to a Radius 1—*continued.*

7 Deg.

′	Sine.	Tang.	Cotang.	Cosine.	′
0	·1218693	·122784	8·144346	·9925462	60
1	·1221581	·123079	8·124807	·9925107	59
2	·1224468	·123375	8·105359	·9924751	58
3	·1227355	·123670	8·086004	·9924394	57
4	·1230241	·123965	8·066739	9924037	56
5	·1233128	·124261	8·047564	·9923679	55
6	·1236015	·124556	8·028479	·9923319	54
7	·1238901	·124852	8·009483	·9922959	53
8	·1241788	·125147	7·990575	·9922599	52
9	·1244674	·125442	7·971755	·9922237	51
10	·1247560	·125738	7·953022	·9921874	50
11	·1250446	·126033	7·934375	·9921511	49
12	·1253332	·126329	7·915815	·9921147	48
13	·1256218	·126624	7·897339	·9920782	47
14	·1259104	·126920	7·878948	·9920416	46
15	·1261990	·127216	7·860642	·9920049	45
16	·1264875	·127511	7·842419	·9919682	44
17	·1267761	·127807	7·824279	·9919314	43
18	·1270646	·128103	7·806221	·9918944	42
19	·1273531	·128398	7·788245	·9918574	41
20	·1276416	·128694	7·770350	·9918204	40
′	Cosine.	Cotan.	Tang.	Sine.	′

Deg. 82.

7 Deg.

′	Sine.	Tang.	Cotang.	Cosine.	′
21	·1279302	·128990	7·752536	·9917832	39
22	·1282186	·129285	7·734802	·9917459	38
23	·1285071	·129581	7·717148	·9917086	37
24	·1287956	·129877	7·699573	·9916712	36
25	·1290841	·130173	7·682076	·9916337	35
26	·1293725	·130469	7·664658	·9915961	34
27	·1296609	·130764	7·647317	·9915584	33
28	·1299494	·131060	7·630053	·9915206	32
29	·1302378	·131356	7·612865	·9914828	31
30	·1305262	·131652	7·595754	·9914449	30
31	·1308146	·131948	7·578717	·9914069	29
32	·1311030	·132244	7·561756	·9913688	28
33	·1313913	·132540	7·544869	·9913306	27
34	·1316797	·132836	7·528057	·9912923	26
35	·1319681	·133132	7·511317	·9912540	25
36	·1322564	·133428	7·494651	·9912155	24
37	·1325447	·133724	7·478057	·9911770	23
38	·1328330	·134020	7·461535	·9911384	22
39	·1331213	·134316	7·445085	·9910997	21
40	·1334096	·134612	7·428706	·9910610	20
′	Cosine.	Cotan.	Tang.	Sine.	′

Deg. 82.

7 Deg.

′	Sine.	Tang.	Cotang.	Cosine.	′
41	·1336979	·134909	7·412397	·9910221	19
42	·1339862	·135205	7·396159	·9909832	18
43	·1342744	·135501	7·379990	·9909442	17
44	·1345627	·135797	7·363891	·9909051	16
45	·1348509	·136094	7·347861	·9908659	15
46	·1351392	·136390	7·331898	·9908266	14
47	·1354274	·136686	7·316004	·9907873	13
48	·1357156	·136983	7·300178	·9907478	12
49	·1360038	·137279	7·284418	·9907083	11
50	·1362919	·137575	7·268725	·9906687	10
51	·1365801	·137872	7·253098	·9906290	9
52	·1368683	·138168	7·237537	·9905893	8
53	·1371564	·138465	7·222042	·9905494	7
54	·1374445	·138761	7·206611	·9905095	6
55	·1377327	·139058	7·191245	·9904694	5
56	·1380208	·139354	7·175943	·9904293	4
57	·1383089	·139651	7·160705	·9903891	3
58	·1385970	·139947	7·145530	·9903489	2
59	·1388850	·140244	7·130419	·9903085	1
60	·1391731	·140540	7·115369	·9902681	0
′	Cosine.	Cotan.	Tang.	Sine.	′

Deg. 82.

IV.—Natural Sines and Tangents to a Radius 1—*continued.*

8 Deg.						8 Deg.						8 Deg.					
′	Sine.	Tang.	Cotang.	Cosine.	′	′	Sine.	Tang.	Cotang.	Cosine.	′	′	Sine.	Tang.	Cotang.	Cosine.	′
0	·1391731	·140540	7·115369	·9902681	60	21	·1452197	·146775	6·813122	·9893994	39	41	·1509733	·152723	6·547767	·9885378	19
1	·1394612	·140837	7·100382	·9902275	59	22	·1455075	·147072	6·799356	·9893572	38	42	·1512608	·153021	6·535029	·9884939	18
2	·1397492	·141134	7·085457	·9901869	58	23	·1457953	·147369	6·785644	·9893148	37	43	·1515484	·153319	6·522339	·9884498	17
3	·1400372	·141430	7·070593	·9901462	57	24	·1460830	·147667	6·791986	·9892723	36	44	·1518359	·153617	6·509698	·9884057	16
4	·1403252	·141727	7·055790	·9901055	56	25	·1463708	·147964	6·758382	·9892298	35	45	·1521234	·153914	6·497104	·9883615	15
5	·1406132	·142024	7·041048	·9900646	55	26	·1466585	·148261	6·744831	·9891872	34	46	·1524109	·154212	6·484558	·9883172	14
6	·1409012	·142321	7·026366	·9900237	54	27	·1469463	·148559	6·731334	·9891445	33	47	·1526984	·154510	6·472059	·9882728	13
7	·1411892	·142617	7·011744	·9899826	53	28	·1472340	·148856	6·717889	·9891017	32	48	·1529858	·154808	6·459607	·9882284	12
8	·1414772	·142914	6·997180	·9899415	52	29	·1475217	·149153	6·704496	·9890588	31	49	·1532733	·155106	6·447201	·9881838	11
9	·1417651	·143211	6·982678	·9899003	51	30	·1478094	·149451	6·691156	·9890159	30	50	·1535607	·155404	6·434842	·9881392	10
10	·1420531	·143508	6·968233	·9898590	50	31	·1480971	·149748	6·677867	·9889728	29	51	·1538482	·155701	6·422530	·9880945	9
11	·1423410	·143805	6·953847	·9898177	49	32	·1483848	·150045	6·664630	·9889297	28	52	·1541356	·155999	6·410263	·9880497	8
12	·1426289	·144102	6·939519	·9897762	48	33	·1486724	·150343	6·651444	·9888865	27	53	·1544230	·156297	6·398042	·9880048	7
13	·1429168	·144399	6·925248	·9897347	47	34	·1489601	·150640	6·638310	·9888432	26	54	·1547104	·156595	6·385866	·9879599	6
14	·1432047	·144696	6·911035	·9896931	46	35	·1492477	·150938	6·625225	·9887998	25	55	·1549978	·156893	6·373735	·9879148	5
15	·1434926	·144993	6·896879	·9896514	45	36	·1495353	·151235	6·612191	·9887564	24	56	·1552851	·157191	6·361650	·9878697	4
16	·1437805	·145290	6·882780	·9896096	44	37	·1498230	·151533	6·599208	·9887128	23	57	·1555725	·157490	6·349609	·9878245	3
17	·1440684	·145587	6·868737	·9895677	43	38	·1501106	·151830	6·586273	·9886692	22	58	·1558598	·157788	6·337612	·9877792	2
18	·1443562	·145884	6·854750	·9895258	42	39	·1503981	·152128	6·573389	·9886255	21	59	·1561472	·158086	6·325660	·9877338	1
19	·1446440	·146181	6·840819	·9894838	41	40	·1506857	·152426	6·560553	·9885817	20	60	·1564345	·158384	6·313751	·9876883	0
20	·1449319	·146478	6·826943	·9894416	40												
′	Cosine.	Cotan.	Tang.	Sine.	′	′	Cosine.	Cotan.	Tang.	Sine.	′	′	Cosine.	Cotan.	Tang.	Sine.	′
Deg. 81.						Deg. 81.						Deg. 81.					

IV.—Natural Sines and Tangents to a Radius 1—*continued.*

9 Deg. | 9 Deg. | 9 Deg.

′	Sine.	Tang.	Cotang.	Cosine.	′	′	Sine.	Tang.	Cotang.	Cosine.	′	′	Sine.	Tang.	Cotang.	Cosine.	′
0	·1564345	·158384	6·313751	·9876883	60	21	·1624650	·164652	6·073397	·9867143	39	41	·1682026	·170633	5·860505	·9857524	19
1	·1567218	·158682	6·301886	·9876428	59	22	·1627520	·164951	6·062396	·9866670	38	42	·1684894	·170933	5·850241	·9857035	18
2	·1570091	·158980	6·290065	·9875972	58	23	·1630390	·165250	6·051434	·9866196	37	43	·1687761	·171232	5·840011	·9856544	17
3	·1572963	·159279	6·278286	·9875514	57	24	·1633260	·165548	6·040510	·9865722	36	44	·1690628	·171532	5·829817	·9856053	16
4	·1575836	·159577	6·266551	·9875057	56	25	·1636129	·165847	6·029624	·9865246	35	45	·1693495	·171831	5·819657	·9855561	15
5	·1578708	·159875	6·254858	·9874598	55	26	·1638999	·166146	6·018777	·9864770	34	46	·1696362	·172130	5·809531	·9855068	14
6	·1581581	·160174	6·243208	·9874138	54	27	·1641868	·166445	6·007967	·9864293	33	47	·1699228	·172430	5·799440	·9854574	13
7	·1584453	·160472	6·231600	·9873678	53	28	·1644738	·166744	5·997195	·9863815	32	48	·1702095	·172730	5·789382	·9854079	12
8	·1587325	·160770	6·220034	·9873216	52	29	·1647607	·167043	5·986461	·9863336	31	49	·1704961	·173029	5·779358	·9853583	11
9	·1590197	·161069	6·208510	·9872754	51	30	·1650476	·167342	5·975764	·9862856	30	50	·1707828	·173329	5·769368	·9853087	10
10	·1593069	·161367	6·197027	·9872291	50	31	·1653345	·167641	5·965104	·9862375	29	51	·1710694	·173628	5·759412	·9852590	9
11	·1595940	·161666	6·185586	·9871827	49	32	·1656214	·167940	5·954481	·9861894	28	52	·1713560	·173928	5·749488	·9852092	8
12	·1598812	·161964	6·174186	·9871363	48	33	·1659082	·168239	5·943895	·9861412	27	53	·1716425	·174228	5·739598	·9851593	7
13	·1601683	·162263	6·162827	·9870897	47	34	·1661951	·168539	5·933345	·9860929	26	54	·1719291	·174527	5·729741	·9851093	6
14	·1604555	·162561	6·151518	·9870431	46	35	·1664819	·168838	5·922832	·9860445	25	55	·1722156	·174827	5·719917	·9850593	5
15	·1607426	·162860	6·140230	·9869964	45	36	·1667687	·169137	5·912355	·9859960	24	56	·1725022	·175127	5·710125	·9850091	4
16	·1610297	·163159	6·128992	·9869496	44	37	·1670556	·169436	5·901913	·9859475	23	57	·1727887	·175427	5·700366	·9849589	3
17	·1613167	·163457	6·117794	·9869027	43	38	·1673423	·169735	5·891508	·9858988	22	58	·1730752	·175727	5·690639	·9849086	2
18	·1616038	·163756	6·106636	·9868557	42	39	·1676291	·170035	5·881138	·9858501	21	59	·1733617	·176027	5·680944	·9848582	1
19	·1618909	·164055	6·095517	·9868087	41	40	·1679159	·170334	5·870804	·9858013	20	60	·1736482	·176327	5·671281	·9848078	0
20	·1621779	·164353	6·084438	·9867615	40												
′	Cosine.	Cotan.	Tang.	Sine.	′	′	Cosine.	Cotan.	Tang.	Sine.	′	′	Cosine.	Cotan.	Tang.	Sine.	′

Deg. 80. | Deg. 80. | Deg. 80.

IV.—Natural Sines and Tangents to a Radius 1—*continued.*

10 Deg.

′	Sine.	Tang.	Cotang.	Cosine.	′
0	·1736482	·176327	5·671281	·9848078	60
1	·1739346	·176626	5·661650	·9847572	59
2	·1742211	·176926	5·652051	·9847066	58
3	·1745075	·177226	5·642483	·9846558	57
4	·1747939	·177527	5·632947	·9846050	56
5	·1750803	·177827	5·623442	·9845542	55
6	·1753667	·178127	5·613968	·9845032	54
7	·1756531	·178427	5·604524	·9844521	53
8	·1759395	·178727	5·595112	·9844010	52
9	·1762258	·179027	5·585730	·9843498	51
10	·1765121	·179327	5·576378	·9842985	50
11	·1767984	·179628	5·567057	·9842471	49
12	·1770847	·179928	5·557766	·9841956	48
13	·1773710	·180228	5·548505	·9841441	47
14	·1776573	·180529	5·539274	·9840924	46
15	·1779435	·180829	5·530072	·9840407	45
16	·1782298	·181129	5·520900	·9839889	44
17	·1785160	·181430	5·511757	·9839370	43
18	·1788022	·181730	5·502644	·9838850	42
19	·1790884	·182031	5·493560	·9838330	41
20	·1793746	·182331	5·484505	·9837808	40
′	Cosine.	Cotan.	Tang.	Sine.	′

Deg. 79.

10 Deg.

′	Sine.	Tang.	Cotang.	Cosine.	′
21	·1796607	·182632	5·475478	·9837286	39
22	·1799469	·182933	5·466481	·9836763	38
23	·1802330	·183233	5.457512	·9836239	37
24	·1805191	·183534	5·448571	·9835715	36
25	·1808052	·183835	5·439659	·9835189	35
26	·1810913	·184135	5·430775	·9834663	34
27	·1813774	·184436	5·421918	·9834136	33
28	·1816635	·184737	5·413090	·9833608	32
29	·1819495	·185038	5·404290	·9833079	31
30	·1822355	·185339	5·395517	·9832549	30
31	·1825215	·185639	5·386771	·9832019	29
32	·1828075	·185940	5·378053	·9831487	28
33	·1830935	·186241	5·369363	·9830955	27
34	·1833795	·186542	5·369699	·9830422	26
35	·1836654	·186843	5·352062	·9829888	25
36	·1839514	·187144	5·343452	·9829353	24
37	·1842373	·187446	5·334869	·9828818	23
38	·1845232	·187747	5·326313	·9828282	22
39	·1848091	·188048	5·317783	·9827744	21
40	·1850949	·188349	5·309279	·9827206	20
′	Cosine.	Cotan.	Tang.	Sine.	′

Deg. 79.

10 Deg.

′	Sine.	Tang.	Cotang.	Cosine.	′
41	·1853808	·188650	5·300801	·9826668	19
42	·1856666	·188952	5·292350	·9826128	18
43	·1859524	·189253	5·283925	·9825587	17
44	·1862382	·189554	5·275525	·9825046	16
45	·1865240	·189855	5·267151	·9824504	15
46	·1868098	·190157	5·258803	·9823961	14
47	·1870956	·190458	5·250480	·9823417	13
48	·1873813	·190760	5·242183	·9822873	12
49	·1876670	·191061	5·233911	·9822327	11
50	·1879528	·191363	5·225664	·9821781	10
51	·1882385	·191664	5·217442	·9821234	9
52	·1885241	·191966	5·209245	·9820686	8
53	·1888098	·192268	2·201073	·9820137	7
54	·1890954	·192569	5·192926	·9819587	6
55	·1893811	·192871	5·184803	·9819037	5
56	·1896667	·193173	5·176705	·9818485	4
57	·1899523	·193474	5·168631	·9817933	3
58	·1902379	·193776	5·160581	·9817380	2
59	·1905234	·194078	5·152555	·9816826	1
60	·1908090	·194380	5·144554	·9816272	0
′	Cosine.	Cotan.	Tang.	Sine.	′

Deg. 79.

IV.—Natural Sines and Tangents to a Radius 1—*continued.*

11 Deg.							11 Deg.							11 Deg					
′	Sine.	Tang.	Cotang.	Cosine.	′	′	Sine.	Tang.	Cotang.	Cosine.	′	′	Sine.	Tang.	Cotang.	Cosine.	′
0	·1908090	·194380	5·144554	·9816272	60	21	·1968018	·200727	4·981881	·9804433	39	41	·2025024	·206786	4·835901	·9792818	19
1	·1910945	·194682	5·136576	·9815716	59	22	·1970870	·201030	4·974381	·9803860	38	42	·2027873	·207090	4·828817	·9792228	18
2	·1913801	·194984	5·128622	9815160	58	23	·1973722	·201332	4·966903	·9803286	37	43	·2030721	·207393	4·821753	·9791638	17
3	·1916656	·195286	5·120692	·9814603	57	24	·1976573	·201635	4·959447	·9802712	36	44	·2033569	·207696	4·814709	·9791047	16
4	·1919510	·195588	5·112785	·9814045	56	25	·1979425	·201938	4·952012	·9802136	35	45	·2036418	·208000	4·807685	·9790455	15
5	·1922365	·195890	5·104902	·9813486	55	26	·1982276	·202240	4·944599	·9801560	34	46	·2039265	·208303	4·800680	·9789862	14
6	·1925220	·196192	5·097042	·9812927	54	27	·1985127	·202543	4·937206	·9800983	33	47	·2042113	·208607	4·793695	·9789268	13
7	·1928074	·196494	5·089206	·9812366	53	28	·1987978	·202846	4·929835	·9800405	32	48	·2044961	·208910	4·786730	·9788674	12
8	·1930928	·196796	5·081392	·9811805	52	29	·1990829	·203149	4·922485	·9799827	31	49	·2047808	·209214	4·779783	·9788079	11
9	·1933782	·197098	5·073602	·9811243	51	30	·1993679	·203452	4·915157	·9799247	30	50	·2050655	·209518	4·772856	·9787483	10
10	·1936636	·197400	5·065835	·9810680	50	31	·1996530	·203755	4 907849	·9798667	29	51	·2053502	·209821	4·765949	·9786886	9
11	·1939490	·197703	5·058090	·9810116	49	32	·1999380	·204058	4·900562	·9798086	28	52	·2056349	·210125	4·759060	·9786288	8
12	·1942344	·198005	5·050369	·9809552	48	33	·2002230	·204361	4·893295	·9797504	27	53	·2059195	·210429	4·752190	·9785689	7
13	·1945197	·198307	5·042670	·9808986	47	34	·2005080	·204664	4·886049	·9796921	26	54	·2062042	·210733	4·745340	·9785090	6
14	·1948050	·198610	5·034993	·9808420	46	35	·2007930	·204967	4·878824	·9796337	25	55	·2064888	·211036	4·738508	·9784490	5
15	·1950903	·198912	5·027339	·9807853	45	36	·2010779	·205270	4·871620	·9795752	24	56	·2067734	·211340	4·731695	·9783889	4
16	·1953756	·199214	5·019707	·9807285	44	37	·2013629	·205573	4·864435	·9795167	23	57	·2070580	·211644	4·714901	·9783287	3
17	·1956609	·199517	5·012098	·9806716	43	38	·2016478	·205876	4·857271	·9794581	22	58	·2073426	·211948	4·718125	·9782684	2
18	·1959461	·199819	5·004511	·9806147	42	39	·2019327	·206180	4·850128	·9793994	21	59	·2076272	·212252	4·711368	·9782080	1
19	·1962314	·200122	4·996945	·9805576	41	40	·2022176	·206483	4·843004	·9793406	20	60	·2079117	·212556	4·704630	·9781476	0
20	·1965166	·200424	4·989402	·9805005	40												
′	Cosine.	Cotan.	Tang.	Sine.	′	′	Cosine.	Cotan.	Tang.	Sine.	′	′	Cosine.	Cotan.	Tang.	Sine.	′
Deg. 78.							Deg. 78.							Deg. 78.					

IV.—Natural Sines and Tangents to a Radius 1—*continued.*

12 Deg. | 12 Deg. | 12 Deg.

′	Sine.	Tang.	Cotang.	Cosine.	′	′	Sine.	Tang.	Cotang.	Cosine.	′	′	Sine.	Tang.	Cotang.	Cosine.	′
0	·2079117	·212556	4·704630	·9781476	60	21	·2138829	·218949	4·567261	·9768593	39	41	·2195624	·225054	4·443376	·9755985	19
1	·2081962	·212860	4·697910	·9780871	59	22	·2141671	·219254	4·560911	·9767970	38	42	·2198462	·225359	4·437350	·9755345	18
2	·2084807	·213164	4·691208	·9780265	58	23	·2144512	·219559	4·554577	·9767347	37	43	·2201300	·225665	4·431339	·9754706	17
3	·2087652	·213468	4·684524	·9779658	57	24	·2147353	·219864	4·548260	·9766723	36	44	·2204137	·225971	4·425343	·9754065	16
4	·2090497	·213773	4·677859	·9779050	56	25	·2150194	·220169	4·541960	·9766098	35	45	·2206974	·226276	4·419364	·9753423	15
5	·2093341	·214077	4·671212	·9778441	55	26	·2153035	·220474	4·535677	·9765472	34	46	·2209811	·226582	4·413399	·9752781	14
6	·2096186	·214381	4·664583	·9777832	54	27	·2155876	·220779	4·529410	·9764845	33	47	·2212648	·226888	4·407450	·9752138	13
7	·2099030	·214685	4·657972	·9777222	53	28	·2158716	·221084	4·523160	·9764217	32	48	·2215485	·227194	4·401516	·9751494	12
8	·2101874	·214990	4·651378	·9776611	52	29	·2161556	·221389	4·516926	·9763589	31	49	·2218321	·227500	4·395597	·9750849	11
9	·2104718	·215294	4·644803	·9775999	51	30	·2164396	·221694	4·510708	·9762960	30	50	·2221158	·227806	4·389694	·9750203	10
10	·2107561	·215589	4·638245	·9775386	50	31	·2167236	·221999	4·504507	·9762330	29	51	·2223994	·228112	4·383805	·9749556	9
11	·2110405	·215903	4·631705	·9774773	49	32	·2170076	·222305	4·498322	·9761699	28	52	·2226830	·228418	4·377931	·9748909	8
12	·2113248	·216207	4·625183	·9774159	48	33	·2172915	·222610	4·492153	·9761067	27	53	·2229666	·228724	4·372073	·9748261	7
13	·2116091	·216512	4·618678	·9773544	47	34	·2175754	·222915	4·486000	·9760435	26	54	·2232501	·229030	4·366229	·9747612	6
14	·2118934	·216816	4·612190	·9772928	46	35	·2178593	·223221	4·479863	·9759802	25	55	·2235337	·229336	4·360400	·9746962	5
15	·2121777	·217121	4·605720	·9772311	45	36	·2181432	·223526	4·473742	·9759168	24	56	·2238172	·229642	4·354586	·9746311	4
16	·2124619	·217425	4·599268	·9771693	44	37	·2184271	·223831	4·467637	·9758533	23	57	·2241007	·229949	4·348786	·9745660	3
17	·2127462	·217730	4·592832	·9771075	43	38	·2187110	·224137	4·461548	·9757897	22	58	·2243842	·230255	4·343001	·9745008	2
18	·2130304	·218035	4·586414	·9770456	42	39	·2189948	·224442	4·455475	·9757260	21	59	·2246676	·230561	4·337231	·9744355	1
19	·2133146	·218340	4·580012	·9769836	41	40	·2192786	·224748	4·449418	·9756623	20	60	·2249511	·230868	4·331475	·9743701	0
20	·2135988	·218644	4·573628	·9769215	40												
′	Cosine.	Cotan.	Tang.	Sine.	′	′	Cosine.	Cotan.	Tang.	Sine.	′	′	Cosine.	Cotan.	Tang.	Sine.	′

Deg. 77. | Deg. 77. | Deg. 77.

IV.—Natural Sines and Tangents to a Radius 1—*continued.*

13 Deg.

′	Sine.	Tang.	Cotang.	Cosine.	′
0	·2249511	·230868	4·331475	·9743701	60
1	·2252345	·231174	4·325734	·9743046	59
2	·2255179	·231481	4·320007	·9742390	58
3	·2258013	·231787	4·314295	·9741734	57
4	·2260846	·232094	4·308597	·9741077	56
5	·2263680	·232400	4·302913	·9740419	55
6	·2266513	·232707	4·297244	·9739760	54
7	·2269346	·233014	4·291588	·9739100	53
8	·2272179	·233320	4·285947	·9738439	52
9	·2275012	·233627	4·280319	·9737778	51
10	·2277844	·233934	4·274706	·9737116	50
11	·2280677	·234241	4·269107	·9736453	49
12	·2283509	·234547	4·263521	·9735789	48
13	·2286341	·234854	4·257950	·9735124	47
14	·2289172	·235161	4·252392	·9734458	46
15	·2292004	·235468	4·246848	·9733792	45
16	·2294835	·235775	4·241317	·9733125	44
17	·2297666	·236082	4·235800	·9732457	43
18	·2300497	·236390	4·230297	·9731789	42
19	·2303328	·236697	4·224808	·9731119	41
20	·2306159	·237004	4·219331	·9730449	40
′	Cosine.	Cotan.	Tang.	Sine.	′

Deg. 76.

13 Deg.

′	Sine.	Tang.	Cotang.	Cosine.	′
21	·2308989	·237311	4·213869	·9729777	39
22	·2311819	·237618	4·208419	·9729105	38
23	·2314649	·237926	4·202983	·9728432	37
24	·2317479	·238233	4·197560	·9727759	36
25	·2320309	·238541	4·192151	·9727084	35
26	·2323138	·238848	4·186754	·9726409	34
27	·2325967	·239156	4·181371	·9725733	33
28	·2328796	·239463	4·176001	·9725056	32
29	·2331625	·239771	4·170644	·9724378	31
30	·2334454	·240078	4·165299	·9723699	30
31	·2337282	·240386	4·159968	·9723020	29
32	·2340110	·240694	4·154650	·9722339	28
33	·2342938	·241001	4·149344	·9721658	27
34	·2345766	·241309	4·144051	·9720976	26
35	·2348594	·241617	4·138771	·9720294	25
36	·2351421	·241925	4·133504	·9719610	24
37	·2354248	·242233	4·128249	·9718926	23
38	·2357075	·242541	4·123007	·9718240	22
39	·2359902	·242849	4·117778	·9717554	21
40	·2362729	·243157	4·112561	·9716867	20
′	Cosine.	Cotan.	Tang.	Sine.	′

Deg. 76.

13 Deg.

′	Sine.	Tang.	Cotang.	Cosine.	′
41	·2365555	·243465	4·107356	·9716180	19
42	·2368381	·243773	4·102164	·9715491	18
43	·2371207	·244081	4·096985	·9714802	17
44	·2374033	·244390	4·091817	·9714112	16
45	·2376859	·244698	4·086662	·9713421	15
46	·2379684	·245006	4·081519	·9712729	14
47	·2382510	·245315	4·076389	·9712036	13
48	·2385335	·245623	4·071270	·9711343	12
49	·2388159	·245932	4·066164	·9710649	11
50	·2390984	·246240	4·061070	·9709953	10
51	·2393808	·246549	4·055987	·9709258	9
52	·2396633	·246857	4·050917	·9708561	8
53	·2399457	·247166	4·045859	·9707863	7
54	·2402280	·247475	4·040812	·9707165	6
55	·2405104	·247783	4·035777	·9706466	5
56	·2407927	·248092	4·030755	·9705766	4
57	·2410751	·248401	4·025744	·9705065	3
58	·2413574	·248710	4·020744	·9704363	2
59	·2416396	·249019	4·015757	·9703660	1
60	·2419219	·249328	4·010780	·9702957	0
′	Cosine.	Cotan.	Tang.	Sine.	′

Deg. 76.

IV.—Natural Sines and Tangents to a Radius 1—*continued.*

14 Deg.

′	Sine.	Tang.	Cotang.	Cosine.	′
0	·2419219	·249328	4·010780	·9702957	60
1	·2422041	·249637	4·005816	·9702253	59
2	·2424863	·249946	4·000863	·9701548	58
3	·2427685	·250255	3·995922	·9700842	57
4	·2430507	·250564	3·990992	·9700135	56
5	·2433329	·250873	3·986073	·9699428	55
6	·2436150	·251182	3·981166	·9698720	54
7	·2438971	·251491	3·976271	·9698011	53
8	·2441792	·251801	3·971386	·9697301	52
9	·2444613	·252110	3·966513	·9696591	51
10	·2447433	·252420	3·961651	·9695879	50
11	·2450254	·252729	3·956801	·9695167	49
12	·2453074	·253038	3·951961	·9694453	48
13	·2455894	·253348	3·947133	·9693740	47
14	·2458713	·253658	3·942315	·9693025	46
15	·2461533	·253967	3·937509	·9692309	45
16	·2464352	·254277	3·932714	·9691593	44
17	·2467171	·254587	3·927929	·9690875	43
18	·2469990	·254896	3·923156	·9690157	42
19	·2472809	·255206	3·918393	·9689438	41
20	·2475627	·255516	3·913642	·9688719	40
′	Cosine.	Cotan.	Tang.	Sine.	′

Deg. 75.

14 Deg.

′	Sine.	Tang.	Cotang.	Cosine.	′
21	·2478445	·255826	3·908901	·9687998	39
22	·2481263	·256136	3·904171	·9687277	38
23	·2484081	·256446	3·899451	·9686555	37
24	·2486899	·256756	3·894742	·9685832	36
25	·2489716	·257066	3·890044	·9685108	35
26	·2492533	·257376	3·885357	·9684383	34
27	·2495350	·257686	3·880680	·9683658	33
28	·2498167	·257997	3·876014	·9682931	32
29	·2500984	·258307	3·871358	·9682204	31
30	·2503800	·258617	3·866713	·9681476	30
31	·2506616	·258928	3·862078	·9680748	29
32	·2509432	·259238	3·857453	·9680018	28
33	·2512248	·259548	3·852839	·9679288	27
34	·2515063	·259859	3·848235	·9678557	26
35	·2517879	·260169	3·843642	·9677825	25
36	·2520694	·260480	3·839059	·9677092	24
37	·2523508	·260791	3·834486	·9676358	23
38	·2526323	·261101	3·829923	·9675624	22
39	·2529137	·261412	3·825370	·9674888	21
40	·2531952	·261723	3·820828	·9674152	20
′	Cosine.	Cotan.	Tang.	Sine.	′

Deg. 75.

14 Deg.

′	Sine.	Tang.	Cotang.	Cosine.	′
41	·2534766	·262034	3·816295	·9673415	19
42	·2537579	·262345	3·811773	·9672678	18
43	·2540393	·262656	3·807260	·9671939	17
44	·2543206	·262967	3·802758	·9671200	16
45	·2546019	·263278	3·798266	·9670459	15
46	·2548832	·263589	3·793783	·9669718	14
47	·2551645	·263900	3·789310	·9668977	13
48	·2554458	·264211	3·784848	·9668234	12
49	·2557270	·264522	3·780395	·9667490	11
50	·2560082	·264833	3·775951	·9666746	10
51	·2562894	·265145	3·771513	·9666001	9
52	·2565705	·265456	3·767094	·9665255	8
53	·2568517	·265768	3·762680	·9664508	7
54	·2571328	·266079	3·758276	·9663761	6
55	·2574139	·266390	3·753881	·9663012	5
56	·2576950	·266702	3·749496	·9662263	4
57	·2579760	·267014	3·745120	·9661513	3
58	·2582570	·267325	3·740754	·9660762	2
59	·2585381	·267637	3·736398	·9660011	1
60	·2588190	·267949	3·732050	·9659258	0
′	Cosine.	Cotan.	Tang.	Sine.	′

Deg. 75.

IV.—Natural Sines and Tangents to a Radius 1—*continued.*

15 Deg.

′	Sine.	Tang.	Cotang.	Cosine.	′
0	·2588190	·267949	3·732050	·9659258	60
1	·2591000	·268261	3·727713	·9658505	59
2	·2593810	·268572	3·723384	·9657751	58
3	·2596619	·268884	3·719065	·9656996	57
4	·2599428	·269196	3·714756	·9656240	56
5	·2602237	·269508	3·710455	·9655484	55
6	·2605045	·269820	3·706164	·9654726	54
7	·2607853	·270132	3·701883	·9653968	53
8	·2610662	·270444	3·697610	·9653209	52
9	·2613469	·270757	3·693346	·9652449	51
10	·2616277	·271069	3·689092	·9651689	50
11	·2619085	271381	3·684847	·9650927	49
12	·2621892	·271694	3·680611	·9650165	48
13	·2624699	·272006	3·676384	·9649402	47
14	·2627506	·272318	3·672166	·9648638	46
15	·2630312	·272631	3·667957	·9647873	45
16	·2633118	·272943	3 663757	·9647108	44
17	2635925	·273256	3·659566	·9646341	43
18	·2638730	273569	3·655384	·9645574	42
19	·2641536	·273881	3·651211	·9644806	41
20	·2644342	·274194	3·547046	·9644037	40
′	Cosine.	Cotan.	Tang.	Sine.	′

Deg. 74.

15 Deg.

′	Sine.	Tang.	Cotang.	Cosine.	′
21	·2647147	·274507	3·642891	·9643268	39
22	·2649952	·274820	3·638744	·9642497	38
23	·2652757	·275133	3·634606	·9641726	37
24	·2655561	·275445	3·630477	·9640954	36
25	2658366	·275758	3·626356	·9640181	35
26	2661170	·276071	3·622244	·9639407	34
27	·2663973	·276385	3·618141	·9638633	33
28	·2666777	·276698	3·614046	·9637858	32
29	·2669581	·277011	3·609960	·9637081	31
30	·2672384	·277324	3·605883	·9636305	30
31	·2675187	·277637	3·601814	·9635527	29
32	·2677989	·277951	3·597754	·9634748	28
33	·2680792	·278264	3·593702	·9633969	27
34	·2683594	·278578	3·589659	·9633189	26
35	·2686396	·278891	3·585624	·9632408	25
36	·2689198	·279205	3·581597	·9631626	24
37	·2692000	·279518	3·577579	·9630843	23
38	·2694801	·279832	3·573569	9630060	22
39	·2697602	·280145	3·569568	·9629275	21
40	·2700403	·280459	3·565574	·9628490	20
′	Cosine.	Cotan.	Tang.	Sine.	′

Deg. 74.

15 Deg.

′	Sine.	Tang.	Cotang.	Cosine.	′
41	2703204	·280773	3·561590	·9627704	19
42	·2706004	·281087	3·557613	·9626917	18
43	·2708805	·281401	3·553644	·9626130	17
44	·2711605	·281715	3·549684	·9625342	16
45	·2714404	·282029	3·545732	·9624552	15
46	·2717204	·282343	3·541788	·9623762	14
47	·2720003	·282657	3·537852	·9622972	13
48	2722802	·282971	3 533925	·9622180	12
49	·2725601	·283285	3·530005	·9621387	11
50	·2728400	·283599	3·526093	·9620594	10
51	·2731198	·283914	3·522190	·9619800	9
52	·2733997	·284228	3·518294	·9619005	8
53	·2736794	·284543	3·514407	·9618210	7
54	·2739592	·284857	3·510527	·9617413	6
55	·2742390	·285172	3·506655	·9616616	5
56	·2745187	·285486	3·502791	·9615818	4
57	·2747984	·285801	3·498935	·9615019	3
58	·2750781	·286115	3·495087	·9614219	2
59	·2753577	·286430	3·491247	·9613418	1
60	·2756374	·286745	3·487414	·9612617	0
′	Cosine.	Cotan.	Tang.	Sine.	′

Deg. 74.

IV.—Natural Sines and Tangents to a Radius 1—*continued.*

16 Deg.

′	Sine.	Tang.	Cotang.	Cosine.	′
0	·2756374	·286745	3·487414	·9612617	60
1	·2759170	·287060	3·483589	·9611815	59
2	·2761965	·287375	3·479772	·9611012	58
3	·2764761	·287690	3·475963	·9610208	57
4	·2767556	·288005	3·472161	·9609403	56
5	·2770352	·288320	3·468367	·9608598	55
6	·2773147	·288635	3·464581	·9607792	54
7	·2775941	·288950	3·460802	·9606984	53
8	·2778736	·289265	3·457031	·9606177	52
9	·2781530	·289580	3·453267	·9605368	51
10	·2784324	·289896	3·449512	·9604558	50
11	·2787118	·290211	3·445763	·9603748	49
12	·2789911	·290526	3·442022	·9602937	48
13	·2792704	·290842	3·438289	·9602125	47
14	·2795497	·291157	3·434563	·9601312	46
15	·2798290	·291473	3·430844	·9600499	45
16	·2801083	·291789	3·427133	·9599684	44
17	·2803875	·292104	3·423429	·9598869	43
18	·2806667	·292420	3·419733	·9598053	42
19	·2809459	·292736	3·416044	·9597236	41
20	·2812251	·293052	3·412362	·9596418	40
′	Cosine.	Cotan.	Tang.	Sine.	′

Deg. 73.

16 Deg.

′	Sine.	Tang.	Cotang.	Cosine.	′
21	·2815042	·293368	3·408688	·9595600	39
22	·2817833	·293683	3·405021	·9594781	38
23	·2820624	·293999	3·401361	·9593961	37
24	·2823415	·294316	3·397708	·9593140	36
25	·2826205	·294632	3·394063	·9592318	35
26	·2828995	·294948	3·390424	·9591496	34
27	·2831785	·295264	3·386793	·9590672	33
28	·2834575	·295580	3·383169	·9589848	32
29	2837364	·295897	3·379553	·9589023	31
30	·2840153	·296213	3·375943	·9588197	30
31	·2842942	·296529	3·372340	9587371	29
32	·2845731	·296846	3·368745	·9586543	28
33	·2848520	·297163	3·365156	·9585715	27
34	·2851308	·297479	3·361575	·9584886	26
35	·2854096	·297796	3·358000	·9584056	25
36	·2856884	·298112	3·354433	·9583226	24
37	·2859671	·298429	3·350872	·9582394	23
38	·2862458	·298746	3·347319	·9581562	22
39	·2865246	·299063	3·343772	·9580729	21
40	·2868032	·299380	3·340232	·9579895	20
′	Cosine.	Cotan.	Tang.	Sine.	′

Deg. 73.

16 Deg.

′	Sine.	Tang.	Cotang.	Cosine.	′
41	·2870819	·299697	3·336699	·9579060	19
42	·2873605	·300014	3·333173	·9578225	18
43	·2876391	·300331	3·329654	·9577389	17
44	·2879177	·300648	3·326141	·9576552	16
45	·2881963	·300965	3·322636	·9575714	15
46	·2884748	·301283	3·319137	·9574875	14
47	·2887533	·301600	3·315645	·9574035	13
48	·2890318	·301917	3·312159	·9573195	12
49	·2893103	·302235	3·308681	·9572354	11
50	·2895887	·302552	3·305209	·9571512	10
51	·2898671	·302870	3·301743	·9570669	9
52	·2901455	·303187	3·298285	·9569825	8
53	·2904239	·303505	3·294833	·9568981	7
54	·2907022	·303823	3·291387	·9568136	6
55	·2909805	·304141	3·287948	·9567290	5
56	·2912588	·304458	3·284516	·9566443	4
57	·2915371	·304776	3·281090	·9565595	3
58	·2918153	·305094	3·277671	·9564747	2
59	·2920935	·305412	3·274258	·9563898	1
60	·2923717	·305730	3·270852	·9563048	0
′	Cosine.	Cotan.	Tang.	Sine.	′

Deg. 73.

IV.—Natural Sines and Tangents to a Radius 1—*continued*.

17 Deg.

′	Sine.	Tang.	Cotang.	Cosine.	′
0	·2923717	·305730	3·270852	·9563048	60
1	·2926499	·306048	3·267452	·9562197	59
2	·2929280	·306367	3·264059	·9561345	58
3	·2932061	·306685	3·260672	·9560492	57
4	·2934842	·307003	3·257292	9559639	56
5	·2937623	·307321	3·253918	·9558785	55
6	·2940403	·307640	3·250550	·9557930	54
7	·2943183	·307958	3·247189	·9557074	53
8	·2945963	·308277	3·243834	·9556218	52
9	·2948743	·308595	3·240486	·9555361	51
10	·2951522	·308914	3·237143	·9554502	50
11	·2954302	·309233	3·233807	·9553643	49
12	·2957081	·309551	3·230478	·9552784	48
13	·2959859	·309870	3·227154	·9551923	47
14	·2962638	·310189	3·223837	·9551062	46
15	·2965416	·310508	3·220526	·9550199	45
16	·2968194	·310827	3·217221	·9549336	44
17	·2970971	·311146	3·213922	·9548473	43
18	·2973749	·311465	3·210630	·9547608	42
19	·2976526	·311784	3·207344	·9546743	41
20	·2979303	·312103	3·204063	·9545876	40
′	Cosine.	Cotan.	Tang.	Sine.	′

Deg. 72.

17 Deg.

′	Sine.	Tang.	Cotang.	Cosine.	′
21	2982079	·312422	3·200789	·9545009	39
22	·2984856	·312742	3·197521	·9544141	38
23	·2987632	·313061	3·194259	·9543273	37
24	·2990408	·313381	3·191003	·9542403	36
25	2993184	·313700	3·187754	·9541533	35
26	·2995959	·314020	3·184510	·9540662	34
27	·2998734	·314339	3·181272	·9539790	33
28	3001509	·314659	3·178040	·9538917	32
29	·3004284	·314979	3·174814	·9538044	31
30	·3007058	·315298	3·171594	·9537170	30
31	·3009832	·315618	3·168380	·9536294	29
32	·3012606	·315938	3·165172	·9535418	28
33	·3015380	·316258	3·161970	·9534542	27
34	·3018153	·316578	3·158774	·9533664	26
35	·3020926	·316898	3·155584	·9532786	25
36	·3023699	·317218	3·152399	·9531907	24
37	·3026471	·317538	3·149220	·9531027	23
38	·3029244	·317859	3·146047	·9530146	22
39	·3032016	·318179	3·142880	·9529264	21
40	·3034788	·318499	3·139719	·9528382	20
′	Cosine.	Cotan.	Tang.	Sine.	′

Deg. 72.

17 Deg.

′	Sine.	Tang.	Cotang.	Cosine.	′
41	·3037559	·318820	3·136563	9527499	19
42	·3040331	·319140	3·133414	·9526615	18
43	·3043102	·319461	3·130270	·9525730	17
44	·3045872	·319781	3·127131	·9524844	16
45	·3048643	·320102	3·123999	·9523958	15
46	·3051413	·320423	3·120872	·9523071	14
47	·3054183	·320744	3·117750	·9522183	13
48	·3056953	·321064	3·114635	·9521294	12
49	·3059723	·321385	3·111525	·9520404	11
50	·3062492	·321706	3·108421	·9519514	10
51	·3065261	·322027	3·105322	·9518623	9
52	·3068030	·322348	3·102229	·9517731	8
53	·3070798	·322670	3·099141	·9516838	7
54	·3073566	·322991	3·096059	·9515944	6
55	·3076334	·323312	3·092983	·9515050	5
56	·3079102	·323633	3·089912	·9514154	4
57	·3081869	·323955	3·086846	·9513258	3
58	·3084636	·324276	3·083786	·9512361	2
59	·3087403	·324598	3·080732	·9511464	1
60	·3090170	·324919	3·077683	·9510565	0
′	Cosine.	Cotan.	Tang.	Sine.	′

Deg. 72.

IV.—Natural Sines and Tangents to a Radius 1—*continued.*

18 Deg. | 18 Deg. | 18 Deg.

′	Sine.	Tang.	Cotang.	Cosine.	′	′	Sine.	Tang.	Cotang.	Cosine.	′	′	Sine.	Tang.	Cotang.	Cosine.	′
0	·3090170	·324919	3·077683	·9500565	60	21	·3148209	·331686	3·014892	·9491511	39	41	·3203374	·338157	2·957205	·9473035	19
1	·3092936	·325241	3·074640	·9509666	59	22	·3150969	·332009	3·011960	·9490595	38	42	·3206130	·338481	2·954372	·9472103	18
2	·3095702	·325563	3·071602	·9508766	58	23	·3153730	·332332	3·009033	·9489678	37	43	·3208885	·338805	2·951545	·9471170	17
3	·3098468	·325884	3·068569	·9507865	57	24	·3156490	·332655	3·006110	·9488760	36	44	·3211640	·339129	2·948722	·9470236	16
4	·3101234	·326206	3·065542	·9506963	56	25	·3159250	·332978	3·003193	·9487842	35	45	·3214395	·339454	2·945905	·9469301	15
5	·3103999	·326528	3·062520	·9506061	55	26	·3162010	·333302	3·000282	·9486922	34	46	·3217149	·339778	2·943092	·9468366	14
6	·3106764	·326850	3·059503	·9505157	54	27	·3164770	·333625	2·997375	·9486002	33	47	·3219903	·340103	2·940284	·9467430	13
7	·3109529	·327172	3·056492	·9504253	53	28	·3167529	·333948	2·994473	·9485081	32	48	·3222657	·340427	2·937480	·9466493	12
8	·3112294	·327494	3·053487	·9503348	52	29	·3170288	·334271	2·991576	·9484159	31	49	·3225411	·340752	2·934682	·9465555	11
9	·3115058	·327816	3·050486	·9502443	51	30	·3173047	·334595	2·988685	·9483237	30	50	·3228164	·341077	2·931888	·9464616	10
10	·3117822	·328138	3·047491	·9501536	50	31	·3175805	·334918	2·985798	·9482313	29	51	·3230917	·341401	2·929099	·9463677	9
11	·3120586	·328461	3·044501	·9500629	49	32	·3178563	·335242	2·982916	·9481389	28	52	·3233670	·341726	2·926315	·9462736	8
12	·3123349	·328783	3·041517	·9499721	48	33	·3181321	·335566	2·980040	·9480464	27	53	·3236422	·342051	2·923535	·9461795	7
13	·3126112	·329105	3·038538	·9498812	47	34	·3184079	·335889	2·977168	·9479538	26	54	·3239174	·342376	2·920761	·9460854	6
14	·3128875	·329428	3·035564	·9497902	46	35	·3186836	·336213	2·974301	·9478612	25	55	·3241926	·342701	2·917990	·9459911	5
15	·3131638	·329750	3·032595	·9496991	45	36	·3189593	·336537	2·971439	·9477684	24	56	·3244678	·343026	2·915225	·9458968	4
16	·3134400	·330073	3·029632	·9496080	44	37	·3192350	·336861	2·968583	·9476756	23	57	·3247429	·343351	2·912464	·9458023	3
17	·3137163	·330395	3·026673	·9495168	43	38	·3195106	·337185	2·965731	·9475827	22	58	·3250180	·343677	2·909708	·9457078	2
18	·3139925	·330718	3·023720	·9494255	42	39	·3197863	·337509	2·962884	·9474897	21	59	·3252931	·344002	2·906957	·9456132	1
19	·3142686	·331041	3·020772	·9493341	41	40	·3200619	·337833	2·960042	·9473966	20	60	·3255682	·344327	2·904211	·9455186	0
20	·3145448	·331363	3·017830	·9492426	40												
′	Cosine.	Cotan.	Tang.	Sine.	′	′	Cosine.	Cotan.	Tang.	Sine.	′	′	Cosine.	Cotan.	Tang.	Sine.	′

Deg. 71. | Deg. 71. | Deg. 71.

IV.—Natural Sines and Tangents to a Radius 1—*continued.*

19 Deg.						19 Deg.						19 Deg.					
'	Sine.	Tang.	Cotang.	Cosine.	'	'	Sine.	Tang.	Cotang.	Cosine.	'	'	Sine.	Tang.	Cotang.	Cosine.	'
0	·3255682	·344327	2·904210	·9455186	60	21	·3313379	·351175	2·847583	·9435122	39	41	·3368214	·357723	2·795453	·9415686	19
1	·3258432	·344653	2·901468	·9454238	59	22	·3316123	·351501	2·844935	·9434157	38	42	·3370953	·358051	2·792891	·9414705	18
2	·3261182	·344978	2·898731	·9453290	58	23	·3318867	·351828	2·842292	·9433192	37	43	·3373691	·358380	2·790333	·9413724	17
3	·3263932	·345304	2·895998	·9452341	57	24	·3321611	·352155	2·839653	·9432227	36	44	·3376429	·358708	2·787780	·9412743	16
4	·3266681	·345629	2·893270	·9451391	56	25	·3324355	·352482	2·837019	·9431260	35	45	·3379167	·359036	2·785230	·9411760	15
5	·3269430	·345955	2·890546	·9450441	55	26	·3327098	·352809	2·834389	·9430293	34	46	·3381905	·359365	2·782685	·9410777	14
6	·3272179	·346281	2·887827	·9449489	54	27	·3329841	·353136	2·831763	·9429324	33	47	·3384642	·359693	2·780144	·9409793	13
7	·3274928	·346606	2·885113	·9448537	53	28	·3332584	·353464	2·829142	·9428355	32	48	·3387379	·360022	2·777606	·9408808	12
8	·3277676	·346932	2·882403	·9447584	52	29	·3335326	·353791	2·826525	·9427386	31	49	·3390116	·360350	2·775073	·9407822	11
9	·3280424	·347258	2·879697	·9446630	51	30	·3338069	·354118	2·823912	·9426415	30	50	·3392852	·360679	2·772544	·9406835	10
10	·3283172	·347584	2·876997	·9445675	50	31	·3340810	·354446	2·821304	·9425444	29	51	·3395589	·361008	2·770019	·9405848	9
11	·3285919	·347910	2·874300	·9444720	49	32	·3343552	·354773	2·818700	·9424471	28	52	·3398325	·361337	2·767499	·9404860	8
12	·3288666	·348236	2·871608	·9443764	48	33	·3346293	·355101	2·816100	·9423498	27	53	·3401060	·361666	2·764982	·9403871	7
13	·3291413	·348563	2·868921	·9442807	47	34	·3349034	·355428	2·813504	·9422525	26	54	·3403796	·361994	2·762469	·9402881	6
14	·3294160	·348889	2·866238	·9441849	46	35	·3351775	·355756	2·810913	·9421550	25	55	·3406531	·362324	2·759960	·9401891	5
15	·3296906	·349215	2·863560	·9440890	45	36	·3354516	·356084	2·808326	·9420575	24	56	·3409265	·362653	2·757456	·9400899	4
16	·3299653	·349542	2·860886	·9439931	44	37	·3357256	·356411	2·805743	·9419598	23	57	·3412000	·362982	2·754955	·9399907	3
17	·3302398	·349868	2·858216	·9438971	43	38	·3359996	·356739	2·803164	·9418621	22	58	·3414734	·363311	2·752458	·9398914	2
18	·3305144	·350195	2·855551	·9438010	42	39	·3362735	·357067	2·800590	·9417644	21	59	·3417468	·363640	2·749966	·9397921	1
19	·3307889	·350521	2·852891	·9437048	41	40	·3365475	·357395	2·798019	·9416665	20	60	·3420201	·363970	2·747477	·9396926	0
20	·3310634	·350848	2·850234	·9436085	40												
'	Cosine.	Cotan.	Tang.	Sine.	'	'	Cosine.	Cotan.	Tang.	Sine.	'	'	Cosine.	Cotan.	Tang.	Sine.	'
Deg. 70.						Deg. 70.						Deg. 70.					

IV.—Natural Sines and Tangents to a Radius 1—*continued.*

20 Deg.

′	Sine.	Tang.	Cotang.	Cosine.	′
0	·3420201	·363970	2·747477	·9396926	60
1	·3422935	·364299	2·744992	·9395931	59
2	·3425668	·364629	2·742512	·9394935	58
3	·3428400	·364958	2·740035	·9393938	57
4	·3431133	·365288	2·737562	·9392940	56
5	·3433865	·365618	2·735093	·9391942	55
6	·3436597	·365948	2·732628	·9390943	54
7	·3439329	·366277	2·730167	·9389943	53
8	·3442060	·366607	2·727710	·9388942	52
9	·3444791	·366937	2·725256	·9387940	51
10	·3447521	·367268	2·722807	·9386938	50
11	·3450252	·367598	2 720362	·9385934	49
12	·3452982	·367928	2·717920	·9384930	48
13	·3455712	·368258	2·715482	·9383925	47
14	·3458441	·368589	2·713048	·9382920	46
15	·3461171	·368919	2·710618	·9381913	45
16	·3463900	·369250	2·708192	·9380906	44
17	·3466628	·369580	2·705769	·9379898	43
18	·3469357	·369911	2·703351	·9378889	42
19	·3472085	·370242	2·700936	·9377880	41
20	·3474812	·370572	2·698525	·9376869	40
′	Cosine.	Cotan.	Tang.	Sine.	′

Deg. 69.

20 Deg.

′	Sine.	Tang.	Cotang.	Cosine.	′
21	·3477540	·370903	2·696118	·9375858	39
22	·3480267	·371234	2·693714	·9374846	38
23	·3482994	·371565	2·691314	·9373833	37
24	·3485720	·371896	2·688919	·9372820	36
25	·3488447	·372227	2·686526	·9371806	35
26	·3491173	·372559	2·684138	·9370790	34
27	·3493898	·372890	2·681753	·9369774	33
28	·3496624	·373221	2·679372	·9368758	32
29	·3499349	·373553	2·676995	·9367740	31
30	·3502074	·373884	2·674621	·9366722	30
31	·3504798	·374216	2·672251	·9365703	29
32	·3507523	·374547	2·669885	·9364683	28
33	·3510246	·374879	2·667522	·9363662	27
34	·3512970	·375211	2·665163	·9362641	26
35	·3515693	·375543	2·662808	·9361618	25
36	·3518416	·375875	2·660456	·9360595	24
37	·3521139	·376207	2·658108	·9359571	23
38	·3523862	·376539	2·655764	·9358547	22
39	·3526584	·376871	2·653423	·9357521	21
40	·3529306	·377203	2·651086	·9356495	20
′	Cosine.	Cotan.	Tang.	Sine.	′

Deg. 69.

20 Deg.

′	Sine.	Tang.	Cotang.	Cosine.	′
41	·3532027	·377536	2·648753	·9355468	19
42	·3534748	·377868	2·646423	·9354440	18
43	·3537469	·378201	2·644096	·9353412	17
44	·3540190	·378533	2·641774	·9352382	16
45	·3542910	·378866	2·639454	·9351352	15
46	·3545630	·379198	2·637139	·9350321	14
47	·3548350	·379531	2·634827	·9349289	13
48	·3551070	·379864	2·632518	·9348257	12
49	·3553789	·380197	2·630213	·9347223	11
50	·3556508	·380530	2·627912	·9346189	10
51	·3559226	·380863	2·625614	·9345154	9
52	·3561944	·381196	2·623319	·9344119	8
53	·3564662	·381529	2·621028	·9343082	7
54	·3567380	·381862	2·618741	·9342045	6
55	·3570097	·382196	2·616457	·9341007	5
56	·3572814	·382529	2·614176	·9339968	4
57	·3575531	·382863	2·611899	·9338928	3
58	·3578248	·383196	2·609625	·9337888	2
59	·3580964	·383530	2·607355	·9336846	1
60	·3583679	·383864	2·605089	·9335804	0
′	Cosine.	Cotan.	Tang.	Sine.	′

Deg. 69.

IV.—Natural Sines and Tangents to a Radius 1—*continued.*

21 Deg.						21 Deg.						21 Deg.					
′	Sine.	Tang.	Cotang.	Cosine.	′	′	Sine.	Tang.	Cotang.	Cosine.	′	′	Sine.	Tang.	Cotang.	Cosine.	′
0	·3583679	·383864	2·605089	·9335804	60	21	·3640641	·390889	2·558268	·9313739	39	41	·3694765	·397611	2·515018	·9291401	19
1	·3586395	·384197	2·602825	·9334761	59	22	·3643351	·391224	2·556075	·9312679	38	42	·3697468	·397918	2·512889	·9291326	18
2	·3589110	·384531	2·600565	·9333718	58	23	·3646059	·391560	2·553885	·9311619	37	43	·3700170	·398285	2·510762	9290250	17
3	·3591825	·384865	2·598309	·9332673	57	24	·3648768	·391895	2·551699	·9310558	36	44	·3702872	·398622	2·508639	·9289173	16
4	·3594540	·385199	2·596056	·9331628	56	25	·3651476	·392231	2·549516	·9309496	35	45	·3705574	·398959	2·506519	·9288096	15
5	·3597254	·385533	2·593806	·9330582	55	26	·3654184	·392567	2·547335	·9308434	34	46	·3708276	·399296	2·504402	·9287017	14
6	·3599968	·385867	2·591560	·9329535	54	27	·3656891	·392902	2·545159	·9307370	33	47	·3710977	·399634	2·502289	·9285938	13
7	·3602682	·386202	2·589317	·9328488	53	28	·3659599	·393238	2·542985	·9306306	32	48	·3713678	·399971	2·500178	·9284858	12
8	·3605395	·386536	2·587078	·9327439	52	29	·3662306	·393574	2·540815	·9305241	31	49	·3716379	·400308	2·498070	·9283778	11
9	·3608108	·386870	2·584842	·9326390	51	30	·3665012	·393910	2·538647	·9304176	30	50	·3719079	·400646	2·495966	·9282696	10
10	·3610821	·387205	2·582609	·9325340	50	31	·3667719	·394246	2·536483	·9303109	29	51	·3721780	·400984	2·493864	·9281614	9
11	·3613534	·387539	2·580380	·9324290	49	32	·3670425	·394582	2·534323	·9302042	28	52	·3724479	·401321	2·491766	·9280531	8
12	·3616246	·387874	2·578153	·9323238	48	33	·3673130	·394918	2·532165	·9300974	27	53	·3727179	·401659	2·489670	·9279447	7
13	·3618958	·388209	2·575931	·9322186	47	34	·3675836	·395255	2·530011	·9299905	26	54	·3729878	·401997	2·487578	·9278363	6
14	·3621669	·388543	2·573711	·9321133	46	35	·3678541	·395591	2·527859	·9298835	25	55	·3732577	·402335	2·485488	·9277277	5
15	·3624380	·388878	2·571495	·9320079	45	36	·3681246	·395928	2·525711	·9297765	24	56	·3135275	·402673	2·483402	·9276191	4
16	·3627091	·389213	2·569283	·9319024	44	37	·3683950	·396264	2·523566	·9296694	23	57	·3737973	·403011	2·481319	·9275104	3
17	·3629802	·389548	2·567073	·9317969	43	38	·3686654	·396601	2·521424	·9295622	22	58	·3740671	·403349	2·479238	·9274016	2
18	·3632512	·389883	2·564867	·9316912	42	39	·3689358	·396937	2·519286	·9294549	21	59	·3743369	·403687	2·477161	·9272928	1
19	·3635222	·390218	2·562664	·9315855	41	40	·3692061	·397274	2·517150	·9293475	20	60	·3746066	·404026	2·475086	·9271839	0
20	·3637932	·390554	2·560464	·9314797	40												
′	Cosine.	Cotan.	Tang.	Sine.	′	′	Cosine.	Cotan.	Tang.	Sine.	′	′	Cosine.	Cotan.	Tang.	Sine.	′
Deg. 68.						Deg. 68.						Deg. 68.					

IV.—Natural Sines and Tangents to a Radius 1—*continued.*

22 Deg.						22 Deg.						22 Deg.					
′	Sine.	Tang.	Cotang.	Cosine.	′	′	Sine.	Tang.	Cotang.	Cosine.	′	′	Sine.	Tang.	Cotang.	Cosine.	′
0	·3746066	·404026	2·475086	·9271839	60	21	·3802634	·411149	2·432204	·9248782	39	41	·3856377	·417967	2·392531	·9226503	19
1	·3748763	·404364	2·473015	·9270748	59	22	·3805324	·411489	2·430193	·9247676	38	42	·3859060	·418309	2·390576	·9225381	18
2	·3751459	·404703	2·470947	·9269658	58	23	·3808014	·411830	2·428186	·9246568	37	43	·3861744	·418650	2·388625	·9224258	17
3	·3754156	·405041	2·468881	·9268566	57	24	·3810704	·412170	2·426181	·9245460	36	44	·3864427	·418992	2·386675	·9223134	16
4	·3756852	·405380	2·466819	·9267474	56	25	·3813393	·412510	2·424180	·9244351	35	45	·3867110	·419334	2·384729	·9222010	15
5	·3759547	·405719	2·464759	·9266380	55	26	·3816082	·412851	2·422181	·9243242	34	46	·3869792	·419676	2·382785	·9220884	14
6	·3762243	·406057	2·462703	·9265286	54	27	·3818770	·413191	2·420185	·9242131	33	47	·3872474	·420019	2·380844	·9219758	13
7	·3764938	·406396	2·460649	·9264192	53	28	·3821459	·413532	2·418191	·9241020	32	48	·3875156	·420361	2·378906	·9218632	12
8	·3767632	·406735	2·458598	·9263096	52	29	·3824147	·413872	2·416201	·9239908	31	49	·3877837	·420703	2·376970	·9217504	11
9	·3770327	·407074	2·456551	·9262000	51	30	·3826834	·414213	2·414213	·9238795	30	50	·3880518	·421046	2·375037	·9216375	10
10	·3773021	·407413	2·454506	·9260902	50	31	·3829522	·414554	2·412228	·9237682	29	51	·3883199	·421388	2·373106	·9215246	9
11	·3775714	·407753	2·452464	·9259805	49	32	·3832209	·414895	2·410246	·9236567	28	52	·3885880	·421731	2·371179	·9214116	8
12	·3778408	·408092	2·450425	·9258706	48	33	·3834895	·415236	2·408267	·9235452	27	53	·3888560	·422073	2·369254	·9212986	7
13	·3781101	·408431	2·448389	·9257606	47	34	·3837582	·415577	2·406290	·9234336	26	54	·3891240	·422416	2·367331	·9211854	6
14	·3783794	·408771	2·446355	·9256506	46	35	·3840268	·415918	2·404316	·9233220	25	55	·3893919	·422759	2·365411	·9210722	5
15	·3786486	·409110	2·444325	·9255405	45	36	·3842953	·416259	2·402345	·9232102	24	56	·3896598	·423102	2·363494	·9209589	4
16	·3789178	·409450	2·442298	·9254303	44	37	·3845639	·416601	2·400377	·9230984	23	57	·3899277	·423445	2·361580	·9208455	3
17	·3791870	·409790	2·440273	·9253201	43	38	·3848324	·416942	2·398411	·9229865	22	58	·3901955	·423788	2·359668	·9207320	2
18	·3794562	·410129	2·438251	·9252097	42	39	·3851008	·417284	2·396449	·9228745	21	59	·3904633	·424131	2·357753	·9206185	1
19	·3797253	·410469	2·436233	·9250993	41	40	·3853693	·417625	2·394488	·9227624	20	60	·3907311	·424474	2·355852	·9205049	0
20	·3799944	·410809	2·434217	·9249888	40												
′	Cosine.	Cotan.	Tang.	Sine.	′	′	Cosine.	Cotan.	Tang.	Sine.	′	′	Cosine.	Cotan.	Tang.	Sine.	′
Deg. 67.						Deg. 67.						Deg. 67.					

IV.—Natural Sines and Tangents to a Radius 1—*continued.*

23 Deg. | 23 Deg. | 23 Deg

′	Sine.	Tang.	Cotang.	Cosine.	′	′	Sine.	Tang.	Cotang.	Cosine.	′	′	Sine.	Tang.	Cotang.	Cosine.	′
0	·3907311	·424474	2·355852	·9205049	60	21	·3963468	·431703	2·316407	·9181009	39	41	·4016814	·438622	2·279865	·9157795	19
1	·3909989	·424818	2·353948	·9203912	59	22	·3966139	·432048	2·314557	·9179855	38	42	·4019478	·438969	2·278063	·9156626	18
2	·3912666	·425161	2·352046	·9202774	58	23	·3968809	·432393	2·312709	·9178701	37	43	·4022141	·439316	2·276264	·9155456	17
3	·3915343	·425505	2·350148	·9201635	57	24	·3971479	·432738	2·310863	·9177546	36	44	·4024804	·439663	2·274467	·9154286	16
4	·3918019	·425848	2·348251	·9200496	56	25	·3974148	·433084	2·309020	·9176391	35	45	·4027467	·440010	2·272672	·9153115	15
5	·3920695	·426192	2·346358	·9199356	55	26	·3976818	·433429	2·307180	·9175234	34	46	·4030129	·440357	2·270880	·9151943	14
6	·3923371	·426536	2·344467	·9198215	54	27	·3979486	·433775	2·305342	·9174077	33	47	·4032791	·440705	2·269090	·9150770	13
7	·3926047	·426880	2·342578	·9197073	53	28	·3982155	·434120	2·303506	·9172919	32	48	·4035453	·441052	2·267303	·9149597	12
8	·3928722	·427223	2·340692	·9195931	52	29	·3984823	·434466	2·301673	·9171760	31	49	·4038114	·441400	2·265518	·9148422	11
9	·3931397	·427568	2·338809	·9194788	51	30	·3987491	·434812	2·299842	·9170601	30	50	·4040775	·441747	2·263735	·9147247	10
10	·3934071	·427912	2·336928	·9193644	50	31	·3990158	·435158	2·298014	·9169440	29	51	·4043436	·442095	2·261955	·9146072	9
11	·3936745	·428256	2·335050	·9192499	49	32	·3992825	·435504	2·296188	·9168279	28	52	·4046096	·442443	2·260177	·9144895	8
12	·3939419	·428600	2·333174	·9191353	48	33	·3995492	·435850	2·294365	·9167118	27	53	·4048756	·442791	2·258401	·9143718	7
13	·3942093	·428944	2·331301	·9190207	47	34	·3998158	·436196	2·292544	·9165955	26	54	·4051416	·443139	2·256628	·9142540	6
14	·3944766	·429289	2·329431	·9189060	46	35	·4000825	·436542	2·290725	·9164791	25	55	·4054075	·443487	2·254857	·9141361	5
15	·3947439	·429633	2·327563	·9187912	45	36	·4003490	·436889	2·288909	·9163627	24	56	·4056734	·443835	2·253088	·9140181	4
16	·3950111	·429978	2·325697	·9186763	44	37	·4006156	·437235	2·287095	·9162462	23	57	·4059393	·444183	2·251322	·9139001	3
17	·3952783	·430323	2·323834	·9185614	43	38	·4008821	·437582	2·285284	·9161297	22	58	·4062051	·444531	2·249558	·9137819	2
18	·3955455	·430668	2·321974	·9184464	42	39	·4011486	·437928	2·283475	·9160130	21	59	·4064709	·444880	2·247796	·9136637	1
19	·3958127	·431012	2·320116	·9183313	41	40	·4014150	·438275	2·281669	·9158963	20	60	·4067366	·445228	2·246036	·9135455	0
20	·3960798	·431357	2·318260	·9182161	40												
′	Cosine.	Cotan.	Tang.	Sine.	′	′	Cosine.	Cotan.	Tang.	Sine.	′	′	Cosine.	Cotan.	Tang.	Sine.	′

Deg. 66. | Deg. 66. | Deg. 66.

IV.—Natural Sines and Tangents to a Radius 1—*continued.*

24 Deg.

′	Sine.	Tang.	Cotang.	Cosine.	′
0	·4067366	·445228	2·246036	·9135455	60
1	·4070024	·445577	2·244279	·9134271	59
2	·4072681	·445926	2·242524	·9133087	58
3	·4075337	·446274	2·240772	·9131902	57
4	·4077993	·446623	2·239021	·9130716	56
5	·4080649	·446972	2·237273	·9129529	55
6	·4083305	·447321	2·235528	·9128342	54
7	·4085960	·447670	2·233784	·9127154	53
8	·4088615	·448020	2·232043	·9125965	52
9	·4091269	·448369	2·230304	·9124775	51
10	·4093923	·448718	2·228567	·9123584	50
11	·4096577	·449068	2·226833	·9122393	49
12	·4099230	·449417	2·225100	·9121201	48
13	·4101883	·449767	2·223370	·9120008	47
14	·4104536	·450117	2·221643	·9118815	46
15	·4107189	·450467	2·219917	·9117620	45
16	·4109841	·450817	2·218194	·9116425	44
17	·4112492	·451167	2·216473	·9115229	43
18	·4115144	·451517	2·214754	·9114033	42
19	·4117795	·451867	2·213037	·9112835	41
20	·4120445	·452217	2·211323	·9111637	40
′	Cosine.	Cotan.	Tang.	Sine.	′

Deg. 65.

24 Deg.

′	Sine.	Tang.	Cotang.	Cosine.	′
21	·4123096	·452568	2·209611	·9110438	39
22	·4125745	·452918	2·207901	·9109238	38
23	·4128395	·453269	2·206193	·9108038	37
24	·4131044	·453620	2·204487	·9106837	36
25	·4133693	·453970	2·202784	·9105635	35
26	·4136342	·454321	2·201083	·9104432	34
27	·4138990	·454672	2·199384	·9103228	33
28	·4141638	·455023	2·197687	·9102024	32
29	·4144285	·455375	2·195992	·9100819	31
30	·4146932	·455726	2·194299	·9099613	30
31	·4149579	·456077	2·192609	·9098406	29
32	·4152226	·456429	2·190921	·9097199	28
33	·4154872	·456780	2·189234	·9095990	27
34	·4157517	·457132	2·187551	·9094781	26
35	·4160163	·457483	2·185869	·9093572	25
36	·4162808	·457835	2·184189	·9092361	24
37	·4165453	·458187	2·182511	·9091150	23
38	·4168097	·458539	2·180836	·9089938	22
39	·4170741	·458891	2.179163	·9088725	21
40	·4173385	·459243	2·177492	·9087511	20
′	Cosine.	Cotan.	Tang.	Sine.	′

Deg. 65.

24 Deg.

′	Sine.	Tang.	Cotang.	Cosine.	′
41	·4176028	·459596	2·175822	·9086297	19
42	·4178671	·459948	2·174155	·9085082	18
43	·4181313	·460301	2·172491	·9083866	17
44	·4183956	·460653	2·170828	·9082649	16
45	·4186597	·461006	2·169167	·9081432	15
46	·4189239	·461359	2·167509	·9080214	14
47	·4191880	·461711	2·165852	·9078995	13
48	·4194521	·462064	2·164198	·9077775	12
49	·4197161	·462417	2·162546	·9076554	11
50	·4199801	·462771	2·160895	·9075333	10
51	·4202441	·463124	2·159247	·9074111	9
52	·4205080	·463477	2·157601	·9072888	8
53	·4207719	·463831	2·155957	·9071665	7
54	·4210358	·464184	2·154315	·9070440	6
55	·4212966	·464538	2·152675	·9069215	5
56	·4215634	·464891	2·151037	·9067989	4
57	·4218272	·465245	2·149402	·9066762	3
58	·4220909	·465599	2·147768	·9065535	2
59	·4223546	·465953	2·146136	·9064307	1
60	·4226183	·466307	2·144506	·9063078	0
′	Cosine.	Cotan.	Tang.	Sine.	′

Deg. 65.

IV.—Natural Sines and Tangents to a Radius 1—*continued.*

25 Deg.

′	Sine.	Tang.	Cotang.	Cosine.	′
0	·4226183	·466307	2·144506	·9063078	60
1	·4228819	·466661	2·142879	·9061848	59
2	·4231455	·467016	2·141253	9060618	58
3	·4234090	·467370	2·139630	·9059386	57
4	·4236725	·467725	2·138008	·9058154	56
5	·4239360	·468079	2·136389	·9056922	55
6	·4241994	·468434	2·134771	·9055688	54
7	·4244628	·468789	2·133155	·9054454	53
8	·4247262	·469143	2·131542	·9053219	52
9	·4249895	·469498	2·129930	·9051983	51
10	·4252528	·469853	2·128321	·9050746	50
11	·4255161	·470209	2·126713	·9049509	49
12	·4257793	·470564	2·125108	·9048271	48
13	·4260425	·470919	2·123504	·9047032	47
14	·4263056	·471275	2·121903	·9045792	46
15	·4265687	·471630	2·120303	·9044551	45
16	·4268318	·471986	2·118705	·9043310	44
17	·4270949	·472342	2·117110	·9042068	43
18	·4273579	·472697	2·115516	·9040825	42
19	·4276208	·473053	2·113924	·9039582	41
20	·4278838	·473409	2·112334	·9038338	40
′	Cosine.	Cotan.	Tang.	Sine.	′

Deg. 64.

25 Deg.

′	Sine.	Tang.	Cotang.	Cosine.	′
21	·4281467	·473765	2·110747	·9037093	39
22	·4284095	·474122	2·109161	·9035847	38
23	·4286723	·474478	2·107577	·9034600	37
24	·4289351	·474834	2·105995	·9033353	36
25	·4291979	·475191	2·104415	·9032105	35
26	·4294606	·475548	2·102836	·9030856	34
27	·4297233	·475904	2·101260	·9029606	33
28	·4299859	·476261	2·099686	·9028356	32
29	·4302485	·476618	2·098114	·9027105	31
30	·4305111	·476975	2·096543	·9025853	30
31	·4307736	·477332	2 094975	·9024600	29
32	·4310361	·477689	2·093408	·9023347	28
33	·4312986	·478047	2·091843	·9022092	27
34	·4315610	·478404	2·090280	·9020838	26
35	·4318234	·478762	2·088720	·9019582	25
36	·4320857	·479119	2·087161	·9018325	24
37	·4323481	·479477	2·085603	·9017068	23
38	·4326103	·479835	2·084048	·9015810	22
39	·4328726	·480193	2·082495	·9014551	21
40	·4331348	·480551	2·080943	·9013292	20
′	Cosine.	Cotan.	Tang.	Sine.	′

Deg. 64.

25 Deg.

′	Sine.	Tang.	Cotang.	Cosine.	′
41	·4333970	·480909	2·079394	·9012031	19
42	·4336591	·481267	2·077846	·9010770	18
43	·4339212	·481625	2·076300	·9009508	17
44	·4341832	·481984	2·074756	·9008246	16
45	·4344453	·482342	2·073214	·9006982	15
46	·4347072	·482701	2 071674	·9005718	14
47	·4349692	·483060	2·070135	·9004453	13
48	·4352311	·483418	2 068599	·9003188	12
49	·4354930	·483777	2·067064	·9001921	11
50	·4357548	·484136	2·065531	·9000654	10
51	·4360166	·484495	2·064000	·8999386	9
52	·4362784	·484855	2·062471	·8998117	8
53	·4365401	·485214	2·060944	·8996848	7
54	·4368018	·485573	2·059418	·8995578	6
55	·4370634	·485933	2·057895	·8994307	5
56	·4373251	·486293	2·056373	·8993035	4
57	·4375866	·486652	2·054853	·8991763	3
58	·4378482	·487012	2·053334	·8990489	2
59	·4381097	·487372	2·051818	·8989215	1
60	·4383711	·487732	2·050303	·8987940	0
′	Cosine.	Cotan.	Tang.	Sine.	′

Deg. 64.

IV.—Natural Sines and Tangents to a Radius 1—*continued.*

26 Deg. | 26 Deg. | 26 Deg.

′	Sine.	Tang.	Cotang.	Cosine.	′	′	Sine.	Tang.	Cotang.	Cosine.	′	′	Sine.	Tang.	Cotang.	Cosine.	′
0	·4383711	·487732	2·050303	·8987940	60	21	·4438534	·495317	2·018908	·8960994	39	41	·4490591	·502583	1·989720	·8935021	19
1	·4386326	·488092	2·048791	·8986665	59	22	·4441140	·495679	2·017433	·8959703	38	42	·4493190	·502947	1·988278	·8933714	18
2	·4388940	·488453	2·047280	·8985389	58	23	·4443746	·496041	2·015959	·8958411	37	43	·4495789	·503312	1·986838	·8932406	17
3	·4391553	·488813	2·045770	·8984112	57	24	·4446352	·496404	2·014486	·8957118	36	44	·4498387	·503676	1·985400	·8931098	16
4	·4394166	·489173	2·044263	·8982834	56	25	·4448957	·496766	2·013016	·8955824	35	45	·4500984	·504041	1·983963	·8929789	15
5	·4396779	·489534	2·042757	·8981555	55	26	·4451562	·497129	2·011547	·8954529	34	46	·4503582	·504406	1·982528	·8928480	14
6	·4399392	·489894	2·041254	·8980276	54	27	·4454167	·497492	2·010080	·8953234	33	47	·4506179	·504771	1·981095	·8927169	13
7	·4402004	·490255	2·039751	·8978996	53	28	·4456771	·497855	2·008615	·8951938	32	48	·4508775	·505136	1·979663	·8925858	12
8	·4404615	·490616	2·038251	·8977715	52	29	·4459375	·498218	2·007151	·8950641	31	49	·4511372	·505501	1·978235	·8924546	11
9	·4407227	·490977	2·036753	·8976433	51	30	·4461978	·498581	2·005689	·8949344	30	50	·4513967	·505866	1·976805	·8923234	10
10	·4409838	·491338	2·035256	·8975151	50	31	·4464581	·498944	2·004229	·8948045	29	51	·4516563	·506232	1·975378	·8921920	9
11	·4412448	·491699	2·033761	·8973868	49	32	·4467184	·499308	2·002771	·8946746	28	52	·4519158	·506597	1·973953	·8920606	8
12	·4415059	·492061	2·032268	·8972584	48	33	·4469786	·499671	2·001314	·8945446	27	53	·4521753	·506963	1·972529	·8919291	7
13	·4417668	·492422	2·030776	·8971299	47	34	·4472388	·500035	1·999859	·8944146	26	54	·4524347	·507329	1·971107	·8917975	6
14	·4420278	·492783	2·029287	·8970014	46	35	·4474990	·500398	1·998405	·8942844	25	55	·4526941	·507694	1·969687	·8916659	5
15	·4422887	·493145	2·027799	·8968727	45	36	·4477591	·500762	1·996953	·8941542	24	56	·4529535	·508060	1·968268	·8915342	4
16	·4425496	·493507	2·026313	·8967440	44	37	·4480192	·501126	1·995503	·8940240	23	57	·4532128	·508426	1·966851	·8914024	3
17	·4428104	·493868	2·024828	·8966153	43	38	·4482792	·501490	1·994055	·8938936	22	58	·4534721	·508792	1·965436	·8912705	2
18	·4430712	·494230	2·023346	·8964864	42	39	·4485392	·501854	1·992608	·8937632	21	59	·4537313	·509159	1·964022	·8911385	1
19	·4433319	·494592	2·021865	·8963575	41	40	·4487992	·502218	1·991163	·8936326	20	60	·4539905	·509525	1·962610	·8910065	0
20	·4435927	·494954	2·020386	·8962285	40												
′	Cosine.	Cotan.	Tang.	Sine.	′	′	Cosine.	Cotan.	Tang.	Sine.	′	′	Cosine.	Cotan.	Tang.	Sine.	′

Deg. 63. | Deg. 63. | Deg. 63.

IV.—Natural Sines and Tangents to a Radius 1—*continued.*

27 Deg.

′	Sine.	Tang.	Cotang.	Cosine.	′
0	·4539905	·509525	1·962610	·8910065	60
1	·4542497	·509891	1·961200	·8908744	59
2	·4545088	·510258	1·959791	·8907423	58
3	·4547679	·510625	1·958383	·8906100	57
4	·4550269	·510991	1·956978	·8904777	56
5	·4552859	·511358	1·955573	·8903453	55
6	·4555449	·511725	1·954171	·8902128	54
7	·4558038	·512093	1·952770	·8900803	53
8	·4560627	·512460	1·951371	·8899476	52
9	·4563216	·512827	1·949973	·8898149	51
10	·4565804	·513195	1·948577	·8896822	50
11	·4568392	·513562	1·947182	·8895493	49
12	·4570979	·513930	1·945789	·8894164	48
13	·4573566	·514298	1·944398	·8892834	47
14	·4576153	·514666	1·943008	·8891503	46
15	·4578739	·515033	1·941620	·8890171	45
16	·4581325	·515401	1·940233	·8888839	44
17	·4583910	·515770	1·938848	·8887506	43
18	·4586496	·516138	1·937464	·8886172	42
19	·4589080	·516506	1·936082	·8884838	41
20	·4591665	·516875	1·934702	·8883503	40
′	Cosine.	Cotan.	Tang.	Sine.	′

Deg. 62.

27 Deg.

′	Sine.	Tang.	Cotang.	Cosine.	′
21	·4594248	·517244	1·933323	·8882166	39
22	·4596832	·517612	1·931945	·8880830	38
23	·4599415	·517981	1·930569	·8878492	37
24	·4601998	·518350	1·929195	·8879154	36
25	·4604580	·518719	1·927822	·8876815	35
26	·4607162	·519089	1·926451	·8875475	34
27	·4609744	·519458	1·925081	·8874134	33
28	·4612325	·519827	1·923713	·8872793	32
29	·4614906	·520197	1·922347	·8871451	31
30	·4617486	·520567	1·920982	·8870108	30
31	·4620066	·520936	1·919618	·8868765	29
32	·4622646	·521306	1·918256	·8867420	28
33	·4625225	·521676	1·916896	·8866075	27
34	·4627804	·522046	1·915537	·8864730	26
35	·4630382	·522417	1·914179	·8863383	25
36	·4632960	·522787	1·912823	·8862036	24
37	·4635538	·523157	1·911469	·8860688	23
38	·4638115	·523528	1·910116	·8859339	22
39	·4640692	·523899	1·908764	·8857989	21
40	·4643269	·524269	1·907414	·8856639	20
′	Cosine.	Cotan.	Tang.	Sine.	′

Deg. 62.

27 Deg.

′	Sine.	Tang.	Cotang.	Cosine.	′
41	·4645845	·524640	1·906066	·8855288	19
42	·4648420	·525011	1·904719	·8853936	18
43	·4650996	·525382	1·903373	·8852584	17
44	·4653571	·525754	1·902029	·8851230	16
45	·4656145	·526125	1·900687	·8849876	15
46	·4658719	·526496	1·899346	·8848522	14
47	·4661293	·526868	1·898006	·8847166	13
48	·4663866	·527240	1·896668	·8845810	12
49	·4666439	·527612	1·895332	·8844453	11
50	·4669012	·527983	1·893997	·8843095	10
51	·4671584	·528356	1·892663	·8841736	9
52	·4674156	·528728	1·891331	·8840377	8
53	·4676727	·529100	1·890000	·8839017	7
54	·4679298	·529472	1·888671	·8837656	6
55	·4681869	·529845	1·887343	·8836295	5
56	·4684439	·530217	1·886017	·8834933	4
57	·4687009	·530590	1·884692	·8833569	3
58	·4689578	·530963	1·883369	·8832206	2
59	·4692147	·531336	1·882047	·8830841	1
60	·4694716	·531709	1·880726	·8829476	0
′	Cosine.	Cotan.	Tang.	Sine.	′

Deg. 62.

IV.—Natural Sines and Tangents to a Radius 1—*continued.*

28 Deg.

′	Sine.	Tang.	Cotang.	Cosine.	′
0	·4694716	·531709	1·880726	·8829476	60
1	·4697284	·532082	1·879407	·8828110	59
2	·4699852	·532455	1·878089	·8826743	58
3	·4702419	·532829	1·876773	·8825376	57
4	·4704986	·533202	1·875458	·8824007	56
5	·4707553	·533576	1·874145	·8822638	55
6	·4710119	·533950	1·872833	·8821269	54
7	·4712685	·534324	1·871523	·8819898	53
8	·4715250	·534698	1·870214	·8818527	52
9	·4717815	·535072	1·868906	·8817155	51
10	·4720380	·535446	1·867600	·8815782	50
11	·4722944	·535820	1·866295	·8814409	49
12	·4725508	·536195	1·864992	·8813035	48
13	·4728071	·536569	1·863690	·8811660	47
14	·4730634	·536944	1·862389	·8810284	46
15	·4733197	·537319	1·861090	·8808907	45
16	·4735759	·537694	1·859792	·8807530	44
17	·4738321	·538069	1·858496	·8806152	43
18	·4740882	·538444	1·857201	·8804774	42
19	·4743443	·538819	1·855908	·8803394	41
20	·4746004	·539195	1·854615	·8802014	40
′	Cosine.	Cotan.	Tang.	Sine.	′

Deg. 61.

28 Deg.

′	Sine.	Tang.	Cotang.	Cosine.	′
21	·4748564	·539570	·1853325	·8800633	39
22	·4751124	·539946	·1852035	·8799251	38
23	·4753683	·540322	·1850747	·8797869	37
24	·4756242	·540698	·1849461	·8796486	36
25	·4758801	·541074	·1848176	·8795102	35
26	·4761359	·541450	·1846892	·8793717	34
27	·4763917	·541826	·1845609	·8792332	33
28	·4766474	·542202	·1844328	·8790946	32
29	·4769031	·542579	·1843049	·8789559	31
30	·4771588	·542955	·1841770	·8788171	30
31	·4774144	·543332	·1840494	·8786783	29
32	·4776700	·543709	·1839218	·8785394	28
33	·4779255	·544086	·1837944	·8784004	27
34	·4781810	·544463	·1836671	·8782613	26
35	·4784364	·544840	·1835399	·8781222	25
36	·4786919	·545217	·1834129	·8779830	24
37	·4789472	·545595	·1832861	·8778437	23
38	·4792026	·545972	·1831593	·8777043	22
39	·4794579	·546350	·1830327	·8775649	21
40	·4797131	·546728	·1829062	·8774254	20
′	Cosine.	Cotan.	Tang.	Sine.	′

Deg. 61.

28 Deg.

′	Sine.	Tang.	Cotang.	Cosine.	′
41	·4799683	·547106	1·827799	·8772858	19
42	·4802235	·547484	1·826537	·8771462	18
43	·4804786	·547862	1·825276	·8770064	17
44	·4807337	·548240	1·824017	·8768666	16
45	·4809888	·548618	1·822759	·8767268	15
46	·4812438	·548997	1·821502	·8765868	14
47	·4814987	·549375	1·820247	·8764468	13
48	·4817537	·549754	1·818993	·8763067	12
49	·4820086	·550133	1·817740	·8761665	11
50	·4822634	·550512	1·816489	·8760263	10
51	·4825182	·550891	1·815239	·8758859	9
52	·4827730	·551270	1·813990	·8757455	8
53	·4830277	·551650	1·812743	·8756051	7
54	·4832824	·552029	1·811496	·8754645	6
55	·4835370	·552409	1·810252	·8753239	5
56	·4837916	·552789	1·809008	·8751832	4
57	·4840462	·553168	1·807766	·8750425	3
58	·4843007	·553548	1·806525	·8749016	2
59	·4845552	·553928	1·805286	·8747607	1
60	·4848096	·554309	1·804047	·8746197	0
′	Cosine.	Cotan.	Tang.	Sine.	′

Deg. 61.

IV.—Natural Sines and Tangents to a Radius 1—*continued.*

29 Deg.

′	Sine.	Tang.	Cotang.	Cosine.	′
0	·4848096	·554309	1·804047	·8746197	60
1	·4850640	·554689	1·802810	·8744786	59
2	·4853184	·555069	1·801575	·8743375	58
3	·4855727	·555450	1·800340	·8741963	57
4	·4858270	·555831	1·799107	·8740550	56
5	·4860812	·556211	1·797875	·8739137	55
6	·4863354	·556592	1·796645	·8737722	54
7	·4865895	·556973	1·795416	·8736307	53
8	·4868436	·557355	1·794188	·8734891	52
9	·4870977	·557736	1·792961	·8733475	51
10	·4873517	·558117	1·791736	·8732058	50
11	·4876057	·558499	1·790512	·8730640	49
12	·4878597	·558881	1·789289	·8729221	48
13	·4881136	·559262	1·788067	·8727801	47
14	·4883674	·559644	1·786847	·8726381	46
15	·4886212	·560026	1·785628	·8724960	45
16	·4888750	·560409	1·784410	·8723538	44
17	·4891288	·560791	1·783194	·8722116	43
18	·4893825	·561173	1·781979	·8720693	42
19	·4896361	·561556	1·780765	·8719269	41
20	·4898897	·561939	1·779552	·8717844	40
′	Cosine.	Cotan.	Tang.	Sine.	′

Deg. 60.

29 Deg.

′	Sine.	Tang.	Cotang.	Cosine.	′
21	·4901433	·562321	1·778340	·8716419	39
22	·4903968	·562704	1·777130	·8714993	38
23	·4906503	·563087	1·775921	·8713566	37
24	·4909038	·563471	1·774714	·8712138	36
25	·4911572	·563854	1·773507	·8710710	35
26	·4914105	·564237	1·772302	·8709281	34
27	·4916638	·564621	1·771098	·8707851	33
28	·4919171	·565005	1·769895	·8706420	32
29	·4921704	·565388	1·768694	·8704989	31
30	·4924236	·565772	1·767494	·8703557	30
31	·4926767	·566156	1·766295	·8702124	29
32	·4929298	·566541	1·765097	·8700691	28
33	·4931829	·566925	1·763900	·8699256	27
34	·4934359	·567309	1·762705	·8697821	26
35	·4936889	·567694	1·761511	·8696386	25
36	·4939419	·568079	1·760318	·8694949	24
37	·4941948	·568463	1·759126	·8693512	23
38	·4944476	·568848	1·757936	·8692074	22
39	·4947005	·569233	1·756747	·8690636	21
40	·4949532	·569619	1·755559	·8689196	20
′	Cosine.	Cotan.	Tang.	Sine	′

Deg. 60.

29 Deg.

′	Sine.	Tang.	Cotang.	Cosine.	′
41	·4952060	·570004	1·754372	·8687756	19
42	·4954587	·570389	1·753186	·8686315	18
43	·4957113	·570775	1·752002	·8684874	17
44	·4959639	·571161	1·750819	·8683431	16
45	·4962165	·571547	1·749637	·8681988	15
46	·4964690	·571933	1·748456	·8680544	14
47	·4967215	·572319	1·747276	·8679100	13
48	·4969740	·572705	1·746098	·8677655	12
49	·4972264	·573091	1·744921	·8676209	11
50	·4974787	·573478	1·743745	·8674762	10
51	·4977310	·573864	1·742570	·8673314	9
52	·4979833	·574251	1·741396	·8671866	8
53	·4982355	·574638	1·740224	·8670417	7
54	·4984877	·575025	1·739053	·8668967	6
55	·4987399	·575412	1·737883	·8667517	5
56	·4989920	·575799	1·736714	·8666066	4
57	·4992441	·576187	1·735546	·8664614	3
58	·4994961	·576574	1·734380	·8663161	2
59	·4997481	·576962	1·733214	·8661708	1
60	·5000000	·577350	1·732050	·8660254	0
′	Cosine.	Cotan.	Tang.	Sine.	′

Deg. 60.

IV.—Natural Sines and Tangents to a Radius 1—*continued.*

30 Deg. | 30 Deg. | 30 Deg.

′	Sine.	Tang.	Cotang.	Cosine.	′	′	Sine.	Tang.	Cotang.	Cosine.	′	′	Sine.	Tang.	Cotang.	Cosine.	′
0	·5000000	·577350	1·732050	·8660254	60	21	·5052809	·585524	1·707871	·8629549	39	41	·5102928	·593363	1·685308	·8600007	19
1	·5002519	·577738	1·730887	·8658799	59	22	·5055319	·585914	1·706732	·8628079	38	42	·5105429	·593756	1·684191	·8598523	18
2	·5005037	·578126	1·729726	·8657344	58	23	·5057828	·586305	1·705595	·8626608	37	43	·5107930	·594150	1·683076	·8597037	17
3	·5007556	·578514	1·728565	·8655887	57	24	·5060338	·586696	1·704458	·8625137	36	44	·5110431	·594543	1·681962	·8595551	16
4	·5010073	·578902	1·727406	·8654430	56	25	·5062846	·587087	1·703323	·8623664	35	45	·5112931	·594937	1·680848	·8594064	15
5	·5012591	·579291	1·726247	·8652973	55	26	·5065355	·587478	1·702189	·8622191	34	46	·5115431	·595331	1·679736	·8592576	14
6	·5015107	·579679	1·725090	·8651514	54	27	·5067863	·587870	1·701055	·8620717	33	47	·5117930	·595725	1·678625	·8591088	13
7	·5017624	·580068	1·723934	·8650055	53	28	·5070370	·588261	1·699923	·8619243	32	48	·5120429	·596119	1·677515	·8589599	12
8	·5020140	·580457	1·722779	·8648595	52	29	·5072877	·588653	1·698792	·8617768	31	49	·5122927	·596514	1·676406	·8588109	11
9	·5022655	·580846	1·721626	·8647134	51	30	·5075384	·589045	1·697663	·8616292	30	50	·5125425	·596908	1·675298	·8586619	10
10	·5025170	·581235	1·720473	·8645673	50	31	·5077890	·589436	1·696534	·8614815	29	51	·5127923	·597303	1·674192	·8585127	9
11	·5027685	·581624	1·719322	·8644211	49	32	·5080396	·589828	1·695406	·8613337	28	52	·5130420	·597697	1·673086	·8583635	8
12	·5030199	·582013	1·718172	·8642748	48	33	·5082901	·590221	1·694280	·8611859	27	53	·5132916	·598092	1·671981	·8582143	7
13	·5032713	·582403	1·717023	·8641284	47	34	·5085406	·590613	1·693155	·8610380	26	54	·5135413	·598487	1·670878	·8580649	6
14	·5035227	·582793	1·715875	·8639820	46	35	·5087910	·591005	1·692030	·8608901	25	55	·5137908	·598882	1·669775	·8579155	5
15	·5037740	·583182	1·714728	·8638355	45	36	·5090414	·591398	1·690907	·8607420	24	56	·5140404	·599278	1·668674	·8577660	4
16	·5040252	·583572	1·713582	·8636889	44	37	·5092918	·591791	1·689785	·8605939	23	57	·5142899	·599673	1·667574	·8576164	3
17	·5042765	·583962	1·712438	·8635423	43	38	·5095421	·592183	1·688664	·8604457	22	58	·5145393	·600069	1·666474	·8574668	2
18	·5045276	·584352	1·711294	·8633956	42	39	·5097924	·592576	1·687544	·8602975	21	59	·5147887	·600464	1·665376	·8573171	1
19	·5047788	·584743	1·710152	·8632488	41	40	·5100426	·592969	1·686426	·8601491	20	60	·5150381	·600860	1·664279	·8571673	0
20	·5050298	·585133	1·709011	·8631019	40												
′	Cosine.	Cotan.	Tang.	Sine.	′	′	Cosine.	Cotan.	Tang.	Sine.	′	′	Cosine.	Cotan.	Tang.	Sine.	′

Deg. 59. | Deg. 59. | Deg. 59.

IV.—Natural Sines and Tangents to a Radius 1—*continued*.

31 Deg. | 31 Deg. | 31 Deg.

′	Sine.	Tang.	Cotang.	Cosine.	′	′	Sine.	Tang.	Cotang.	Cosine.	′	′	Sine.	Tang.	Cotang.	Cosine.	′
0	·5150381	·600860	1·664279	·8571673	60	21	·5202646	·609205	1·641482	·8540051	39	41	·5252241	·617210	1·620192	·8509639	19
1	·5152874	·601256	1·663183	·8570174	59	22	·5205130	·609604	1·640408	·8538538	38	42	·5254717	·617612	1·619138	·8508111	18
2	·5155367	·601652	1·662088	·8568675	58	23	·5207613	·610003	1·639335	·8537023	37	43	·5257191	·618014	1·618085	·8506582	17
3	·5157859	·602049	1·660994	·8567175	57	24	·5210096	·610402	1·638263	·8535508	36	44	·5259665	·618416	1·617033	·8505053	16
4	·5160351	·602445	1·659901	·8565674	56	25	·5212579	·610801	1·637191	·8533992	35	45	·5262139	·618818	1·615982	·8503522	15
5	·5162842	·602841	1·658809	·8564173	55	26	·5215061	·611201	1·636121	·8532475	34	46	·5264613	·619221	1·614932	·8501991	14
6	·5165333	·603238	1·657718	·8562671	54	27	·5217543	·611601	1·635052	·8530958	33	47	·5267085	·619623	1·613882	·8500459	13
7	·5167824	·603635	1·656629	·8561168	53	28	·5220024	·612000	1·633984	·8529440	32	48	·5269558	·620026	1·612834	·8498927	12
8	·5170314	·604032	1·655540	·8559664	52	29	·5222505	·612400	1·632917	·8527921	31	49	·5272030	·620429	1·611787	·8497394	11
9	·5172804	·604429	1·654452	·8558160	51	30	·5224986	·612800	1·631851	·8526402	30	50	·5274502	·620832	1·610741	·8495860	10
10	·5175293	·604826	1·653366	·8556655	50	31	·5227466	·613201	1·630786	·8524881	29	51	·5276973	·621235	1·609696	·8494325	9
11	·5177782	·605224	1·652280	·8555149	49	32	·5229945	·613601	1·629722	·8523360	28	52	·5279443	·621638	1·608652	·8492790	8
12	·5180270	·605621	1·651196	·8553643	48	33	·5232424	·614001	1·628659	·8521839	27	53	·5281914	·622041	1·607609	·8491254	7
13	·5182758	·606019	1·650112	·8552135	47	34	·5234903	·614402	1·627597	·8520316	26	54	·5284383	·622445	1·606567	·8489717	6
14	·5185246	·606417	1·649030	·8550627	46	35	·5237381	·614803	1·626536	·8518793	25	55	·5286853	·622848	1·605526	·8488179	5
15	·5187733	·606814	1·647949	·8549119	45	36	·5239859	·615204	1·625476	·8517269	24	56	·5289322	·623252	1·604485	·8486641	4
16	·5190219	·607213	1·646868	·8547609	44	37	·5242336	·615605	1·624417	·8515745	23	57	·5291790	·623656	1·603446	·8485102	3
17	·5192705	·607611	1·645789	·8546099	43	38	·5244813	·616006	1·623359	·8514219	22	58	·5294258	·624060	1·602408	·8483562	2
18	·5195191	·608009	1·644711	·8544588	42	39	·5247290	·616407	1·622302	·8512693	21	59	·5296726	·624465	1·601370	·8482022	1
19	·5197676	·608408	1·643633	·8543077	41	40	·5249766	·616809	1·621246	·8511167	20	60	·5299193	·624869	1·600334	·8480481	0
20	·5200161	·608806	1·642557	·8541564	40												
′	Cosine.	Cotan.	Tang.	Sine.	′	′	Cosine.	Cotan.	Tang.	Sine.	′	′	Cosine.	Cotan.	Tang.	Sine.	′

Deg. 58. | Deg. 58 | Deg. 58.

IV.—Natural Sines and Tangents to a Radius 1—*continued.*

32 Deg.

′	Sine.	Tang.	Cotang.	Cosine.	′
0	·5299193	·624869	1·600334	·8480481	60
1	·5301659	·625273	1·599299	·8478939	59
2	·5304125	·625678	1·598264	·8477397	58
3	·5306591	·626083	1·597231	·8475853	57
4	·5309057	·626488	1·596198	·8474309	56
5	·5311521	·626893	1·595167	·8472765	55
6	·5313986	·627298	1·594136	·8471219	54
7	·5316450	·627704	1·593107	·8469673	53
8	·5318913	·628109	1·592078	·8468126	52
9	·5321376	·628515	1·591050	·8466579	51
10	·5323839	·628921	1·590023	·8465030	50
11	·5326301	·629327	1·588997	·8463481	49
12	·5328763	·629733	1·587973	·8461932	48
13	·5331224	·630139	1·586949	·8460381	47
14	·5333685	·630546	1·585926	·8458830	46
15	·5336145	·630953	1·584904	·8457278	45
16	·5338605	·631359	1·583883	·8455726	44
17	·5341065	·631766	1·582862	·8454172	43
18	·5343523	·632173	1·581843	·8452618	42
19	·5345982	·632581	1·580825	·8451064	41
20	·5348440	·632988	1·579807	·8449508	40
′	Cosine.	Cotan.	Tang.	Sine.	′

Deg. 57.

32 Deg.

′	Sine.	Tang.	Cotang.	Cosine.	′
21	·5350898	·633395	1·578791	·8447952	39
22	·5353355	·633803	1·577776	·8446395	38
23	·5355812	·634211	1·576761	·8444838	37
24	·5358268	·634619	1·575747	·8443279	36
25	·5360724	·635027	1·574735	·8441720	35
26	·5363179	·635435	1·573723	·8440161	34
27	·5365634	·635844	1·572712	·8438600	33
28	·5368089	·636252	1·571702	·8437039	32
29	·5370543	·636661	1·570693	·8435477	31
30	·5372996	·637070	1·569685	·8433914	30
31	·5375449	·637479	1·568678	·8432351	29
32	·5377902	·637888	1·567672	·8430787	28
33	·5380354	·638297	1·566666	·8429222	27
34	·5382806	·638707	1·565662	·8427657	26
35	·5385257	·639116	1·564659	·8426091	25
36	·5387708	·639526	1·563656	·8424524	24
37	·5390158	·639936	1·562654	·8422956	23
38	·5392608	·640346	1·561654	·8421388	22
39	·5395058	·640756	1·560654	·8419819	21
40	·5397507	·641167	1·559655	·8418249	20
′	Cosine.	Cotan.	Tang.	Sine.	′

Deg. 57.

32 Deg.

′	Sine.	Tang.	Cotang.	Cosine.	′
41	·5399955	·641577	1·558657	·8416679	19
42	·5402403	·641988	1·557660	·8415108	18
43	·5404851	·642399	1·556663	·8413536	17
44	·5407298	·642810	1·555668	·8411963	16
45	·5409745	·643221	1·554674	·8410390	15
46	·5412191	·643632	1·553680	·8408816	14
47	·5414637	·644044	1·552688	·8407241	13
48	·5417082	·644456	1·551696	·8405666	12
49	·5419527	·644867	1·550705	·8404090	11
50	·5421971	·645279	1·549715	·8402513	10
51	·5424415	·645691	1·548726	·8400936	9
52	·5426859	·646104	1·547738	·8399357	8
53	·5429302	·646516	1·546751	·8397778	7
54	·5431744	·646929	1·545764	·8396199	6
55	·5434187	·647341	1·544779	·8394618	5
56	·5436628	·647754	1·543794	·8393037	4
57	·5439069	·648167	1·542810	·8391455	3
58	·5441510	·648580	1·541828	·8389873	2
59	·5443951	·648994	1·540846	·8388290	1
60	·5446390	·649407	1·539865	·8386706	0
′	Cosine.	Cotan.	Tang.	Sine.	′

Deg. 57.

IV.—Natural Sines and Tangents to a Radius 1—*continued.*

′	33 Deg. Sine.	Tang.	Cotang.	Cosine.	′	′	33 Deg. Sine.	Tang.	Cotang.	Cosine.	′	′	33 Deg. Sine.	Tang.	Cotang.	Cosine.	′
0	·5446390	·649407	1·539865	·8386706	60	21	·5497520	·658127	1·519463	·8353279	39	41	·5546024	·666496	1·500382	·8321155	19
1	·5448830	·649821	1·538884	·8385121	59	22	·5499950	·658544	1·518501	·8351680	38	42	·5548444	·666917	1·499436	·8319541	18
2	·5451269	·650235	1·537905	·8383536	58	23	·5502379	·658961	1·517540	·8350080	37	43	·5550864	·667337	1·498492	·8317927	17
3	·5453707	·650649	1·536927	·8381950	57	24	·5504807	·659378	1·516579	·8348479	36	44	·5553283	·667758	1·497548	·8316312	16
4	·5456145	·651063	1·535949	·8380363	56	25	·5507236	·659796	1·515620	·8346877	35	45	·5555702	·668178	1·496605	·8314696	15
5	·5458583	·651477	1·534972	·8378775	55	26	·5509663	·660213	1·514661	·8345275	34	46	·5558121	·668599	1·495663	·8313080	14
6	·5461020	·651891	1·533996	·8377187	54	27	·5512091	·660631	1·513703	·8343672	33	47	·5560539	·669020	1·494722	·8311463	13
7	·5463456	·652306	1·533021	·8375598	53	28	·5514518	·661049	1·512746	·8342068	32	48	·5562956	·669441	1·493782	·8309845	12
8	·5465892	·652721	1·532047	·8374009	52	29	·5516944	·661467	1·511790	·8340463	31	49	·5565373	·669863	1·492842	·8308226	11
9	·5468328	·653136	1·531074	·8372418	51	30	·5519370	·661885	1·510835	·8338858	30	50	·5567790	·670284	1·491903	·8306607	10
10	·5470763	·653551	1·530102	·8370827	50	31	·5521795	·662304	1·509880	·8337252	29	51	·5570206	·670706	1·490965	·8304987	9
11	·5473198	·653966	1·529130	·8369236	49	32	·5524220	·662722	1·508927	·8335646	28	52	·5572621	·671128	1·490029	·8303366	8
12	·5475632	·654381	1·528160	·8367643	48	33	·5526645	·663141	1·507974	·8334038	27	53	·5575036	·671550	1·489092	·8301745	7
13	·5478066	·654797	1·527190	·8366050	47	34	·5529069	·663560	1·507022	·8332430	26	54	·5577451	·671972	1·488157	·8300123	6
14	·5480499	·655212	1·526221	·8364456	46	35	·5531492	·663979	1·506071	·8330822	25	55	·5579865	·672394	1·487222	·8298500	5
15	·5482932	·655628	1·525253	·8362862	45	36	·5533915	·664398	1·505121	·8329212	24	56	·5582279	·672816	1·486288	·8296877	4
16	·5485365	·656044	1·524286	·8361266	44	37	·5536338	·664817	1·504171	·8327602	23	57	·5584692	·673239	1·485355	·8295252	3
17	·5487797	·656460	1·523320	·8359670	43	38	·5538760	·665237	1·503222	·8325991	22	58	·5587105	·673662	1·484423	·8293628	2
18	·5490228	·656877	1·522354	·8358074	42	39	·5541182	·665657	1·502275	·8324380	21	59	·5589517	·674085	1·483491	·8292002	1
19	·5492659	·657293	1·521389	·8356476	41	40	·5543603	·666076	1·501328	·8322768	20	60	·5591929	·674508	1·482561	·8290376	0
20	·5495090	·657710	1·520426	·8354878	40												
′	Cosine.	Cotan.	Tang.	Sine. Deg. 56.	′	′	Cosine.	Cotan.	Tang.	Sine. Deg. 56.	′	′	Cosine.	Cotan.	Tang.	Sine. Deg. 56.	′

IV.—Natural Sines and Tangents to a Radius 1—*continued.*

34 Deg.						34 Deg.						34 Deg.					
′	Sine.	Tang.	Cotang.	Cosine.	′	′	Sine.	Tang.	Cotang.	Cosine.	′	′	Sine.	Tang.	Cotang.	Cosine.	′
0	·5591929	·674508	1·482561	·8290376	60	21	·5642467	·683433	1·463200	·8256062	39	41	·5690403	·692002	1·445081	·8223096	19
1	·5594340	·674931	1·481631	·2288749	59	22	·5644869	·683860	1·462287	·8254420	38	42	·5692795	·692432	1·444183	·8221440	18
2	·5596751	·675355	1·480702	·8287121	58	23	·5647270	·684287	1·461374	·8252778	37	43	·5695187	·692863	1·443286	·8219784	17
3	·5599162	·675779	1·479773	·8285493	57	24	·5649670	·684714	1·460463	·8251135	36	44	·5697577	·693293	1·442389	·8218127	16
4	·5601572	·676202	1·478846	·8283864	56	25	·5652070	·685141	1·459552	·8249491	35	45	·5699968	·693724	1·441494	·8216469	15
5	·5603981	·676626	1·477919	·8282234	55	26	·5654469	·685569	1·458642	·8247847	34	46	·5702357	·694155	1·440599	·8214811	14
6	·5606390	·677050	1·476993	·8280603	54	27	·5656868	·685996	1·457732	·8246202	33	47	·5704747	·694586	1·439704	·8213152	13
7	·5608798	·677475	1·476068	·8278972	53	28	·5659267	·686424	1·456824	·8244556	32	48	·5707136	·695018	1·438811	·8211492	12
8	·5611206	·677899	1·475144	·8277340	52	29	·5661665	·686852	1·455916	·8242909	31	49	·5709524	·695449	1·437918	·8209832	11
9	·5613614	·678324	1·474221	·8275708	51	30	·5664062	·687281	1·455009	·8241262	30	50	·5711912	·695881	1·437026	·8208170	10
10	·5616021	·678749	1·473298	·8274074	50	31	·5666459	·687709	1·454102	·8239614	29	51	·5714299	·696313	1·436135	·8206509	9
11	·5618428	·679174	1·472376	·8272440	49	32	·5668856	·688137	1·453197	·8237965	28	52	·5716686	·696745	1·435245	·8204846	8
12	·5620834	·679599	1·471455	·8270806	48	33	·5671252	·688566	1·452292	·8236316	27	53	·5719073	·697177	1·434355	·8203183	7
13	·5623239	·680024	1·470535	·8269170	47	34	·5673648	·688995	1·451388	·8234666	26	54	·5721459	·697609	1·433466	·8201519	6
14	·5625645	·680450	1·469615	·8267534	46	35	·5676043	·689424	1·450485	·8233015	25	55	·5723844	·698042	1·432578	·8199854	5
15	·5628049	·680875	1·468696	·8265897	45	36	·5678437	·689853	1·449582	·8231364	24	56	·5726229	·698474	1·431690	·8198189	4
16	·5630453	·681301	1·467778	·8264260	44	37	·5680832	·690283	1·448680	·8229712	23	57	·5728614	·698907	1·430803	·8196523	3
17	·5632857	·681727	1·466861	·8262622	43	38	·5683225	·690712	1·447779	·8228059	22	58	·5730998	·699340	1·429917	·8194856	2
18	·5635260	·682153	1·465945	·8260983	42	39	·5685619	·691142	1·446879	·8226405	21	59	·5733381	·699774	1·429032	·8193189	1
19	·5637663	·682580	1·465029	·8259343	41	40	·5688011	·691572	1·445980	·8224751	20	60	·5735764	·700207	1·428148	·8191520	0
20	·5640066	·683006	1·464114	·8257703	40												
′	Cosine.	Cotan.	Tang.	Sine.	′	′	Cosine.	Cotan.	Tang.	Sine.	′	′	Cosine.	Cotan.	Tang.	Sine.	′
Deg. 55.						Deg. 55.						Deg. 55.					

IV.—Natural Sines and Tangents to a Radius 1—*continued*.

35 Deg.

′	Sine.	Tang.	Cotang.	Cosine.	′
0	·5735764	·700207	1·428148	·8191520	60
1	·5738147	·700641	1·427264	·8189852	59
2	·5740529	·701074	1·426381	·8188182	58
3	·5742911	·701508	1·425498	·8186512	57
4	·5745292	·701943	1·424617	·8184841	56
5	·5747672	·702377	1·423736	·8183169	55
6	·5750053	·702811	1·422856	·8181497	54
7	·5752432	·703246	1·421976	·8179824	53
8	·5154811	·703681	1·421097	·8178151	52
9	·5757190	·704116	1·420220	·8176476	51
10	·5759568	·704551	1·419342	·8174801	50
11	·5761946	·704986	1·418466	·8173125	49
12	·5764323	·705422	1·417590	·8171449	48
13	·5766700	·705858	1·416715	·8169772	47
14	·5769076	·706294	1·415840	·8168094	46
15	·5771452	·706730	1·414967	·8166416	45
16	·5773827	·707166	1·414094	·8164736	44
17	·5776202	·707602	1·413222	·8163056	43
18	·5778576	·708039	1·412350	·8161376	42
19	·5780950	·708476	1·411479	·8159695	41
20	·5783323	·708913	1·410609	·8158013	40
′	Cosine.	Cotan.	Tang.	Sine.	′

Deg. 54.

35 Deg.

′	Sine.	Tang.	Cotang.	Cosine.	′
21	·5785696	·709350	1·409740	·8156330	39
22	·5788069	·709787	1·408871	·8154647	38
23	·5790440	·710225	1·408003	·8152963	37
24	·5792812	·710663	1·407136	·8151278	36
25	·5795183	·711100	1·406270	·8149593	35
26	·5797553	·711539	1·405404	·8147906	34
27	·5799923	·711977	1·404539	·8146220	33
28	·5802292	·712415	1·403674	·8144532	32
29	·5804661	·712854	1·402811	·8142844	31
30	·5807030	·713293	1·401948	·8141155	30
31	·5809397	·713732	1·401086	·8139466	29
32	·5811765	·714171	1·400224	·8137775	28
33	·5814132	·714610	1·399363	·8136084	27
34	·5816498	·715050	1·398503	·8134393	26
35	·5818864	·715489	1·397644	·8132701	25
36	·5821230	·715929	1·396785	·8131008	24
37	·5823595	·716369	1·395927	·8129314	23
38	·5825959	·716810	1·395069	·8127620	22
39	·5828323	·717250	1·394213	·8125925	21
40	·5830687	·717691	1·393357	·8124229	20
′	Cosine.	Cotan.	Tang.	Sine.	′

Deg. 54.

35 Deg.

′	Sine.	Tang.	Cotang.	Cosine.	′
41	·5833050	·718131	1·392501	·8122532	19
42	·5835412	·718572	1·391647	·8120835	18
43	·5837774	·719014	1·390793	·8119137	17
44	·5840136	·719455	1·389940	·8117439	16
45	·5842497	·719897	1·389087	·8115740	15
46	·5844857	·720338	1·388235	·8114040	14
47	·5847217	·720780	1·387384	·8112339	13
48	·5849577	·721222	1·386534	·8110638	12
49	·5851936	·721665	1·385684	·8108936	11
50	·5854294	·722107	1·384835	·8107234	10
51	·5856652	·722550	1·383986	·8105530	9
52	·5859010	·722993	1·383139	·8103826	8
53	·5861367	·723436	1·382292	·8102122	7
54	·5863724	·723879	1·381445	·8100416	6
55	·5866080	·724322	1·380600	·8098710	5
56	·5868435	·724766	1·379755	·8097004	4
57	·5870790	·725210	1·378910	·8095296	3
58	·5873145	·725654	1·378067	·8093588	2
59	·5875499	·726098	1·377224	·8091879	1
60	·5877853	·726542	1·376381	·8090170	0
′	Cosine.	Cotan.	Tang.	Sine.	′

Deg. 54.

IV.—Natural Sines and Tangents to a Radius 1—*continued.*

36 Deg.

′	Sine.	Tang.	Cotang.	Cosine.	′
0	·5877853	·726542	1·376381	·8090170	60
1	·5880206	·726987	1·375540	·8088460	59
2	·5882558	·727431	1·374699	·8086749	58
3	·5884910	·727876	1·373859	·8085037	57
4	·5887262	·728321	1·373019	·8083325	56
5	·5889613	·728767	1·372180	·8081612	55
6	·5891964	·729212	1·371342	·8079899	54
7	·5894314	·729658	1·370504	·8078185	53
8	·5896663	·730104	1·369667	·8076470	52
9	·5899012	·730550	1·368831	·8074754	51
10	·5901361	·730996	1·367995	·8073038	50
11	·5903709	·731442	1·367161	·8071321	49
12	·5906057	·731889	1·366326	·8069603	48
13	·5908404	·732336	1·365493	·8067885	47
14	·5910750	·732783	1·364660	·8066166	46
15	·5913096	·733230	1·363827	·8064446	45
16	·5915442	·733677	1·362996	·8062726	44
17	·5917787	·734125	1·362165	·8061005	43
18	·5920132	·734573	1·361335	·8059283	42
19	·5922476	·735021	1·360505	·8057560	41
20	·5924819	·735469	1·359676	·8055837	40
′	Cosine.	Cotan.	Tang.	Sine.	′

Deg. 53.

36 Deg.

′	Sine.	Tang.	Cotang.	Cosine.	′
21	·5927163	·735917	1·358848	·8054113	39
22	·5929505	·736366	1·358020	·8052389	38
23	·5931847	·736814	1·357193	·8050664	37
24	·5934189	·737263	1·356367	·8048938	36
25	·5936530	·737712	1·355541	·8047211	35
26	·5938871	·738162	1·354716	·8045484	34
27	·5941211	·738611	1·353891	·8043756	33
28	·5943550	·739061	1·353068	·8042028	32
29	·5945889	·739511	1·352244	·8040299	31
30	·5948228	·739961	1·351422	·8038569	30
31	·5950566	·740411	1·350600	·8036838	29
32	·5952904	·740861	1·349779	·8035107	28
33	·5955241	·741312	1·348958	·8033375	27
34	·5957577	·741763	1·348139	·8031642	26
35	·5959913	·742214	1·347319	·8029909	25
36	·5962249	·742665	1·346501	·8028175	24
37	·5964584	·743117	1·345683	·8026440	23
38	·5966918	·743568	1·344865	·8024705	22
39	·5969252	·744020	1·344049	·8022969	21
40	·5971586	·744472	1·343233	·8021232	20
′	Cosine.	Cotan.	Tang.	Sine.	′

Deg. 53.

36 Deg.

′	Sine.	Tang.	Cotang.	Cosine.	′
41	·5973919	·744924	1·342417	·8019495	19
42	·5976251	·745377	1·341602	·8017756	18
43	·5978583	·745829	1·340788	·8016018	17
44	·5980915	·746282	1·339975	·8014278	16
45	·5983246	·746735	1·339162	·8012538	15
46	·5985577	·747188	1·338350	·8010797	14
47	·5987906	·747642	1·337538	·8009056	13
48	·5990236	·748095	1·336727	·8007314	12
49	·5992565	·748549	1·335917	·8005571	11
50	·5994893	·749003	1·335107	·8003827	10
51	·5997221	·749457	1·334298	·8002083	9
52	·5999549	·749911	1·333490	·8000338	8
53	·6001876	·750366	1·332682	·7998593	7
54	·6004202	·750821	1·331875	·7996847	6
55	·6006528	·751276	1·331068	·7995100	5
56	·6008854	·751731	1·330262	·7993352	4
57	·6011179	·752186	1·329457	·7991604	3
58	·6013503	·752642	1·328652	·7989855	2
59	·6015827	·753098	1·327848	·7988105	1
60	·6018150	·753554	1·327044	·7986355	0
′	Cosine.	Cotan.	Tang.	Sine.	′

Deg. 53.

IV.—Natural Sines and Tangents to a Radius 1—*continued.*

37 Deg. | 37 Deg. | 37 Deg.

′	Sine.	Tang.	Cotang.	Cosine.	′	′	Sine.	Tang.	Cotang.	Cosine.	′	′	Sine.	Tang.	Cotang.	Cosine.	′
0	·6018150	·753554	1·327044	·7986355	60	21	·6066824	·763175	1·310314	·7949444	39	41	·6112969	·772423	1·294627	·7914014	19
1	·6020473	·754010	1·326242	·7984604	59	22	·6069136	·763636	1·309523	·7947678	38	42	·6115270	·772887	1·293848	·7912235	18
2	·6022795	·754466	1·325439	·7982853	58	23	·6071447	·764096	1·308734	·7945913	37	43	·6117572	·773352	1·293071	·7910456	17
3	·6025117	·754923	1·324638	·7981100	57	24	·6073758	·764557	1·307945	·7944146	36	44	·6119873	·773817	1·292294	·7908676	16
4	·6027439	·755379	1·323837	·7979347	56	25	·6076069	·765018	1·307157	·7942379	35	45	·6122173	·774282	1·291517	·7906896	15
5	·6029760	·755836	1·323036	·7977594	55	26	6078379	·765480	1·306369	·7940611	34	46	·6124473	·774748	1·290742	·7905115	14
6	·6032080	·756294	1·322237	·7975839	54	27	·6080689	·765941	1·305582	·7938843	33	47	·6126772	·775213	1·289966	·7903333	13
7	·6034400	·756751	1·321437	·7974084	53	28	·6082998	·766403	1·304796	·7937074	32	48	·6129071	·776679	1·289192	7901550	12
8	·6036719	·757209	1·320639	·7972329	52	29	·6085306	·766864	1·304010	·7935304	31	49	·6131369	·776145	1·288418	7899767	11
9	·6039038	·757666	1·319841	·7970572	51	30	·6087614	·767327	1·303225	·7933533	30	50	·6133666	·776611	1·287644	·7897983	10
10	·6041356	·758124	1·319044	·7968815	50	31	·6089922	·767789	1·302440	·7931762	29	51	·6135964	·777078	1·286871	·7896198	9
11	·6043674	·758582	1·318247	·7967058	49	32	·6092229	·768251	1·301656	·7929990	28	52	·6138260	·777544	1·286099	·7894413	8
12	·6045991	·759041	1·317451	·7965299	48	33	·6094535	·768714	1·300873	·7928218	27	53	·6140556	·778011	1·285327	·7892627	7
13	·6048308	·759499	1·316655	·7963540	47	34	·6096841	·769177	1·300090	·7926445	26	54	·6142852	·778478	1·284556	·7890841	6
14	·6050624	·759958	1·315861	·7961780	46	35	·6099147	·769640	1·299308	·7924671	25	55	·6145147	·778946	1·283786	·7889054	5
15	·6052940	·760417	1·315066	·7960020	45	36	·6101452	·770103	1·298526	·7922896	24	56	·6147442	·779413	1·283016	·7887266	4
16	·6055255	·760876	1·314273	·7958259	44	37	·6103756	·770567	1·297745	·7921121	23	57	·6149736	·779881	1·282246	·7885477	3
17	·6057570	·761336	1·313480	·7956497	43	38	·6106060	·771030	1·296964	·7919345	22	58	·6152029	·780349	1·281477	·7883688	2
18	·6059884	·761795	1·312687	·7954735	42	39	·6108363	·771494	1·296185	·7917569	21	59	·6154322	·780817	1·280709	·7881898	1
19	·6062198	·762255	1·311895	·7952972	41	40	·6110666	·771958	1·295405	·7915792	20	60	·6156615	·781285	1·279941	·7880108	0
20	·6064511	·762715	1·311104	·7951208	40												
′	Cosine.	Cotan.	Tang.	Sine.	′	′	Cosine.	Cotan.	Tang.	Sine.	′	′	Cosine.	Cotan.	Tang.	Sine.	′

Deg. 52. | Deg. 52. | Deg. 52.

IV.—Natural Sines and Tangents to a Radius 1—*continued.*

38 Deg.

′	Sine.	Tang.	Cotang.	Cosine.	′
0	·6156615	·781285	1·279941	·7880108	60
1	·6158907	·781754	1·279174	·7878316	59
2	·6161198	·782222	1·278407	·7876524	58
3	·6163489	·782691	1·277641	·7874732	57
4	·6165780	·783161	1·276876	·7872939	56
5	·6168069	·783630	1·276111	·7871145	55
6	·6170359	·784100	1·275347	·7869350	54
7	·6172648	·784570	1·274583	·7867555	53
8	·6174936	·785040	1·273820	·7865759	52
9	·6177224	·785510	1·273057	·7863963	51
10	·6179511	·785980	1·272295	·7862165	50
11	·6181798	·786451	1·271534	·7860367	49
12	·6184084	·786922	1·270773	·7858569	48
13	·6186370	·787393	1·270013	·7856770	47
14	·6188655	·787864	1·269253	·7854970	46
15	·6190939	·788336	1·268494	·7853169	45
16	·6193224	·788808	1·267735	·7851368	44
17	·6195507	·789280	1·266977	·7849566	43
18	·6197790	·789752	1·266219	·7847764	42
19	·6200073	·790224	1·265462	·7845961	41
20	·6202355	·790697	1·264706	·7844157	40
′	Cosine.	Cotan.	Tang.	Sine.	′

Deg. 51.

38 Deg.

′	Sine.	Tang.	Cotang.	Cosine.	′
21	·6204636	·791170	1·263950	·7842352	39
22	·6206917	·791643	1·263195	·7840547	38
23	·6209198	·792116	1·262440	·7838741	37
24	·6211478	·792590	1·261686	·7836935	36
25	·6213757	·793064	1·260932	·7835127	35
26	·6216036	·793537	1·260179	·7833320	34
27	·6218314	·794012	1·259426	·7831511	33
28	·6220592	·794486	1·258674	·7829702	32
29	·6222870	·794961	1·257923	·7827892	31
30	·6225146	·795435	1·257172	·7826082	30
31	·6227423	·795911	1·256421	·7824270	29
32	·6229698	·796386	1·255672	·7822459	28
33	·6231974	·796861	1·254922	·7820646	27
34	·6234248	·797337	1·254174	·7818833	26
35	·6236522	·797813	1·253426	·7817019	25
36	·6238796	·798289	1·252678	·7815205	24
37	·6241069	·798765	1·251931	·7813390	23
38	·6243342	·799242	1·251184	·7811574	22
39	·6245614	·799719	1·250438	·7809757	21
40	·6247885	·800196	1·249693	·7807940	20
′	Cosine.	Cotan.	Tang.	Sine.	′

Deg. 51.

38 Deg.

′	Sine.	Tang.	Cotang.	Cosine.	′
41	·6250156	·800673	1·248948	·7806123	19
42	·6252427	·801151	1·248204	·7804304	18
43	·6254696	·801628	1·247460	·7802485	17
44	·6256966	·802106	1·246716	·7800665	16
45	·6259235	·802584	1·245974	·7798845	15
46	·6261503	·803063	1·245232	·7797024	14
47	·6263771	·803541	1·244490	·7795202	13
48	·6266038	·804020	1·243749	·7793380	12
49	·6268305	·804499	1·243008	·7791557	11
50	·6270571	·804979	1·242268	·7789733	10
51	·6272837	·805458	1·241529	·7787909	9
52	·6275102	·805938	1·240790	·7786084	8
53	·6277366	·806418	1·240051	·7784258	7
54	·6279631	·806898	1·239313	·7782431	6
55	·6281894	·807378	1·238576	·7780604	5
56	·6284157	·807859	1·237839	·7778777	4
57	·6286420	·808340	1·237103	·7776949	3
58	·6288682	·808821	1·236367	·7775120	2
59	·6290943	·809302	1·235631	·7773290	1
60	·6293204	·809784	1·234897	·7771460	0
′	Cosine.	Cotan.	Tang.	Sine.	′

Deg. 51.

IV.—Natural Sines and Tangents to a Radius 1—*continued.*

39 Deg. | 39 Deg. | 39 Deg.

′	Sine.	Tang.	Cotang.	Cosine.	′	′	Sine.	Tang.	Cotang.	Cosine.	′	′	Sine.	Tang.	Cotang.	Cosine.	′
0	·6293204	·809784	1·234897	·7771460	60	21	·6340559	·819948	1·219588	·7732872	39	41	·6385440	·829724	1·205219	·7695853	19
1	·6295464	·810265	1·234162	·7769629	59	22	·6342808	·820435	1·218865	·7731027	38	42	·6387678	·830216	1·204505	·7693996	18
2	·6297724	·810747	1·233429	·7767797	58	23	·6345057	·820922	1·218142	·7729182	37	43	·6389916	·830707	1·203793	·7692137	17
3	·6299983	·811230	1·232696	·7765965	57	24	·6347305	·821409	1·217419	·7727336	36	44	·6392153	·831199	1·203081	·7690278	16
4	·6302242	·811712	1·231963	·7764132	56	25	·6349553	·821896	1·216698	·7725489	35	45	·6394390	·831691	1·202369	·7688418	15
5	·6304500	·812195	1·231231	·7762298	55	26	·6351800	·822384	1·215976	·7723642	34	46	·6396626	·832183	1·201658	·7686558	14
6	·6306758	·812678	1·230499	·7760464	54	27	·6354046	·822871	1·215256	·7721794	33	47	·6398862	·832675	1·200947	·7684697	13
7	·6309015	·813161	1·229768	·7758629	53	28	·6356292	·823359	1·214535	·7719945	32	48	·6401097	·833168	1·200237	·7682835	12
8	·6311272	·813644	1·229038	·7756794	52	29	·6358537	·823847	1·213816	·7718096	31	49	·6403332	·833661	1·199527	·7680973	11
9	·6313528	·814128	1·228308	·7754957	51	30	·6360782	·824336	1·213097	·7716246	30	50	·6405566	·834154	1·198818	·7679110	10
10	·6315784	·814611	1·227578	·7753121	50	31	·6363026	·824825	1·212378	·7714395	29	51	·6407799	·834648	1·198109	·7677246	9
11	·6318039	·815095	1·226849	·7751283	49	32	·6365270	·825314	1·211660	·7712544	28	52	·6410032	·835141	1·197401	·7675382	8
12	·6320293	·815580	1·226121	·7749445	48	33	·6367513	·825803	1·210942	·7710692	27	53	·6412264	·835635	1·196693	·7673517	7
13	·6322547	·816064	1·225393	·7747606	47	34	·6369756	·826292	1·210225	·7708840	26	54	·6414496	·836129	1·195986	·7671652	6
14	·6324800	·816549	1·224665	·7745767	46	35	·6371998	·826782	1·209508	·7706986	25	55	·6416728	·836624	1·195279	·7669785	5
15	·6327053	·817034	1·223938	·7743926	45	36	·6374240	·827271	1·208792	·7705132	24	56	·6418958	·837118	1·194573	·7667918	4
16	·6329306	·817519	1·223212	·7742086	44	37	·6376481	·827762	1·208076	·7703278	23	57	·6421189	·837613	1·193867	·7666051	3
17	·6331557	·818004	1·222486	·7740244	43	38	·6378721	·828252	1·207361	·7701423	22	58	·6423418	·838108	1·193162	·7664183	2
18	·6333809	·818490	1·221761	·7738402	42	39	·6380961	·828742	1·206646	·7699567	21	59	·6425647	·838604	1·192457	·7662314	1
19	·6336059	·818976	1·221036	·7736559	41	40	·6383201	·829233	1·205932	·7697710	20	60	·6427876	·839099	1·191753	·7660444	0
20	·6338310	·819462	1·220312	·7734716	40												
′	Cosine.	Cotan.	Tang.	Sine.	′	′	Cosine.	Cotan.	Tang.	Sine.	′	′	Cosine.	Cotan.	Tang.	Sine.	′

Deg. 50. | Deg. 50. | Deg. 50.

IV.—NATURAL SINES AND TANGENTS TO A RADIUS 1—*continued.*

40 Deg.

′	Sine.	Tang.	Cotang.	Cosine.	′
0	·6427876	·839099	1·191753	·7660444	60
1	·6430104	·839595	1·191049	·7658574	59
2	·6432332	·840091	1·190346	·7656704	58
3	·6434559	·840587	1·189643	·7654832	57
4	·6436785	·841084	1·188941	·7652960	56
5	·6439011	·841581	1·188239	·7651087	55
6	·6441236	·842078	1·187538	·7649214	54
7	·6443461	·842575	1·186837	·7647340	53
8	·6445685	·843073	1·186136	·7645465	52
9	·6447909	·843570	1·185437	·7643590	51
10	·6450132	·844068	1·184737	·7641714	50
11	·6452355	·844567	1·184038	·7639838	49
12	·6454577	·845065	1·183340	·7637960	48
13	·6456798	·845564	1·182642	·7636082	47
14	·6459019	·846063	1·181944	·7634204	46
15	·6461240	·846562	1·181247	·7632325	45
16	·6463460	·847062	1·180551	·7630445	44
17	·6465679	·847561	1·179855	·7628564	43
18	·6467898	·848061	1·179159	·7626683	42
19	·6470116	·848561	1·178464	·7624802	41
20	·6472334	·849062	1·177769	·7622919	40
′	Cosine.	Cotan.	Tang.	Sine.	′

Deg. 49.

40 Deg.

′	Sine.	Tang.	Cotang.	Cosine.	′
21	·6474551	·849563	1·177075	·7621036	39
22	·6476767	·850064	1·176382	·7619152	38
23	·6478984	·850565	1·175688	·7617268	37
24	·6481199	·851066	1·174996	·7615383	36
25	·6483414	·851568	1·174303	·7613497	35
26	·6485628	·852070	1·173612	·7611611	34
27	·6487842	·852572	1·172920	·7609724	33
28	·6490056	·853075	1·172229	·7607837	32
29	·6492268	·853577	1·171539	·7605949	31
30	·6494480	·854080	1·170849	·7604060	30
31	·6496692	·854583	1·170160	·7602170	29
32	·6498903	·855087	1·169471	·7600280	28
33	·6501114	·855591	1·168782	·7598389	27
34	·6503324	·856095	1·168094	·7596498	26
35	·6505533	·856599	1·167407	·7594606	25
36	·6507742	·857103	1·166720	·7592713	24
37	·6509951	·857608	1·166033	·7590820	23
38	·6512158	·858113	1·165347	·7588926	22
39	·6514366	·858618	1·164661	·7587031	21
40	·6516572	·859124	1·163976	·7585136	20
′	Cosine.	Cotan.	Tang.	Sine.	′

Deg. 49.

40 Deg.

′	Sine.	Tang.	Cotang.	Cosine.	′
41	·6518778	·859629	1·163291	·7583240	19
42	·6520984	·860135	1·162607	·7581343	18
43	·6523189	·860641	1·161923	·7579446	17
44	·6525394	·861148	1·161240	·7577548	16
45	·6527598	·861655	1·160557	·7575650	15
46	·6529801	·862162	1·159874	·7573751	14
47	·6532004	·862669	1·159192	·7571851	13
48	·6534206	·863176	1·158511	·7569951	12
49	·6536408	·863684	1·157830	·7568050	11
50	·6538609	·864192	1·157149	·7566148	10
51	·6540810	·864700	1·156469	·7564246	9
52	·6543010	·865209	1·155789	·7562343	8
53	·6545209	·865718	1·155110	·7560439	7
54	·6547408	·866227	1·154431	·7558535	6
55	·6549607	·866736	1·153753	·7556630	5
56	·6551804	·867246	1·153075	·7554724	4
57	·6554002	·867755	1·152397	·7552818	3
58	·6556198	·868265	1·151721	·7550911	2
59	·6558395	·868776	1·151044	·7549004	1
60	·6560590	·869286	1·150368	·7547096	0
′	Cosine.	Cotan.	Tang.	Sine.	′

Deg. 49.

IV.—Natural Sines and Tangents to a Radius 1—*continued.*

41 Deg.

′	Sine.	Tang.	Cotang.	Cosine.	′
0	·6560590	·869286	1·150368	·3547096	60
1	·6562785	·869797	1·149692	·7545187	59
2	·6564980	·870308	1·149017	·7543278	58
3	·6567174	·870820	1·148342	·7541368	57
4	·6569367	·871331	1·147668	·7539457	56
5	·6571560	·871843	1·146994	·7537546	55
6	·6573752	·872355	1·146321	·7535634	54
7	·6575944	·872868	1·145648	·7533721	53
8	·6578135	·873380	1·144976	·7531808	52
9	·6580326	·873893	1·144304	·7529894	51
10	·6582516	·874406	1·143632	·7527980	50
11	·6584706	·874920	1·142961	·7526065	49
12	·6586895	·875433	1·142290	·7524149	48
13	·6589083	·875947	1·141620	·7522233	47
14	·6591271	·876462	1·140950	·7520316	46
15	·6593458	·876976	1·140281	·7518398	45
16	·6595645	·877491	1·139612	·7516480	44
17	·6597831	·878006	1·138944	·7514561	43
18	·6600017	·878521	1·138276	·7512641	42
19	·6602202	·879037	1·137608	·7510721	41
20	·6604386	·879552	1·136941	·7508800	40
′	Cosine.	Cotan.	Tang.	Sine.	′

Deg. 48.

41 Deg.

′	Sine.	Tang.	Cotang.	Cosine.	′
21	·6606570	·880068	1·136274	·7506879	39
22	·6608754	·880585	1·135608	·7504957	38
23	·6610936	·881101	1·134942	·7503034	37
24	·6613119	·881618	1·134277	·7501111	36
25	·6615300	·882135	1·133612	·7499187	35
26	·6617482	·882653	1·132947	·7497262	34
27	·6619662	·883170	1·132283	·7495337	33
28	·6621842	·883688	1·131620	·7493411	32
29	·6624022	·884206	1·130957	·7491484	31
30	·6626200	·884725	1·130294	·7489557	30
31	·6628379	·885244	1·129632	·7487629	29
32	·6630557	·885763	1·128970	·7485701	28
33	·6632734	·886282	1·128308	·7483772	27
34	·6634910	·886801	1·127647	·7481842	26
35	·6637087	·887321	1·126987	·7479912	25
36	·6639262	·887841	1·126327	·7477981	24
37	·6641437	·888361	1·125667	·7476049	23
38	·6643612	·888882	1·125008	·7474117	22
39	·6645785	·889403	1·124349	·7472184	21
40	·6647959	·889924	1·126690	·7470251	20
′	Cosine.	Cotan.	Tang.	Sine.	′

Deg. 48.

41 Deg.

′	Sine.	Tang.	Cotang.	Cosine.	′
41	·6650131	·890445	1·123032	·7468317	19
42	·6652304	·890967	1·122375	·7466382	18
43	·6654475	·891489	1·121718	·7464446	17
44	·6656646	·892011	1·121061	·7462510	16
45	·6658817	·892534	1·120405	·7460574	15
46	·6660987	·893056	1·119749	·7458636	14
47	·6663156	·893579	1·119094	·7456699	13
48	·6665325	·894103	1·118439	·7454760	12
49	·6667493	·894626	1·117784	·7452821	11
50	·6669661	·895150	1·117130	·7450881	10
51	·6671828	·895674	1·116476	·7448941	9
52	·6673994	·896199	1·115823	·7446999	8
53	·6676160	·896723	1·115170	·7445058	7
54	·6678326	·897248	1·114518	·7443115	6
55	·6680490	·897773	1·113866	·7441173	5
56	·6683655	·898299	1·113214	·7439229	4
57	·6684818	·898825	1·112563	·7437285	3
58	·6686981	·899351	1·111912	·7435340	2
59	·6689144	·899877	1·111262	·7433394	1
60	·6691306	·900404	1·110612	·7431448	0
′	Cosine.	Cotan.	Tang.	Sine.	′

Deg. 48.

IV.—Natural Sines and Tangents to a Radius 1—*continued*.

42 Deg.

′	Sine.	Tang.	Cotang.	Cosine.	′
0	·6691306	·900404	1·110612	·7431448	60
1	·6693468	·900930	1·109963	·7429502	59
2	·6695628	·901458	1·109314	·7427554	58
3	·6697789	·901985	1·108665	·7425606	57
4	·6699948	·902513	1·108017	·7423658	56
5	·6702108	·903041	1·107369	·7421708	55
6	·6704266	·903569	1·106721	·7419758	54
7	·6706424	·904097	1·106075	·7417808	53
8	·6708582	·904626	1·105428	·7415857	52
9	·6710739	·905155	1·104782	·7413905	51
10	·6712895	·905685	1·104136	·7411953	50
11	·8715051	·906214	1·103491	·7410000	49
12	·6717206	·906744	1·102846	·7408046	48
13	·6719361	·907274	1·102201	·7406092	47
14	·6721515	·907805	1·101557	·7404137	46
15	·6723668	·908336	1·100914	·7402181	45
16	·6725821	·908867	1·100270	·7400225	44
17	·6727973	·909398	1·199628	·7398268	43
18	·6730125	·909930	1·198985	·7396311	42
19	·6732276	·910461	1·198343	·7394353	41
20	·6734427	·910994	1·197702	·7392394	40
′	Cosine.	Cotan.	Tang.	Sine.	′

Deg. 47.

42 Deg.

′	Sine.	Tang.	Cotang.	Cosine.	′
21	·6736577	·911526	1·097060	·7390435	39
22	·6738727	·912059	1·096420	·7388475	38
23	·6740876	·912592	1·095779	·7386515	37
24	·6743024	·913125	1·095139	·7384553	36
25	·6745172	·913659	1·094500	·7382592	35
26	·6747319	·914192	1·093861	·7380629	34
27	·6749466	·914727	1·093222	·7378666	33
28	·6751612	·915261	1·092584	·7376703	32
29	·6753757	·915796	1·091946	·7374738	31
30	·6755902	·916331	1·091308	·7372773	30
31	·6758046	·916866	1·090671	·7370808	29
32	·6760190	·917402	1·090034	·7368842	28
33	·6762333	·917937	1·089398	·7366875	27
34	·6764476	·918474	1·088762	·7364908	26
35	·6766618	·919010	1·088126	·7362940	25
36	·6768760	·919547	1·087491	·7360971	24
37	·6770901	·920084	1·086857	·7359002	23
38	·6773041	·920621	1·086222	·7357032	22
39	·6775181	·921159	1·085588	·7355061	21
40	·6777320	·921696	1·084955	·7353090	20
′	Cosine.	Cotan.	Tang.	Sine.	′

Deg. 47.

42 Deg.

′	Sine.	Tang.	Cotang.	Cosine.	′
41	·6779459	·922235	1·084322	·7351118	19
42	·6781597	·922773	1·083689	·7349146	18
43	·6783734	·923312	1·083057	·7347173	17
44	·6785871	·923851	1·082425	·7345199	16
45	·6788007	·924390	1·081793	·7343225	15
46	·6790143	·924930	1·081162	·7341250	14
47	·6792278	·925470	1·080532	·7339275	13
48	·6794413	·926010	1·079901	·7337299	12
49	·6796547	·926550	1·079271	·7335322	11
50	·6798681	·927091	1·078642	·7333345	10
51	·6800813	·927632	1·073013	·7331367	9
52	·6802946	·928173	1·077384	·7329388	8
53	·6805078	·928715	1·076756	·7327409	7
54	·6807209	·929257	1·076128	·7325429	6
55	·6809339	·929799	1·075500	·7323449	5
56	·6811469	·930342	1·074873	·7321467	4
57	·6813599	·930884	1·074246	·7319486	3
58	·6815728	·931428	1·073620	·7317503	2
59	·6817856	·931971	1·072994	·7315521	1
60	·6819984	·932515	1·072368	·7313537	0
′	Cosine.	Cotan.	Tang.	Sine.	′

Deg. 47.

IV.—Natural Sines and Tangents to a Radius 1—*continued.*

43 Deg | 43 Deg. | 43 Deg.

′	Sine.	Tang.	Cotang.	Cosine.	′	′	Sine.	Tang.	Cotang.	Cosine.	′	′	Sine.	Tang.	Cotang.	Cosine.	′
0	·6819984	·932515	1·072368	·7313537	60	21	·6864532	·944001	1·059320	·7271740	39	41	·6906721	·955064	1·047049	·7231681	19
1	·6822111	·933059	1·071743	·7311553	59	22	·6866647	·944551	1·058703	·7269743	38	42	·6908824	·955620	1·046440	·7229671	18
2	·6824237	·933603	1·071118	·7309568	58	23	·6868761	·945102	1·058086	·7267745	37	43	·6910927	·956177	1·045831	·7227661	17
3	·6826363	·934147	1·070494	·7307583	57	24	·6870875	·945653	1·057470	·7265747	36	44	·6913029	·956734	1·045222	·7225651	16
4	·6828489	·934692	1·069870	·7305597	56	25	·6872988	·946204	1·056854	·7263748	35	45	·6915131	·957291	1·044613	·7223640	15
5	·6830613	·935238	1·069246	·7303610	55	26	·6875101	·946755	1·056238	·7261748	34	46	·6917232	·957849	1·044005	·7221628	14
6	·6832738	·935783	1·068623	·7301623	54	27	·6877213	·947307	1·855623	·7259748	33	47	·6919332	·958407	1·043397	·7219615	13
7	·6834861	·936329	1·068000	·7299635	53	28	·6879325	·947859	1·055008	·7257747	32	48	·6921432	·958965	1·042790	·7217602	12
8	·6836984	·936875	1·067377	·7297646	52	29	·6881435	·948411	1·054394	·7255746	31	49	·6923531	·959524	1·042183	·7215589	11
9	·6839107	·937421	1·066755	·7295657	51	30	·6883546	·948964	1·053780	·7253744	30	50	·6925630	·960082	1·041576	·7213574	10
10	·6841229	·937968	1·066134	·7293668	50	31	·6885655	·949517	1·053166	·7251741	29	51	·6927728	·960642	1·040970	·7211559	9
11	·6843350	·938515	1·065512	·7291677	49	32	·6887765	·950070	1·052553	·7249738	28	52	·6929825	·961201	1·040364	·7209544	8
12	·6845471	·939062	1·064891	·7289686	48	33	·6889873	·950624	1·051940	·7247734	27	53	·6931922	·961761	1·039758	·7207528	7
13	·6847591	·939610	1·064271	·7287695	47	34	·6891981	·951178	1·051327	·7245729	26	54	·6934018	·962321	1·039153	·7205511	6
14	·6849711	·940157	1·063651	·7285703	46	35	·6894089	·951732	1·050715	·7243724	25	55	·6936114	·962881	1·038548	·7203494	5
15	·6851830	·940706	1·063031	·7283710	45	36	·6896195	·952287	1·050103	·7241719	24	56	·6938209	·963442	1·037944	·7201476	4
16	·6853948	·941254	1·062411	·7281716	44	37	·6898302	·952842	1·049492	·7239712	23	57	·6940304	·964003	1·037340	·7199457	3
17	·6856066	·941803	1·061792	·7279722	43	38	·6900407	·953397	1·048880	·7237705	22	58	·6942398	·964565	1·036736	·7197438	2
18	·6858184	·942352	1·061174	·7277728	42	39	·6902512	·953952	1·048270	·7235698	21	59	·6944491	·965126	1·036133	·7195418	1
19	·6860300	·942901	1·060556	·7275732	41	40	·6904617	·954508	1·047659	·7233690	20	60	·6946584	·965688	1·035530	·7193398	0
20	·8662416	·943451	1·059938	·7273736	40												
′	Cosine.	Cotan.	Tang.	Sine.	′	′	Cosine.	Cotan.	Tang.	Sine.	′	′	Cosine.	Cotan.	Tang.	Sine.	′

Deg. 46. | Deg. 46. | Deg. 46.

IV.—Natural Sines and Tangents to a Radius 1—*continued.*

44 Deg.						44 Deg.						44 Deg.					
′	Sine.	Tang.	Cotang.	Cosine.	′	′	Sine.	Tang.	Cotang.	Cosine.	′	′	Sine.	Tang.	Cotang.	Cosine.	′
0	·6946584	·965688	1·035530	·7193398	60	21	·6990396	·977564	1·022950	·7150830	39	41	·7031879	·989006	1·011115	·7110041	19
1	·6948676	·966251	1·034927	·7191377	59	22	·6992476	·978133	1·022355	·7148796	38	42	·7033947	·989582	1·010527	·7107995	18
2	·6950767	·966813	1·034325	·7189355	58	23	·6994555	·978702	1·021760	·7146762	37	43	·7036014	·990158	1·009939	·7105948	17
3	·6952858	·967376	1·033723	·7187333	57	24	·6996633	·979272	1·021166	·7144727	36	44	·7038081	·990734	1·009352	·7103901	16
4	·6954949	·967939	1·033122	·7185310	56	25	·6998711	·979842	1·020572	·7142691	35	45	·7040147	·991311	1·008764	·7101854	15
5	·6957039	·968503	1·032520	·7183287	55	26	·7000789	·980412	1·019978	·7140655	34	46	·7042213	·991888	1·008178	·7099806	14
6	·6959128	·969067	1·031919	·7181263	54	27	·7002866	·980983	1·019385	·7138618	33	47	·7044278	·992465	1·007591	·7097757	13
7	·6961217	·969631	1·031319	·7179238	53	28	·7004942	·981554	1·018792	·7136581	32	48	·7046342	·993042	1·007005	·7095707	12
8	·6963305	·970196	1·030719	·7177213	52	29	·7007018	·982125	1·018199	·7134543	31	49	·7048406	·993620	1·006420	·7093657	11
9	·6965392	·970761	1·030119	·7175187	51	30	·7009093	·982697	1·017607	·7132504	30	50	·7050469	·994199	1·005834	·7091607	10
10	·6967479	·971326	1·029520	·7173161	50	31	·7011167	·983269	1·017015	·7130465	29	51	·7052532	·994777	1·005249	·7089556	9
11	·6969565	·971891	1·028921	·7171134	49	32	·7013241	·983841	1·016423	·7128426	28	52	·7054594	·995356	1·004665	·7087504	8
12	·6971651	·972457	1·028322	·7169106	48	33	·7015314	·984414	1·015832	·7126385	27	53	·7056655	·995935	1·004080	·7085451	7
13	·6973736	·973023	1·027724	·7167078	47	34	·7017387	·984987	1·015241	·7124344	26	54	·7058716	·996515	1·003496	·7083398	6
14	·6975821	·973590	1·027126	·7165049	46	35	·7019459	·985560	1·014651	·7122303	25	55	·7060776	·997095	1·002913	·7081345	5
15	·6977905	·974156	1·026528	·7163019	45	36	·7021531	·986133	1·014061	·7120260	24	56	·7062835	·997675	1·002329	·7079291	4
16	·6979988	·974724	1·025931	·7160989	44	37	·7023601	·986707	1·013471	·7118218	23	57	·7064894	·998256	1·001746	·7077236	3
17	·6982071	·975291	1·025334	·7158959	43	38	·7025672	·987282	1·012881	·7116174	22	58	·7066953	·998837	1·001164	·7075180	2
18	·6984153	·975859	1·024738	·7156927	42	39	·7027741	·987856	1·012292	·7114130	21	59	·7069011	·999418	1·000581	·7073124	1
19	·6986234	·976427	1·024141	·7154895	41	40	·7029811	·988431	1·011703	·7112086	20	60	·7071068	1·00000	1·000000	·7071068	0
20	·6988315	·976995	1·023546	·7152863	40												
′	Cosine.	Cotan.	Tang.	Sine.	′	′	Cosine.	Cotan.	Tang.	Sine.	′	′	Cosine.	Cotan.	Tang.	Sine.	′
				Deg. 45.						Deg. 45.						Deg. 45.	

CPSIA information can be obtained
at www.ICGtesting.com
Printed in the USA
LVHW092304230322
714114LV00005BA/188

9 783752 577204